Vintage Attraction

ALSO BY CHARLES BLACKSTONE

The Week You Weren't Here

The Art of Friction: Where (Non) Fictions Come Together (co-editor)

Vintage Attraction

CHARLES BLACKSTONE

PEGASUS BOOKS
NEW YORK LONDON

VINTAGE ATTRACTION

Pegasus Books LLC
80 Broad Street, 5th Floor
New York, NY 10004

For Alpana Singh and Haruki Murakami

Hitch your agony to a star.

—Saul Bellow, *Herzog*

But the way it works, you get what you get and the rest you have to do yourself.

—Philip Roth, *Zuckerman Unbound*

Vintage Attraction

Saturday, March 20

On the El ride to the airport, Izzy wouldn't even look at me. How had things gotten so crazy between us? It was as though Chicago's celebrity sommelier and I, her husband of almost five weeks, were complete strangers. She sat across the train car, reading her book, checking e-mail. Any job leads? When her BlackBerry rang, I feared it was Pacer Rosengrant, Izzy's sommelier protégé and ex-boyfriend, calling. I wanted to believe that nothing was going on between them again, but part of me couldn't. I'd found him in our bed one recent morning. The other master candidates had gone home after the blind tasting Izzy conducted. He spent the night. She slept on the couch—ostensibly. Pacer Rosengrant's return to town, coming almost as quickly as Izzy's and my falling in love, buying an apartment together, and eloping, almost decanted us. It might have even already done damage we were incapable of fleeing. Yet here Izzy and I were, going to Greece for ten days.

"Who was that?"

"*Peter*," she said, in that urgent, annoyed—and annoying—way few people aside from my parents and student loan creditors ever pronounced my given name.

"What?"

"Don't you think now that we're separated you kind of have no right to know who I'm on the phone with?"

I didn't answer, and instead tried a new tactic. "Are you hungry?" I asked.

Izzy looked at the paper bag in my lap and nodded. "I can't stop smelling that guy's fries."

I passed her our lunch. She inspected the three peanut butter and banana sandwiches I'd made before we left and selected one. She threw the bag back over the aisle. I barely managed to catch it.

2 · CHARLES BLACKSTONE

"Why are we taking this trip, again?" I asked.

There was a throng at the terminal so dense I was certain that by the time we'd get checked in, we'd miss our flight. Never mind making it through security. Not going wouldn't have been an entirely terrible scenario. At least to me.

"Psst."

This sort of impasse had been plaguing us since the night we met. "Don't look," I whispered, but it was too late. Izzy began to turn her head.

A TSA agent, seated on a bar stool at an opening in between the Retracta-Belt stanchions, said, "You're that girl, ain't ya?" Izzy smiled. The agent waved his hand. "Come this way."

He led us to a corner of the maze and unabashedly released a lock on one side of the barrier. It sprang a length of prohibitive cloth and freed a space for Izzy and me to enter. We now were advanced on the line by a good fifteen minutes' worth of passengers waiting for tickets.

"I love your show. As soon as you recommend a wine, my wife runs right out to buy it."

"Thank you"—she looked at his silver tag—"Malcolm. That's sweet."

He emitted a hearty, rumbling laugh. "Now, that's where I draw the line. When you had that one time that pink wine—I forget what it's called—I was like, 'Baby, you're drinking that one yourself.' I may be willing to try a lot of things, but pink wine? Uh-uh. If I want something sweet, I'll eat a cupcake."

"Rosé," she said. "And, actually, that kind is dry, so I think you'd like it."

"Not sweet?"

"Give it a try."

"Okay, okay. If Isabelle Conway says it's good, you know what? I'm gonna try it."

"I appreciate that, Malcolm."

"Have a good trip, Miss Conway. Be sure to drink a lot of wine."

Malcolm reminded me, in a distant way, of myself, five months ago. It was then that I, sleep deprived and love starved, and nothing more to her than a fan, wrote an e-mail to Izzy. The subject line was "An impassioned plea (I think) for attention." *So, I'm sort of just guessing that this is your address, I'd typed last fall, and also that even if this were your address, that you check this account, given the fact that there have probably been at least 35,214 people who at one point tried reaching you this way. Okay, it's more like hoping—reckless optimism perhaps—but my cause is a worthy one: you have to get your* Vintage Attraction *producers to cast me. I think I'm perfect for the part. I'm skeptical, curious, ready to learn, like restaurants and wine bars, have an eclectic cellar in my kitchen (two bottles, of dubious French provenance, stowed above the stove). I'm also quite charming, contentious, and always hungry for a good debate. I've been catching up on reruns, and let's face it, in the last season or two, most of the guests have been kind of dogmatic and a little overdramatic. A logician would have a field day with the rabbi who answered charges of "mediocre pairing" with a stammered, "But that's what we serve at shiva!" Bring me in to shake things up a bit. Please. I want to help the sommelier with the, er, mostellier make good TV. Truthfully, I'm just interested in meeting you and figured this whole trying-to-get-on-the-show thing (and, with any luck, this e-mail) might make for a good entree, no pun intended.* I signed off, *Yours in Champagne, Peter Hapworth, Conceptualist, Teacher, Chicagoan, Swashbuckler, Eater, Drinker, Butcher, Baker, Candlestick Maker.* She replied, eight minutes later. *My goodness! This is definitely one passionate plea to get on the show. I don't actually pick the guests but I will forward your note directly to the producer. I'm thrilled that you enjoy* Vintage Attraction *and appreciate your enthusiasm in trying to get on. Your e-mail really made me laugh, and that's always a good thing. Plus if you really are a butcher, that's even better. I don't think we have ever had a butcher on before.* I never made it as far as an audition, but ended up with something even better: a date with the host several hours later. We'd spent few nights apart since.

The airline ticket agent at the counter also recognized Izzy. He printed our coach-fare boarding cards, stapled luggage claim coupons to the envelopes, and snuck us into the first-class security lane, which again bought us some extra time.

Once we'd put our shoes and jackets back on and reclaimed our messenger bags, Izzy said, "Well, that wasn't so bad."

"It pays to be you sometimes, I guess."

"Sometimes."

We wandered the dark international terminal. It was a bazaar of languages, smells, and food-court stalls. Duty-free shops for cartons of cigarettes and gallon jugs of vodka lined the path to the gates. Snacks were available in vending machines. A few umbrella-covered carts served a small selection of bottled beer, wine, and spirits. I had no cash in my pocket, but found an operator with a sign announcing that he accepted a spectrum of transatlantic credit cards.

"Want to get a drink?"

"Sure."

People had been telling me about the show for a long time, about how much they not only enjoyed it but also actually learned something about wine in the process. Before I moved to Humboldt Park, though, I'd never actually seen it. I conflated Izzy's with another program that featured a popular lilt-voiced, panic-eyed Chicago restaurateur who'd become notorious with recipes he was rumored to have stolen at a *parrila* while on vacation in Buenos Aires. From a sound-stage set built to look like his home kitchen, he broadcasted alongside an overacting dancer he'd imported from the Palermo's nightly tango show. With the *porteña* in a one-shoulder ballroom dress, the chef, costumed in a campy coat and toque, now rather sanctimoniously, and lucratively, shared the Argentine dishes with a national audience. "His" famous menu was available for consumption across the country by way of an eponymously-branded frozen foods line, featured in heavy advertising rotation. Their show put me in mind of a strung-up hyperbolic duo on *The Muppet Show* making *empanadas*. Izzy's would change my life.

Vintage Attraction's premise wasn't terrifically revolutionary: each week, three everyday Chicagoans—salesmen and computer consultants and kindergarten teachers and marketing specialists who'd never met each other—gathered around a table to drink and talk extemporaneously about all things wine, as though good friends whose cocktail hour bantering wasn't being recorded by two television cameras. Between their recommendations of favorite varietals and reviews of the bottle lists and menus at area restaurants and wine bars, Isabelle Conway revealed her unique perspective. Herein lay the real reason for the show's popularity. She was the sommelier with whom everyone in the city that liked wine—pretty much the entire city—most wanted to sit at a candlelit bistro table or on the living room couch and chat over a bottle or two. And for good reason: Izzy let her empaneled enthusiasts (and, by extension, the viewers at home) in on secrets of the trade. She introduced her audience to alternative selections and exciting unexplored wine regions. She debunked the perpetuated myths. She offered advice on practical domestic matters, such as storage, serving techniques, and wine and food pairings for dinner parties. And she managed to do it all in a way that made everyday people feel smarter about wine, smarter about life. The guests were modestly engaging, their anecdotes sometimes amusing, and the issues they came to the table to raise were largely germane. But they were ultimately *mise-en-scène*. As numerous magazine articles and blog posts concurred, it was the host who was the true television rarity. With her vast knowledge—exalted for years by industry and consumers alike—and inimitable unscripted personality by which she conveyed that knowledge, Isabelle Conway was what made the show uniquely compelling.

The first time I saw *Vintage Attraction*, shortly after discovering I was getting cable, I was struck. Izzy was answering in medium-shot a complex question about how it is white wine can be made from red grapes, and somehow it felt like she was talking directly to me. Absurd as it was to think, I was suddenly overtaken by the notion that she and I could know each other. I didn't know how. I didn't know why. It just seemed possible. She was a conceptualist just like I was, but her ideas were more than just fancies, bound to the province of dreams. She was taking it somewhere, doing something with what she dreamt. Isabelle Conway wasn't just pouring wine into people's glasses. She poured wine into consciousness, into the world.

She was also very beautiful, and I'd been frustratingly single. Part of it was my exacting standards, as esoteric as they were unrealistic. On Craigslist, I posted Casual Encounters ads that sought "someone who knows the difference between Shiraz and Merlot, because I don't; someone who knows the difference between metaphor and metonymy, because I do." My Nerve.com profile called for, in the words of Liz Phair, an "average everyday sane psycho supergoddess." Who else besides Izzy would ever come close?

So I resolved to meet her. I'd use my charm and intellect and figure out a way to draw Isabelle Conway from my screen and into my life. For research, I programmed the VCR to catch all the reruns, which, fortunately for me, aired often. At the end of an episode, I'd turn off the TV, but found it hard not to think about her. And that's how I got the idea to apply to be a guest on the show. The scene played as vividly in my head as if I were watching a film: we'd meet on the set, I'd tell 150,000 cable-access viewers where I liked to have a glass of wine after a long day at work, or when my parents and sister came to town, and I'd make Izzy laugh throughout the taping. *With so many vagaries and uncertainties, how do regular people make sense out of any of it? How's a guy supposed to get a drink in this town?* Then I'd ask her out and we'd fall in love. That was my dream. Instead, she invited me to a wine tasting.

That October afternoon, something else I never imagined also began: my vinification. My experiences with grapes up to that point had been few, yet indelible: I could still taste the syrupy kiddush cup I'd hefted at the bar mitzvah that declaimed me an Upper West Side man. In college, after leaving New York for Chicago, there was kiwi-lemon Mad Dog 20/20, procured from Cornell Liquors with a fake ID I'd laminated with an iron, smuggled into the Reg, and drunk in the reserve stacks. It was with the help of jug Burgundy that I was able to fortify my way through not one but two grad degrees in English, back on the East Coast. In the years since returning to the blustery city to teach at UIC, I'd attended liquor store demos, but those late-afternoon gatherings of timid customers were always too awkward to enjoy or to learn anything. Between the pedantic store employees masquerading as winery advocates and the small samples, I always walked away with a sharp headache instead of the dull buzz I'd sought. What was worse, everyone feared sounding unsophisticated by voicing disapproval of the *Wine Spectator* pronouncements the "connoisseurs" recycled. *Even I hear people talk about wine sometimes and wonder what the hell they're referring to,* Izzy confided in our e-mail thread. *"Ah, yes, it's a dainty little thing. Perfect balance, good legs, and a strong will to survive." It's all pretty silly.* Over and over that day, and for many days afterward, I told myself, *You can't fuck this up.*

On the flight to Munich, Izzy watched movies—*Atonement, Michael Clayton, National Treasure*—while I sketched concepts in my Rhodia. I flitted from idea to idea like a teenaged slacker poet with combination skin and attention deficit. I knew I should focus if I really expected anyone to take me seriously as a restaurant conceptualist, but I couldn't help it. For the first time in months, everything around seemed to inspire me. The babbling high school orchestra that flooded the dozen rows in front of us, their ingratiating chaperones, myriad backpacks and iPods and plastic accordion folders. The meticulous, austere flight crew. The militaristic aluminum meal containers and tiny bullets of Coke and Coke Light. There's a restaurant in this somewhere, I thought, again and again as we crossed the Atlantic Ocean. No matter how good a concept I'd come up with, though, I'd never be able to do much beyond describing it in a notebook without Izzy. I'd once told her, *I need to have you in my life to be whole, to be anything.* It couldn't have been truer now.

It was six thirty in the morning when we landed for our connecting plane stopover. A gray, snowy, yet bright European day was just starting to render itself tangible. We found some seats near our next departure gate and Izzy put her head in my lap and fell asleep. My body couldn't decide if it was rested or tired. It was hard to reconcile this feeling like I was in two places simultaneously—both here in the morning of a Friday in Germany, bleary, but more or less present, and there, ready for bed back on a Thursday night in Chicago. And it definitely didn't feel like my birthday. Somewhere on the planet I was still thirty-seven, even though here I was thirty-eight.

The Aegean Airlines ride from Munich was far shorter in duration, the ATR 72 jet less grand. We descended the airstairs and walked into a deliriously balmy Thessaloniki afternoon. Inside the terminal, we pushed our bags through customs and got our passports hastily inspected and stamped. Then we met George. George was the trip's coordinator from the Greek Wine Council, and our tour guide. He led us to a sputtering, rusty blue taxi. Our driver smoked cigarettes as leisurely as he sped the seventeen kilometers on A25. While I stared at the sprawl of wild shrubs and renegade trees, the interspersing tan, rectangular industrial buildings, and the aging but fuel-efficient cars that we passed, George gave some introductory remarks about the island. Thessaloniki, known for its culture, home to museums, universities, and of course, numerous delicious restaurants, was in the northernmost part of the country, three hundred kilometers from Athens at the opposite end down south.

My wife, across the ramshackle taxi's warm vinyl backseat, ignored me and talked about wine with George, who sat in front. Then, with her eyes trained on the landscape ahead, she reached for my hand.

As much as it felt like the contrary, the evidence I'd amassed against her really wasn't proof of anything at all. I could hear my mother's defensive lawyering: *Maybe the young man merely had too much to drink and passed out. It's possible, Peter.* It was true; I'd need more than a sole shirtless sommelier in our bed to convince a jury. But life wasn't a courtroom. My heart, the venal partisan jurist that it was, could hand down a conviction on the basis of a lot less. Here in Greece I'd learn the answer to a lately persistent question: Was what Izzy and I had together also just as much as my heart needed to acquit?

In vino, veritas.

Even though I was pretty much the last person anyone would have expected to end up the guest of an international government touring wineries five thousand miles away from home, let alone married to someone famous, I still loved Izzy. *When did you first fall in love with me?* she'd memorably asked. *When I first saw you,* I said. *It must have been later,* she said, *like on our first real date, when I had my hair down. Then, too,* I said. *Also the first time I heard you laugh.* This Grecian expedition would have to be about undoing what she'd done, what we'd done. It was our only chance.

Vino

I

THE METROPOLITAN CLUB MEMBERS AND THEIR GUESTS—MEN IN chalk- and pinstriped suits and women beneath coruscating black and gold—mingled around charcoal-jacketed waiters bearing trays of drinks and amphitheatrically arrayed cocktail shrimp that they circulated in step with the rhythm of a combo's Miles Davis and Benny Goodman renditions. Meanwhile, I, in my campus regalia consisting of a blue button-down shirt and jeans, ersatz Princeton Club tangelo-colored tie, and a well-worn but adequately presentable blazer, stood in a narrow space between a round table and an expanse of Sears Tower windows overlooking the lesser skyscrapers and the city sixty-seven floors below. I sipped a glass of Champagne and waited for Isabelle Conway, someone I'd never met but had seen many times on television, to arrive.

Above the din of banter and languorously jazzy instrumental, I could hear Izzy's and my final e-mail exchange of the afternoon parrying and riposting in my ears. *All this talk about wine is making me thirsty. Might you be interested in having a drink with me tonight?* I asked. Two hours and fifty-nine minutes later, her reply: *Tonight I will be hosting a tasting. It sounds much fancier than it really is, but we can hang out there if you like. I could use the entertainment. I'll be there at 6. This invitation is all based on the assumption that you are not a psycho killer stalker with unmarked graves in your backyard.* It was now five fifty-seven.

Before long, I felt a presence inhabit an empty space to my left. The new arrival accepted, in a familiar-sounding voice, the glass a waiter offered her. With numb fingertips and a pounding heart, I took this cue to turn.

Isabelle Conway was even more remarkable in person than TV depicted. Her eyes were the color of coffee beans and lacked the vapidity attending those belonging to the sort of girl I typically flirted with. Her long hair was wound into a shimmery bittersweet chocolate–colored updo.

"Well, hello there," I said, in my best impersonation of the opening gambit of a tuxedoed Humphrey Bogart sort of character.

She cracked up.

I smiled.

"Peter," she said a little hesitantly. "You keep making me laugh."

A commotion of inquiry brought on by others of the evening's attendees who crowded in behind us made off with her notice. While they questioned her, I waited patiently. I couldn't help staring, recording her for posterity. She was tall yet stately, with precise shoulders that managed to appear expansive without detracting from the minimalist ethos of her proportions. She was also elaborately made up and costumed. Her face had a sheen of healthy, indolent tan, an ochre cosmetic applied to her symmetrical nose, square chin, and provocatively elevated cheekbones almost imperceptibly, as though she'd spent a long day reclining in a beach chair on an island sand. It was the hue women of my grandmother's generation spent the summers of their youth striving to achieve. The garnet on her lips turned her mouth into that of an RKO Radio Pictures actress's: sturdy yet delicate, alternately brash and elegant. Her outfit was a uniform belonging to a rarefied profession. It consisted of a suit top that looked like a jacket, with gold buttons running down the tautly tailored front. The long sleeves that clung to her arms concluded in identical buttons. Below was a square black skirt and matching lacquered heels.

Finally she was able to break away from her interrogators and return to me. This time when our gazes connected, they remained. "Sorry about that, Peter. Want to start over?" She extended a small hand.

"Hapworth," I returned. "Call me Hapworth."

"Have you been here long?" she asked me. "Traffic was crazy and I couldn't get an express bus."

"You took the bus here?"

A large chef I'd watched entering the room now stood making imperious throat-clearing sounds behind Izzy. The chef's coat he wore was larger than any garment that I'd ever beheld this close, as though fashioned out of an entire tablecloth. It had a bleached starkness that gave the impression of having never been used in actual service.

She turned, and the chef looked at Izzy importunately. Distress telegraphed his face. "Sommelier," he said in a putatively genuine French accent. "Maybe it's time you talk to the people?" His tinted English sounded to me like the halting, self-contradictory production of an unrehearsed impressionist, whose lack of forethought reduced his channeling to that of a porcine cartoon character's.

"Do you smell that?" Izzy asked then. "The perfume?"

I sniffed the air. "I don't think so."

She inhaled a measure of staccato eighth notes. "It's Estée Lauder."

An older woman turned around. "How did you know?"

"Her nose has a photographic memory," a man interjected.

Izzy shrugged. "You work in fine dining long enough, and eventually you'll smell everything."

When the chef stepped back a few feet, I followed. Immediately others descended and took our places in order to commandeer Izzy's attention.

"She is, after all, why they paid extra for this VIP reception," he said.

"I would have guessed for these gigantic shrimp," I teased.

"I am Dominique," the chef said then. He reached over a meaty paw. "Isabelle's business partner."

"Chef Dominique, of course," I said. "My parents took me to Bistro Dominique once for my birthday. Seven or eight years ago, I think?" I gave my name, which he seemed to dimly receive, as though he'd already known who I was. "My mother says your food is better than anything in New York."

"Well, certainly," the chef said. "We have won many, many awards."

"It really is quite a thrill to meet you." I gestured across. "And her."

"Yes, yes," he replied. "Sommelier is really quite something, isn't she?"

More VIPs clambered over to her. It was an opportunity for me to watch Izzy, study her in wide-angle. It appeared she knew some of them, restaurant regulars. I listened to her instantly recall precise details of the wines she'd poured and they'd drunk at dinners in the distant past. How the hell did she do that? She periodically met my gaze as the growing crowd put more space between us. Somehow, her focus obliquely, yet squarely, was me. I didn't mind being banished.

Upon a waiter's approach, Chef Dominique reached up a glass of Champagne in each hand. One he gave me. We toasted. I'd lost count of how many glasses I'd already had. I never recalled enjoying effervescent wine this much before. I usually found it impenetrably tart. Tonight it tasted sweeter somehow.

"I think that dinner was the last time I had Champagne," I said. I stared at my glass, turning it in my hand by the stem.

"It's cava," the chef said.

"Excuse me?"

"Spanish."

A gong clang signaled the cocktail reception was coming to an end. The chef excused himself, leaving me to drink more cava and watch Izzy and survey the proceedings. The servers pulled apart the curtains of a partition, which revealed a new quadrant. At the front of the expanded room, situated upon a dais, two chairs sat on either side of a small, low coffee table. Behind was a warm-colored backdrop. Facing the cozy and gently lit (spotlights notwithstanding) living room set, long tables with place settings had been arranged on the floor. On each plate were little canapés that reminded me of hors d'oeuvres my mother and father served at cocktail parties in our apartment on Riverside Drive when I was growing up. Around the plates stood six glasses of different wines: three whites on the left, three reds off to the right, each filled a couple of inches up from the bottom. Beside the place settings was an empty plastic cup, and between each pair were a black plastic bucket, a carafe of water, and a basket containing crackers. There didn't seem to be assigned seats, so I chose a setup in a middle row, to the right of the aisle, on what would turn out to be Izzy's side of the stage.

Izzy hadn't taken the chair that was obviously set aside for her across from Chef Dominique's, and instead stood in front of the darkened podium adjacent. She smiled and thanked the applauding crowd into stillness. "Okay, so I'm going to introduce you to the six basic styles of wines and some foods you can pair with them. We'll start with the whites: light whites, sweet whites, and heavy whites."

A few in the group stared ahead. Others nodded tentatively but agreeably.

"What are we supposed to eat this with?" a geriatric shouted, much more powerfully than one might have expected on the basis of his frangible physiognomy.

Izzy said into the microphone, "Could we please have some forks? Thank you."

Without delay, several servers began to orbit the room with baskets of cutlery. They distributed a handful to the guests seated on the aisles, with the implicit instruction to take a fork and pass the rest down.

"I'd like for you to pick up the glass of wine all the way on your left and tell me what you smell." The noses went in and out. Some shrugged. Others mumbled uncertain descriptors to those seated closest—"cat piss," I was pretty sure I heard one doyenne declare—but nobody ventured to offer a noun or an adjective to the entire group.

"Kind of hard to say, right?" Izzy said. "Let me show you why."

Izzy's brief technical but intimate primer in the basics of wine tasting began with how to swirl. The introduction of oxygen to the glass was what really brought wine to life. Swirling aerated the wine, Izzy told the room, and drove its quiescent particles into motion, so that you could smell (and taste) them. This was a smaller-scale version of what took place when one decanted a bottle. I struggled with the maneuver. Holding the glass a few inches into the air, I couldn't coax its contents into as smooth a typhoon as I saw Izzy make from the stage. My wine sloshed up only one side of the glass. I tried with my opposing hand and almost capsized. I was glad that I wasn't sitting in Izzy's line of vision. Many of the club members were also having difficulty transposing what they saw into actions of their own, and so Izzy offered an alternative method: planting the stem of the glass on the smooth surface to propel from a steady base. While we practiced, Izzy said, "You've actually already tasted the first wine on the program."

Some in the audience looked at each other with exaggerated expressions of astonishment, inhibitions clearly relaxed by the effects of consuming several glasses of said first wine.

Here Chef Dominique rose from his chair and lurched down-stage. He moved in an unsteady manner, but in doing so managed to release himself from the background sequestration in which he'd somehow ended up. "The cava," he offered. This was his first contribution to the presentation.

Izzy nodded. "We'd usually pair this sparkling wine with a *gougère*—a cheese puff. Spanish cava's perfect for everything from hors d'oeuvres at your grand receptions to simple light-bites when you gather some friends in your living room. Oysters are also a good choice. The cava's tartness balances the saltiness of the oysters."

"We had shrimp," a rotund woman with a gravelly voice blurted out.

"Yes," Izzy said, undeterred. "Well, there's another rule of entertaining, which actually contradicts what I've just said. If you don't have shrimp, your guests won't be happy. And if you don't have happy guests, there's no sense in continuing the party, wine or not. Ladies and gentlemen, if you take away nothing else from tonight, remember this: shrimp trumps all."

Cackles and guffaws and high-pitched trills of laughter burst out around the room. The sound escalated counterclockwise, like a choreographed fireworks detonation.

"Okay, now pick up that glass of wine all the way on your left and give it a swirl *before* you smell it." We went for the glasses. "A little citrusy, a little grassy, freshly cut herbs, maybe? This part's tricky, because we're not even really *smelling* grapefruit or tomato leaf. It's just how our brain decodes the compounds in the wine that aerating sweeps up. The brain can only translate what's going on in the glass by comparing it to something we've already been exposed to and logged in our scent memory banks."

It made sense, I thought, and sounded easy enough. I lifted my glass again to see if I could decode any of its compounds. It just smelled tangy.

"Go ahead and take a sip—don't just swallow it right away; I want you to really wash it around your mouth, like it's Listerine—and tell me what you taste."

Back to the glasses. "It's lemony," someone behind me went.

"Yes," Izzy exclaimed. "And the food we have for you to try alongside is a cucumber canapé topped with smoked salmon, black caviar, and crème fraîche. This wine has a high acidity, so we like to pair it with dishes you'd squeeze lemon juice on, like salmon. Think of the wine as you would a condiment."

Words of delight and amazement came forth from the audience. It could just have been the booze talking, but out of this small measure of demystification, something was definitely starting to cohere. I took a bite of the canapé.

Izzy said to the room, "I have another question for you. What is the consistency of this wine? If you had to compare it to, let's say, milk, would this wine have the texture of whole milk? Two percent? Or would you say it most closely resembled nonfat?"

I took a sip. Whole milk?

"Nonfat milk, right?" Izzy said. There were nods and faint articulations of agreement. "Does anybody want to guess what the wine is?" Silence. "This light-bodied white is Sauvignon Blanc, from New Zealand."

Another canapé was next described, this time by Chef Dominique. "Here we have a tartare of beets. The beets are tossed with, eh . . . olive oil, balsamic vinegar, fresh basil, salt, and pepper. This we serve to you on a point of toast."

Izzy, holding her tartare, gently added a detail he'd omitted, "Yes, and Chef, a schmear of goat cheese on the top."

Along with the scarce Semites in the room, I chuckled.

"The wine in your corresponding glass is a Pinot Gris from Alsace, actually one of my favorite wines," she continued. I almost finished the tiny, elegant tartare before remembering to introduce some of it to the Pinot Gris. "You'll notice this very noble wine has sweetness, but, just to make sure you don't typecast it as a wine lacking in seriousness, there is an earthy quality here."

I concentrated, with what little of my allotment remained, to pick up the flavors. The fruits eluded, but I could taste something sweet. I returned to Izzy mid-analysis: " . . . peach, apricot, and honey, combined with the wine's residual sugar left over after fermentation, all of these play with the sweetness and earthiness of the beets. The goat cheese provides refreshing acidity." Honey, I thought. Honey. What was the texture like? This wine had a more substantial weight than nonfat milk, like honey. Was I actually getting this?

As Izzy went on to tell everyone, you could ascertain many things about how a wine would taste before it even reached nose or palate, just by assessing the color of the juice. The Pinot Gris's brownish-gold tint resembled honey. Izzy next introduced a California Chardonnay. The Chardonnay's intense, dark-yellow tone was dramatic. "Reminds you of pineapples and guava and ripe peaches," Izzy said. Those juicy tropical fruits were precisely the flavors of this style. A sip revealed it was definitely heavier than the Sauvignon Blanc. This Chardonnay also had a characteristic texture, or "mouth feel," caused by a process during the winemaking, or vinification, called malolactic fermentation. Oh, did I love this terminology! Malolactic fermentation brought about the creaminess of the wine. "It tastes like butter, right?" Izzy asked the audience. "Here, too, there's complexity; the minerality gives that slight soil taste. This all plays off of the richness and earthiness of the mushrooms in the quenelle, which were sautéed in butter, garlic, and fresh thyme."

And it was very good.

"Okay," she said. "I know most of us are more familiar with red wines, so I'm sure you're raring to go with these."

A few happy hecklers, whose ties had become loosened and whose suit jackets now hung on the shoulders of their chairs, hooted. I straightened my spine and cleared my throat warningly to compensate—and offer symbolic rebuke—for the gentlemen's lack of comportment.

"Just as we saw a progression of weights and differing concentrations of fruit and balancing acidity among the whites that we tasted, this group's corresponding categories are light reds, spicy reds, and heavy reds."

I suspected I was one of few in the room who continued to watch Izzy intently, as everyone else had become so engrossed in personal tasting experiments. Some had even gone ahead of the group and begun the next sequence of wines, trying the Oregonian Pinot Noir and an Austrian-style Zweigelt, which had been cellared on Canada's Niagara Peninsula. It was a shame many ignored the duck pâté and roast beef–wrapped asparagus spear pairings on the plates. At least most were aerating and inhaling the scent compounds in their glasses before gulping.

But before long, I, too, found my mind wandering. Was I a little more inebriated than I realized? The contents of my brain were swimming in a sea of new denotations and sense-memories, tastes, smells, honey, earth, acid. I felt smarter for having undertaken this. I had to will myself to stay present, to fight the desire to just stare at Izzy, with whom I decided I was now unredeemably smitten. There were more wines to be evaluated. I took a restorative breath.

An unclaimed item loomed on the plates, like the solipsistic party guest who'd been yammering to his host for so long he'd failed to realize that everyone else had gone home. This was a chocolate dessert. "Lava cake," Chef Dominique called out, from his new seat in the audience, fork in hand.

"Zinfandel and chocolate," Izzy said to her smiling, serotonin-and-knowledge-and-alcohol-imbued admirers. "You can't do much better than that when it comes to dessert pairings." I had only recently learned from a supermarket stocker that this heavy red was a legitimate grape variety, not stigmatized and repudiated like the notorious "white" version, a favorite of many an undergrad comp student. Those who'd begun working at their cakes had chocolate molten streaming out and down the sides. I brought my fork into the center of my cake and only found more cake. Nothing erupted.

"Americans consumed over seven hundred million gallons of wine last year," Izzy told the room. "That's, like, the equivalent of almost four *billion* bottles. And yet wine is the one beverage, the one beverage out there, that requires a special tool to open. A special tool that only one out of every three kitchens has. I say, 'Corkscrew that!' Wine isn't supposed to be about points and scores. And I don't really think it should be about collecting and aging. Nine out of every ten bottles are drunk within six days of purchase. I can tell you you'll enjoy that Silver Oak you've been saving a lot more in your glass tomorrow night than you will keeping it buried away in your cellar for millennia. Wine's not a big mystery. It's a journey. You've begun a journey tonight. It began here. But tonight is not where it ends."

While we applauded, the houselights returned. Izzy stepped down from the dais to meet the growing multitude accumulating to confer with her. The chef followed behind. I stood on the periphery, back along the bank of windows. When the room had emptied out, Izzy came over to me. "I hope that wasn't too boring," she said.

"No," I replied. "Not at all. In fact, I thought it was quite fascinating."

Chef Dominique appeared with his and Izzy's coats. He handed me hers, and I helped her into it. "Well, Peter Hapworth. You must be hungry. Why don't you join us?"

"Really?" I looked at Izzy. "I mean, you know, if it's all right. I wouldn't want to intrude."

"Don't be silly," she said. She leaned toward my ear. "We can get a drink later, too."

"So, we go, then," Chef said.

"Wollensky's?" she asked.

I couldn't tell if Izzy had directed the question to me or to Chef Dominique, but I replied anyway. "Sounds good to me."

We trudged in the cold along Wacker, across the bridge, to Smith & Wollensky, which sat in Marina City and overlooked the river. I followed Izzy down the stairs to the grill below the expensive steakhouse, and revolved inside.

The place was packed. People with domestic beer bottles and mixed drinks were double-parked at the bar, watching the White Sox game from one or both of the screens. They talked, laughed, ordered more cocktails from the bartenders who never seemed to stop moving, and occasionally cheered on the baseball players. All the tables thrummed with conversations and the clinking of silver and glassware. I watched a fraternity of similarly sized and shaped servers, smiling tightly, emerge from the kitchen with a *slam* and a *creak* of the swinging door. They ported to the martini-sodden an endless parade of charred steaks and tall burgers beside heaps of fries and salads and plates of mashed potatoes and creamed spinach. I couldn't remember the last time I'd eaten in a restaurant that wasn't a campus food stand.

A manager quickly came over and greeted us. "Miss Conway, Chef, step up, step up. Right this way. Sorry to keep you waiting. We just finished setting your favorite table."

As much as I tried to pretend this was just a typical Friday night, it was still surreal. I was out, on a chaperoned date of sorts, with a celebrity. First dates were strange enough. The goal always was to pretend like the sudden juxtaposition of two strangers was the most ordinary, comfortable pairing in the world. But when your first date was with someone who was on television, and when there was another man at the table alongside you to oversee the proceedings and make sure you weren't a psycho stalker, there was little mistaking the situation for an everyday occurrence. Still, I enjoyed being here with Izzy and Chef Dominique. Somehow we made an effortless trio—then, anyway.

Izzy scanned her menu and selected a burger. "Rare," she said, after the waiter inquired how she wanted it cooked. When it was my turn, I asked for the same. I figured the unusually low degree of doneness and choice of Swiss cheese instead of my cafeteria customary American would win me culinary sophistication points with Izzy and also with the chef.

"When did you first become interested in wine?" I asked. "It's not exactly something you can major in at college."

"When I was six," Izzy said.

Chef Dominique laughed. "Tell him, tell him," he said.

"I grew up in Carbondale, Illinois," Izzy began. "Three hundred and thirty three miles south of the city, population twenty-five thousand. And the people who raised me weren't wine drinkers. They knew one beverage for all occasions: beer. Football games, summer barbeques, weddings, wakes, birthday parties, Saturday nights, Monday nights, Tuesday nights. Beer, beer, beer. Classy, right? But at parties, our neighbor Shirley refused to partake. Absolutely refused. She said ladies only drank *wine*. My dad—my foster dad—Ernie ran a liquor store, so he'd always have something for her. This wasn't sophisticated wine, by any means. We're probably talking Bartles & Jaymes."

"I think that's how a lot of us first got to know alcohol," I said. The chef squinted at me.

"So, anyway, there was this one Super Bowl Sunday and Ernie had brought home these peach-flavored wine coolers. And I remember looking at the bottles and thinking this sounded like the most delicious drink I'd ever heard of. I snuck one out of the six-pack in the refrigerator, went off to my room, and had a sip. Well, as you can imagine, I didn't find the peach pie I was expecting, but instead discovered something that tasted . . . pretty unpalatable. Still, though, I couldn't get it out of my head that the label said 'peach.' Who'd drink this and taste that? And what was wrong with me that I couldn't? I didn't pick up wine again for quite a few years, but I guess you could say the curiosity always stuck with me.

"I've worked in restaurants since I was sixteen. It's, like, the only world that's ever made sense to me. So, after I got waitressing down, I started attending staff trainings about wine. I memorized the lists and could recite all the descriptors better than anyone, but it took me forever to figure out how the other servers were getting all these peaches and apples and blueberries they said they were tasting. I was thinking very literally and just didn't understand it at all. I was like, 'Do they put peaches and bananas and blueberries in the wine?'"

I smiled and nodded, miming my sympathy for the uninitiated, but was aware as I did that until a few hours ago, I might have asked the same question. I hadn't even realized—before tonight—there'd been a gap in my comprehension, that wine was supposed to taste like anything other than, well, wine.

"And then one day it just clicked," she said.

"Just like that?"

"Just like that."

Rallying to rejoin the discussion, Chef Dominique recited, in ascending order, the awards he and Bistro Dominique had won. The list referenced professional organizations, publications, and associations (some of which were now defunct). I'd never heard of many of them, but nodded after each as though I had. The last culinary distinction had been conferred four years prior. I got the feeling he was trying to downplay the enological accolades that Izzy had brought more recently.

As Izzy and the chef regaled each other and me with their stories, I periodically looked at those who sat around us. I sensed they were watching our table in return. I wondered how many of the patrons at the bar, waiters, and valet parkers huddled by the door had already seen the *Vintage Attraction* season premiere, which, Chef Dominique had reminded me as we walked, aired tonight. It might even have been played here before the baseball game tyrannized the screens. A woman peered in our direction, silently gasped, and threw her lips and cupped hands to her friend's ear. Was she whispering, "Oh my god, that's her! That's the girl from TV!"? It certainly appeared so. Were these people who recognized Izzy also sizing me up, speculating about who I was, what connection I had to a famous sommelier and her accomplished chef, what had brought me to sit at their table like this? These were the very same concerns that, if I allowed myself to sober up, would have perplexed me, too.

I was full after half a burger. I usually ate like an ascetic and subsisted on monastery fare devoid of garnishes and seasoning, bowls of oatmeal or condensed soups, peanut butter sandwiches on dry whole wheat. My former student and occasional paramour Talia, a vegan, occasionally made me Trader Joe's boxed organic mac and soy cheddar, which I'd become oddly fond of (both the product and the gesture). This sudden shift to brioche and ground beef and mayo and ketchup and lettuce and real cheese was an embarrassment of richness. On an adjunct instructor's salary, it made sense to eat out as seldom as possible, but I wasn't about to pass up the invitation tonight. When the check came, I didn't want to seem like I couldn't afford a share.

I dug out my moldering billfold and reached a gold American Express, largely unfamiliar to me, despite its bearing my name. My parents had opened the account for me when I graduated from the University of Chicago. They hadn't cancelled it and had been quietly paying the bills ever since. I only allowed myself to accrue charges in truly dire emergencies befitting a consummate bachelor of arts, like a foundering Craigslist Casual Encounter, or dining with a television celebrity. "We have the same card. It's a sign," Izzy said. She randomly followed with, "Do you speak Spanish?"

"French," I said. "I *took* French, through college, not that I have much to show for it now. I started in third grade. I had to choose between French and German, and my father thought French would be much handier in restaurants."

Chef Dominique seemed to find this very amusing, possibly even trenchant. "You can say that again," he said.

Izzy said, of the chef, "He's from Alsace, which was, at one point, part of Germany. We've never actually been able to get him to tell us when he was born, but depending on the occupation"—she put her hand on his shoulder—"Chef, you could be German and serving even more sauerkraut at the bistro."

"*Nous disons 'choucroute,*' Sommelier. *Choucroute.* I'm no Sherman."

"We can Pinot Gris to disagree."

"That's good," I told Izzy. "Did you just come up with that?"

A large woman, moving sideways and wearing what appeared to be a running suit underneath an unzipped fur coat, came over to the table. "Excuse me," she said, "I hate to bother you while you're having dinner, but you're Isabelle Conway."

Izzy, gradually looking up from her unfinished burger, and Chef Dominique both nodded. The chef grinned proudly.

"My name is Nancy Podolsky." She and Izzy shook hands. To Chef Dominique she turned and said, "Nancy Podolsky," and they touched palms. I thought it was funny that she kept repeating her full name. "Yes, honey," she said to the ceiling. It was then I noticed she had a Bluetooth headset affixed to her ear. "I'll make sure they have barbeque sauce, and horseradish sauce for the fries, which I shouldn't be having anyway, and can you just wait a second? I'm standing, yes, I'm standing right in front of her." She lowered her head, setting her sights back on Izzy, whose building exasperation subtly revealed itself only in the rigidity of her mouth. "Can you say something to your biggest fan?"

"How, um . . ."

Did this Nancy Podolsky woman really expect Izzy to put her diseased earpiece into—

"Here, wait." She slapped a button on the headset, and the device screeched. The noise startled several of those at the table adjacent, but Nancy Podolsky was, it seemed, steeled to the terrible sounds. "Okay, Byron, can you hear me? It's on speaker. Yes, honey, please. I hear him. Can you hear her, honey? Okay, it's okay."

Izzy tried to put in, "I think you have to—"

"Just say something," she barked at Izzy. Her bald haughtiness was surprising. Chef Dominique straightened his back.

Izzy took her napkin from her lap and began to fold it into rectangles and then squares. "Hi there," she said, in the theatrical voice that she used when speaking from the dais at the club tonight.

Nancy Podolsky ripped the Bluetooth out of her ear. It started emitting a series of unrelentingly high-pitched error tones. "Disconnected," she huffed.

"Well, I'm sure—"

"Okay, okay, how about this. How about a photo?" She drew her cell phone out of her coat pocket.

Izzy rose and asked me to take the picture of them standing in a narrow space that had opened in front of the bar. Amid the mortifying stares of those both chary and intrigued dining around us, I agreed, feigning cheerfulness. "How do I—"

"Just press the button that looks like a camera. And then hold down the round button in the middle when it looks good."

Chef Dominique sighed. I was the only one to turn in his direction. He took the cocktail straw he'd transferred to his water glass and blew air through it.

"Are you her publicist?" Nancy Podolsky then asked me.

As Izzy's wine got warm and burger cold, I snapped the digital shutter a couple of arbitrary times and returned the phone. Nancy shook her head, as though displeased, after assessing my shots. "Not the best lighting, but I guess it will do." It wasn't my fault she was trying to use a shitty camera phone for a photo shoot in a basement restaurant.

I suggested a retake, but Chef Dominique shook his head. "She wants a picture with Sommelier, she should pay for it."

"Excuse me, ma'am?" a waiter interjected, too quietly to be effective, before sidestepping away.

Nancy Podolsky bleated, "I know, I know. How about an autograph?"

"Sure, but I don't have—" Izzy looked at Chef Dominique for assistance. The only thing he offered was thinly veiled scorn.

"Here, in my purse. Here," Nancy said.

She produced a ballpoint pen, and Izzy grabbed one of the unused cocktail napkins on our table. The woman received the autograph Izzy handed her, as though a subpoena.

"That's great, honey, but, I don't know, could you maybe write something funny? Something about wine. Ooh, I know. I know. How about 'I'm drinking Champagne and you're not'? That would be so terrific."

"Except she's not drinking Champagne," Chef Dominique growled.

Izzy's eyes begged him not to make this even more unpleasant than it had to be, but Chef Dominique, it was quite obvious, really wanted to tear into this woman for some reason. "I think you've wasted enough of her time," Chef Dominique said then. "How about you just get the hell out of here?"

Izzy appeared horrified. "Look, if you want me to—"

The manager shouldered in, handling ameliorating take-away packages. With an affected flourish, Nancy Podolsky snatched the brown and white paper bags from him and stomped off.

"The mediocracy drives me crazy," Chef Dominique said to the manager, who smiled wanly and turned away. Mediocrity? The chef took a sip of water, and blotted his forehead with a corner of his napkin. After a moment, he excused himself to find the manager and speak to him.

"Sorry about Chef," Izzy said once we were alone. "He shouldn't have done that."

"Does that kind of thing happen a lot?" I gestured in the direction of the balled-up napkin, on top of which leaned the cocktail straw, as though a child had been recently sitting with us. The chef hadn't even bothered to push in his chair before he left. "People coming to the table like that?"

She shrugged and fastened a lock of hair behind her ear. "Dominique's just drunk and being overly sensitive. He doesn't usually mind if fans bother me, as long as they make an appropriately big deal out of him first. I just wish he'd think about my reputation before getting hysterical."

"You didn't even get to finish your burger."

"You know what? I've had enough of Dominique for one night, if not one life. You want to get a drink somewhere else? Just the two of us?"

"Yeah. Let's."

Izzy and I said polite but fraught good nights to the chef in front of Marina City, and she hailed a taxi. It was only a dozen or so blocks to the bar Izzy suggested, and we probably could have walked, yet I didn't object. I was happy to follow along, enjoying the ride, literally and figuratively, wherever it took us.

We chose an open table at Bijan's by the window. Almost simultaneous to our ascent, a harried-looking Teutonic cocktail waitress presented us with menus. Izzy excused herself to the ladies'. Once she was out of the room, I illuminated my Timex with Indiglo and took an inconspicuous glance at my wrist under the table. *Tempus fugit*—it was already after one in the morning. I was surprised at this late hour I was still conscious. I'd subbed an eight o'clock for Berkal, my grad student officemate; taught my own classes; drank wine through the tasting and vodka at dinner; and hadn't even once needed to mask a yawn behind a gulp of water or dissembling smile. But for most of the evening, I'd largely only needed to be responsible for a third of the conversational momentum. There was no falling asleep at the table now. Izzy and I, here, were officially on a date.

Since deciding I needed to be on her television show in order to win her heart, I'd learned, via Google, about Izzy. I knew she was thirty-two. She had, intrepidly, moved from Southern Illinois to the city to take a job working the fine-dining floor at Bistro Dominique, a position that came with a starting salary four or five times what I picked up at UIC, even after all these semesters of parsing flawed introductory clauses and indicting generalities. Within a few years she'd seen her picture on the covers of *Wine Spectator* and *Cellar Temperature*, been profiled in a *Times* feature on rising young enological talent across the country, and received a James Beard Foundation Outstanding Wine Service award years ahead of many of her significantly older and more experienced colleagues on the shortlist. All of this had brought Isabelle Conway unparalleled acclaim, and made her the object of food and drink bloggers' relentless, gossipy scrutiny. She'd want to know things about me, too. What would I share about myself?

There really wasn't a lot to tell. These days, I mostly taught my English composition classes, languished in my office, and drove home in the Mustang I'd had since undergrad with a seemingly bottomless pile of papers to grade. I'd Foreman Grill some chicken I'd eat alongside microwaved frozen vegetables. A glass of warm Côtes du Rhône in hand, I'd watch the evening's *Vintage Attraction* rerun, recasting the day's failures with more fruitful outcomes, not in a classroom with my indifferent students but at a dinner table, with someone else, someone who'd get me, who'd inspire me—Sommelier Isabelle Conway.

Following the waitress's departure with our cocktail orders, Izzy asked, "So, what exactly is a conceptualist?"

It took me a bemused second to recall that I had included "conceptualist" among my other occupations when I signed my first e-mail to her this afternoon. The eventual need to define the term for a date wasn't a surprise. My Nerve.com girls, after a couple of dirty martinis and the opening statements, when things began to slow, frequently probed for clarity the vague occupation I'd listed on my profile. I'd produce my Rhodia, the pumpkin-colored pad in which I jotted my ideas, and share my favorite entries: *I Have a Beef with You: civil procedure and steakhouse. For the Hitchcock fan who has a predilection for overly salty meats: Pork by Porkwest, where even the menu comes wrapped in bacon. Rawwwwr: hipster vegan, chic raw foods, screaming Howard Dean mascot. Sushi bar-meets-strip club: Pandora's Bento Box.* Nobody in recent romantic memory had received this with anything to suggest we might be kindred spirits. "So," one of the sharper ones once asked, "'if you have no intention of starting the business, what's the point? What do you hope to achieve?" I had no answer.

This time I left the notebook in my messenger bag. "Picture a tiny space," I told Izzy. "Like a New York bar, something you'd find in the East Village, but really concealed, hidden to keep the tourists away. Maybe like only ten tables, mostly for two people, and a bar, but with only four or five seats. And all the tables have little tea-light candles, nothing bright anywhere, everything soft . . ."

"Romantic," she finished. "That sounds like a perfect place for wine."

"Yeah," I said. "I actually came up with this one tonight, during the tasting. When you talked about the Zinfandel and the lava cake."

"Dimly lit, people sitting close to each other," she prompted. "What kind of food?"

"It's a dessert place. Little pastries, petit fours, macarons, and hazelnut tarts."

"And port," she added. "Do you have a name for it?"

I beamed. "That's pretty much how I always start." Remembering the instant it came to me, a moment in which I was gazing up at Izzy's electric performance, swirling my glass of Zinfandel offhandedly, almost finally, nearly, maneuvering with precision, brought a similar pulse. Her rapt eyes and mouth further swelled my heart. The captivated attention she paid made me feel as though she were one of the audience and I the one mesmerizing the room. "The naming is the best part," I was able to tell her in a steady voice.

"So, what is it called? The suspense is killing me."

"Monogamousse."

Delight and adrenaline coursed through my roughened romantic pipes, which had, until tonight, lain dry for months. Izzy began to smile, really smile, not just widening her mouth out of courtesy. Whereas my Internet dates might have privately dismissed me as being entirely frivolous, a half-wit, I had finally found someone who'd receive a performance like this and might just think I was a genius. And an e-mail had brought us together.

"Not bad," she said. "So many restaurants today seem to have everything *but* a brilliant concept behind them."

It was all I could do not to get up and throw my arms around her. I wanted to kiss her.

"Wine could definitely work there."

"How?"

"Dessert wine is very sexy," she said. "I could see a delicious tawny port pairing quite nicely with that beautiful hazelnut tart. A couple of small glasses of port—and you'd only need to serve a little bit, in keeping with the diminutive charm of things—and tarts? It would be love at first bite."

"That's not a bad slogan," I said.

"Yes, it is," she said.

"You're really good at this," I said, "and you've gotten me thinking. Not just about Monogamousse." I pushed my drink aside, clearing a narrow space between us, and laid my hand on top of hers. I pressed with the assurance that only this much booze could instill. She looked down at what I was doing, but didn't comment, as though I'd made no more serious of an overture than to reach for a packet of Splenda. Then she flipped her palm to touch mine. With our fingers interlaced, I stared seriously into her eyes. "How come there's never a pen around when you find yourself sitting across the table from a wellspring of inspiration?"

She looked away. "I've always wanted to be somebody's muse," she said.

I paid the check. Outside at the intersection, we waited for the light to change so we could cross the street and hail a southbound taxi. It was freezing out here. I moved my toes and heels and clenched my calves to keep warm. Bouncing around amplified my buzz. We held hands now. When we became still for a moment, I leaned forward to kiss her. She pulled away.

"Wait," she said.

The wind suddenly turned much colder.

"You can't kiss me here."

"Why not?"

"Look." She turned around, to the pornographically illuminated White Hen Pantry behind us. "It's a convenience store. That's not very romantic. That's not the kind of place where you want to say your first kiss happened. Right?"

Vodka sloshed around in my stomach, climbed up my veins, and spilled into my head. I felt myself leaning and pitched forward faster than my eyes could refocus. For a moment I couldn't see anything, only smell her coat. I aligned my hips and stood straight once again. The light for westbound traffic on Erie had changed to green, and we crossed the street.

"What about here?" I asked. We stood before a brick building with an out-of-business restaurant on its ground floor. I moved in once more.

She raised a hand to my chest. This was now a bit acted out by a comedy duo. "Look at the address."

We raised our heads in unison. 666 North State.

"You can't kiss me in front of six-six-six," she said. "That definitely doesn't bode well."

"I'm out of ideas," I said. I looked up the street for taxis. A few came, but they had darkened roof lights and didn't slow down. My teeth began to chatter from standing still, and I jammed my hands into my jeans pockets.

"You remind me of Woody Allen. Has anyone ever told you that before?"

I laughed. "I mostly get Jeff Goldblum, because of the hair. I prefer to think of myself as a young Dustin Hoffman, with glasses. Or Yale, Woody's best friend in *Manhattan*, though I guess—"

She tilted her head, as though appraising me. "I love *Annie Hall*," she said. "It's, like, the most romantic movie."

"I have it at my apartment," I said. "On DVD. If—"

"If?"

"If you wanted to, you know, come over and see it."

"Okay, tell you what," she said. "If we get in the cab and NPR is on, we'll go to your place."

"Okay."

"And you can kiss me."

"It's a deal."

I flagged down a dusty white for-hire taxi with a faded purple logo on its rear door. It lurched over to the curb so quickly that I thought it might end up plowing us down. Izzy slid in, and I followed. Idling there, we listened to the radio. Wordless African music, rhythmic with tribal-sounding drums, played. She frowned an apology.

I realized something. "Wait a minute," I said. "This is NPR. They have music at night. It's *World Beat*."

"Nice try," she said.

"It *is* NPR. I swear." I leaned forward to address the driver through the opening in the bulletproof partition. "Is this NPR?" I asked.

"NPR?"

"Ninety-one point five. WBEZ? The radio station?"

"Ninety-one point five, yes, yes," the driver said with a Caribbean lilt that complemented the instrumental.

I grinned. "I told you so."

I slurred my cross streets in Humboldt Park to the driver. Izzy held up her hands for a moment in capitulation before opening her arms to receive me.

And then I kissed her.

We reached a corner market that sold cheap brewed Cafe Bustelo in miniature foam cups and the three-story brick building to which it was Siametically attached. I'd been subletting a one-bedroom on the ground floor from an associate professor on a research sabbatical. It was my first residence since my parents' with central air, cable (illegal basic), and an in-sink disposal. I opened the door and let us inside. I began leading a brief walk around the open areas of the apartment. Izzy paused in front of the kitchen counter piled with books. At the coffee table in the living room flooded with DVDs, she picked up *Annie Hall* and smiled. We passed my cluttered desk in the back alcove between the bedroom and bathroom. "I have to show you my cellar," I said. I directed Izzy again to the kitchen, where we'd begun, and opened a cabinet high above the range. I couldn't see into it, but knew for what I reached. I took out the two dusty bottles of French wine Talia had left behind at the beginning of the summer.

"Are these any good?" I asked.

She ran her fingers over one label. The clearing didn't render the text any more comprehensible than it was before. "Oh, sure," she said, "if you like Two Buck Chuck."

"You know, after tonight, I think I'm ready to move on to . . . to bigger and better reds," I said.

"I think you are, too," she said. "So, how about the rest of the tour?"

"I think you may have seen everything."

"Not quite everything."

We fell into my bed and were greeted by a fusillade of high-, medium-, and low-pitched squeaks and screeches. Izzy cracked up. I, susceptible to late-hour giddiness, emitted several gleeful measures of chromatic, staccato eighth notes.

In the morning, we went to brunch at a spot in Bucktown I knew was trendy. We had to stand on a long queue and order at the counter. Izzy wanted muesli and fruit. The occasion seemed to merit a splurge, so I chose the peanut butter and banana pancakes. I paid for everything and we found a small table by the wall. Izzy sat with her back to the room. I picked up our flatware and napkins from a service bar and brought over mugs of coffee. I went back up for a small cup of each dairy and nondairy complement they offered, since I didn't know what she liked. It turned out she took Splenda and nonfat milk, just as I did.

"You know, I don't remember the last time I . . . went out with someone who wasn't in the restaurant business," she said while we waited for our food.

I had consciously avoided asking about her romantic life last night. My Google research hadn't unearthed anyone to whom she was linked. What would I have done if she hadn't been single? "Oh yeah?" I asked.

"My last boyfriend was a sommelier at the bistro. Pacer Rosengrant."

"Is it awkward working with . . . an ex?"

"Actually," she said, "he's not—I mean, he's not at the restaurant anymore. I've heard he went to Las Vegas to work with this master the Palazzo owns who he convinced to mentor him." She spoke as though informing herself for the first time, sounding a new idea out loud. "I haven't really had time for dating since."

"You haven't missed much."

"We're supposed to ask each other more questions, right? Like about brothers and sisters and things?"

"It's a popular approach. Okay, so how many siblings do you have?"

"None," she said. "My mother was sometimes a waitress but mostly a drunk and a drug addict and was always getting arrested. Dealing, prostitution. The DCFS took me when I was, like, one."

"She never got cleaned up?"

"She died of an overdose."

"I'm sorry."

"It's okay," she said. "The truth is, I don't really remember her at all. It's weird talking about this with someone who knows me from TV. That you were an abandoned kid from a tiny town and tossed from foster home to foster home isn't really what your big-city fans want to hear about at their window tables. Not really the kind of thing that gets them in the mood to spend two hundred dollars on a bottle of wine."

"Weird, as in weird-talking-about-this-bad?"

"Weird-kind-of-nice, actually."

It *was* nice that she felt she could confide in me, but also somewhat bewildering that she'd share this much, this soon. I'd had dates who'd armored themselves in candor, in order to remain at a safe distance. But if Izzy didn't genuinely like me, if I was nothing more than a fan with whom she'd gotten a little carried away, what was she still doing with me? She could have easily gotten out of my bed and called a taxi instead of sleeping over, or before I drove us to Milk & Honey. I got the sense that there was another meaning to all of this, something yet to be assessed in magazine advice columns. By staying with me, by revealing the unpleasant parts of her past, Izzy was doing quite the opposite of trying to pull away. She was gauging my capacity to love her.

"I have an older sister," I said. "She's a criminal lawyer, in New York. Just like my mom."

"And your father? A professor?"

"He's a Freudian psychologist. Semi-retired. Which is kind of Freudian, I guess."

"Are you close?"

"Not really," I said. "They come to Chicago to visit once a year and stay in a hotel. We speak on the phone occasionally. My mother prefers e-mail. I kind of have always thought of myself as an orphan with parents. I think they never really forgave me for leaving New York and not coming back. Or for getting an MFA in fiction." I coughed. "I have another question for you."

"Okay, go."

"What's it like being on TV?"

She slowly shook her head. "I don't know whether all of this has helped my wine career, or just turned grocery shopping without a baseball hat into a major ordeal."

"Chef Dominique mentioned that it was his idea to start *Vintage Attraction*."

"He's always looking for ways to publicize the bistro when covers are down. We began as kind of this low-budget informercial. I expected it would run at two A.M. a few times, nobody would see it, and that would be that. Then people started writing, calling, e-mailing, demanding more . . . Before long, we had a show for real, sponsors, advertisers, and at the restaurant, reservations filling weeks and weeks on the books. He was a television producer, and I became Chicago's sommelier Isabelle Conway."

"That's crazy."

"The wine world is a freak show," Izzy told me then. "I think that has a lot to do with the draw. Customers think sommeliers' lives are so glamorous, but the truth is, we're utterly contemptible. Standing behind the accolades and expensive vintages is a lot of unhappiness. Affairs, failed marriages, failed Court exams, abortions, lawsuits, debts, fraud charges, corked bottles . . ."

"A few semesters ago, an adjunct in my department got fired for charging booze to the reading series account at Liquor Mart. The alias he used was Kazuo Ishiguro."

Her face lit up. "*Remains of the Day* is my favorite novel. I mean, I couldn't explain all the metaphors, but I liked how the words stuck with you."

"They're pretty much the only thing that's ever stuck with me."

"I'm kind of jealous of your students," she said. "I used to dream about going to college. I took a few classes back when I was waiting tables at the Cattle Company, but it got to be too much."

"I can teach you everything you need to know about literature," I said.

"Really?" she asked.

"No, not really."

She laughed and then took a charming tone of put-on disappointment. "And to think, I was going to offer you wine lessons in trade."

"I doubt I could learn everything there is to know about wine."

"I think I could show you enough to be dangerous."

A waitress called our number. I tottered back from the counter with our food on a perilously packed tray.

"Hey, I have another question," Izzy said, before we began eating.

"Okay."

"How come you've never tried to pitch a restaurant for real?"

When we were finished, I drove her home. She directed me to her building, and I parked the Mustang in an alley behind it. We said our good-byes. Then I leaned in to kiss her. Off and on since we'd gotten up this morning, I'd feared that what I thought had begun last night and was still going on between us had been entirely of my own drunken invention. With our lips colliding—for the first time in sober daylight—something nebulous calcified. This kiss made the concept of us as a couple real somehow.

The sunlit sky faded quickly after I returned to the sublet. I scribbled some perfunctory comments on flimsy essay pages I'd neglected while Izzy and I were at brunch. By the time I finished, the abbreviated day had leapt into deep evening. An important hour was near. I microwaved a frozen plastic bowl purporting to contain lamb vindaloo and sat down in front of the television. From the moment *Vintage Attraction* came on, I was mesmerized by the likeness of the girl who, that morning, had lain in my bed. I was now seeing the program through different eyes, eyes theretofore not mine. I witnessed Izzy holding court on her set as the well-regarded famous host of the show, just as I always had, but now she also was someone real, someone whose phone number lay on my kitchen counter. At an amateurishly shot and edited commercial for a sketchy liquor store downtown on Chicago Avenue, I got the paper and held her handwriting close to my eyes. She'd been here. She'd written it. And she had my phone number, too.

A fitful, insomniac night of nonsleep followed. Groggy the next day, I read the *Times*, pretending it was a Sunday like all those in my life that had preceded it. I wanted to call Izzy, but it was still too early. She may have liked me, but I couldn't risk startling her at eleven the morning after we last saw each other. Waiting, however wrenching, would prove, in some small but significant way, that I hadn't completely lost my mind. Yet.

Late that night, my cell began buzzing. Before I checked the display, I hoped, illogically, that it was Izzy. Instead, it was her diametrical opposite, Talia. This time I'd be the one to not answer the phone.

2

IT HAD BEEN COMPLETELY QUIET FOR NEARLY AN HOUR WHEN THE TRILL clanged in the next morning. I was on campus, on duty—office hours—and thus required by English department law to pick up. It could have been one of my students. Though undergraduates' preferred method of communication was the grammatically indifferent e-mail, sometimes they rang up to relay elaborate excuses about the car trouble or roommate's food poisoning that had forced them to skip a previous hour's lecture. The incidence of trial depositions and relatives' sudden deaths and funerals that caused them to be late for or absent from class was particularly high when a paper was due. I hefted the receiver. Talia. She caught me.

"What can I do for you?" I asked.

"Are you pissed about me not calling you back last weekend? My phone died at the Riv."

"What were you doing there?"

"Seeing Rilo Kiley."

"Was he in my 212? The one with the orthopedic shoes who smelled like maple syrup?" She didn't answer. "The plagiarist who always agreed with you?"

"I was at a show. Indie *rock*, Hapworth."

"Oh, right. You went by yourself?"

"I went with someone. A boy."

"Who? Which boy?"

"No one you know. So it was late when I saw your text."

"It's no big deal," I said. It really wasn't anymore. "And, for the record, it was, like, three weekends ago."

"Can we have dinner tonight?" she asked.

"Where?"

"Marché."

"I'm not dressed for it."

"Come on, Hapworth. It won't be too expensive. There's a three-course *prix fixe* on Mondays."

I was silent, still thinking about my clothes.

"Okay, *fine*, dude, I'll pay," she said. "By the way, what *are* you wearing?"

I pulled my sweater off. The blue button-down looked as though I'd been wearing it since Friday, and sleeping in it just as long, which were both true. I was only in front of students three times a week this semester, which meant I could often delay laundry, but since I was only teaching one class instead of three, there was considerably less money in the dry-cleaning budget. Things would be better in the spring—I thought—but for now I had to ration.

"My shirt has seen better days," I said. "If I tuck it in, it should be okay."

She laughed. "We really are going to have to work on you, aren't we? What would you do without me?"

"Probably pretty much what I always do without you."

When Berkal came back from his 161 section, he dropped a pile of index cards likely belonging to one of his research-paper-writing Comp Two students. He unbuttoned his blazer before he bent down to pick the cards up. I quickly seized upon an opportunity I wasn't expecting to find.

"Hey, Berkal," I said. "How was class?"

"It's Ber*quelle*," he returned.

"Whatever," I said. "I need a favor."

"I'm so glad I'm not teaching this shit next semester," he grumbled, dusting the cards.

"Hey, listen, can I borrow your blazer?"

"Excuse me?"

"Your blazer. Your jacket."

Berkal bent his arms and showed off the corduroy elbow patches in lieu of responding.

"I need it."

"For what?"

"To wear. To see . . . someone."

"Be more specific or else no costume."

Though it peeved me to have to share any of the details of my life with a colleague as undeserving as Ber*quelle*, I always ended up telling him everything. He wasn't even truly a colleague. He was a grad student with a teaching assistantship. In keeping with the rest of his GPTI cohort from the PhD program, at his classroom podiums and here in our office, he impersonated a professor, in the hopes of getting the routine down such that he could someday work an actual career out of it. When, with two shiny master's degrees still sanguine in my sock drawer, I was an optimistic adjunct (before I had a chance to discover that was an oxymoronic state), I'd done the same thing. "I have to break up with Talia," I said.

"Yes," Berkal said. "It's been, what, a couple of months?" He grinned tauntingly. "She might want you to move in with her."

I let this go. "We haven't been exclusive. Anyway, I'm done with it. I met someone else the other night."

He sat on the edge of his desk and crossed his arms. "Craigslist?"

"No," I said stiffly. "As a matter of fact, the Internet had nothing to do with it. Maybe it had a little to do with it. I was at a wine tasting."

"How did you end up there?"

"Do you know Isabelle Conway?"

Berkal threw his head back. "The sexy sommelier from TV? No, not personally."

"I had a date with her."

"Yeah, right."

"Fine, don't believe me. So I can have it?"

The blazer, once on me, hugged my chest and stomach tightly. The sleeves hung down and covered my extended hands a little more than they were supposed to.

Berkal sized me up after I sought his opinion. "You're a college professor. Everyone expects you to be unshaven and disheveled. It's part of the charm."

"Adjunct professor. Adjunct *lecturer*, if you want to get technical."

"When are you supposed to see her?"

"Seven."

"You have plenty of time."

"Not really. I have to go shopping first."

"For what? I thought you said she was on the Pill."

"A bouquet. What do you think? Roses? Carnations? I can't show up empty-handed."

Berkal rubbed the chin-end of his goatee. "You're planning to break up with this girl, and you're contemplating a botanical hand prop?"

"I'm not a complete asshole, Berkal. I just—"

He cackled. "You just what?"

"You know what I was thinking, when I was driving Izzy home?" I swirled my coffee cup, as though a wineglass.

"Izzy, as in Isabelle Conway, as in the sommelier from TV you had an imaginary date with?"

"I need this to work because . . . because I need my adulthood to begin. Look at me. I'm thirty-seven years old. I don't have job security. I'm living in a city I didn't grow up in. I'm not even committed to a real apartment lease. Don't you think it's time I was in a real relationship with someone with whom I could actually see spending the rest of my life?"

Berkal shrugged. "Good luck breaking the news to Talia."

"She's twenty, Berkal. She'll understand."

"She's twenty, Hapworth," he mocked. "Precisely why she *won't* understand."

A few hours later, and only about a mile from campus, I was hunched over a corner of the long bar at Marché. As West Loop architects in North Face jackets and entrenched lawyers strode from their loft offices with commuter fervor on the other side of the windows, I tried to select a glass of wine. The list presented a thicket of mysterious amalgamated grape variety choices Izzy hadn't talked about the other night. Sauvignon Blanc-Semillon-Muscadelle, Marsanne-Viognier, Malbec-Tempranillo—which one was I supposed to choose? I ended up with a Belvedere on the rocks. (Grey Goose, Izzy had alerted me the other night, was more appropriate for car dealers.)

Talia entered the restaurant, in a long, ruffled gossamer dress. Instinctively, I hid in my jacket pocket the green plastic swizzle stick I'd been oaring through the vodka. She made her way past the host stand and to the bar. Tension circumscribed her round, pale face and the glossy-lipped smile with which she acknowledged my wave. Her hair was down, seeming to intensify the patches of blonde, rose, pomegranate, and Northern Spy apple I'd come to know over the summer as more than simply the mottled auburn I appraised from an appropriate distance across the classroom during the spring term. The dense colors of her highlights became further magnified in the sharp light that descended from the ceiling and spotlighted the bar. Her arrival caused me to feel a surge of self-consciousness from which I wasn't certain I'd recover. While she officially was no longer an undergraduate, and I no longer her creative writing teacher, or anyone's, I was still a little frightened when we were in such close proximity. Even though we'd slept together, her eyes could still pierce mine with a rather ferocious and almost blinding blue ice.

"Can I get you something?" I asked. I turned to try to signal the bartender so I'd have to stop following the plunge of Talia's neckline to abundant breasts.

"Let's just go sit down."

An intricate architectural infrastructure of columns that had been gessoed with decades-faded *Le Monde* front pages ensconced our table. I took the seat facing elegantly rusted shelves of baubles that filled an entire juxtaposing southern wall. Across from me, Talia cautiously—yet appreciatively—accepted the orchids I'd had sent over ahead of us. She peered into a small vent at the top of the brown paper and cellophane. "Wow," she said flatly, though her face bore the first immoderate smile of the evening, "are you asking me to prom?" After she put them aside, we studied our menus for an overly long time. Periodically I lifted mine up, screening out my face. I felt like I was sinking, that my store of resolve was dwindling by way of a small leak. My power to steer this breakup in an auspicious direction seemed to spill out through an invisible hole in my pilling khakis. I couldn't possibly have still had feelings for her, could I? I needed another drink.

"Do you want a cocktail?" I blurted. "Or some wine?" I had hoped she'd want to order a bottle, so I could show off a little of what I'd recently learned. Then I recalled the impenetrability of the list I wrestled at the bar. Perversely, I almost wished Izzy were here to make a recommendation that would pair well with our *plats principaux*.

Talia looked at her empty glass. "I don't really want any wine. I kind of have something I should tell you."

"I have something to tell you, too."

But before either of us could start, our waitress was back. Talia ended up asking for a dirty gin martini with the olive juice on the side. I'd been chewing my ice and was grateful for the opportunity to order more vodka. The waitress peered in the direction of the flowers and asked, "Is tonight a special occasion?"

"Um," I began. "We're, I—"

"I'm moving to Iowa," Talia said. "For grad school."

I almost choked on the cube in my mouth. "You got in?"

"Congratulations," the waitress said.

I was so relieved, but probably looked utterly shocked.

"To you," I toasted Talia when we lunged our glasses.

"To your glowing letter of recommendation."

We ate with little fanfare. She didn't seem particularly taken with any of the courses we had. The vinaigrette on her pear, walnut, endive, and soy Gorgonzola salad was too salty. The dairy-free butter substitute she put on a swatch of baguette tasted tangy, slightly spoiled. Talia declined a fork of my Caesar, saying, "Dude, there's anchovy in that." I didn't solicit her ratatouille nor offer any of the asparagus or mushrooms I'd been careful to keep from coming into contact with my salmon.

We were nearing the end of the meal when I said, "I'm really glad, you know, that"—I extended my hand, as risky a gesture as it was, across the table—"we're here. You're going to Iowa next fall, and that's—that's really outstanding. The fiction program is nearly impossible to get into."

As I spoke, the scenes of the afternoon our harrowing flirtation materialized were indelible in my mind. It began when she'd picked me up in a salt-dusted red Volkswagen Jetta with out-of-state plates. The sedan's plush interior smelled like Crayolas. She brought us to a bagel place in a strip mall on the edge of campus. We were there to discuss ideas for her next story, if anyone happened to ask. She'd taken my hand when we left. I still could feel how my fingers felt laced between hers. Now she put her hand on top of mine and patted firmly, conclusively.

"Spring semester," she said. "I'm starting early to take an instruction practicum. I'm moving now. I might as well, right?"

I nodded, the corners of my mouth struggling not to ascend.

"I guess we'll always have University Hall."

My cocktail was empty again, so I lifted my water glass. "To Iowa. You'd better write your ass off."

"I could say the same to you."

I smirked. "I'm not a writer. That's ancient history."

"You're not an artifact," she said, and unfixed herself from her chair.

While she was off in the bathroom, I sent the waitress for the check. The bill was astronomical—almost half a week's salary—and we hadn't even gotten wine. I scratched in a hyperbolic tip, just in case Talia happened to open up the leather presenter and inspect the figures. She returned and saw the completed credit card receipt peering out from the presenter. "Dude." She brought a hand to her little jaw. "You didn't have to do that." I shrugged. "What was it you wanted to tell me before?"

"Oh, just that I wanted to pick up dinner," I said, looking up at her. I was aware of Talia's tense shifting from present to past as I spoke. Really, it had occurred long before now. "It's getting late. You probably should get those in some water."

She reached for the bundle of orchids, which had been languishing in the empty seat on her other side. "Hapworth," she said, "I've had a really good time."

"Me, too," I said.

We stood outside, in front of the revolving door, waiting for a taxi. Talia handed me the cumbersome parcel to hold while she took a plastic Urban Outfitters child's wallet from her bag. She began wrenching free a credit card. Her averted eyes allowed me a puerile chance to check her out. In doing so, I was again put in mind of the occasion of our unofficial first date at the bagel place. The counter barista had been so transfixed by the sight of her chest her open coat and low-cut top had afforded that he delivered Talia her change *and* the cash she'd paid him for her coffee with a tremulous hand. When she said to the lanky kid with Brillo-pad hair who reminded me a lot of myself at that age, "Um, dude, I'm pretty sure *I'm* supposed to pay *you*?" it only made things more awkward. I recalled how rapidly the patches of freezer-burnt skin on the kid's face reddened, in the time he reached to recollect the pair of dollar bills she held out for him. Everything had worked out according to plan—better than according to plan, since I hadn't really arrived with a plan. I knew I'd finally found the right time to call Izzy. But standing there I also found the familiar and unfamiliar abundance of Talia's physicality eliciting a shade of incapacitation similar to that of the nerdy barista's on my own cheeks now.

It was inordinately frustrating that despite how I felt about Izzy, Talia still had some kind of hold on me. Things with me and the host of the city's most watched cable-access television show couldn't have been more promising in juxtaposition with this sexual perversity in Chicago. How had I gotten so attached to a twenty-year-old vegan with dyed hair, a music blog, Facebook page, and a Brazilian wax? During the semester, both because of how I felt and of the inevitable institutional repercussions for feeling, I was wary of even venturing close enough to hand back assignments, but when she began to come on to me, I didn't resist. I couldn't. She wore ethereally iridescent purple and blue thongs. She sprayed thrift-store sweaters with anachronistic Exclamation perfume. She had a Mac. She read Pynchon and kept T. S. Eliot and Nabokov on her bedside table in off-campus student housing. During our illicit months together, we drank wine (the French provenances she always pronounced unflinchingly), made out in my Mustang, in her Jetta, ate at pancake houses, fucked breathlessly and without condoms. Once, when I was sick, she bought and prepared me instant asparagus risotto—the outcome of which was far more successful than when she tried to cook without a boxed mix—and hot lemon Theraflu. I could argue about philosophy and summary-to-scene ratios in short stories with the precocious underclassman poised to graduate in just two years, three fewer than the average UIC English major. But our connection, like everything else within the speciously protective confines of academia, was, even then, already finite. At the time, being with Talia was everything I needed, but I didn't want it anymore. No matter how drunk I ever got, I knew how I operated: I stumbled into entanglements, tumbled from one romance with a girl I'd offhandedly select to the next, haphazardly—I always had—but when I fell in love, I catapulted. I was in love with somebody else. And luckily for me—as far as I could see then, anyway—things with Talia were over for good.

The taxi into which I helped her climb took off and vanished into the night before I'd finished saying good-bye. I was left standing at the curb. I realized that I was still holding the paper-and-plastic-bound bouquet. The orchids, through the vent, looked a little less energetic than they'd been when the clerk first armed me with them. It didn't matter that Talia had relinquished the gift. With her gone, and out of my life, the flowers had served their purpose. I deposited the bundle into a black-painted sidewalk receptacle.

Unencumbered, and commensurately emboldened, I revolved back into the restaurant. From an inconspicuous corner by the coat check, I dialed Izzy from my cell phone. I made up something preposterous about having just finished a meal with a visiting poet and some of the faculty and not feeling quite ready to make my way to the Blue Line station to begin the four-mile trek home.

"Let me buy you an after-dinner drink," she said.

She showed up in a blue-and-white taxi fifteen minutes later. "Pilsen isn't that far from here," she said. I reached for her hand as we walked along Randolph, headed for The Tasting Room. To my surprise, she didn't object. The street was empty. This part of town was full of warehouses and delivery trucks and wholesale meat and produce purveyors that operated early in the day and then were dead at night.

We took two seats in the center of the mahogany bar. There was wood everywhere: the tables, the walls, the floors. Everything was dark and polished. The lights were kept dim and obfuscating, except for the higher-wattage glow from the bulbs haloing the liquor bottles against the backsplash. A server equipped us with menus and decorated our allocation of space with silver and napkins and a small tea-light candle in a squat, unadorned container that could have doubled as a shot glass.

I barely had a chance to handle my menu before the bartender, a blonde woman with spiky platinum hair, swept it away. After only a second's consideration, Izzy ordered a flight of dessert wine. The bartender brought over a narrow rectangular paper placemat that had a row of circles on top of which glasses would eventually be placed. Beneath each circle, a small caption indicated what they would contain: Hungarian Tokaji, Australian Muscadelle, and white port from the Upper Douro Valley—regions of the world I knew nothing about, much less their *digestifs*. A spectrum of hues soon stood before Izzy and me. We passed the portions back and forth, spending a moment or two sniffing and sipping microscopic fractions, and then exchanging again. I was surprised how sweet the dessert wine was. The alcohol burn, though unremitting, began to warm my chest.

"Beats vodka," I said, turning the glass I held.

"Old-school cocktails are really hot right now."

"I can't believe how many people are out this late on a Monday."

"Industry night," the eavesdropping bartender put in with her faint Texas twang. "Monday is the restaurant world's Sunday."

"What's their Saturday?" I asked.

"Sunday," Izzy replied.

"What about Friday?"

"They don't get a Friday."

"That is a confusing calculus," I said. "Here's to Monday nights."

"Monday's actually a popular date night."

"Makes sense, with all the half-priced-bottle deals in the city. Nothing says love like *prix fixe*."

"At the bistro, I've seen cheap wine backfire. I've seen expensive wine backfire. Did you catch those orchids in the garbage we passed? I don't even want to know what happened on that date."

I'd almost completely forgotten about them, and laughed. "Something tells me those flowers are going to end up the subject of a Craigslist Missed Connections post tomorrow, one way or another."

"I read those, too," she said. "They're hilarious."

"It never ceases to amaze me how badly people misinterpret insignificant gestures. 'I was riding the Red Line, and you asked me if you could sit down in the space my bag was hogging. I felt like we really connected. Drinks sometime?' She only spoke to you because she wanted your seat. It wasn't love at first transfer."

Izzy nodded. "And, okay, let's say it was love, right? Let's just say that such an absurdity were possible. How do they really think the other person is going to, like, drop everything and fall for them?"

"I sometimes wonder if they even really expect that," I said. "It could just be more like leaving notes for god at the Wailing Wall. You know, in Jerusalem? There are all these little scraps of paper stuck in the cracks, requests in a billion languages, for who knows how many different conceptions of god, to cure an aunt's cancer or find a kidney for the second cousin, twice removed. I mean, I'm sure they'd *like* it to work, but nobody could really expect it to."

We sat close on our neighboring barstools, leaning in, our legs angled toward each other's. "I'm actually kind of shocked nobody's posted one for me. I feel completely left out," she said then.

"This," I said, "is a problem. Perhaps you've not been reading as closely as you should."

"Perhaps," she said.

I rarely stayed out this late, ate this much, drank this much on weeknights—or any nights. Accordingly, my muscles ached and my head pulsed as we walked a sobering, windswept walk down Halsted and back to my lot at UIC on Harrison. I was grateful the Mustang started after a few panicking hesitations on the second level of the mostly empty concrete parking structure. Izzy didn't object to a kiss from me before she climbed the stairs to her apartment. I missed her instantly. I hated to see her go, didn't want us to be apart, and was glad she hadn't refused my offer to take her home so that I could extend our impromptu date another fifteen minutes. Driving to my place in Humboldt Park, my feet were cinder blocks against the clutch and the accelerator, and my shifting was inelegant. Once in the apartment, however, I couldn't sleep.

It was at insomniac times like these that I usually pulled out the Rhodia and sketched a concept or two, but on this occasion, it was a monologue of sorts I wrought. I sat at my little kitchen table, hovering over a legal pad. Even though I was exhausted, all that transpired tonight—finally being freed from Talia's spell; sharing, unencumbered, the port with Izzy—had energized me. My sentences blazed. At four thirty in the morning, I had a draft. I continued to edit as I plugged the text into the Craigslist form from my office Mac Performa on campus the next morning before submitting. I entered the URL the automatic responder sent a moment later, and read my Missed Connections post, entitled "Because it was Monday night at The Tasting Room—m4w":

I'd never in the five minutes I'd known you seen you looking so amplified, and the fact that I wasn't the one making you glow tore me into impossible shreds. I tried to ignore your date, the young artist—postmodern restaurateur maybe, or was he an indie film actor?—a cross between Jeff Goldblum and F. Scott Fitzgerald, with returned-to-vogue chunky Woody Allenish glasses, sagaciously—or slovenly—cantilevered, because I was immensely jealous. I could tell by the way he held your gaze that he was a formidable opponent.

The way he felt about you was apparent in irrefutable, unimpeachable physiognomy as you made your way out. Your date stood a little straighter, his hair free to cascade whichever way it wanted, his chin stronger, more sure of itself. It was as though his entire picture had been retouched. His smile grinned larger, his ardor more ardent. I think his blazer even fit a little better. How did you do it? How did you manage to change him? After you departed, I needed to grab something, to still myself, but there was nothing I could reach; it was all too far from me. I stood from my little table and found everything inside me had shifted, moved, reorganized. Things had been bought, sold, an internal organ garage sale. I had a heart shard, a lung cross section, and a kidney encased in glass, but most disconcerting was that I had ceased to possess truth, a priori or posteriori, because of you, because you were gone, *and you were the truth. I need to have you in my life to be whole, to be anything.*

May I see you again?

I e-mailed Izzy: *I think someone was following us last night* and then pasted the web address. Below that I signed off simply, *Hapworth.*

A reply was waiting for me when I got back from class.

Peter, that is the most amazing thing anybody has ever written me. You are sweet. I had a splendid time last night. Can't wait to see you again. Izzy.

3

AROUND THE CONFERENCE TABLE IN SHELLEY SCHULTZ'S OFFICE SAT next semester's new adjuncts—and me. There was Bearded Sweater Dude, a pudgy Wicker Park hipster who exuded a sickening air of conscientiousness not made any easier to endure by his environmentally responsible metallic coffee tumbler and serious-looking spiral notebook. To his left was Senegalese Woman, a mid-forties first-grade teacher sort, with a fabric-covered journal and a vacant but present look on her face. In between her fingers, she had a Bic pen. Its white plastic shell seemed even brighter against her dark skin. She nodded a lot, even when nobody was speaking. To Senegalese Woman's left sat Short Haired. Though her blue eyes and Mandy Moore haircut connoted a much younger person, her tiny, lusterless features betrayed signs that her twenties took place in an analog era. Orange Corduroy Pants had a high forehead and lipstick spilling over the boundaries of her mouth. She was the sort of person I'd have expected to find working at a holistic acupressure clinic. It wasn't beyond the realm of possibility that she'd come to UIC from such a position. Next to her stood Schultz, the coordinator, in an age-inappropriate miniskirt and department-issue turtleneck.

I always hated having to see Schultz, let alone attend her super-fluous, disorganized meetings. I wasn't sure why she'd even invited me to this one, since I'd been adjuncting for almost ten years. I would have blown it off, like I usually did, but I showed up today to find out what Schultz had assigned me for the coming semester. No matter how much I disliked her, to have a livelihood, even a meager one, depended on my receiving at least two sections a term. I was annoyed, but resigned to suffer through. If at the end of it I could get what I wanted, I'd have no need to interact with her, corporeally, for a few months at least. Her e-mails and mailbox memos were an unrelenting scourge.

Bearded Sweater Dude spoke in jazzy cadences. "I, like, start them out, you know, like, free associating, just to kinda get them in the groove of brainstorming." What the hell was he talking about?

Orange Pants, for a full two minutes, rambled an anecdote about a former student of hers. The student had been having trouble writing a resume and come to a number of her office-hours sessions seeking guidance on the topic. By the end of the term, "they" emerged victorious. Schultz, visibly pleased and not at all fettered by the pronoun-antecedent disagreement, unveiled her plan for us to teach this spring a full three-week unit on "practical writing," with lectures on resume fonts, paper stocks, and personal website designs. "I have some handouts on using Microsoft Mail Merge macros, for students that want to maximize the reach of their cover letters," Orange Pants told us. Senegalese Woman made a note of this and drew several emphatic asterisks beside it.

"Mr. Hapworth, you've been quiet," Schultz said. "Do you have anything to add?" She put a hand to her mouth. "Everybody, I forgot to introduce Peter Hapworth. Mr. Hapworth is, dollars to donuts, one of our longest-surviving adjuncts. Three or four years now, right? Peter has a creative writing background, so, as you can imagine, he always has unique and creative approaches to teaching comp."

While some tenured faculty solicited feedback from us transients at occasional departmental meetings and on-campus happy hours just to foster the illusion of academic democracy, which we all pretended existed in spite of the oligarchic hierarchy, I knew, "dollars to donuts," that Schultz wasn't putting up a pretense. She was an administrator in the worst way. She had a master's in education, not in English, and accordingly unrealistic expectations of the students. She actually really did need suggestions from adjuncts, as it had been years since she'd bothered to read any pedagogy in journals. Her source for inspiration was, in keeping with the undergraduates, Google.

For comic relief—what else could have prompted it?—Bearded Sweater Dude stood up here. I didn't even look in the vicinity of his face while he spoke. Instead I stared at the guy's flat-fronted khakis, which fit him poorly, like he'd bought them without even trying them on. "I like to have the students trace themselves on a big piece of butcher paper, and then cut out the silhouette and make a collage on it, using pieces of newspapers and pictures from magazines that they feel describe themselves."

"You could also just have them write something," I said.

"Sorry, man?" Bearded Sweater Dude sat down again.

"Like, I don't know, instead of wasting time with the magazines and collages, just, you know, assign a paragraph or two of self-reflection. Writing." He stared at me with unfocused eyes. "Writing? Pens, paper, sentences, that sort of thing?"

Bearded Sweater Dude shook his head slowly. My very obvious suggestion had, it appeared, sent his lesson plan, or what passed for one, into revolution.

Schultz must have sensed there was nowhere the meeting could possibly go from here. She abruptly and awkwardly dismissed us with benedictions. I watched the new adjunct hires collect their notebooks, shoulder their bags, and walk, single-file, out of her office. They waited to begin conversing until they had cleared the threshold, as though timid undergraduates.

"Is there a problem, Peter?" Schultz asked when we were alone. Her voice was affectless. "Are you happy working here?"

"Happy?" I asked. "This is academia. Liberal arts academia. English department liberal arts academia, no less. What does being happy have to do with it? We're naturally a disgruntled sort."

She cleared her throat. "I think you saw a room full of enthusiastic young teachers who would disagree with you."

"You want to know something, Shelley? I've realized—okay. I've been thinking a lot about Beethoven. You know, the composer?"

She nodded, though I seriously doubted she would have been able to name one sonata.

"Beethoven gradually started going deaf, but he continued to compose after he'd become fully deaf. Deaf. And he was writing music that would continue to be relevant for hundreds of years to come. Deaf. What excuse do we have to advocate, to champion mediocrity? Is it just because some of us are mediocre? I certainly am not."

She didn't remark, as though I'd given a soliloquy. "I wanted to speak with you about this, Mr. Hapworth." She clicked her computer mouse weakly several times and turned the monitor to me. There was an e-mail I'd sent weeks ago.

From: Peter Hapworth <hapworth@uic.edu>
Date: Tue, Sep 11, 2007 at 11:36 AM
To: Adjunct Coordinator <shelleys@uic.edu>
Subject: RE: ENG161 mandatory handouts!!!

Could you possibly leave hard copies of future items we're to distribute somewhere where those of us with limited computer access can get them? Once again, I couldn't read the descriptive essay attachment because it was in PDF format, and the computer the department placed in my

office back in 1997 is now too ancient to open these files. A
kind departmental administrator with access to a terminal
manufactured in the twenty-first century printed it for me
and I was able to provide my students with copies after that.

I'm really glad I took a look at it on my walk across
campus, as it contained a number of overly simplistic
assumptions about showing vs. telling in narrative, as well
as a laughable usage error in its second sentence. Considering the author had so pompously heralded himself a professional, we appreciated the irony of his misusing "affect"
and "effect," but presenting such flawed models to students
is inordinately embarrassing. I've been using a new textbook
called *Teaching Composition to Dummies*, and I'm sure after
perusing it for a few minutes, we could come up with a more
useful handout than a download from a specious, random
website offering "instruction."

I withdrew and Schultz took this as a cue to angle the screen
back to where only she could view it. I was silent until she spoke.

"Your tone in this message came across as extremely conde-
scending, Peter," she said, gaze fixed on the monitor, "and I don't
believe that was your intention. I know that often it is hard to
convey what we mean in written communication, where we don't
have voice inflections to help us decode—"

"I'm sorry for the e-mail, Shelley." I sighed. "For the tone, I mean.
I've just been a little preoccupied lately, I guess."

Shelley Schultz pivoted her empty head, which signaled my
dismissal. So I left. The next time I'd visit would be the last time.

Back at my desk, I pulled up the note I'd sent to Schultz from
my webmail folders. I spent a number of minutes wondering if I
should have said "during" the twenty-first century instead of "in"
when I juxtaposed my elderly office terminal with receptionist
Charles Wilcox's iMac. The matter I should have been pondering
was what exactly I thought pissing off Shelley Schultz was going to

accomplish. I knew I was already disliked around here. This was my job, my only discernible means of having an income, but it had become hard to care too much about the politics. I was largely a department outsider. Possibly I'd always been. I began adjuncting, I supposed, as a phasic placeholder, a space-filler for my life. I never imagined it to be anything beyond temporary. And on the nineteenth floor I still was.

In the early days, still marginally professionally naïve, I'd apply for tenure-track jobs at area schools from time to time. Once, some years ago, an entry-level assistant professor line opened up here. I submitted the paperwork, the myriad transcripts and recommendations and a statement of teaching philosophy, by the deadline, but didn't get an interview. It wasn't a complete shock to have not made it beyond the first round, if I'd actually progressed *that* far. The disorganized department never sent a letter to acknowledge receipt of my dossier. A few months later, they hired Shelley Schultz.

Even though the adjunct coordinator lacked a degree beyond her MEd, I knew my unsuccessful candidacy had much to do with the fact that I didn't have a PhD. Sometimes I regretted I'd ended up without one. But after two master's degrees, the idea of taking the GRE subject exams the doctoral program application prerequisites required had seemed inconceivable. I'd barely done well enough on the regular test to get into grad school in the first place. And there was the two-foreign-languages requirement. As an undergrad, I'd struggled with French, and couldn't imagine having to go through that again with Spanish or Greek. Oral exams? A dissertation longer than my eighty-eight-page MFA short-story-collection thesis I threw together the week before it was due at Cornell? So, I never applied and instead ended up a University of Illinois at Chicago part-time adjunct lecturer. It was in this position that, at some point I could no longer recall, I'd resigned myself to remain.

With my face close to the monitor, I continued to stare at the paragraphs (did people still paragraph e-mails?) I'd sent Schultz until the words blurred into antiquated Performa pixels. My cell phone's ringing broke the digital spell.

"Hi," Izzy said, after I greeted her. "I hope I didn't catch you at a bad time."

"No, no," I returned. "It's nice to hear your voice."

"I want you to come somewhere with me this weekend."

Ever since that monumental evening in the not-so-distant past, Izzy and I had been gradually but eagerly accumulating dates. We'd seen Truffaut double features at the Siskel Center, drunk Brachetto d'Acqui by candlelight in a private corner of a River North osteria that was open late. At my place we'd had a living-room screening of *Annie Hall* and half of *Manhattan*, followed by a meal of taqueria takeaway and chilled Cru Beaujolais, a night we fondly called Mexicallen. We'd gone to dim sum brunches, taken strolls along crowded downtown avenues and through quaint neighborhood side streets, and made out for quite a few hours atop my IKEA couch. Every time I saw her, I was reminded of how I'd felt about Izzy when I first beheld her in person almost three weeks ago. I was immediately taken with her beauty, her dark-brown hair, statuesque height and broad shoulders, her remarkably resilient onstage persona, and smart and expensive-looking Chanel ensemble, which demonstrated an equally remarkable next-day resilience. Just as impressive was her offstage persona. I'd never failed to feel comfortable or happy in her presence, and so I'd wandered a measure blindly through our times together, just as I'd blindly and unthinkingly sent her that first e-mail. Now, together, we moved from this burger to that burrito to this glass of wine to that potsticker in a perpetual fog of thrill and delight. Doing so was serving me well. I didn't want to analyze how things were going, sabotage her willingness—or mine—with suffocating preoccupation and skepticism. After a life of anticlimax and blunders in love, I knew it was indisputably smarter to let things progress and stay in the moment.

"Where?" I asked.

"I have to give a talk at this food and wine thing," she said. "In Kohler, Wisconsin."

"As in the Kohler that makes toilets?"

"Let's hope among other things."

Even in our headlong nascence, a time well before I'd ever have real cause to, I caught myself occasionally wondering what the hell she was doing with me. Now was one of those times.

4

A FEW NIGHTS LATER, IZZY FINALLY TOOK ME TO HER APARTMENT IN Pilsen. Chris, Dominique's general manager, and, for the last few years, Izzy's roommate, was still at the bistro. With the oversight of the waiters' sidework, vacuuming, end-of-shift inventory, and, most crucially, a few sake bombs at the sushi bar down the block ahead of him, he was unlikely to return for at least several hours. This meant we'd have privacy otherwise unavailable to us here. But it didn't mean we were actually by ourselves. In the dusty flat, which was warm and cluttered with furniture, Izzy turned on lights as she went ahead of me to a bedroom. After she entered, a honey-colored furry rocket shot out, and began frantically zigzagging, glancing off the walls. Ishiguro spotted me, the interloper, right away, but made several circuits of the kitchen and a launch into the living room before coming back to inspect. He stood in front of me on his hind paws. His front pair batted the legs of the faded, loosely-fitting jeans I'd had to wear to the Hard Rock Hotel because there wasn't enough time to get from campus to my place before meeting Izzy and Chef Dominique downtown.

"Nice to meet you," I said to the pug. He inhaled and exhaled and yipped and sneezed before me. "Izzy's told me a lot about you."

He growled, a low, serious rumble, evidently wary.

"Just ignore him," Izzy said, now behind the dog. She'd changed into a T-shirt and sweatpants, but looked no less magnificent than she did earlier, all dressed up. Ishiguro conducted a final inspiration and granted my presence his approval. He then went off in search of amusement in the back rooms.

"So, this is your place," I said.

"For now," she said, somewhat dejectedly. "I'm too old to have a roommate. I need something a little more permanent."

"I think I'll be renting for life," I said, distracted by an array of outdated sports team calendar magnets on the beige refrigerator.

We sat on the couch and watched TV. I couldn't see the time on a clock across the room, but Izzy was obviously single-digit tired. She apologized for an immoderate yawn.

"These silly events take a lot out of me," she went on. "They don't sound like much, on paper, but with all the talking and talking, it might as well be a twelve-hour shift at the bistro all over again."

I hoped this wouldn't sound like prying. "Do they . . . pay well, at least?"

"Yeah," she said. "Very well. That's why Dominique wants me to do it all. The restaurant, the TV show, the appearances, the speaking engagements, the trips."

"As long as you're getting a good percentage, right?"

"Half."

"He takes *half*?"

Tonight at the Hard Rock, I'd watched Chef Dominique canting with the servers and others exhibiting attention deficits at the buffet while his sommelier and Jim Williams, her charismatic newscaster counterpart on the stage, read name after name of what seemed like a million different regional Emmy-award nominated segments (Outstanding Achievement Within a Regularly Scheduled News Program: "Elmwood Park Accident," "Plane Off Runway,"

"Tempting Toxins," "Catholic School Rabbi"). However tedious the performance, it should have been accorded the focus—or at least the quiet. What was Chef Dominique even doing at these things with Izzy? She recited her lines beneath a spotlight and engaged the crowd. He stood in the dark audience and talked loudly. She kept an operatic smile near-continuously affixed to her face. He stuffed his with desserts and cava from the open bar. The disparity in their work had been apparent the night we met at the Metropolitan Club, and nothing had changed as long as I'd been around them. He was hardly a partner. He didn't even make a charming sidekick. It seemed abundantly unfair for him to receive a manager's ten percent, let alone to split the proceeds a partnership fifty-fifty. I had a feeling, which would someday be confirmed, that the true take-home figures weren't even *that* equitable.

"How did you end up hooking up with Dominique, anyway?" I asked.

I listened to the story, my hand on Ishiguro's spine moving fore and aft and back again. There'd been a food and wine event Izzy had found online, which needed pourers for a weekend gig. The pay wasn't much. What she'd spend in getting herself to Chicago and staying in a youth hostel for two days and three nights to work was almost twice the amount of the check to turn up eight weeks later at the apartment she shared with three other waitresses downstate. But working the event would give her something more important than money: an opportunity to put herself in the orbit of chefs and sommeliers, and to taste some wines that didn't ever seem to make it to Carbondale. At the close of the second night, the cognoscenti ended up convening at a winery's table in the tasting tent. They didn't seem at all provoked to leave by the anonymous staff's dismantling taking place around them, and nobody was about to send them back to their rooms. Izzy knew all the chefs' faces from trade magazines. There was Jean-Louis Palladin, Chef Dominique, Michel Richard, Jacques Pépin. Without obvious impetus, Palladin, who'd been the acclaimed culinary genius behind Jean-Louis at the Watergate Hotel in Washington, DC, turned to Izzy, who was then collecting abandoned glassware. He and Dominique were arguing about a wine and Palladin asked her to blind-taste it. Izzy took the challenge by the stem, held the glass this way and that, looked into the liquid from a variety of angles of the harsh light available at that late hour, and swirled up the contents. She inhaled deeply and took a short but deft sip. After only having the wine there to corporeally process a picosecond before she'd swallowed it, she said, "That's easy. It's Pinot Noir."

The winemaker pantomimed putting a medal over Izzy's head.

All night, Izzy couldn't keep herself from gaping at Palladin, and not just because he was a celebrity she'd read so much about. He and his date were completely mismatched, an incongruous pair. She was a blonde siren of a young lady in a blue cocktail dress. With his big glasses and bushy moustache and eighties blowout near-shoulder-length hairstyle, the chef resembled Weird Al Yankovic. This could only have meant the girl was a hooker or a relative. And now here they stood.

Izzy shook hands all around. "It's such an honor to meet you, Chef Palladin," Izzy said. She once more caught sight of the girl's glossy pink lips, bearing no indications of having touched a single glass. Her charcoaled eyelids gradually drew nearer to each other as she stood there without word. "And your beautiful daughter."

Everybody laughed and laughed.

"Oh, she's his daughter, all right," Chef Dominique said. "Tell her, tell her," he demanded of the other chefs. They ignored him, so he pressed Izzy, "They look alike, no?" Palladin, face reddening, informed Izzy who his companion was. "What, you think I'm not man enough?" And, without even a beat of awkwardness, Izzy returned, "Well, Chef, if she's your girlfriend, your foie gras must really be good."

He nodded, pleased, and waved at Chef Dominique. "You fat German, why do you just stand there? What kind of shit host are you? Get *mademoiselle* a glass. *Vite, vite!*" The winemaker had opened another bottle, and they invited Izzy to stay for a drink.

The talk that unfurled revealed that Dominique was looking to hire a sommelier. He liked Izzy and said she should give him a call the following week. And she did.

A month later, she had a room in Chicago and a job at the bistro. Chef Dominique didn't care that her wine knowledge had come from waiting tables at a chain steakhouse and reading library books. He was impressed. He knew she knew what she needed to in order to run his program. Whatever she didn't know, she could learn. He was the first person who'd taken a chance on her. And it was high time to go; there was no future for her downstate. Nobody in Carbondale had ever really given a shit. If she was to have a life, a future, she was going to have to go out there and create it for herself.

But somewhere along the way, she'd made the mistake of becoming famous in her own right. It wasn't long before she'd eclipsed the chef and his restaurant in popular culture. She'd never wanted that, but it had happened. "I sometimes seriously don't know what I'm doing here," she said, by way of epilogue. "I've fantasized about telling Dominique to fuck off and going back to Carbondale and getting my old job waitressing at the goddamn Cattle Company."

"I wouldn't make any sudden southward moves," I said when her head met my shoulder. "These people want you for the gigs, and you can use the money right now, especially if you're going to buy a place. You know?"

"Yeah," she said. "What would I do without you, Hapworth? You're my stalwart. You're my voice of reason."

I grinned. "It has to get easier, at some point, right?"

Izzy got up and walked behind the couch, as though trying to pace her way to an answer. "Oh, sure," she finally said, "if you can figure out a way to clone me."

"Don't you know? I'm a scientist, a scientist and a CIA operative, Wine Service Division. I've been sent to study you and to secret away samples of your genetic material."

"Well, you can tell your bosses that it's no secret. I'm a vampire." She came behind me, put her hands on the back of the couch, leaned down, pressed her lips to my neck, and stage-bit it. I played along. I improvised her suck to be a much more forceful vacuum than the gentle sensual embrace it actually was and let my head hang over the edge of the couch, as though she were draining me. I pleaded theatrically for her to stop, but she only returned comic maniacal laughter. All of this frightened the pug and he skittered over to intercede. He leapt to my side and barked—the first time I'd heard him make any sounds of the seriously aggrieved—until Izzy pulled away. The dog, now silent again, with a paw that resembled a hand on my leg, glared at her like she'd gone mad, which got her apologizing to him, amid our avalanching laughter.

"That's so sweet," Izzy said to me once she'd collected herself. "He was trying to protect you."

"I appreciate your coming to my rescue," I said to the dog. He grumbled intermittently, still unconvinced I hadn't been harmed. I was touched by the pug's instant unequivocal endearment, which I couldn't help reciprocating. "I owe you one."

"He likes you," Izzy said. She coyly added, "I think you'll have to spend the night now."

Ishiguro snorted and sneezed in agreement and jumped down from the couch. He sat facing me, a pragmatically sober yet amply hopeful expression on his face. With his head angled up, he held my eyes in his.

"I think you're probably right."

Friday afternoon, I couldn't get out of teaching in time to ride along with Chef Dominique and Izzy to Kohler in Chef's Range Rover. So I'd had to drive up to the sleepy, rarefied, moneyed town, one-hundred-forty-five miles from Chicago, alone. Armed with nothing more than dubious MapQuest directions I could barely make out on the poorly illuminated side roads I took after I'd gotten off the highway, I feared getting lost in the Wisconsin hinterlands. I also doubted the Mustang would survive the trip. It did, and I eventually found my way to town, though not before missing the first event of the weekend, a cocktail reception held at the Kohler Design Center, the brightly lit loft that showcased all the latest bathroom fixtures and appliance prototypes. When Izzy told me about the party, I was actually disappointed not to have been able to attend. I cheerfully complained about the unique and wry opportunity to eat a canapé under an abeyant rain shower and to drink a glass of sparkling wine while seated, in mixed elite company, atop a toilet, now gone for me. "You didn't miss much," she said. "It was fairly ridiculous."

Izzy had come to the ritzy golf and tennis resort destination to present a menu of budget pairings at this fall's Kohler Food and Wine Experience, a bucolic paean to consumption held each October. Upper-middle-class epicures—"foodies," as they were commonly known—traveled the country and beyond to sample the cuisine of the latest celebrated chefs and seek the advice of the touted sommeliers. This festival drew thousands of them.

On Saturday, between her seminars, Izzy and I were at Riverbend, a historic mansion that provided its members-only guest quarters to the Kohler dignitaries for the weekend. In our luxury-grade suite, we sat on the bed that raised us nearly four feet above the ground and drank most of a bottle of Krug that a Moët rep had handed Izzy and I smuggled back. By the time we finished the Champagne, we were starving.

"Do you think there's time for room service?" I asked.

"Probably not," she said. "See what's in the basket."

We routed around in the gift basket that the promoters from *Cellar Temperature* magazine had delivered before we arrived. Along with several wines, a jar of sesame seeds, a bag of coffee, a silver Grey Goose bottle stopper, a set of Kitchen Aid measuring cups, spatula, and cheese slicer, it contained a bevy of snacks. We shared an apple and a banana. Izzy mined the mixed nuts for cashews. I impeached the nutritional facts on the side of an organic granola bar.

"Can you believe this?" she asked. She unwrapped a brownie and tore off a corner. "Isn't it all kind of crazy? And you don't even want to know how much these people paid for tickets."

"They seem very pleased with themselves," I said.

"Okay, so they have money. We *get* it. They're what we call Window Tables at the bistro. Always trying to show off, handing out cash to the maître d' and the captains and flashing their capped teeth and Black Cards. As if anybody really cares where they're sitting or what cliché wine they're drinking so proudly. Those silly sleeveless fleece things with the embroidered Kohler Experience logo the three guys from Chicago in the front row had on? Total Window Table move. Do they think they're going to forget they're here? Or that anyone else might have missed noticing they're here?"

"I don't think I've ever seen so many golfers in one place."

"They just like wearing the polo shirts and khakis."

"I guess if you break a sweat crossing from one end of the tasting tent to the other, it's kind of a sport. Oh, I was meaning to ask: what's up with those holster necklace things?"

"How else can you hold your wineglass while you have a fork in one hand and a plate in the other?" She shook her head and put the uneaten brownie half back in the basket. "Guerrilla buffet warfare."

I laughed. "You're bad."

"Don't tell anyone I talk like this," she said. "I'm supposed to be grateful they admire me and support me and watch the show and everything, and I am, but sometimes it's just so—"

"Your secret's safe with me," I said.

Her BlackBerry buzzed and she spent several interminable seconds taking in the information the screen presented.

"What is it?" I ventured to ask. "You're staring like gapers' block."

"Oh, nothing," she said quickly. She flung the phone onto the bed, where it landed facedown. "Just a random text." She continued to eye the device, as though anticipating its starting to move again. "Young sommeliers. They're all freaking out about next year's master's exam."

"How come you never took it?"

"They've been trying to get me to for years," she said, "since the Court has so few female masters, but it wouldn't do anything for my career at this point. I don't have a problem helping candidates study, though."

"Should you be concerned? About the message?"

"No," she said. "Not at all." She looked down at the BlackBerry again. It hadn't vibrated a second time. "In fact, I'm not going to reply."

"Should I be concerned?"

"You? No. You definitely should not be. You should enjoy yourself." She ran her hand down the buttons of my shirt. "And let me enjoy yourself before this next damn talk."

"On today's episode of *Lifestyles of the Rich and Fermented*," I said in Leach parody.

"Seriously, Hapworth, are you ready for this?"

"You're kind of stuck with me now."

"What do you think brought us together?" Izzy asked. The question surprised me. "Like, do you think it was fate?"

"Do you believe in that?"

"Sometimes," she said. She turned her head to the chandelier that loomed over us. "And other times I think things just happen." Then her eyes came back to me. "Or is that the same thing?"

My inner English major was tempted to debate connotations, but I offered a humble shrug.

"You sit through my songs and dances."

"I happen to think you're amazing. Though," I teased, "that could just be an effect of Kohler's intoxicating charms."

"It's beautiful here, isn't it? Hapworth, what if we could leave our lives behind and stay here forever?"

"Someone would probably miss us."

"You know who I really miss?" she asked.

"Who?"

"Ishiguro."

The Kohler Experience attendees cooed in mock deference around Izzy, but you could tell, above all, they were here to be entertained. They hadn't spent thousands merely to come learn about Spanish Monastrell and Rhone-style blends from the Languedoc, alternatives to fifty-dollar Napa Valley Cabernet that could be had at a third of the price. It created a very skewed power dynamic within the proceedings. The second presentation consisted of an hour and a half talk through a tasting, almost identical to the earlier installment. Following that, Izzy answered myriad idiotic questions. "Which wines should I decanter?" "'97 Robert Mondavi. Drink or sell? Saving a mag since my son's 'destination' wedding—Oakville—still paying that bad boy off—it's a reserve." Didn't foodies know how to use Google, too? Then—*then*—came another twenty minutes of autograph signing, picture taking, and a barrage of even more puerile interrogations than those given before the full room. The numerous sips I hadn't spit steeled me for the outlandishness of some propositions: "I got a whole vertical of Opus One. Screaming Eagle, Harlan, Bryant. The best. The best! And a guesthouse! Anytime you want to come down to Wichita, say the word. We'll get hammered!"

A few tarrying Window Tables, glass holsters swinging, finally shambled off elsewhere for more eating, drinking, and bragging about the depth and breadth of their basement cellars. Their purple-lipped wives followed behind with their festival tote bags jammed with trade wine spec sheets that might as well have been printed in Greek for all the use they had for them. From a phone in the empty lecture hall, Chef Dominique called for the complimentary shuttle service. Within a few moments, a black hybrid Lexus sedan skated halfway through the circular driveway at the entrance. The driver delivered us to the Kohler Waters Spa, in the Carriage House next door to the American Club, where Izzy had made a massage appointment. Chef Dominique said he was going to the sauna. I thought about wandering the town—I doubted I'd get very far beyond the hotels, as the paved walking paths were almost nonexistent—or returning to Riverbend to stare at the crimson and green and gold leaves that had fallen to the ground and scattered picturesquely from a comfortable chaise on the patio, but when Izzy suggested I join Chef Dominique, I cheerfully agreed. Even though sweating in a small airless chamber with the chef was probably just about the last thing I could have wanted to do that afternoon, I accepted the proposal because I wanted to give Izzy the impression that I was an easygoing, up-for-anything sort of guy. It was more important than my own happiness. Why would she want to be with anyone who was a drag in paradise?

I changed out of my button-down and khakis, wrapped a heavy towel around my waist, enveloped myself in a luxurious robe, and met Chef Dominique in a sensory-assaulting, epithelium-eroding tiled box. The hulking enabler of Izzy's fame and misfortune was amply frightening in the semi-nude. I struck up uncomfortable chitchat with the chef, but he did most of the talking. He didn't seem at all concerned whether or not his audience of one remained attentive—or even present—and prattled away. The balmy viscosity in the air made it increasingly difficult to see his face. Soon all I could perceive was a giant talking stomach.

"What's the meaning of life?" the stomach suddenly asked me.

"I think . . . You know, the usual things. Being able to love, to be loved, to produce something of lasting significance—"

The steam stopped flowing. Without the ambient hissing noise the heat brought, the box became alarmingly quiet. We just sat there as the air began to dry up and clear. Neither of us seemed to have any idea of what to do, whom to seek for help. Then there was a sharp, jarring clang, and a rusty-sounding rumble, and the steam began to pump in again.

"All my years of the restaurant, all of my awards, it is meaningful to me, *absolument*, but it is . . . eh, Peter Hapworth, how do I say? That is all behind me. Now I am TV producer and business manager."

"Do you ever miss cooking?"

"Ah, Peter Hapworth. To be executive chef is not the same. You're a celebrity. All you do is hug and kiss and smile for the cameras and then you die one day. If you live like me"—he patted his belly here—"maybe one day is sooner than you think?" He chortled complacently. The amplified sounds reverberated exponentially as they bounced against the tiles.

"Izzy doesn't really strike me as the type who needs a manager," I said. "You trusted her to run your wine program, to order and stock and sell thousands of dollars' worth of inventory every night, for years. Isn't she capable of handling her speaking engagements, now that she's off the floor, just as well? Besides, wouldn't it free you up to do other things?"

"Ah, *mon ami*, she is only the sommelier." He snorted crudely. "And a sommelier knows wine, but not about life."

The smugness was almost as difficult to inhale as the steam. "Isn't that kind of . . . I don't know . . . a little patronizing?"

Chef Dominique laughed again, so strongly and for such an extended duration that I was almost certain he was going to asphyxiate. Then he said he was done. We returned to the locker room.

"You want to know the meaning of life, Peter Hapworth?" he asked. I looked at him. "There is no meaning of life. That's what it means."

An attendant reminded Chef of his own massage appointment, which, apparently, he'd completely forgotten. He excused himself, and I dried off in the locker room alone—able to breathe for the first time since I got to the sauna—changed into a clean robe, and went to wait for Izzy.

Later on, after Izzy and I returned to our room, I kept thinking about what the chef said in the haze. His caustic remarks were bewildering. I hoped it was just that something had gotten lost in translation, or that the chef—or I—was having a momentary grandiose delusion brought on by the surplus heat. This was too nice a weekend to have bad feelings.

Izzy wanted to take a shower—with me. We stood, romantically entwined, in the glass-and-marble Kohler booth big enough to rain on us in comfortable tandem. Following that, we tried out the separate Jacuzzi. We leaned against each other, a fusillade of water jets firing against our torsos. I stared at the gilded faucets and toilet handles in the bathroom. After a long soak, none of the day's—none of life's—accrued indignities seemed that outrageous after all.

The *Cellar Temperature* dinner that night had us first boarding a shuttle bus to take us deep into the dark country night. The neighboring River Wildlife private club's Lodge Restaurant was in a log cabin at the edge of a forest. There was little that hadn't been hunted on the menu. A loaded rifle rack (fortunately chained up) stood by the wine cellar to underscore the theme. The guest list included a spiky-haired, trendily suited columnist and some PR girls from the magazine in black and pink Forever 21 dresses. Also at the table were, I'd learn later, some other food and wine world celebrities: Michael Lomonaco, a genial but reserved New York chef who'd once run Windows on the World; a mixologist and redoubtable chronicler of cocktail culture with an equally redoubtable Double Windsor, Anthony Giglio; and Laura Werlin, "The Cheese Lady," who'd published a number of preeminent domestic and imported volumes. Izzy knew them all from the festival circuit.

While plates of appetizers I didn't recall anyone having ordered appeared and moved from hand to hand, people spoke casually about the Kohler Experience, the panels on which they'd sat, the presentations and demos they'd performed, and other cities they'd visited and would visit in the coming year. I obviously had little to offer a discussion like this, and was grateful they allowed me to just listen and quietly eat and drink. I looked, intermittently, at the empty seat across from me. Chef Dominique had received a last-minute invitation to have drinks with a Food Network executive he'd been stalking, and stayed behind at Riverbend.

The entrees went down (not yet aware that the magazine was picking up the tab, I'd chosen the duck, which, for $46, was the least expensive option), and the diners began to pick and praise and offer bites of this and that to their neighbors. Servers decanted more bottles of wine and served them to us in giant glasses.

As people ate, a table-wide lull befell. The sounds of silver touching plates had superseded the conversations. Then The Cheese Lady turned and asked Izzy how long she and I had been dating. We'd anticipated this question and rehearsed an answer before we'd even gotten to Kohler: we agreed to tell people who inquired that we'd been together "going on a year." It seemed reasonable enough a courtship duration that we wouldn't run the risk of panicking anyone with what might have appeared to be unchecked romantic impetuousness—only together a millisecond and now travel companions to boot? But Izzy, admittedly never one who lied well, stammered and unearthed the truth before I even had a chance to deliver our party line.

"Three weeks," she confessed to The Cheese Lady. Amid neighboring gasps, she said Izzy was putting her on. Then she looked to me to correct the figure and end the gag. I couldn't, of course, and nodded.

"I've dated men for three *years* and haven't felt ready to go on a trip together," The Cheese Lady said. She raised her wineglass to toast us. "There's a phrase that comes to mind to describe a whirlwind courtship like yours, and that's 'holy shit.'"

After getting up late the next morning, we checked out of Riverbend, had Bloody Marys served with beer backs for brunch in a pub, and set out for Chicago as the day's sun was effusing from the Wisconsin sky. Though this time Izzy rode with me, the chef wasn't far behind us. We managed to lose him, briefly, when we turned off at a roadside shack for apple pie and cider and to admire the kitschy rural souvenirs. During this interlude, he made his own detour to a Culver's drive-thru for butter burgers and a pint of frozen custard he'd finish in the Range Rover. He was once again on our trail almost as soon as we were back on the highway.

◄○►

Izzy continued to invite me to events in the weeks that followed. Together we went to cocktail parties and store openings and celebrations of new fashion lines at Saks. In a new suit, one of three new shirts, and one of four new ties she bought me, I sat beside Izzy at strategically placed ballroom tables at charity dinners that she also emceed. There were lunches at which she was bestowed an award. I accompanied her to receptions organizers wanted her to attend for no reason other than to "be seen." I enjoyed these occasions, especially the ones that featured an open bar and, though they occurred more infrequently, a live band and dancing. Our pictures began to appear regularly in the scene section of the *Sun-Times* and in the about-town society pages of *Chicago Social* and *Today's Chicago Woman*, coverage essentially dedicated to regaling readers with glimpses of fantastic events most would only be able to dream of experiencing in person. It made less and less sense to photograph her with anyone else or on her own. People were talking about *us*. Someone had even updated Izzy's Wikipedia entry to reflect her new entanglement with me, Peter Hapworth, "a Chicago-area entrepreneur." My far less sensational role of college comp teacher had been revised out of the narrative. I received a number of astonished (and some baldly disbelieving) wall posts when I linked my Facebook page to Izzy's and our status turned to "in a relationship." "The same Isabelle Conway? The one from TV?" some of the messages read.

And I wasn't only to be Isabelle Conway's in-town companion. We traveled frequently over the next months. We went to Miami for the South Beach Wine and Food Festival. We visited Seattle twice. First to attend Taste Washington, and then again, a few weeks later, so Izzy could lead a tasting at a law firm's client appreciation night. In Jacksonville and Silicon Valley, Izzy hosted events for another law firm's satellite bureaus. She spoke at a little regional festival in Traverse City, Michigan that drew, surprisingly, some big-name chefs and wine talent. We only spent a night in New York, so we didn't tell my parents. One Saturday, I had a bagel and read *American Rhapsody* in a completely desolate downtown Cleveland mall while Izzy judged a sommelier competition. Chef Dominique, who'd made brief, superfluous appearances at a few of the Chicago functions, never passed up the opportunity to "be there" for Izzy when the destinations involved a change in time zone. He had no qualms about demanding the liquor distribution syndicate sponsor or law firm or bank or nonprofit hosting the event pay for his airfare and hotel room and lavish meals, in addition to those of the guest of honor's.

But Izzy always insisted on charging my plane tickets to her own AmEx. My guilt over it eventually wore away. I was adding to Izzy's quality of life by tagging along. She called me her "voice of reason" and "stalwart." The same could not be said of her "manager" and "business partner." And the adventures were vastly improving my viticultural life, socially, as well as professionally. The data I amassed on these trips! I filled Rhodia page after page with annotated transcripts of Izzy's tastings. When she'd respond to a sniff and a swish of a wine she'd selected for her talk, or one we'd drink at a hotel bar, or another that an assistant lounge manager sent up with room service when we dined in our suite at the end of a harried evening, with descriptors like "intense," "grippy tannins," "fruity," and "big potential," I'd scribble these immediate reactions of hers, as though a journalist conducting an interview. I wasn't always using the information to develop restaurant concept sketches, *per se*, but the scenes I took always struck me as being useful in a way I couldn't yet see. Capturing Izzy's assessments, embodying them, making the facts permanent parts of my imagination's arsenal, would only fortify a concept that at some point down the wine line I'd construct. Her words weren't just words. They went beyond concepts. They were consequential. What if this experience helped me find my way to opening a *real* restaurant?

The morning after we got back from Kohler, Izzy and I were seated on opposing sides of a plastic booth, at a Pilsen taqueria.

The narrow dining room was painted a once bright and now fading yellow. The color seemed even more conspicuously absent behind the dark tint of the laminated tables, which were held up by wobbly metal stilts. Not quite in the corner, there was a hulking Spanish music-spinning jukebox, festooned with dry hanging aloe and potted jade plants. The waitress presented us with inflexible plastic menus, described some highlights, and gasped when Izzy took off her sunglasses.

"Are you—" She interrupted herself when Izzy smiled. "Wow," she said, "I don't know anyone who doesn't watch your show."

"Thanks," Izzy said, and followed with, "Two coffees?" She ordered for both of us, by number, and our jubilant server flip-flopped off for mugs.

I craned my neck to read the descriptions on the wall behind the counter. "Baja shrimp," I said. "Daring."

"Exhaustion emboldens me."

"I hope the weekend wasn't too crazy. You'd think Dominique could give you a day off after a trip."

She sighed. "The Alsatians don't believe in such things. Leisure is expensive."

Our dishes arrived within minutes. Izzy emptied a packet of non-dairy creamer into her coffee, stirred, and tapped the spoon on the mug three times, as though signaling the end of a round. We exchanged plates. "Do you teach today?" she asked.

I declined my head theatrically. "Yeah. And office hours. In case any students with etymological crises seek counsel. Nobody ever shows up. Not that I mind the quiet, though."

She took her first sip of coffee, now sufficiently cooled. "I still have no idea what English comp is all about."

"Okay, okay," I said. "Do you have a pen in your purse?" She nodded, dug around for one, and produced a blue Bic. "Hold that for a second." I took several napkins from the tabletop dispenser and passed them over. "What I want you to do is to write out your life in three sentences. I'll tell you what's wrong with it."

"My life?"

"Your paragraph."

"I don't know if I want you editing my life."

I smiled. "Well, that's pretty much it. That's what I do."

"You're so much better than three sentences, Hapworth. You know that, don't you?"

"It's hard to be sure sometimes," I said.

Izzy paid the check at the counter and we stepped outside, back into the day. "Are you sure you don't want a ride?" I asked. "We could take a cab to my car and—"

"No," she said. "It's not too difficult for me to get to the studio on the El."

"Woman of the people, I remember. I'm accompanying you to the station at least."

We were waiting at the corner for the walk light when I heard whispering from behind. I stiffened my back to keep myself from turning around. I pretended like I wasn't listening when a voice said, "That's the girl from *Vintage Attraction*." We began moving again, but a four-way stop sign soon halted us.

"Excuse me," a shrill elder pitched forward. "Miss. Are you on television?"

"It's crazy how people never leave you alone," I said, after our privacy had been restored. "How do you deal with the constant interruptions?"

"It's always a little surreal," she said. "They feel like since they've had me in their bedrooms, they know me, that we're old friends, even though they're strangers."

"Failing to recall TV only works one way. I hear you."

"I mean, it's tolerable if I'm prepared for it, which I have to be pretty much any time I'm in public, but I won't lie; it's nice to be able to go home and close the door."

"Fortunately, they're not showing up in your living room or anything. Yet."

"Are you sure you're ready for this?" she asked again.

At the El station, Izzy turned to me sharply, as though having just recalled something she'd meant to say. "I was thinking maybe next weekend we could go look at some places," she said.

We were standing in front of the staircase that descended to the Blue Line subway. Facing each other, we slid, unconsciously, over to one side to clear the way. A cross cascade of passengers accessed and egressed. Some of them, no doubt, gaped.

"Places?"

5

PILSEN, CHICAGO'S LITTLE MEXICO, HAD BEGUN A SLOW COURSE OF gentrification around the time I moved back to Chicago eleven years ago. Garbage and shambling alcoholics still clung to the streets, but a number of trashed buildings on those streets had been swept, retrofitted, and repainted. The onetime Section 8 apartments within were now "gut-rehabbed" condominiums for sale. Stories of empty industrial factories had turned into luxury lofts plugged with consumer appliances, gleaming hardwood lining the once untenable concrete floors. Pilsen didn't appeal to all gringos. Many only passed through to buy drugs. To the urban pioneers that it did, like Izzy, the confluence of progress and unsanctioned sidewalk cart vendors formed an irresistible part of the city, desirable like no other.

There was a lot of living space to be had behind the tamales and *horchata* on the Lower West Side of Chicago for around three hundred thousand dollars. There were also a ton of *spaces* on the market. After three or four Saturday afternoon outings last summer with her realtor, Izzy couldn't make a decision about which one to buy. She was overwhelmed by the profusion of possibilities—and implications. This wasn't like choosing an apartment to lease for a year. Selecting was a commitment for the foreseeable, and unforeseeable, future. So she'd put her plans to become a homeowner on hold. She recently made an appointment to resurrect the search. This morning she enlisted me to come along, in the hopes that I might be able to make the process a little less daunting and help lead her to a conclusion. Safety in numbers.

Izzy's realtor, Leslie, took us past store windows that advertised cut-rate merchandise on neon poster paper and grimy doc-in-a-box clinics to see a new listing in a four-story loft complex on South Blue Island Avenue. The building, as recently as a half century ago, had been a biscuit factory. The "true loft" we saw had visible concrete pillars holding the place up and exposed copper pipes stained with industrial shades of rust overhead in the absence of a finished ceiling. There were views of the Chicago skyline from east-facing windows, limestone on the floor and walls in the master bathroom, his and her closets, a guest room that was larger than my current bedroom, a foyer, cherry hardwood floors, and in-unit washer and dryer. It was a great apartment. It was the kind of place in which I could imagine myself, or the person I wished I were, living. I could tell Izzy also really liked it here. She took in each new room with an excitement that animated her hands. Her brightened face had the mien of a child's, a child who'd never endured anything even remotely infelicitous. The open kitchen with its new GE appliances and raised bar, garbage disposal in the sink, and forty-two-inch "Shaker-style" cabinets, it seemed, provided her with the greatest charge of any of the architectural features and convenience facets we'd glimpsed today.

Leslie read a document she procured from the breakfast bar. She nodded and muttered to herself awhile. Finally she said aloud, "Your elementary school is St. Procopius. Point twelve miles from here."

Izzy laughed. "Ishiguro still has a few years to go before kindergarten."

"Does the sheet say which saint Procopius was?" I asked.

Leslie fumbled with the paper. "It doesn't," she said. She concocted a spurious smile out of Real Estate 101.

"I'm guessing the Saint of Procreation," I said. Leslie laughed tightly.

"BlackBerry," Izzy said. She asked Leslie, "What did we do before these things?"

With the device out of her purse, Izzy called up Google on a miniature Internet browser. From where I stood behind her, I could see a red progress bar as it chugged along for a few seconds, struggling to channel information through the signal-depleting concrete that surrounded us. "Procopius of Caesarea was a martyr," Izzy said then. "'The first victim of persecution of the Church in Palestine by Emperor Diocletian. He was born in Jerusalem but moved to Scythopolis.'" She flicked the trackball with her index finger a couple of swipes to advance, I supposed, through some boring biographical debris. She resumed, at what sounded like the end of the entry: "'Procopius was a reader in Scythopolis at the time of his arrest by Roman authorities. He was beheaded.'"

"Let's hope the school is a little more Montessori than Diocletian in its disciplinary practices," I said. "I bet they have one hell of a church casino night. Caesarea's Palace."

Izzy put a hand on my shoulder. "You should totally pitch that to them. They'd raise a ton of money."

I pretended to have found something intriguing near the handle of one of the Shaker cabinets in the kitchen. Here I began to conjure a restaurant with a gambling theme. I envisioned slot machines, roulette wheels, and dice slamming against the shock-absorbing felt of game tables. Then a patter of some sort sounded over our heads. The images in my mind were so vivid that I barely comprehended the noise. It took me several moments after the commotion had died out to register it. "What was that?" I asked. "Nothing," Izzy said quickly, and plunked the BlackBerry she still held back into her bag.

On the terrace, we took in the panorama. In front of the building, parked cars lined the street. A courtyard apartment complex facing us was in the process of condo-conversion. The biscuit factory's communal yard below had sod slowly taking root. Standing here we discovered the source of the outbreak we'd heard: there were people living upstairs. I was about to put my arm around Izzy when a voice spoke. I looked up at a woman on an identical terrace one floor above. Her face was pointed down at us. "Hi, guys!"

"Hello," Izzy said tentatively. I snatched my arm back and shook away a shiver of adolescent embarrassment.

"I'm Sheryl," the woman said. Her accent was brusque, thickly Midwestern, the kind often belonging to a diner waitress or a Chicago traffic cop. Also her forehead had been shot up with a substantial quantity of Botox. "Are you two moving in?" she asked. "Because this is a *great* neighborhood."

"Thinking about it," Izzy said.

"Well, I *absolutely* think you should. We could use some more cool people like you two. Has anyone ever told you you look like that wine lady on TV?"

Sheryl continued to lean over the edge and describe Pilsen in bombastic superlatives. The more she effused, the more she turned into a cartoon character.

Izzy remarked succinctly throughout. I knew she was scouring the brief pauses Sheryl left for a way to end the conversation. Before she could, Sheryl exclaimed, "Wait! I'll be right down!"

While Sheryl and Izzy chatted by the door, I returned to the terrace. I felt a little guilty about not correcting Sheryl's misapprehension that Izzy and I were shopping as a couple. A part of me didn't really want it to be untrue.

I stepped back into the empty living room. "I'll take it, Leslie," Izzy said.

Ten minutes later, Izzy and I were once again in the Mustang. We were on our way to Leslie's office to draw up the paperwork.

"What do you think of Pilsen?" she asked me.

"I like it. I like it a lot, in fact," I said.

"Enough to live here?"

At a stop sign, my eye caught a mailbox on the corner that was strangling with spray paint. "Sure. In theory."

"What about in practice?"

"What do you mean?"

"Well, maybe we should do this together."

"How would that work?" I asked. "Would I . . . pay you rent?"

"I was kind of hoping you'd let them put both our names on the mortgage."

"I don't . . . I don't really think I make the kind of money that can pay half the mortgage on a place like this." I was getting flustered. I had to pull over and park the car.

"So, fine, you won't pay half. I just . . . I don't know, I've been thinking about how much I've loved these weeks we've been spending together and how much . . . I don't know . . . how much I'd just like to . . . do this with you."

"Well, I love this, too. And my sublease is up in a couple months. But Izzy, my credit, my credit's never going to pass. I still make payments on *two* grad school degrees. I barely even get approved to *rent*. Plus there's going to be a down payment and—"

"Just forget about that. I have a ton of cash saved, and I'll take care of it and whatever else."

I turned her head to face mine and pushed the hair out of her eyes. "You really want me to live with you that badly?" I asked.

She looked at me with the guileless, liquid eyes of a five-year-old. "Yes."

My focus pinned to something nonexistent on her lapel. In a small voice I asked, "Is it really dense of me to wonder why?"

She put my hand between hers. "Easy. You inspire me. I feel like with you I can do anything."

"Izzy, I have to say, you've never struck me as one who's hindered by much. You did quite a lot before I came along."

"I did," she said dully. "And that's the problem. I had to raise myself. I've always had to take care of myself. Everything I've gotten in life, I've gotten because I've been the one to go out there and get it."

"Same here."

"But the funny thing is, it's not like I regret it. It's kept me real. It's kept me from thinking I was better than I really am. Hapworth, I never thought celebrity could ever change me, but what if someday it does? I like who I am with you."

"Same here."

"And ever since we got together, I keep thinking, what's the point of having everything and being able to do everything—especially when it comes to wine, and this wine life of mine—if you can't share it with someone? I have awards, I have knowledge, my name generates seventeen thousand hits on Google." She sighed. "But what the hell good is any of it without . . . without my person?"

"And I'm that someone? I'm your person?"

"As long as you want to be."

I smiled. "You want to marry me or something?" I teased in deadpan.

"I don't know," she returned, in a similar tone of feigned indifference, "are you asking?"

Several dark nights later, I was to meet Izzy at the mortgage office. I arrived first. Ramona, the broker, began to distribute schedules and brochures. Receiving them without Izzy there made me uneasy. What did I know of itemizations, declarations, and PMI? Izzy showed up. She'd come directly from the studio, in a long blue dress and silver costume pearls. Her face still had on theatrical makeup, and her hair spilled down from the thin silk scarf that wrapped around it. She sat between Ramona and me. Facing the computer, we gave a deposition that required both of us to recite names of employers, years of graduation, to estimate outstanding debts, bank account balances, assets, gross incomes. When my numbers lined up next to Izzy's on Ramona's screen, the disparity in the figures was laughable. After more than a decade, the minimum payments on my student loans hadn't even tickled the principal. In the event we'd have to liquidate our portfolios, I could produce a handful of overripe fifty- and hundred-dollar Series E savings bonds. My teaching salary was, to put it mildly, gross. It was hard to pretend we were getting this loan jointly.

Though Izzy had said it didn't matter what I contributed financially, and would shortly to that end issue a check for our hundred-thousand-dollar down payment with intrepidity and without having to pawn a single piece of stereo equipment, for me to even nominally cosign on a mortgage for the two-hundred-thousand-dollar balance meant I'd have to set aside the juvenile philosophies—an ethos born of insecurity—that had, if not stood in the way, at least hovered over my ability to love and have a life to a defying degree since I was a teenager.

Dating before Izzy, I always paid for everything. I couldn't admit to Ramona that it took me a year to vacate the sizable debt I'd managed to amass funding my high school girlfriend Sydney's and my frequent treks down to the Village for cheeseburgers and Export A's and carne asada at Las Mañanitas on Bleecker Street. She had plenty of allowance—her father was a gentleman mobster with a wall safe in the library off the living room filled with guns, porn, and stacks of freshly laundered cash—but I insisted. When I was seeing Amy in college, I also adamantly refused to let her pick up a single check, despite the fact that her job as editor-in-chief of the *Maroon* had a restaurant review expense account. At meals, at concerts, at movies, I'd drawn my credit card as instantly as I'd been approved for it at a Reynolds Club table offering students the choice of a Frisbee or complimentary Kit Kat in exchange for applying. I knew that the source of the compulsion went beyond merely thinking that's what the guy in a couple was supposed to do. The reason I couldn't let a girlfriend buy something for me was because I never could say what apprehensible thing I brought to the relationship. I'd always thought, if I wasn't spending money—money I didn't even have—could these women and those that would succeed them, particularly the accomplished ones, ever see me as a *sine qua non* in their lives, or would I always just be a charming, affectionate, solicitous, witty, but ultimately inconsequential transient?

All of that thinking fell away last October. Izzy changed me. I no longer felt like I had to justify my existence materially. So what if I couldn't pay half the mortgage? My contribution was more significant. Getting this loft wasn't just something Izzy wanted. It was something she *needed*. But she didn't need my help to get it. Somehow I'd ended up the catalyst, the *sine qua non*. She needed me.

I needed this, too. The risk I was about to take to prove how much I loved somebody wasn't a student Visa with a $1,500 limit for which there could be easy absolution in the aftermath of reck-lessness. The stakes were the highest they'd ever been in my life. I was signing up for, potentially, decades of relying on someone else, someone with whom I was romantically involved, a woman. And yet it didn't trouble me. Instead, I saw only opportunity. Here was a chance to take something I'd started somewhere beyond the safety of the merely theoretical. For the first time since my bar mitzvah, I, with mighty pen in hand, was to become a man.

We submitted our mortgage application and left Ramona's office. It was all a little surreal. Who'd believe that someone I'd been dating not quite six weeks put my name on a loft title? We weren't even engaged. And why weren't we? I'd been searching for someone this brilliant, this beautiful, this *real*, since, what, seventh grade? If it was right between us, right enough to buy real estate, why put it off, why not just propose now?

I drove us to a fragrant, steamy late-night restaurant in China-town. A host led Izzy and me to a small table in the back. She and I held hands and could hardly stop smiling at each other long enough to send for the dim sum cart.

"I don't get why people are so afraid to get married," Izzy said uncannily. "Home ownership is way more of a serious commitment."

"Yeah," I said. I watched the tea I poured cascade into the dingy white miniature cup.

"Thirty years."

"Fixed," I said, a thread of tension festooning my voice.

"Are you scared?" she asked.

"Honestly?"

"Honestly," she said.

"No."

"Neither am I."

"Should we get married, too, while we're at it?"

"Hapworth, are you proposing?"

I took a sip of tea and burnt my tongue. "Yes."

"Well, do it properly, if you're going to do it, and then it will be official."

"Hold on a second." I got up from the table, rounded the corner, and sped over to a pantry I'd noticed between the bathrooms. Isabelle Conway wasn't Sydney or Amy or Talia or a Nerve.com girl or Craigslist Casual Encounter I'd see once and never again. Izzy mattered. I grabbed a cellophane-wrapped fortune cookie from a teeming box and returned to her.

"What's this for?"

"Open it."

She took the cookie out of its crinkly package.

"Isabelle Conway, will you marry me?"

She snapped the cookie in two. "'*Now is the time to try something new*,'" she read.

"Is that a yes?"

"Of course. Yes."

"I hope you're going to save that fortune forever."

Following our engagement, Izzy's and my having separate residences in the interim was more of a technicality and not that pestering of an impediment. We slept in the same bed each night. Still, we heartily looked forward to the condo closing, the loft apartment we'd soon jointly own, and to moving in together.

Even Ishiguro seemed unable to corral his Christmas-morning impatience, his eyes unusually perspicacious and his curly tail unfurled and darting practically every second he wasn't having his meal or taking a nap.

We couldn't wait to get started on the future, and so spent a series of evenings that late fall shopping in Lincoln Park. We began, modestly enough, with the intention of buying a TV. The set at Izzy's belonged to Chris, and my ancient tube had outlived its usefulness. Izzy planned to relegate it and my bachelor pad–green IKEA pullout, book boxes, and record crates to the second bedroom (office, storage "garage," guest room). She was also ready to replace her heavy, battered thrift-store dresser, cocoa-colored queen-size headboard, matching bed frame, mattress, and box-spring. A lot more work lay ahead of us.

In each furniture store and housewares boutique we visited up and down Halsted and across Armitage, Izzy sought and appraised and juxtaposed while I nodded and tried not to think too much about the rising ache in my back and rumble in my stomach. I was innately bored by shopping and fearful of the tab, which seemed to increase exponentially like the national debt clock sign near Times Square with each second we were held consumer captives. Our final stop, Ethan Allen, was the most customer-labor intensive. Like a good fiancé, I remained present before the color swatches and floor sample wood and silver and glass and Oriental rug. I was intent on bearing sangfroid throughout this. I could fake it until dinner. We strode the floors, following our designer. She wasn't terribly concerned with sublimating her indisposition for buyers' uncertainty or the fact she was working on commission. Izzy hastily selected major items that would be ready for delivery in eight to twelve weeks. Why couldn't the designer have just said two months, I wondered. By the end, Izzy had maxed out a credit card for our new bed and tables and lamps and wall hangings. She handled and returned a Torah's worth of computer-printed scrolls requiring almost as many signatures as our mortgage application itself.

And before long, it was January. We closed on the place on a Wednesday morning and celebrated with pizza and Prosecco in a neighborhood trattoria afterward. Barely a week later, a moving truck made a stop in front of my Humboldt Park sublet and another at Izzy's building. Then it delivered the boxes of things we'd accumulated separately, which from here on out would be our mutual possessions, to the new place, followed closely behind by a large, gray delivery rig from a remote warehouse. I'd always remember, as we purchased and packed and pared, sending our quiescent particles into motion, how blissfully unaware I was during those joyful, auspicious days of what life was to decant next.

6

THE MORNING AFTER VALENTINE'S DAY, IZZY, IN A SIMPLE BLACK evening gown, and I, in my event suit, went before a judge at City Hall to repeat-after-me and say-I-do. Chris, our solely attending "best man of honor," stood behind us in a tag-concealed Brioni tux he planned to return to Neiman Marcus before work that afternoon. Izzy had to slip Chris's silver Superman ring onto my finger during the ceremonial exchange since he'd let me leave the apartment without the wedding band she bought me at a jewelry store in Chinatown the night I proposed. I smiled at her through the short round of clapping that followed the kissing of the bride and groom. The jubilance the collective hands of the registrar, the judge, the bailiff, Chris, and the two or three random people in the courtroom generated was unexpectedly touching. With the documents signed, we were ready to go to lunch. Izzy chose a trattoria that was a short walk from 121 North LaSalle. It had so-so food, she told us, but plenty of cheap, bubbly Prosecco. It sounded perfect for our budget that, since buying real estate, couldn't as comfortably accommodate Champagne.

Bea Corton joined us at the trattoria. Bea was the sommelier at Osteria Via Stato and Izzy's first friend in the city. I'd met her on one of our earliest dates. For our celebration, or for her upcoming shift on the restaurant floor, Bea was dressed impeccably. She wore a black-gray Chanel suit and matching patent leather Mary Janes. Her dark hair was blow-dried and styled. It bore the glossy sheen of fresh meringue, just like Izzy's, but was trimmed several inches shorter. They saw the same stylist, Ingrid. Bea presented me a small, rectangular Tiffany box.

"You didn't have to get me anything," I said, tugging on the shimmery ribbon.

Her gift was a waiter's corkscrew—a wine key—with a handle that matched the color of its packaging. Izzy had taught me how to use the industry-standard opener, and I could now finally retire my old rabbit ears. "Something borrowed, something blue?" I asked.

"You'll need one of these now," she said.

The trattoria's general manager was so amused to have guests who'd just gotten married that he didn't seem to detect that Isabelle Conway was not just one of the party, but the *bride*. He bought us a bottle of Piper Heidsieck, which a server shortly brought out and poured. Once the fury of fizz atop the amber-tinged Champagne in the flutes around the table subsided, I held my glass aloft and drew it to Izzy's. "To you," I said.

We clinked, sipped, and then kissed. "This is much better than a wedding," she said.

I looked at the portion of the upended red label that extended beyond the rim of the ice bucket. "Much better." I took another sip and swished the contents around my mouth. "It's toasty," I said. "I'm getting it! The toast!"

She smiled. "It comes from the oak barrels the wine aged in."

I was almost too stunned to speak. I sipped again and confirmed the slightly charred buttery brioche. "I mean, I've gotten some of the other things: the weight of wines, two percent milk, whole milk, acid . . . usually after you point them out. I think this is the first time I've really *picked up* something in a wine. Like I can really taste the toast."

"I'm proud of you. My sommelier protégé is learning." She chuckled. "I can always tell you've gotten acid after you've had too much Pinot Noir and cheese and spend most of the night hurling."

"Right," I said, and forced a small grin. I tried not to recollect spending an evening, after a tasting event Izzy did for Harris Private Bank, sleeping on the bathroom floor at the intervals I wasn't deploying the contents of my fractious stomach. I stared into my glass. It was remarkable. "Toast."

She raised her flute. "To us."

When we got back to the apartment, Izzy kicked off her shoes and repaired down the hall to the bedroom to dislodge herself from her makeshift wedding dress. I watched my bride—*my wife*—through the eyes of the newly contextualized.

It was strange being home at this hour. With our neighbors away, at work, shopping at Costco, off on camping trips, it was almost as though nobody else resided at the Biscuit Lofts but Izzy and me, and the pug I now officially co-parented. The most pleasing absence was that of the equanimity terrorist Laheys and their volatile three-year-old son from upstairs. Scott and Sheryl had been disingenuous nuisances from their first official visit to introduce themselves five weeks ago, all fake smiles and triteness and self-consciously manicured hair. They claimed to welcome us to the factory, but were quite transparently there to poke around. Scott had a franchise insurance agency in Tri-Taylor and began to hawk off-brand homeowner's policies within sentences. Sheryl tried to cadge distributors' samples of cheap Pinot Grigio before the movers had even finished unloading the truck. We could tell right away they were a supremely odd couple. Sheryl was older, Scott wore toe rings. In front of us, they feigned affection for each other, but at home, amid the toys and extension cords and family portraiture, they argued, violently and often. Cassidy ran up and down their uncarpeted floors when they fought, and also when they didn't.

After she was free from her binding garments and had changed into a T-shirt and some sweatpants, Izzy arranged herself comfortably on the couch. She dug the remote control out from the small of her back and commenced a survey of the afternoon television options. Ishiguro came over, stretched, yawned, and then resituated himself atop her rose colored–cotton legs.

I began sending text messages reporting the news of our getting hitched, to old grad school girlfriends ("You're so cool, Hapworth," Jessie fired back); to Ari Marks, a former student who was now a local journalist; to my campus sub for the afternoon, Berkal. I left voice mails at my mother's office, telegraphic haiku with my father's and sister's answering services.

"I should probably tell Dominique," Izzy said, though she didn't sound very eager to enact the plan. She was petting the snoozing dog and glancing at the television with little interest. She seemed perfectly content doing nothing more than basking in the afternoon's tranquillity. Izzy's bistro absence must have infuriated the tyrannical chef, though he'd begrudgingly granted permission. I was glad she'd taken the entire day off. These rare hours of freedom she had from commotion and disturbance were precisely what Izzy needed to detoxify from her celebrity and its attendant annoyances, to reconcile accounts, to be able to gird herself for future trials.

I was standing at the breakfast bar. I freed my shirttails from my suit pants and stared at my reflection in the darkened screen of the new MacBook Izzy had bought me. My phone buzzed while I was loosening my tie. I discerned from the Caller ID that it was Ari Marks. I answered and sat down on a barstool.

"Congratulations, Professor."

"Thanks," I said. I looked over at Izzy again. "I can't believe we actually did it."

"Let me read you your wedding present." It was a draft of a short article about Izzy that he'd just submitted to make the deadline for next week's *Daley Machine* issue. I was touched by my old student's abiding reverence for the teacher he'd so patently eclipsed.

My mouth opened involuntarily, in the overdramatic manner of a seventies sitcom character, at some of the more tumescent bits.

"I can't believe you called me a restaurateur," I whined with mock exasperation.

"They don't fact-check," Ari said. "And besides, I didn't say you *worked* in Chicago."

"You said 'acclaimed.'"

"Oh, who cares? You got married. *Married.* To Isabelle Conway, a prominent Chicagoan. That makes you prominent by association."

"So we have a prommon-law marriage?"

I hung up my suit and changed into a pair of jeans and a long-sleeved gray T-shirt. Beside Izzy I fell asleep. I dreamt I was sitting courtside at a Bulls game, more concerned with the hot dog and its yet-to-be boiled marketing potential than I was with the play, but attuned to the sounds nonetheless. I woke up, returned to the couch in my post-wedding real life. The game noise had followed me out of the dream and morphed. Scott and Sheryl were embroiled in a fight that now rained down from the invisible rafters. I got the gist of the conflict when Sheryl screamed, "*Go back to your fucking slut, you bastard! I'm gonna find a man who knows how to fuck me!*" Meanwhile, Cassidy, to whom his parents were oblivious, cried away in his room. The new false drywall ceiling we'd installed was supposed to muffle the Laheys, but their melodrama came at nearly as ferocious a pitch as ever.

Izzy was shaking a cocktail in the kitchen. She glared at me when I sat up. "I still think he's gay," she said, pointing at the ceiling.

I shook my head. At least she was being somewhat lighthearted about it. "Do you want to go somewhere? Have a drink somewhere?"

"We can't go out every time they start up."

"No," I said, "I don't suppose we can."

Despite the unlikelihood of our ever doing anything to make living below the Laheys tolerable, we'd tried to implement a variety of approaches. We went upstairs to talk. At first we approached with sympathy, open to discussion. Nothing changed. We began to emerge from the discussions astonished, embarrassed. Often Izzy was crying by the time we returned to the apartment. Our sentiments turned vengeful and fulminating. "That kid's an asshole," she shouted over our heads, following one scathing negotiation regarding the toddler's incessant—and incessantly reverberant—toddling. "A *Cass*hole," I returned. Many nights Izzy stayed up with the computer for hours after Ishiguro and I had passed out. She read document after document, website message board after message board, Googled phrase after phrase that she thought could offer some insight, a way out of this suffocating mess. A single promising lead emerged: to have a ceiling installed. It was a messy and expensive proposition, but the pulverized newspaper insulation blasted into it supposedly absorbed all echoing sound. Twenty thousand dollars and a dozen vacuumings later, we could still hear everything just as before. The only thing left to do was to resign ourselves to the fact that this living situation wasn't going to be everything we'd dreamed it would be. We had to get used to the unplanned cohabitation. *You make do*, I could hear my grandmother saying in her Jersey accent. But for Izzy, it wasn't going to be that easy.

She grabbed her martini from the counter. The vodka spiraled up in a splash, but managed to catch itself. I marched behind her down the long hall. Once inside our bedroom, I observed what looked to be a disaster site, a small village that had been ravaged by war, an island decimated by nuclear explosion, a West Side women's clothing store that had been looted after the second Bulls championship in Rodney King–besmirched 1992. Izzy's dresses lay on the floor, pantsuits on the unmade bed. Over the back of a chair were a number of T-shirts. Cashmere sweaters, inside out, practically balled up, were strewn about. The disarray kicked a faction in my brain to which I hadn't been yet introduced that mandated a degree of order in our life into high alert mode.

"What happened?" I asked.

She didn't respond to my question. Instead she announced, "We'll just sit in here. If they're going to be down there, we can hide here."

This didn't sound like a very promising plan. "Izzy, there's no TV here. What are we going to do? Listen to the radio?"

"Read," she said. "You can read."

"You're not being very reasonable. It's our wedding day. Is this the honeymoon you envisioned? Marooned in a bedroom?"

She drew in a deep breath and let it out slowly. Then she took another sip of vodka from her sweaty glass.

"Okay. Let's go get a drink," she finally said.

I realized I was standing on the black evening dress Izzy wore at the City Hall courtroom this morning. "What about this?" I asked.

"What about what?" she replied testily.

I knew from women's cable TV that some brides shipped their wedding costumes off to the garment taxidermists long before the Donna Summer song at the end of the reception. Most probably at least zipped theirs back up in plastic bags and hung them in their closets. And here Izzy had abandoned hers like some kind of hospital gown.

"This," I said. "Your dress is under my foot."

"Well," she said, "then address it."

I picked the lifeless exoskeleton up and stood there, stupefied.

"What?" she asked. "Do you know how much that fucking false ceiling cost?"

"I'm sorry it didn't work."

She reached for the dress. She took it from me so forcefully I feared it might end up in two pieces. We'd been so happy this morning, taking our vows before the judge, at the trattoria afterward. Now we were being practically chased out of our home by some loud morons upstairs. Did Izzy really want to spend the rest of our lives locked in a constant battle, like they were?

Several hours and many drinks later, I pretended to sleep as Izzy gathered the dog from the corner of the bed. I listened to her pad down the hall. I supposed she was headed to stow Ishiguro for the night in his crate in the spare room. As I expected, she came back alone. The Pottery Barn *Melrose Place* drama on the third floor had abated while we were *emborrachandonos con margaritas* at Mamacita's. At long last, the building stood in utter silence. Regrettably, the opposite was the case on the set of my internal soap opera. Something about the afternoon weighed on my mind. And it wasn't just the aftershock of the fighting upstairs that continued to rankle. My eyes were still shut when I felt Izzy climbing on top of me.

"Izzy," I said.

"What," she whined. The word, slippery with tequila, fell from her mouth and landed, palpably, on my cheek. "We don't need to bother with condoms anymore."

"That's not exactly—I just . . . I can't . . ."

There was nothing going on between my legs. It was as though I didn't have a dick. I imagined myself a longhaired paraplegic Ron Kovic, railing against my malfunctioning equipment before a frightened hooker in *Born on the Fourth of July*. Emotion had never gotten in the way of erection before. I was astonished, and not astonished, that this had happened to me, on my wedding night, of all nights. For the last twenty years, save the occasional performance anxiety that one-night stands and recreational drug use used to sometimes engender, I could always count on one invariable: I could fuck whenever, wherever: grimy food court unisex bathrooms, the backseats of compact cars, cabana showers. For twenty years, my cock had stood at perpetual attention, stoic, compliant, dimly guileless, smiling dumbly, yet capable, in theory, of wreaking great havoc, like an armed and overweight bank branch rent-a-cop. I had always been, even in the face of adversity, virile.

She wrenched herself away and rolled onto her side. Her rigid back walled me off.

My eyes, I realized then, were still closed.

Her breathing evened out to an involuntary degree and the tautness in her muscles went slack. Izzy was asleep. I wriggled myself out from beneath the covers. I tiptoed down the hall and sprung Ishiguro from his gratuitous exile.

—◄◦►—

My first morning of marriage to Izzy began when Scott Lahey got on his treadmill at five thirty in the morning—on a Saturday, no less—and powerwashed our apartment with a relentless hip-hop bass line. After one particularly impolite stretch of ceiling shaking, Ishiguro stood up in bed. He stretched himself out, announcing, in his typical pug fashion, that he was ready to go outside. Even though the sun hadn't completed its rising, I stepped into my jeans and socks, pulled a green argyle sweater over the Connells T-shirt I'd slept in, and followed Ishiguro to the door. I looked back at Izzy before we left the room. She remained in the position in which she'd slept, with a pillow covering her face, but I could tell, like the rest of us, she was now awake.

By the time we returned, she had relocated to the couch. Though Scott's marathon "training" run had extinguished itself after only fifteen minutes, Izzy lay with her eyes open, head propped up, legs stretched out on the couch. My old Ithaca blanket buried her form below her neck. A hand bearing a remote control extended out from underneath. The television screen hopscotched from one barely distinguishable morning news show to another. She acknowledged the pug and me with a halfhearted nod. This wasn't like Izzy. Something beyond the unscheduled wake-up call was evidently bothering her. Did she harbor hard feelings about my missile's failure to launch? Not screwing in the nuptial twilight, according to the tenets of the Oxygen network, was an unfathomable sin. It was a nightmare scenario, much the same as failing to distribute copies of the syllabus on the first day of class.

"Do you want coffee?" I asked.

"Yes, please."

I poured Ishiguro's kibble and managed to pull myself from the intersection of pug and food critical seconds prior to certain collision. While the kettle heated, I sat down at the breakfast bar and logged onto Facebook. I sifted my inbox. The messages were mostly junk from groups I regretted joining. And there was one from Talia.

I nearly deleted it along with the others. After reading the note, I wished I had.

I'm coming to Chicago. Can I see you?

I replied via text message from my cell phone: *I can't see you.*

Why not? she returned, seconds later.

Because I got married.

WTF when?

Yesterday.

Whoa.

Talia, Talia, Talia. I'd suspected she could read my mind from the beginning. I'd never mentioned in our recent brief and forgettable exchanges about writing exercises that I was even dating someone, but she must have intuited where I was headed. Possibly she'd sensed I'd already replaced her the last night we saw each other at Marché. Izzy or no, Talia was completely wrong for me. She was too young, she thought she was smarter, she was crazy. She had no idea of what she wanted. All of that had been true long before I had a wife who was the complete opposite. Izzy was someone successful, someone stable, wine's glinting, award-winning TV face. She was a deeded co-owner of property, *an adult*. As far as I could tell then, she'd remain so forever. Why did Talia even want to see me now? If a nostalgia-fueled tryst with an old flicker was what she sought, she was too late. With the vows I took yesterday, there wasn't to be any future of even a second's duration for Talia and me.

At least that was what I'd spend the next weeks of my life trying to convince myself.

I went back into the kitchen. The dog's bowl was empty, cleaned with scientific precision, as though it had never once contained anything. I French pressed coffee, and brought a mug, doctored with a Splenda and splash of nonfat milk, to the living room. Izzy accepted the coffee appreciatively, bent her knees, and withdrew her legs a measure in order that I could sit down at the end of the sofa.

"Sorry about last night," I said.

"It's okay," she said. She blew on her coffee.

"We said we weren't going to make a big deal about eloping."

"It's not that. It's not you. I was just kind of preoccupied yesterday."

"Why?"

She sighed an inordinately lugubrious sigh. "Chef Dominique wants to go to Carbondale to shoot a segment."

I couldn't decide if I should feel perturbed she'd kept something important from me. The reappearance of Carbondale in her dialogue was also unsettling. She hadn't referenced it in months. I asked, "Why didn't you say something?"

"I was getting married."

I flashed back to all the smiling. How delighted it made me to see her so unencumbered, so unguarded. The feeling of triumph that the future I'd offhandedly imagined for the two of us following our first date had actually, by virtue of who knew what, come true.

"Of all the places, why Carbondale? What enologically news-breaking topic could he possibly want to cover in Southern Illinois? A White Zinfandel revival?"

She muted the television and dropped the remote control onto her blanketed lap. "There are actually close to five hundred boutique wineries in the state," she said. "Next week is Frontenac Festival and—why do I have to explain this to you?"

I rubbed my eyes and tried to bring my campus schedule to mind. It followed no pattern I could commit to memory. It was a haphazard, illogical arrangement that one could safely assume had been generated either by a slot machine or by an incompetent adjunct coordinator. "I think . . . I can get someone to cover class for me, but that—"

"With the camera guy and the equipment and everything, there's not going to be enough room in the Range Rover for another person."

"I could drive you separately."

"In the 'Stang? We'd be lucky to make it to I-57."

"I have it on good authority that there are cars manufactured postbellum to be rented."

"Just stop it, okay? We don't have to go everywhere together."

"We used to go to festivals together."

"Well, we're married now."

"I'll drive up by myself, after I'm done teaching."

"I don't want you to."

"Why?" I asked.

"Because I started out there alone," she said, "and I want to finish there alone." She switched the television back on. "Did I ever tell you about Ernie?" she asked. "My stepfather?"

"Foster father."

She threw the remote in my direction. I ducked, instinctively. It landed on the floor before it had a chance to reach my head. "Foster father, stepfather, you know what I mean." She stared down at her hands, as though a FedEx delivery of new information had arrived at her brain, priority, guaranteed before ten thirty, and she'd excused herself to sign for it. Her hands fell to her sides. "He ran a liquor store. I used to work there, on weekends, in high school. You know, I never really thought about it before, but that was kind of my first job in the wine business."

"Are you sure this is a good idea? You haven't been back to Carbondale since you moved away."

"At least it's quiet there."

"We have the rest of the weekend together, though, right? When are you leaving? Monday?"

"Tomorrow."

"Great," I mumbled.

This honeymoon was getting better and better. I felt like I should fight her decision, make her see why I, her new husband, should come. Clearly, the prospect of returning to the site of her impoverished youth was harrowing Izzy—all the more reason to have her so-called stalwart accompany her. She was supposed to now be able to lean closer to me, and not have to turn deeper into herself. At the same time, I really didn't *want* to go to Carbondale, especially not for a celebration of a hybrid grape variety of which I'd never heard, alongside a film-school crew and a chef masquerading as the director. Letting a childish emotional whim like that govern me, I realized, was not the sort of thing to which I, an adult, a man, was supposed to succumb, but what else was there for me to do? All of this hurt.

I finished my now-cold coffee and returned to the kitchen for a refill. I purposely avoided asking Izzy if she wanted more. I poured the last of the lukewarm, glazed-over contents of the French press into my sooty mug. After a few tortured swigs, I sat down at the breakfast bar and pulled over the MacBook so I could load up Face-book. From the message queue, Talia's profile picture thumbnail stared at me. Irony would have had no choice but to return her to me now. Was the look in her eyes, frozen in microscopic digital still frame, one offering compassionate salvation or one betraying supercilious mockery?

"Do you want to go have brunch or something?" Izzy asked. "We can go to Milk & Honey. Get those peanut butter and banana pancakes you like. It is our honeymoon, after all."

I nodded. "Those pancakes *you* like. And I can bring you coffee with five different creamer options, just like when I didn't know any better. Whole, nonfat, vanilla soy . . . Lactaid."

"Now you know what I like. And that's only four options."

I shot an index finger over my head. In Chef Dominique's inarticulate put-on Franco-Prussian accent, I exclaimed, "Get me half-and-half!"

It was the first time I'd heard her laugh, really laugh, in a while.

Rustling summoned me from repose. It was five in the morning. I assessed my surroundings and found that there was only a narrow portion of the huge queen-size bed available for me. Izzy was positioned in the center. Unconsciously, she'd put her hands behind her head, as though she dreamt of lying alone in a hammock. Her arms and forearms formed forty-five-degree akimbo angles. The near elbow pointed, hovering, at my cheek. Between us lay an unraveled Ishiguro. He traced the contour of Izzy's side with his rangy body. His even, innocuous snoring resembled a toy machine gun's emptying of its magazine of plastic bullets back into itself.

Driven by what had to be an intuitive canine sense of solidarity, Ishiguro soon was awake, too. He arched his back to stretch it out, just as Talia's cat Mildred did after a lengthy spell of repose, and then vaulted over Izzy. She remained asleep, or feigning so. Ishiguro leapt out of bed. At the closed bedroom door, the pug issued a plaintive whimper.

"Izzy," I whispered. I nudged her gently in the side. "Izzy."

"Wha?" she half-spoke.

"I think Ishiguro needs to go out."

Silence.

I followed the pug along a rectangular route of the north and south sides of the block. He analyzed and catalogued a number of frozen organic and inorganic objects that littered the sidewalk in myriad textures and colors and states of decomposition. Before each item he poked and sniffed, he was immobile. I tugged on the lead, asked him politely to come so we could go home, but he refused to move forward until he'd completed the inspection. His fixity seemed a pretty clear message: every smashed plastic lighter and sodden Chase ATM receipt and greasy, stomped take-away food tin was a matter deserving of his—and my—full consideration. It made me wonder if the dog was also trying to tell me something else. Perhaps I'd been moving through this new life of mine with Izzy a little too easily, too casually, too much like a blithe-breed canine or like one of my incurious undergraduates. Maybe I needed to start sniffing more than just the wines to which my sommelier continued to introduce me. The time had come for me to stop taking the things that presented themselves along the ways of our relationship for granted. I was fucking married. I owned half a condo. I was thirty-seven years old and needed to learn how to be skeptical again and scrutinize life just as I had when I was an idealistic MFA student and still believed someday I'd end up a writer.

When we returned to the apartment, the sun was coming up. The light flooded in through the windows here so strongly, much more so than it had ever entered my old sublet, with the necessarily inadequate vantages of the bachelor pad it was. Even in the city, where illumination, in one highway billboard form or office building or twenty-four-hour diner other, never ceased, the return to day from impenetrable night was provocative. The pug, too, appeared dazzled by it. Standing there, it was as though we were being embraced by a lion's room-sized golden arm. I divested Ishiguro of his harness and we made our way back to the bedroom. Izzy was still fast asleep, but had narrowed herself. The pug and I resumed our poses of repose without a sound.

7

ISHIGURO AND I GOT UP SEVERAL HOURS LATER ALONE. IZZY WAS already in the living room, primed to leave. Her suitcase and messenger bag were packed. She'd put on her stage makeup and blown out her hair. A new Burberry trench cinched her waist.

"Not even a good-bye?"

"Hapworth, you were sleeping."

"So?"

"Let's just . . ." She looked at her baggage. "I just want to get to the part when this trip is over and I can come back. Okay?"

"Okay," I said quietly. I thought about asking if she'd at least call me when she got to Carbondale, but I didn't know if I wanted to hear her answer.

With Izzy at the Frontenac Festival, the Biscuit Factory was somehow even more untenable. This was due, in part, to a series of absurd incidents. First, Amanda, from the garden apartment, distributed "warning" memos under each of our doors. She cautioned the residents against "suspicious activity"—enterprising kids selling ice creams and tamales from their grandparents' ramshackle carts. According to her handwritten and Xeroxed screed, this sort of unlicensed vending could only contribute to the overall decline of public health. She entreated us to abstain from patronizing. The illiterate propaganda's philosophical underpinnings thoroughly disgusted me. We lived in Pilsen. Xenophobia wasn't supposed to be an urban pioneer trait. Amanda's note also offended me grammatically. The resident comp teacher "anonymously" corrected and graded his copy. I returned it to her doorstep wadded into a ball. Yet most disconcerting was how insensible she was of the dangers on the very premises. Amanda had suggested we call the non-emergency 3-1-1 police line whenever children were being "obstinate" and couldn't be "shooed away." Could I call 3-1-1 on Casshole? He'd taken up driving a foot-powered red and yellow plastic toy car inside the loft. The Laheys had *recently* bought the Little Tykes Cozy Coupe for him. Even though he'd abandoned hammering, for those beneath the highway, it was to be death by a thousand excruciating tiny stomps. Again and again, I planned to put Ishiguro in his crate and go to Mamacita's for the evening. There I could drown my grievances in a few hours' worth of tequila. By the time I'd return, Casshole's gas tank would have been empty. But I didn't leave the loft. Running, the Laheys were ever reminding us, only worsened matters. Plus I had no interest in going out without Izzy. I missed her. Her abrupt and bewildering departure left me listless. Were my wife and I unraveling already? How could a marriage begin and end so quickly? To compound my unhappiness and confusion, I'd let myself fall into a messages-long Facebook conversation with Talia. At the end of it, we'd agreed to have a drink one afternoon.

We met at Third Coast, a wine bar on the Near North Side. I'd gone there a lot after I moved back to the city in the mid-nineties. We sat at a table in the back where she could smoke. I inquired about Mildred, the calico cat she promised to leave in my care before she went to grad school. I asked after the stack of my beloved cellophane-wrapped Modern Library editions she'd absconded with to

Iowa City. That was pretty much all I had left to say. So I let her talk, while I stared at her. She'd lost a considerable amount of weight, and, as a result, had gotten older. Her face was more angular than I'd remembered. Her baby-fat cheeks had pulled taut. I concentrated on her pale eyes, more gray here than they were blue. I could tell she hadn't washed her hair, now dyed blonde throughout, since she'd been back from Iowa, but I wanted to reach up and inhale it never-theless. Under an unbuttoned man's flannel, she wore a tight wife-beater, which revealed a suitably provocative amount of cleavage. I wondered if Talia approved of the Prada shirt, two-hundred-dollar Diesel jeans, and black blazer from H&M I had on.

As we drank our glasses of Malbec, I imagined that afternoon last year, when we first succumbed to each other. There was snow on the ground, just like now, and raw coldness in the air. I'd never be able to get that ride in her red Jetta with out-of-state plates out of my head. In my brain's nose was the scent of waxy, paper-covered crayons the upholstery exuded and the Exclamation perfume on her skin (I knew what kind it was from her earlier fiction's foreshad-owing). I watched us hurry into the bagel place in a strip mall near campus. We got coffee and she gave me the story. She claimed to have spent hours on it. Discussing the two double-spaced pages of disjointed exposition was our purported purpose for meeting. We only got through a sentence before the context took an unrecover-able turn for the ill-considered. I was beyond the teacherly point of caring. I just wanted to fuck her.

"How are things with Izzy?" she asked now. She'd been going on about Iowa and her workshops and her untalented undergrads while I reminisced, and seemed content with my participating in no more significant way than nodding. This question brought me back to the conversation. "You were kind of weird on the phone."

"I'm fine. Things are fine," I said.

"You don't sound too convinced."

I sighed. "We're going through something right now. Domestic disturbances."

"Meaning?"

"Our neighbors are terrible. Upstairs, downstairs. We're sand-wiched between two slices of hell." She looked at me like I was being ridiculous. "It's a strain on things."

"A strain on you?"

"Yeah, it's a strain on me." Then Amanda's stupid memo came to mind. I smiled. "They're obstinate. They can't be shooed away."

"You can't shoo people away, Hapworth."

"Yeah," I said, my eyes to her Camel Lights packet. "I'm begin-ning to notice."

"So, is that why you didn't want to see me?"

"What are you talking about? I *wanted* to see you. It's just that, you know, I didn't get your message for a while because I didn't recognize the number you were dialing from and didn't check the voice mail and then when you called—"

"When I called, you were married," she completed.

I nodded.

"Maybe you're not allowed to see me," she said quietly.

"Of course I am," I said emphatically, but with a pang. *Seeing* her was just about all I was allowed to do. I was married. No matter what I'd imagine could happen between us, it was a foregone con-clusion how this would have to go, where it would end up. I was now prohibited by social mores (and possibly even certain litigable formal norms) from having intentions beyond wine and conversa-tion. More important, I couldn't bring myself to do something that would hurt Izzy. Sure, we were having problems. I hadn't gotten over the feeling that she'd *left me* when she left me. But it would have been madness to just throw it all away, for sex with my old student Talia, someone with whom I had little significant connection otherwise. We weren't soul mates. We'd hardly even been entangled. I was still single during those two months we were sleeping together, and so was she. We'd owed nothing to anyone then, but that was no longer the case for me. If anything were to happen with Talia now, even if Izzy never found out, I'd be breaking a promise I made. I had to remind myself that though sitting across from Talia helped me pretend I was someone I else, I was no longer that person. I sat here as someone she didn't know and whom I was just getting to know, someone monumentally different beyond fancy clothes, someone married. I had to be.

"So what do you want to do now?" she asked.

I glanced at the silver band on my finger that Izzy and I had picked up in Chinatown after we got engaged, the ring I forgot to bring to the City Hall ceremony when we eloped. "Say good-bye?"

"Is that really what you want?"

"It doesn't matter if I do or not," I said. I wasn't looking at her face. I could feel my resolve slipping again, as it was wont to do in her proximity. Goddamn it. My eyes lingered around an arbitrary fixture behind the chrome and glossy cherrywood bar. I couldn't even make out what it was. It was too late to find out.

"Oh, Hapworth," she said. "What would you do without me?"

When I got home that night, Izzy's still-packed suitcase stood on its wheels by the breakfast bar. There was an open bottle of DeKalb County Chambourcin on the counter. Beside it lay the cork, which had fractured in the middle, with the key Bea Corton gave me at the wedding still screwed through it, holding the two pieces together. My wife was back, but the luggage and the wine were the only indications. She wasn't on the couch. The TV was off. The pug was snoring in his crate.

I found Izzy in our room. She lay on her side of the bed, reading a novel. Even absent its dust jacket, I recognized the hardcover I'd bought at O'Gara's in 1992 from the doorway: *Crazy Cock*. I said hello. She closed the book without marking her page and set it on the night table beside a full glass of wine. Then she pulled back a corner of the comforter and gestured for me to get under the covers with her. She was only wearing her bra and underwear.

"How did it go?" I asked. "Are you okay?"

"Will you just lie down with me?"

"Right now?"

Those first couple of weeks after we'd begun dating, we did it at Izzy's place or mine (and *really* early on, both) every day. It began without preamble. We just started in, wherever we were, *in medias res*, like teenagers. But after we moved into the Biscuit Factory, our sex life tapered. There were still some nap breaks between seminars at a food and wine festival and recumbent tussles after speaking engagements here and there. Though at home, it was just too absurd and distracting to commence while the Laheys carried on. Izzy wouldn't even shut off the television and turn in for the night until the fight ended, usually after Scott drove off to go sleep in his office or they'd gone to bed at opposite ends of their loft. Rest for us was certainly out of the question prior to that, let alone fucking. In the aftermath, neither of us was much in the mood to get in the mood. I didn't think I'd lost interest. I'd just let the obstacles get in the way of this, too.

"They went to Costco. It will be quiet for a couple of hours. Come on, Hapworth, let's not waste it."

I took my shirt and jeans off and spooned her. Pressing my thicket of chest hair against her back, the lengths of our torsos aligned, my knees filling the divots in the hollows behind hers like that, brought me to a state of rapt priapic attention. She reached around, drew down my boxers, and took it into her hand.

"Tell me what happened," I heard myself whisper.

"You don't want to hear," she whispered back. She clung to my dick tighter.

"I want to."

She let go of me and began to get up, but I reeled her back and climbed on top of her. She relented. I pulled down her underwear. The bare surface above her crotch was slippery against my abdomen.

"I missed you," she said.

"I missed you, too."

I obviated her bra and landed my mouth over a pert nipple. I took my tongue to it and encircled. She clamped down her eyelids. I curled my fingers and pushed into her.

"Keep doing that," she said. "Make me come." She interspersed the words with throaty vocalizations.

I finished with my hand and was inside her now. She jammed her tongue against mine. The harder I pushed, the harder she pushed, but her push felt like a pull. As she rose, she was simultaneously falling. I was driving her down instead of resurrecting her. And she, me.

After a while, she wanted me behind her and pulled me out of bed. Trying to find my way into her vertically, I flailed around. She directed, righted my course. I could see through a gap between the venetian blind slats that the Laheys' SUV was still gone. How much longer would they stay away? I suddenly felt like I was on an orgasm deadline. I had to make Izzy come before they came home. Once the running and screaming started up, there'd be nothing to keep her from falling apart. I didn't want her to be reminded of how she'd imploded after the wedding. I didn't want either of us to have to return to that scene, even though I knew it was inevitable. She was against the wall beside the door that slid open onto our back porch, above the parking spaces. I was disappointed screwing like this—it was as though we were strangers doing it in an alley—but she was into it. Obviously I had to keep going. Her hands against the concrete balanced the tripod our fused limbs made. The only sound besides our breathing was the hum of the humidifier.

When we were done, we fell back onto the mattress. Our limbs lay like battered, cast-aside merchandise that remained after the Christmas shopping stampede. We'd been thrown from the shelves and trampled into unfamiliarity in the aisles. My ears buzzed. Eventually Izzy tore herself away from me. From under the bed, she pulled a pack of American Spirits I hadn't known was there. She lit a cigarette with a match from a box on the nightstand, heretofore used in the apartment for the sole purpose of igniting Pottery Barn cherry-and-lavender scented candles.

I let this smoking go without comment. Izzy was so placid. I couldn't imagine disturbing her with reproof. Periodically she turned to ash on Henry Miller. The building was still silent.

"I don't want you to leave again," I said. I waited for her to tell me she wouldn't. I wanted her to tell me that if she had to go somewhere, she'd take me with her, just as she'd always done before.

But she didn't.

8

I'd hoped we could spend a few days together, but Izzy returned to work the next morning, and the mornings following. There were tastings to lead and talks to give. There were private dinners to host and fans to greet at the bistro. As though that weren't enough to keep her busy, she had episodes of *Vintage Attraction* to film. The most arduous show she described to me was a three-part series on serving wine at parties. It covered how to open a bottle of Champagne without blinding your friends. "Use a towel and rotate the bottle, not the cork," she said. One guest wanted to know what wine to pair with heat-and-serve Costco hors d'oeuvres. Izzy's It-Tip: pour a New Zealand Sauvignon Blanc, the crisp acidity of which does wonders to mask the freezer burn that attends the reconstituted Bagel Bite. She also gave suggestions about how to keep tarrying party guests from sneaking into your stash after everyone else has left and availing themselves of prized bottles. "As soon as you decide a vintage should be saved rather than drunk, open it immediately." In lieu of that, hide collectibles among the empties, where no guest would ever look. Just be careful to check the capsules before making a trip to the recycle bin. I was glad for the stories. It was heartening to see her industrious. It was also lonely without her around. Izzy often didn't return to the loft until well after midnight. I had conversations with Ishiguro while I graded papers. He and I ordered a lot of pizza.

One night I arrived home to find digital music playing on the television. Izzy was in the kitchen. She diced tomatoes on a white IKEA cutting board. When I entered the alcove, she kissed me without stopping what she was doing with her hands.

"No bistro?" I asked.

"No," she said. She sounded rather pleased. "I actually get a night off. How about that?"

"That's excellent," I said. I scanned the cupboard. "Do you want a glass of wine? There's a Cabernet."

Izzy touched the bottle and clamped her lips together.

"I could put it in the freezer." Chilling a room-temperature bottle down to cellar degrees was a trick of hers. This heightened the fruit and softened the alcohol burn, which was always sharper when wine was warm, like with vodka.

She pointed at the refrigerator. "Get the Albariño back there. That would work. We're having paella. I don't want any yet, though."

I opened the door and retrieved the bottle. Izzy was cleaning shrimp, deep in a cooking trance. She said nothing when I poured myself a glass or when I left for the couch to laze with Ishiguro.

Even though a part of me really wanted to know, I purposely didn't ask what had happened in Carbondale, what old haunts Izzy had reconnoitered, or whom she'd seen, or what she'd done. Aside from what there was to interpolate from the footage recorded at the wine festival that would end up in a package on an episode of a cable-access TV show I'd someday watch, I'd never find out how the going back into her past and the returning to the current life she'd built from the ashes in Chicago had affected her. I didn't need to know. Her resurfacing—not to mention the sex with which we toasted it—seemed to suggest she was ready to begin our marriage, this new life of ours. Plus, what reason would I have yet had to think any ghosts she'd have worked to elude could provoke her from anywhere but three-hundred-thirty-three miles away? As for my own erstwhile provocations, the presence of a self-collected, affectionate, dinner-preparing Izzy made me feel even guiltier about having flirted with disaster in her absence. I didn't want to dwell on my own brief devolutive foray. There was as little sense in my dredging it up as in Izzy's. And I'd have been happy to forget the entire meeting with Talia had even taken place. Unfortunately, she was still very much in mind of it. When Joe Walsh began strumming, *ba bah ba ba baah*, the sound, as if a watch alarm, reminded me to take the note I'd found in my mailbox at school out of my back pocket.

Now Izzy added Valencia rice to the paella pan roiling on the range. She reduced the heat and arranged the prepared shrimp and clams from her *mise en place*. It was doubtful she would be able to see what I was reading from across the room. To err on the side of caution, I flattened the paper and arranged it between two pages of *Wine Spectator* ads for temperature-controlled cellars I could have installed in my basement or in the galley of my yacht. Then Izzy peered into the oven to check on the gilding of the apple tart she'd made from scratch, crust and all. Her back was to me. I read the note's text quickly. Then I folded the document back up again.

The words circled my brain involuntarily. *I can't go back to Iowa yet . . . everything seems heavy now . . . caused me to question the relationships I've had with men over the past few years . . . so what are we supposed to do? Reminisce the good old days and meet for wine again . . . or what?*

To begin to determine the *"or what?"* required me to remember everything I could about our brief dalliance. She'd been my student, my beautiful student with the wild hair. She was always dyeing it. The shades often matched the color of the paper onto which she had Charles Wilcox in the department office mimeograph her draft copies when it was her turn to present work to the group. While the rest of the class packed up their bags and filtered out of the room at the afternoon's end, she'd stay behind to talk. We could converse effortlessly. Sometimes she followed me back to the office. All of this was, outwardly, very innocuous. For a time, I diligently tried to keep her off my libidinous radar. Our relationship could have been easily explained then. That changed when I started coming to her off-campus apartment, and she to mine.

"Dinner's almost ready," Izzy called out. "Want to set the table?"

I arranged the plates and knives and forks and water goblets and wine stems in two adjacent places on our screw-it-together-yourself (yet fashionably expensive) dinette. I was still thinking about Talia. In those months we were sleeping together, she would show up at my apartment at night. Wordlessly, she'd walk the length of my junior one-bedroom after closing the front door. She shed her clothes as she went. By the time she reached the green IKEA pullout couch or the bedroom and my squeaky mattress, she was naked. We'd share a joint after sex. I felt the situation warranted breaking the landlord's no-smoking-indoors policy. Mostly because of Talia's urging, I was moving out of the place I'd stubbornly occupied for close to a decade at the end of the semester. Then we were starving and plotting the procurement of dinner. We usually ordered cheeseless pizza from Domino's. If the mood struck, we'd get dressed and take off in my Mustang and have pancakes at the Golden Nugget. There were the boxes of pasta and packets of instant risotto she brought and affectionately heated. Once, she announced she wanted to *make* something—for me. Wary, but resigned to indulge her, I drove to the Dominick's. She picked out strange ingredients I couldn't even recognize. These were things I wouldn't have had any idea how to incorporate into a dish. I pushed the cart and said nothing. I paid for everything. We went back to my place. I carried the groceries upstairs. There she set about a long, spiraling cooking process. It ended up accomplishing pretty much everything except producing a meal. She cursed and sputtered and clanged from the start, only to give up halfway through. She claimed that the recipe she was using was faulty, and blamed the mishaps—a scalded onion, an overly salty sauce, a tripped smoke detector—on my dorm room appliances and Salvation Army dollar pots. I was left to clean everything up. She went to sit on the porch in one of my rusty beach chairs and sulked and smoked cigarettes and listened to indie rock songs on her giant white iPod. All the wasted expensive gourmet products, the produce, the organic proteins in the garbage bin made me furious. By the time I finished getting my small, inefficient kitchen back in order, seething and muttering pronouncements to myself, I was ready to throw her out. Of course then, at almost precisely the same moment I was riled enough to give her "the talk," she came in from outside, a blue-gray cloud of Camel Light smoke trailing. She looked even more beautiful than before she'd left, with these big, mournful eyes, and all this multicolored hair, and this ghostly pale skin. She came over to me. We started kissing. All I could think about was how much I never wanted her to leave, never wanted to find myself in this apartment alone, never ever again. We kissed some more. She started to take off her clothes. Then gone were my own. We lay down, in the living room on the carpeted floor. I inserted myself, gradually and suddenly, my cock jumping the Brazilian waxed turnstile, and plunged into the subway. There, I pommeled away for as long as I possibly could. Always after the detonation I felt embarrassed that I couldn't have made it for another ten or fifteen minutes, but the profusion of sensation brought on by having my unadorned dick devoured by her relatively pristine nougat was just too much. Just too much. A porn star I was not. She smiled though, and swiped sweat from her brow, as if to say, *You're not so bad.* Before she got dressed and back into her red Jetta, she sparked another joint from my stash. I didn't object. When she was gone, I crashed into the bedroom and squeaked my way onto the unmade bed, still vaguely redolent of our fucking the night before, exhausted, delirious, and appreciative.

"This looks good," I said. I took my seat across the dinette from my wife, a person who mere months ago was only a recognizable face on a popular television program to me.

"Sorry it took so long," Izzy said. She removed an empty mussel shell from her bowl, but wasn't eating.

"Rough day?"

She swirled her Albariño. "You could say that."

I played tag with saffron-tinted rice grains. It was a rare opportunity to eat without Ishiguro's scheming and cajoling for an edible fragment. He snoozed blissfully on the couch. But when Izzy's BlackBerry began convulsing and chirping on the table, he awoke right away, sat up, and stared at us. Izzy inspected the display and read a text message. "I have to go out later," she said. She looked crushed.

"Why?"

"Put in an appearance at a dinner Chef Dominique's doing."

"Where?"

She returned to the screen. "The Peninsula."

"How are you going to get there?"

She seemed taken aback for a moment. "I don't know . . . I mean, I'd hoped you'd drive me, but I guess I could take a cab or whatever."

"Izzy," I said. "Of course I'll drive you. But that's not the point. Why does he think he can just drag you out whenever he wants? You haven't had a night off since the wedding. Whatever happened to downtime? Peace, relaxation, and the rest?"

She pointed at the ceiling. Scott and Sheryl had begun arguing. The latter was already in Sicilian hysterics. "Hardly what I'd consider relaxing."

"So, you want me to get the car keys?" I looked with regret at our interrupted meal. After all of that intricate prep work, she'd barely had three bites of the finished product. My cultural DNA hated to see it go to waste. I could always microwave and eat the paella leftovers with the pug while Izzy was gone.

"Yeah, fine," she said. "I'll put away Ishiguro."

At the sound of his name, the dog jumped off the couch. He came over with a perplexed look on his face that didn't understand why someone was planning to go out at this late hour.

"Okay," I said.

"Stop pouting," she said.

"I wasn't pouting."

"Yes, you were. If it's such a big deal for you to take me, I'll get a taxi."

"That's crazy. It would cost you like forty dollars from here."

She scoffed. "It would not." She took her wallet from the breakfast bar. I watched her count a ten and a number of singles.

"Twenty?"

In a smaller voice, she said, "Maybe twenty." The pug looked up at her incredulously.

"That's a lot of money so you can stay there ten minutes and then turn around and come right back."

She pushed one of the empty dinette chairs, nearly knocking it over. "I haven't decided how long I'm going to stay."

"I want to talk to him. I've had enough of this. I'm your husband. It's not like he's just taking you away from some . . . some boyfriend."

"I don't want you talking to him. You'll just piss him off and then . . . then there'll be no bookings, and no money to pay for this mortgage or fill that kitchen with food."

"You'd get more bookings without him."

"Do you have to disagree with me about everything?"

"I don't disagree with you about everything."

"See what I mean?"

"Izzy, I may not be able to earn what it takes to keep this household running, but you have a family, a life outside the restaurant and appearances now, and the mighty and powerful Chef Dominique needs to learn to respect that."

It was several long moments before she spoke again. Finally, she said, "It is really infuriating when you fight me on these things. You don't know what I have to do. You don't know what goes on."

"You're right, I don't, because you don't tell me. Tell me what I don't understand."

"You don't know how much bullshit goes into getting these clients. Tonight he's arranging some more speaking work for me. The National School Boards Association is coming to town next month, then the Kitchen and Bath Industry Show, and the Green Party is having their national convention in Chicago in July . . ."

"The Green Party," I said. The image of a wine tasting amidst the nomination of a candidate for president staunched my melancholy. I found a smile returning to my face.

She laughed. "I know. The funny part is that it makes more sense than at the kitchen and bath thing. What am I supposed to do? Pour wine samples from a tub?"

My heartbeat began to resume the lazy amble of the unprovoked. "Maybe they'll use toilets for spit buckets."

"That's not a bad idea."

"Oh, Izzy," I began, "I'm sorry to get so . . . I don't know . . ."

"Overprotective?"

"Overprotective."

"Jealous?"

"Let's go with 'frustrated.'"

She put her arms around me. "I'm sorry. I really am. But the truth is, it helps for me to be there, and another truth is, one more hour I don't have to be here listening to that craziness upstairs is one more hour I don't have to be unhappy."

"Is it really that bad? You're not getting at all used to it?"

She took a deep breath and exhaled it through her nose. "I . . . am. I guess I am. On some levels. But . . . it's hard."

"I know. It is for me, too."

"Well, let's not make this any worse than it has to be. Okay? You and Ishiguro stay here, and I'll go and come back soon."

The dog's pleading eyes turned to me. It seemed he was in favor of the plan. I was the last holdout. "Fine," I said.

After Izzy went downstairs and to the taxi she'd called, I cleaned the table. I washed and put away the paella pan. I loaded the dishwasher with our plates and utensils. I turned off the kitchen lights. Then I went in search of the dog, to capture and suit him up.

Ishiguro refused to walk in a slow and orderly fashion once we were outside. He was a bucking calf. He kept darting from one edge of the sidewalk to the other. He sniffed every frozen plant and patch of dead grass and pissed-on rusty fence we passed. His erratic motions were giving me a headache. I gave up on trying to steer our course. I'd planned to take the dog north, to Addams Park, which was our usual evening destination. We began in that direction, but then Ishiguro rerouted us. He had another idea about where we'd go on this particular outing. The pug pushed ahead vigorously. He led me down a strange and seemingly arbitrary series of streets. First we went southwest on diagonal Blue Island Avenue until it spilled into Loomis. Then we went down Loomis to Nineteenth Street. We took a right at Throop, a left at Cullerton. Where were we going? We were blocks and blocks from our building. This was a part of Pilsen that I didn't recall having ever walked. I certainly had never brought Ishiguro here. I couldn't figure out to what he was heading with such unwavering certainty and furry four-legged force.

The dog stopped in front of the door to a narrow apartment house. He was panting. His pastrami tongue unfurled to slice the air. He pulled himself and me closer to the glass and tapped the pane with a paw. A frenzied determination had overtaken him. He wanted to get inside.

"What's in there?" I asked him. Ishiguro now batted the wooden frame. I asked, facetiously, "Is someone expecting you?"

The hysterical way Ishiguro clawed and smacked the old, heavy door could only mean that the pug had gone mad. On occasion I'd witnessed him so eager to return home that he nearly cannonballed through his harness. We clearly weren't standing at the entrance to the Biscuit Factory. It wasn't like cautious Ishiguro to be so adamant about wanting to venture into unfamiliar enclosed spaces. I read down the list of names on the intercom registry. *Talbot/Shrum 3B, Ascarrunz-Ramierez 3A, Carroll/Averill/Kenney 2B, Rosengrant/ Zukowski 2A, Dennis 1B, Geller/Smith 1A.*

I immediately recalled the name Rosengrant from the conversation I'd had with Izzy the morning after we met. The night before, when I was drunk enough to want to introduce her to my silly conceptualizing, and somehow we ended up back at my place, in my bed, I'd avoided the conversation about whom she'd dated before. With or without alcohol, it was always awkward to talk about past attachments at any point in an involvement. The matter asserting itself at such an early phase, one decidedly inhospitable to honesty, compounded the feeling. It was a time when fear of scaring the other person off necessitated a careful selection of topics. Only those determined to be shiny and hopeful, nothing even remotely imperfect or disquieting, were typically granted admittance to discussion. But would there really have ever been a better time? When she brought it up at brunch the next day, I'd received the information with the unconditional acceptance also crucial to that nascent stage. I veiled my displeasure, not knowing what else to do. That day I catalogued away the name and that for which it stood. One might have suspected—hoped—Izzy had, too. Each month we'd been together had buried the relic deeper and deeper into our romantic archeology. Nothing previous to this buzzer roster had given her words reason to present themselves again to me.

"*My last boyfriend was a sommelier—is a sommelier, I guess. Pacer Rosengrant. We met at the bistro. I've heard he went to Las Vegas to work with this master the Palazzo owns—*"

That motherfucker was back in town, living a half mile from our house. A half mile.

And Izzy, goddamn her, what was she doing here? And why the hell would the dog know this skeezy tenement?

Had the dog been here, too??

As was his want, Ishiguro tarried, but I cajoled mightily to keep him focused and on course so we could get back to the apartment. There, I got on Facebook and found a page for Pacer Rosengrant. I couldn't see much, since we weren't friends. But I could tell, from a previous wall narration, that his network had changed to Chicago, Illinois two weeks ago. How many times had Izzy seen him since then? This was just too much to deal with.

I logged out and keystroked the computer back into its slumber. I sat at the breakfast bar with my head in my hands. I remained in this position until Ishiguro became alarmed. He whimpered and nipped at my black sock. "Fine," I said, after the dog had wrought persuasive pinching pain on my big toe.

I removed my glasses and lay on the floor in the unfurnished space between the kitchen alcove and the front entrance. Ishiguro, without hesitation, began licking my face. He performed an ethnic cleansing of my large Semitic nose and weak chin with ritualistic, dispassionate precision. Once the pug was complete, he inspected his work. His snout was barely a millimeter from my right eye. Satisfied, he trotted off. I remained where he left me, the wetter for wear. With my face drying in the air, I stared at the new white ceiling and let the austerity transfix me. This was the same game I used to play when I was a child: I'd lie on the shag carpeting in my apartment on Riverside Drive and stare at the ceiling and pretend it was the floor. Beside the oval dining room table, I imagined that my parents had packed up all our belongings and moved off somewhere, without me. Gone were the Hasidic rococo-framed oil paintings, my father's opera records, the leather-bound Shakespeare folios. Gone were my mother's ancestral plastic-covered chairs and the stiff-cushioned couches. Gone were the embroidered pillows. Gone were my older sister and her porcelain dolls. Just a broad expanse of white was left. Except for the chandelier. Inverted, it was a solitary crystal palm tree with a spindly silver trunk, standing on an empty, icy beach. I sometimes lay like this for hours. I had no idea—at seven or thirty-seven—why the simple act of staring at a blank canvas could be so engaging, but it was. In this quasi-self-hypnosis, I reviewed the events of the night. The meditative lull concluded with my shocking discovery that Pacer Rosengrant had returned to Izzy's life—which now meant he was part of my life, too. And Talia. What the fuck had I done to make someone who'd never been anything but coolly equanimous and affectedly coy the entire time we'd known each other suddenly so plainly melodramatic? And atavistic: she, who'd taught me how to text and gotten me on Facebook, was leaving analog-era folded, handwritten, maudlin notes in campus mailboxes? What the fuck was I doing that managed, now, after all this time, to draw out the ludicrousness of her desires—to draw palpable desire of any sort out of her? And, worst of all, why now and not when I would have wanted it? It all worked to vanish any tranquility the trance delivered and replace it with anguish. I couldn't make any sense out of this heartbreaking pileup of so many realities.

The only thing I could do then was drink. I refilled my wineglass, left behind from dinner. I remained in the kitchen until I finished the Albariño and the warm Cabernet I opened after it. The strafe of drunken hunger that came next had me remembering the apple tart. Izzy left it resting in the oven. I paired it with a half pint of Ben and Jerry's Cinnamon Buns and ate everything, to try to defuse the alcohol and keep from throwing up. When I was done, I flung myself onto the couch. Ishiguro, an infirmary heating pad, climbed onto my stomach. I turned on the television and scanned the Comcast video-on-demand listings for a film. None of the offerings appealed to either of us. Shortly, my cell phone trembled. It took a considerable amount of effort to reach it. The front pocket of my jeans had been barricaded by a mass of unyielding, tawny port–colored fur. I read the text message that had been delivered: *wht is yr address im cmng over* and promptly deleted it.

9

BECAUSE I'D PASSED OUT BEFORE SHE GOT HOME, I DIDN'T KNOW WHAT time Izzy finally returned last night. I suspected it had been quite late. She'd slept through both alarms this morning. What I did know was that I felt like shit. My brain was still bruised from the evening's bottle-and-a-half bacchanal. Yet I made Izzy some coffee before she left for work. Whether she'd admit it or not, she needed all the help she could get to deal with Chef Dominique and his gauntlet of a production schedule.

Izzy emerged from the bedroom at an intermission in her preparations. She'd shadowed her eyes. Part of her hair was blow-dried. The other part was still in giant bright-red curlers.

"That must have been some meeting."

"Hapworth, please don't start with me."

I really wasn't going to. Though my wife had been the one who'd ostensibly physically transgressed, I nevertheless couldn't bring myself to interrogate her. I was guilty, too, in thought, if not in deed. And we were supposed to trust each other. Admitting I knew Pacer Rosengrant was back and that she'd been to his place would betray my fear that she was capable of cheating. If you read the situation through my father's Freudian lens, my largely unfounded suspicion suggested that I was uncertain about my own propensity for betrayal. This was not so much of a reach if you knew about my surreptitious Facebooking while Izzy was away. In my mother's profitable parlance, the wine assignation with Talia was inculpatory evidence. Transference theory and adjudicative implications aside, I didn't like Izzy's and my sleeping apart in the same house.

I rubbed my neck. "I think the couch killed my back," I said.

"I didn't want to wake you up."

"Whatever. Do you want coffee?"

She nodded. I ran the French press and presented her with a mug. She inhaled sharply twice, just like Ishiguro did when he uncovered an unfamiliar fragrant spot on the sidewalk. "Dunkin' Donuts?"

"Yeah," I said.

"It's horrible."

Her rejection stung. "It was all I could find. It was that or nothing."

"We still have it *because* it's horrible," she said. She handed the mug back to me and returned to the bedroom to finish dressing.

I tried the coffee. I couldn't fault her for not wanting it. There was something peculiar about the taste. An unpleasant metallic acidity had corrupted the water. I cleaned out the press and started over. She was sitting on the bed, her makeup half done, when I delivered my revised draught. She squinted intently at her BlackBerry screen. It was a tape day, when Izzy filmed her TV show. Accordingly, there were always a lot of e-mails before she even made it to the El. Chef Dominique apparently couldn't wait to begin ordering her around until she'd gotten to the studio.

She took a sip. "It tastes weird," she said. She looked at me kindly, however. "It's sweet of you to keep trying."

I tested the sample Izzy's professional tongue deemed completely unpalatable. Now it tasted like Dunkin' Donuts coffee: bold, milky, unctuous, with only a remote tanginess. I was sluiced with nostalgia. It brought me back to the Hyde Park Dunkin' Donuts on Fifty-third Street. I'd spent an entire Saturday reading *The Garden of Eden* there. I was a second-year with a black Members Only jacket and Jewfro to match. I drank fifty cups of coffee over those dozen or so hours. I sat in a chair bolted to the floor. It was an uncomfortable painted-metal seat. I could only turn left or right. I was too engrossed in the novel to care. *The Garden of Eden* was the first book to show up on a syllabus that would become a lifelong favorite of mine.

My cell phone buzzed. A two-page-long text message from Berkal. *Tell Sommelier to dress you up for dept cocktail party. Need not worry abt lunch money. Grad din Greektown after gratis + heavily liquored. In vino veritas, SJB.*

"Fuck," I said aloud.

"What?" Izzy asked.

"I forgot about this thing I'm supposed to do tonight."

"What is it?"

"A stupid English Department get-together at the Alumni Center. The one time of the year they roll out the open bar and get everyone drunk and stuffed with bacon-wrapped scallops and pathetic conversation about issues in twenty-first-century literature and the dwindling readership."

"I guess I don't need to put the pork shoulder in the Crock-Pot, then." She said this almost sadly, like she'd really been looking forward to it.

"A group is going to the Parthenon or something after."

"Well, have some *baklava* for me."

"What will you eat?"

"I can have family meal at the bistro before service." Her eyes turned wistful. "Just like the old days."

"Don't stay out too late," I said. "Ishiguro gets sad when we're both gone too long."

"You either," she said.

I picked up Izzy's repudiated coffee mug. In the kitchen, I poured out what was left. I watched the coffee spill down the drain in a warm, murky-colored rapid. Atop that rapid, my hope for the day rafted away. I knew what to expect. There were no surprises left. I'd go do what passed for teaching. I'd return to University Hall after class and sit around for office hours. Not a single student would show up. Probably not even my grad student officemate.

There was a gathering of some indeterminate sort in front of University Hall's revolving doors. I read paper signs bearing Sharpie-scrawled indictments and protestations, but the aggrieved students weren't holding them. They ate Subway sandwiches and drank Pepsis and updated their Facebook statuses from their phones. Inside, it was a relief to find the arriving elevator car empty.

Dark mornings seemed even darker from within this building. It was a surprise to find Berkal at his desk. He was reading student stories for his 212. Berkal's lamp was on. He had the overhead fluorescents off. The warmer light made the place look a little more congenial.

"How do you explain to an engineering major that just because something happened in your life doesn't mean it belongs in short fiction?" Berkal asked.

"Don't ask me. Do you realize it's been a year since I got to teach a workshop?"

Berkal stood up. "It hasn't been that long."

"It has," I said. "It's been that long since I've even been able to get more than two *comp* classes."

"Schultz is doing the summer schedule now. You could get in and—"

Hearing the name of the adjunct coordinator and chief departmental course distributor made me wince. "Fuck no," I said. "I hate teaching summer classes. It's always either too cold or too hot in the building, nobody wants to be there, everyone wants to have class outside, which you say is a bad idea for acoustic and general comportment reasons, but nobody cares. People just see you as the overdressed asshole who won't let them enjoy the weather."

"I always have class outside," Berkal offered unhelpfully.

"Of course you do," I said, "because you're a grad student, and, by definition, brilliant and infallible. The times I've tried it, it's been a disaster."

"You want me to talk to Schultz? I am lead GPTI."

"Since when? And no. I'm sure she's already slotted me in for whatever the shittiest fall class is, in the worst room on campus, with the students who won't have even passed the admissions requirements, but will matriculate for the sole purpose of—"

"Of tormenting you," Berkal interrupted. "Right. It's all for your benefit, or whatever the opposite of benefit is. It all seeks to destroy you."

"I'm not entirely convinced it isn't. I've been teaching here a long time."

"And?"

"How much longer do you have?"

"Coursework is done. I'm basically ABD."

"My advice? Don't rush to terminate that terminal degree. A lot of good an MFA does me."

"It says you can write, and that at least at some point in your life, you did."

"It doesn't matter. I'm never going to end up on the tenure track with it."

"And you think I will? Even with a PhD, I'll be lucky to get a couple of adjunct gigs at the city colleges. I doubt UIC would ever look at me as anything more than a grad student. This, my friend, is about the best I'm gonna get."

He had a point. The chances of full-time employment for post-grads in English had been bleak even back when I'd finished my *first* master's. Prospects had become further dire in the many years since I was a newly minted MFA. Forget about a full-time job with benefits and security. Now my meager, tenuous role here was actually desirable and possibly even sought-after.

"Hapworth, why do you think you have to have a PhD to get on the tenure track?" Berkal asked. "Because academics can't write and writers can't teach. You choose one or the other. Or one or the other chooses you. It's as simple as that."

"What's chosen me?"

"The right thing will come along."

"I think I better not quit my day job in the meantime, as the cliché goes."

"I'll make you an appointment to see Schultz. How's Friday?" He printed a reminder for me on the blank side of a student's old index card.

I folded it and put it in my back pocket. "Thanks," I said.

"No problem. Maybe it's not too late."

"Too late for what?"

"To—to—you know, to get a smart room. Have you been in one of them? Computer, Internet, audio, video, dry erase boards with clean erasers. Twenty-first century, dog. You can do a film-as-literature unit and spend a week or two showing the director's cut of *Heaven's Gate*. Is—is—that what you're wearing tonight?"

"I have a tie in my bag. I didn't want to teach in anything too bureaucratic. Scares the kids, you know."

My officemate turned off his lamp. He packed his messenger bag and put on his coat and hat. I followed him into the hallway. "What about Izzy?" Berkal asked.

"What about her?"

"Haven't you ever thought about doing something with her?"

"Like getting married? We did that. For what it's worth."

"Like working together."

I shrugged.

"*Carpe diem.*"

On my way out of University Hall and to the library, my mind was on Izzy and the bad Dunkin' Donuts this morning and *The Garden of Eden*. When I was a grad student teaching assistant and had my own classes, I put several chapters on the reading list. Some students who'd never even read any Hemingway before told me they were "fired up" and "super psyched" by the preview. They wrote outstanding response papers and ran off to the library to check out the entire book. Only then did I ever feel like I was actually accomplishing something in a classroom. The students listened. They took notes. They let themselves be galvanized by the texts. In so doing, they galvanized them in return. It was just as I had experienced my life-changing Modern Lit winter quarter in that musty, heady little lecture room back in Harper Library, on my beloved ivied and gargoyle-adorned first campus. But teaching comp at a commuter school designed with the austerity of a Bergman film, embodying the practicality and earnestness of a Minnesota congressman, it wasn't at all like that. Now I considered it a major accomplishment if I was able to induce a majority of the kids convening for my course to even angle their faces in my direction for an appreciable duration. One early semester at UIC, I tried swapping out the syllabus boilerplate "Hills Like White Elephants" for an excerpt from *Eden*. Few even bothered to read it. Several copies I reeled out of the wastebasket after everyone had left. I still kept them in my desk drawer as a reminder, because it was horrible. I swore I'd never again attempt to teach prose that really meant anything to me. What was the point? The remotely insightful were outnumbered. The arrogant and entitled rest just didn't care. I wasn't going to be able to do much to improve things. *If you cannot respect the way you handle your life then certainly respect your trade.*

Two minutes before the library classroom clock read the official commencing hour, I dropped myself into the chair at the head of the long conference table. Teaching was just about the last thing I wanted to do right now. I was hungover. I was pissed off at Izzy. Whether or not she actually cheated on me, I couldn't stop feeling I'd been betrayed. I missed Ishiguro. And I had nothing prepared. It was going to take days to get through this class. Even if I started fifteen minutes late, ordered some in-class writing, and then had a generously untimed break afterward, I still would struggle. For the next two and a half hours, I'd have to be here, my knotted brain arteries throbbing, my fingertips slightly numb, my heart chagrined.

As though presaging my mood, the students, shuffling in, looked more despondent than usual. They wordlessly claimed seats, more or less the exact positions they'd staked out on the first day of the semester. My favorites, the grade-favor curriers, the ass-kissers, ambled in first, as always. They took their places around mine at the head of the table. Ordinarily, I appreciated the proximity. Today they just seemed a little too near. I kind of wished they'd go over and sit with the Trench Coat Mafia. I wasn't ever sure why these Goths, burnouts, and militants enrolled in English classes. Weren't they usually business majors? Though the Mafia Midwest chapter members sat with crossed arms, torsos and legs encased in perennially heavy leather, and sneers permanently affixed to their ever-so-unsubtly lipsticked mouths, they were harmless and mostly kept their distance. Even so, a part of me always feared they might beat the shit out of me or blow up Norlin Library when I returned their inarticulate paragraphs stippled with red objections.

The Trio, Lindsay, Lindsey, and Lindsie, sat near each other at the far end of the room. I still considered it a skill worthy of bragging that I could precisely correspond the spelling and girl. AY was beautiful. She styled her long, dark hair in a variety of ways. This afternoon, it curtained her face. Her tresses tumbled down her white open-buttoned shirt and concluded at her breasts. When I first took in her frighteningly alluring eyes, encased in don't-fuck-with-me black mascara, I decided she'd get an A whether or not she chose to do any work in this class. She must have sensed this. She paid me little attention from then on. EY, with her ponytail and Iowa farm-girl freckles and soft eyes, was dim but attentive. Despite her unabashed lack of sophistication, or because of it, she was precociously trenchant. And IE was a hippie with long, dirty dreads. She wore no makeup on her face. Her lips were always cracked. She carried a black handbag with a silver closure that I once believed toted her lunch. She told me later in passing that it actually contained the handmade bongs she sold on campus.

Heather, Sally, Nikki, Dave, David, Seth, and Stereo came in. The noise level in the room was high with the collective volume of all of the separate conversations taking place. I directed a finger around the conference table, attempting to count the heads, but I kept losing my place. Finally I gave up and reached for my attendance book. Checking off their names seemed easier.

"Where's Adam?" I asked the grid.

T. J.'s was always one of the first arms in the air. He chimed, "Adam dropped."

"He did not," I said.

"Wait," T. J. said. He was never easily contradicted. "Which Adam?"

My eyes bulged in front of the list. Could I really have gone all this time without knowing I had multiple Adams?

"You should say last names. You never call last names," T. J. said. Generally I was cheerful in the face of T. J.'s smugness. He seemed to like and respect me, even if his officiousness sometimes felt mocking. Today I was diminished to the point that the gangly boy with insincerely mussed hair, thick Weezer glasses, and a cliché of a goatee might just have finally found his chance to usurp my authority.

"Let's move on. I'd like us to do some writing today," I said. I spoke loudly, in as strong a voice as I could offer.

At the sound of the word *writing*, a cacophonic symphony of academic sounds commenced. The prepared kids opened the notebooks already before them. They flipped past the pages they'd previously filled until they landed at a blank opportunity. Accompanying this was the music of the unready. Piles of undesired books slammed down onto the table. Zippers on messenger bags pierced the air with high-frequency vibrations. Velcro closures that secured backpack compartments ripped apart. They scavenged for pens in pockets and jackets, borrowed from neighbors if necessary, and then uncapped or clicked into action. T. J. unsheathed a battered white iBook with a very large screen and deployed its initializing Mac chime.

"Okay," I began, when the fourth movement had concluded. "I know we've been talking a lot about research papers over the last few weeks, developing theses, finding and cataloging sources, but I'd like to move on to a different form of essay, the narrative."

T. J. had the syllabus in hand. He said, "But you have on here that today we're going to be learning how to . . . use MLA format."

"Yes," I said. "And MLA format is very important. But I kind of feel it would be of more use to us now to return to a simpler mode of thought." I was catching my stride. I cleared my throat and spoke more assuredly. "I'd like us to take a moment to diverge."

"But what about the syllabus?"

"What the adjunct coordinator doesn't know won't hurt her?"

"Nice," went Heather. T. J. nodded his unqualified approval.

"Are we going to turn this in at the end of class?" David asked.

I sighed. "If you want to. If you want to keep working, you can have it for me—"

"Can we e-mail it to you?"

"I'm not going to be here next Tuesday, so can I give it to you after—"

"Look," I said testily. Then I quickly corrected my tone with a stock good-natured grin. "I haven't even told you what I want you to write about."

"About what you want us to write," T. J. said. Was he trying to be funny?

"Yes. Right. And if anyone ends any sentences with prepositions, he or she must answer to T. J."

The three or four who didn't have their eyes to their notebooks stared at me confusedly.

"Never mind," I answered their searching gazes. "Okay, here is the prompt. I want you to write about a time when you were deceived."

Lindsey raised her hand. Her pen still seesawed between two fingers. I nodded for her to go ahead. "Like, you mean when a boy-friend cheats on you?"

"That makes an instant *ex*-boyfriend," Lindsay coolly added.

I immediately envisioned Pacer Rosengrant, twisted up in elec-trified embrace with Izzy at his new apartment within walking distance of hers—*ours*. Then I saw him later, cashed, a shell buried under the sheets as Izzy pried herself away to return to me, her husband. "Could be. Sure. Yeah, of course. But not limited to that."

"Like if we got ripped off on eBay?"

"Yes," I said. "Right. Like Sally says. There are probably times you recall having been swindled in a transaction."

"This one time, I was, like, fucking this hooker, but she couldn't make me come, so I, like, didn't want to pay her," Kevin, one of the thugs, offered. It was a rare moment of volubility for him. The guys in the room laughed. Most of the girls looked off to the bookshelves that lined the perimeter between the windows. I shook my head, my official response to an interruption. I was secretly pleased that I'd gotten one of the thugs to speak.

"What I'd like you to concentrate on," I began, once the students were no longer amused or appalled by Kevin and returned their attention to the front, "is an instance in your life when someone led you to believe something was one way and you found later on that the situation was something quite different."

A girl with a square face and a rectangular torso said, "Like . . . when somebody starts dating a guy and finds out he's still hooking up with his ex-girlfriend?"

"Yes, Dana. That's a good example."

"Danielle."

"Sorry?"

"My name is Danielle."

"Shit," I said. A few nervous giggles fired around me. "Sorry. Danielle. What did I say?"

"You called me Dana."

"Did you once go by . . . Dani?"

She rolled her eyes.

"Anyway, yes, Danielle. *Danielle* had a very good example, everyone. Hello? I'm glad to see you've already gotten started. Can I have just one more moment of your time? Hello? Guys? *Please?*"

The pens came down after this last exhortation. Most of the eyes turned to me.

"Thank you," I said, sincerely appreciative. I was in no condition to battle unruliness. "Just write about a time when you got cheated. Fooled. Misled. Basically any opportunity you've had to disabuse yourself of misconceptions about a situation you were in. Okay?" I waited for someone to ask me to define "disabuse." Luckily for me nobody did.

"Is it only if we've *been* cheated on by someone else? What if we did the cheating?" T. J. asked. By this point everyone else had begun working. I answered T. J. individually, with a consenting wave of the hand. We both knew he was going to write what he wanted to regardless of whether or not I approved. But in the classroom, ceremony triumphed.

I pretended to scrutinize a piece of departmental junk as though it contained critical information. It was a flyer for a talk. An emeritus professor lectured on "The Declining Significance of Prose." A Q-and-A, light refreshments, and non-alcoholic beverages followed. I'd found it newly delivered to my mailbox a week after the event was scheduled to take place. "Because sometimes that happens," T. J. continued.

"Yes, T. J. Sometimes we do cheat and lie and swindle."

T. J. looked scandalized. I thought I was only agreeing with the boy. "Are you writing yet?"

He pointed at his iBook. "Already done."

"Yeah, right."

"I'm serious," T. J. said, his voice low. He leaned in my direction as though we were buddies chatting next to each other over beers at a pub. "I started writing about this pyramid scheme for fiction workshop. I can just add to it."

"Well, do something with that," I said. I had to cut him off. I simply didn't have the wherewithal to argue with T. J. I returned to the flyer in front of me. The boring but, strangely, soothing design of the Microsoft Word template the advertiser—Shelley Schultz—used to frame the event details put me into a moiré trance.

Twenty minutes later, the students with little sympathy for those still locked in concentration started to get itchy. First two whispered back and forth. Then another two turned to each other. I ignored them. The conversations joined forces. Before long, most of the students were chatting, even those whose scribbling pens suggested they probably still had more to write. It was too loud for me to keep pretending I didn't hear.

"It seems like you're more or less done, so who wants to read?" I asked.

Danielle raised her hand first. I was panicked by the earlier name mix-up and stammered when I went to call on her.

"Danielle?" she gave me, with a linguistic hip shake. Some of the other girls snickered.

"Yes. Read yours."

She opened her mouth, but I stopped her.

"Do you want to tell us what it's about first?"

T. J. looked at me disapprovingly.

"I'd rather just read it, Mr. Hapworth."

God, she really was pissed off. "Okay, fine. Let's hear it."

"Do I have to stand up?"

"Do you ever?"

We were silent as she breathed. It appeared to take a great deal of effort for her to ready herself to recite. She'd only used one side of a piece of lined paper. I could see through the translucence when she held it up that the text was dense enough to keep us occupied for a while. One of the thugs opened a bottle of Pepsi. The crack of the plastic top separating from the safety ring and the carbonated high-fructose hiss that followed jarred me. He leaned back in his chair, as if at a theater, settling in to see an action film.

"'His name was Conrad,'" Danielle opened. The sentence was likely an unconscious nod to the well-anthologized Joyce Carol Oates story we'd spent two classes at an earlier point in the semester, along with every other entry-level comp course around the planet, attempting to learn how to deconstruct.

The discussion of Danielle's draft began haltingly. A thug spoke first. He mumbled something I couldn't make out. The thug was a boy I was fairly certain slept through entire lectures. I'd never completely seen his face, since he'd never taken off his sunglasses. I assumed his contribution was a derisive remark about the basketball team Danielle referenced. I offered *"Okay, okay,"* in a sharp, admonishing pitch, which was surprisingly effective in keeping everyone else from coming unglued. The thug offered no more and lapsed back into the silence we were accustomed to.

Lindsay asked, "What happened after that?"

Danielle seemed almost surprised to find that she had ended without concluding. She performed a short forensic examination of her paper. "I guess I stopped writing then."

"I wanna know what happened, though." There were murmurs of concurring.

"I don't know. He wouldn't delete her number from his phone."

"Damn," Lindsay said softly.

The essay had very obviously shaken the guys. Either they were embarrassed by their gender collectively or felt inadvertently exposed for romantic misdeeds of their own. To mask their discomfort, they made obscene gestures. They mercilessly excoriated Danielle for being so naïve in the first place.

I slapped my sweaty palm on the conference table. This immediately commanded Danielle's—and everybody else's—attention. "And you broke up with him."

She looked out the window.

"This is what I'm trying to get at, people."

One of the thugs asked, "What is?" His question betrayed an earnest curiosity.

"I can't believe I just called you 'people.'" I shook my head, in an attempt to return to diction that more closely resembled my own. "The point of this exercise, the point of writing these narrative essays, of writing anything, is to take something confusing from life and, through language, and distance, try to see if the character—"

"You mean us, if it's a personal essay," T. J. said.

"Well, that's probably an ideological discussion for another class, but for our purposes at the moment, you, the character, whomever's narrating, *whatever*, has an opportunity to reassess before . . . before . . ."

"Before we fuck up again?"

Out from behind her intricate canvas of freckles, Lindsey opined, "Guys like that always do." She shivered, almost imperceptibly, as though shaking away an unpleasant recollection. "She was better off losing him."

"Actually, she didn't say whether she did or not yet," canny T. J. pointed out.

"Professor Hapworth?"

"Yes, Nikki?"

"Can I go to the bathroom?"

I groaned. "Nikki, this is college. You don't have to ask my permission."

"But what if I have to go?"

"You just . . . go."

Her cheeks reddened. She remained in her seat until I resumed speaking. It allowed for an exit that went mostly undetected.

"Where was I?"

"We can learn about ourselves from writing."

"Yes. Thank you. I mean, I'm oversimplifying here, but I think there's something we can take away. Oh, yeah. I remember the point I was trying to make: Why is this important?"

Silence.

"Discovering, like, you know, that you thought you knew someone and then you didn't?"

"Have any of you seen *Manhattan*?" I asked the class.

Those weeks Izzy and I were first dating, when we didn't have to go to a food and wine festival or a dinner or a law firm or bank speaking engagement or a shortbread cookie launch party, we stayed in and watched movies on my couch. It was a phase we'd moved on from so quickly that we'd already taken to reminiscing it. She called it "When Our Love Was New." We covered much of Woody Allen's early oeuvre. In my mind now was the famous concluding scene of my favorite of his films. It was a part Izzy didn't know. We'd gotten too tired that night to watch the second half and had never returned to it. I conjured the shots I had mostly memorized from having had in front of my eyes easily fifty times along the past twenty-nine years. As I did, Danielle, with her dark-blonde hair and tragicomically prosoponic face, began to channel Mariel Hemingway. She had even vaguely echoed the actress's youthful soubrette register while she read her consciousness stream's most vulnerable admissions to us.

"Scorsese?" Stereo asked.

"No, not exactly, Stereo. It's an older movie, from the seventies, which I'm sure you haven't heard of. Anyway, the film ends with this line: 'You have to have a little faith in people.'"

"So my essay sucked?" Danielle asked.

"No," I said. "It didn't suck. It was actually quite engaging. But think about that line for a second." It was a long second. "Does anybody see the connection?"

"She could have forgiven him. If she really wanted to be with him."

"That's the question. Did you really want things to be over?" I asked her.

"Do I have to tell you in order to get full credit?"

"Forget about the assignment. What did you do after the point where the story left us?"

"You mean the narrator?"

"Ha, ha. Yes, I meant the narrator. Does more of the story remain to be told?"

"I guess."

"And do you guys know why?"

"Why?" Danielle asked, in Mariel's guilelessly chirpy voice.

"Because there's always more. That's what the line means. That, ladies and gentlemen, is why you take these silly English classes. That's why there's narrative. It reminds us, if we bother to read it, that there's always another way of looking at things, because there's always more to see. We just can't always see it immediately. But if we don't jump to conclusions, if we don't make irrevocable decisions, if we give peace a chance—I think you don't need me to tell you it's . . . it may very well be the meaning of life."

"Mr. Hapworth?"

"Yes?"

"Would you like me to read mine?"

"Yes, Seth. Thanks."

"David."

"Dave. I'm sorry. I think I didn't get enough sleep last night."

"*David.* He's Dave."

"Oh, fuck."

I ended class fifteen minutes early. The quorum had lapsed into unanswerable restlessness long before that. I wanted them gone as soon as possible. I remained in my seat as my students tore pages out of their notebooks and passed their papers forward. They reorganized their backpacks, capped their pens, and left the conference table without pushing in their chairs. They mumbled good-byes or nodded in my general direction as they made for the door. Lindsie flashed me a peace sign. I accepted it with an instinctive and regrettably dorky thumbs-up. I tried to keep my head down as they shambled out. I wished to avoid the looks. I knew the kids' faces would reflect either disappointment or disgust. T. J. must have sensed I didn't feel like talking. Usually he hung around for at least ten minutes of babble before decamping. He took off without remark. Lindsay and Lindsey were less willing to accept my detaching. They deflected my nonverbal cues and tactlessly issued frantic questions about previously collected exercises, looming deadlines.

I sat in the empty room and put my hands over my eyes. It didn't help. Even shielded from the world, my brain spun a myriad of scenes. There projected onto the TV screen behind my eyelids was a slickly edited montage of all that had happened to me over the last weeks and months, the waning triumphs and the recently fast-accumulating disasters. My e-mail to Izzy, meeting, falling in love, the movies, Ishiguro, the pork bao, the trips, buying the loft, buying furniture, moving in together, Chef Dominique and the neighbors driving us crazy, eloping, Talia, Pacer Rosengrant, my teaching career careering off the edge of a comp class cliff, all the wines drunk during and in between. The good, the bad—was there even a difference? Most of the mental video offered ugly junctures of the two. It all presented itself to me again so clearly. I desperately wished to change the channel. But I couldn't. This was my life.

Outside it was raining. Heavy, gray mist clung to the air, erasing the upper portions of tall buildings. My umbrella was, predictably, missing from my Timbuk2. I started walking quickly. I avoided the grassy shortcuts, which were already mud. My walk turned into a little jog. After only a few yards, a searing pain in my ankles slowed my pace back down to a purposeful trot. I reached University Hall, soaked. Inside I brushed water off the arms of my jacket, from the top of my messenger bag. I could feel my wet socks clinging to my feet and cold toes. My sneakers squished and splattered the elevator and the hallway.

At my desk, I logged into the campus webmail. I wasn't in the mood for the inane mass mailings to the adjunct teaching pool from Schultz that filled my inbox. I couldn't help feeling like she was trying to send me an encoded direct message with subject lines like "Online Networking Tools and Finding Employment" and "Great Rundown of How-To's for Cover Letters." I selected her e-mails without opening them and changed their status marks to "read." I was grateful that Berkal hadn't come back to campus yet.

The party wouldn't start for a few hours. I wanted to do nothing but disappear in the silence and try to take a nap.

But the tranquillity was punctured before long. Two knocks came to the door. A winsome coed brought the first of them. Her blonde hair, side-parted and gathered into a ponytail, appeared as annoyed by the rain as my own hair felt. Her clothes were dry, even though she wasn't wearing a coat. The small pendant dangling from a thin gold string on her neck fell forward as she leaned over my shoulder to squint into the office. She almost, but not quite, pressed against me. Instead of asking the girl what she wanted, I just stared at her long-sleeved white T-shirt and jeans. I touched my hair again. I pulled away wet fingertips.

"Is Dr. Berkal here?"

I repeated the interrogation, aghast. "Does he make you call him that?"

Her eyelids widened, as though she were shocked by my shock. "We can call him Stephen," she said in a small voice.

"But he said 'Dr. Berkal' was among the other possibilities?"

"I don't . . . I don't really remember."

"Because you know he's just a PhD student, right?"

She nodded.

"So you can call him 'Qualifying-Examined Berkal,' or 'Dissertation-in-Progress-at-Least-Officially Berkal.' But not 'Doctor Berkal.' Not for another ten years or so. Okay?"

"I can't call him anything since he's not here."

I felt my cheeks heating up. I attempted to chuckle. Only sputter came forth. "No, I don't suppose . . . I suppose you're right."

"Is he coming back?"

I pretended like I didn't know the answer. I inspected the index card taped to our door. "Um . . . it looks like he's not in. It's just me for the rest of the day." I smiled then. "Anything I can help you with?"

"What do you know about mood?"

"You don't want to know."

"I'll just come back later."

She turned to leave. I bellowed after her, "Don't call him Dr. Berkal again, okay? And don't let anybody else, either."

She didn't respond.

I closed the door.

Before I could slump back to my desk, the other knock came. It was Talia. Her hair was damp. The heavy, wet dark of it made her face appear even lighter than it was. She'd already taken off her J. Crew mackintosh and laid it over the back of a chair someone left in the hall. She looked absolutely unhinging in a white, collared oxford shirt with a short black dress over it.

"Dude, I think you traumatized that girl."

I ushered her into the office and shut the door. "What are you doing here?" I asked. We were alone in the small rectangle with a popcorn ceiling and dull tiled floor. She smiled archly, which was both frightening and exciting at the same time. I took my seat, but then got up and went over to Berkal's floor lamp. I turned it on and sat down again. Talia looked at me like I was crazy.

"Dude."

"It makes me nervous when you call me 'Dude.'"

"Like it makes you nervous when little girls call Stephen J. Berkal 'Doctor'?"

"Something like that. No. Nothing like that. I don't give a shit about him."

"What was with the upbraiding, then?"

"I'm having a hard day and everything is pissing me off."

"How was your class?"

I responded truthfully. "I was a parody of meaningful instruction." I had no other way of answering.

She pouted her sympathy. Then she pulled the empty guest chair from beside the desk and positioned it close to my feet. I had to withdraw my legs when she plunked down. Our knees still touched. I wondered if she could feel my damp jeans through her black stockings. Thunder rumbled outside, thrumming the office. The weather sounded its percussion intermittently, but persistently. It gathered severity with each successive rise.

She looked in the direction of the window, but there wasn't anything there on the other side to see. The view was a sheet of gray. It was almost as though the glass had been painted over, or had never existed at all. "It's shitty out there."

"If the elevators go down, we'll have to sleep here tonight." Another bass drum sounded a round measure.

"No, we won't," she said with a scoff. After a moment of silent contemplation, she took a pink mini iPod from her bag. She shook loose the snarl of blue waterproof headphones attached to it. "Has that ever happened before?" she asked in a less certain tone.

"Probably." I heard miniature sounds coming through the earpieces. "Indie rock?"

"*Exile in Guyville.*"

"I love that album."

"I know you do. Why do you think I was flying into Chicago at night?"

"'Watching the lake turn the sky into blue-green smoke.' The first scene of the story you brought to my workshop. The character was listening to 'Stratford-on-Guy' as her plane descended. I remember."

"I wrote that to get your attention."

"It worked."

"Do you think anyone's ever had sex in the offices?"

I winced. "I hope not in this one."

She laughed. She reclaimed her eyes momentarily and powered off the iPod. "So you know of such things."

"I've heard some rumors. I've taught here a long time."

"How long?"

"Too long."

"Working on your PhD?" she teased.

I rolled my eyes.

"How do you think it would go down?" she asked me then. "Like over here?" She pointed at eroded tiles on the floor. I found a dark spot I hadn't noticed before on a square. It might have been a circle of spilled red nail polish or a chewed stick of cinnamon gum tamped again and again over the last few centuries. "Or there?" Yeah, sure, I thought. What said cupidity like Berkal's desk? "If I had to choose," she said, "I'd do it there, up against the window." I shrugged, pretending this was still just a theoretic anthropological discussion. With each option she presented, the languorousness in her voice compounded. The whole thing was turning me on. Even though she sat so close, there was still distance separating us. I concentrated on the distance. I was grateful for it. I sought refuge in the scarce inches keeping us discrete. It was probably best. It wasn't a good idea for me to answer Izzy's conjectured betrayal with tangible reprisals. At another moment in my life, sure, it would have made sense to exploit this deliciously coincidental opportunity. If we were in high school. If I weren't almost thirty-eight. If Izzy and I weren't married. If my name weren't on a fucking mortgage that I couldn't even begin to pay if she stranded me. Regardless of romantic inclination or disinclination, I could no longer just succumb to temptation. I couldn't just throw my life at the mercy of desire.

I stared at the empty mug on my desk. It was one Izzy and I had gotten together, driving back to Chicago after the weekend in Kohler, at a roadside pie, cider, and Christmas tree ornament shack off the highway. That Sunday outside of Milwaukee, when our love was new, the fall afternoon sky was leaden with dusk. We planned to collect a souvenir from each speaking engagement city or food and wine festival we'd visit. So far we had just the one mug, which we began with there at Apple Holler.

"Do you want some coffee?" Talia asked.

"No. Do you?"

"No."

I considered it a small victory I was able to resist the urge to press myself against Talia until we lost ourselves in symbiosis.

"My head hurts."

Her touching of my forehead coincided with the next menacing thunderclap. Her fingers gave palpable form to the electricity that I followed as it burned through the fog. The blinding current flared in the sky only a millisecond. Long after it was gone, lightning continued to torch and singe the inside wall of my chest.

"Is that better?" Her hand was a little cold, and agonizingly soothing.

"Why are you doing this?"

"Because you're not."

Of course I realized my feigned indifference was all just an increasingly transparent pretense. Everything she said, had ever said, fractured my resolve. She'd gradually been pushing my guard farther and farther out to sea since the day I met her. The thunder's next declamation caused the lights to flicker. It was the first time I considered seriously the possibility that I might end up trapped here, with her. I'd never witnessed an interruption of power on campus from this high. And here I was yoked to Talia, as though we'd planned it.

"Do you want me to leave?"

"Don't be crazy."

"It's crazy for me to be here. I shouldn't have come." She stood up. I followed. "Is this the first time that's occurred to you?"

"No. Not the first time."

"So if you had second thoughts, why are you here?"

"It's stupid."

"Tell me."

"You don't want to know."

"I do."

"How about I'll tell you I made a mistake and I'm going before I can do anything else wrong?"

I stepped closer. I could now see the topography of her lips. They were glossed, likely with the pomegranate and fig botanical butter from Portland she ordered online. I could smell Exclamation on her skin. "You don't want to fuck around with those elevators."

"Goddamn it. When will it motherfucking stop raining?"

"Probably never."

We faced each other, frozen, as though reflections waiting for a gesture to mirror. But neither of us moved. My limbs were paralyzed. My heart thumped. Rain sheeted the window. The glass still afforded dark opacity, only the suggestion of a vantage. Whether or not we were trapped here had little to do with the storm. Something else refused to relinquish us. Something impossible to relinquish rendered each of us inextricable to the other. That something was the motherfucking past.

At the department party, in a checked shirt and navy blazer, I hung around the middle room of the Koenig Alumni Center, where the bar was situated. I didn't want to be too far from the booze. I bantered with tenured professors who sipped cocktails that contained amounts of alcohol that recalled World War II Stateside butter and sugar rationing. Some of the acclaimed grad student creative writing instructors sauntered in for a beer or glass of jug wine. They worked themselves into the chat. The pleasantly inconsequential conversation topic segued to Kafka and the election and contemporary novelists I was ashamed to admit I'd heard of. These ingratiating talking points peeved me and turned my discourse rancorous. "Well, I mean, would anybody really give a shit about Nick Laird if it weren't for Zadie Smith?" I figured I could get away with it in the spirit of good-natured intellectual inquiry. Garrulity was a departure for me from my typical mild-mannered demeanor at these unpleasant annual events. I'd never before imbibed this liberally at an on-campus function. I'd been downing well vodkas since five o'clock.

The professors became more interested in the grad students, so I turned away and shortly found The Pregnant Lady at the bar. She'd given birth semesters ago, but the nickname endured. Together we declined the warm Cabernet Sauvignon when the bartender attempted to spill it into our stems. We opted instead for his heavily oaked Chardonnay. The bartender withdrew a new bottle from a bin of ice beneath his station. The white and the red were equally execrable, but at least with the Chard, The Pregnant Lady reminded me, we were guaranteed a more felicitous serving temperature. (She watched *Vintage Attraction* regularly, and this rationale was a famous party tip of Izzy's from the show.) T. Stoddard shortly joined our adjunct coterie. He was an unshaven, pugilistic, foul-mouthed, couplet-wielding, tortured-spirited Bukowskiesque drunk. T. Stoddard drove a rusty El Camino with expired tags to and from school. His comp class "insurance policy" was never to teach without having a scotch and soda in his Starbucks tumbler. He ordered us tequila. I was already spinning from vodka and wine when the first shots (and the second shots) arrived, but what the hell.

Berkal was in rare form. He looked like a politician in a black suit and a red tie. He spent a large portion of the evening chatting up the department head. I had no doubt he was procuring for himself every last undergraduate fiction workshop UIC would offer from now until fall 2018. I tried diligently to ignore him in order to preserve my buzz.

A trio of beleaguered adjuncts stopped me at the unfortunate moment my plastic glass was empty. I'd noticed they'd been rambling in pairs and triplets all night. Why did the underemployed always travel in groups? Was there job security in numbers? Without anything to drink, I quickly tired of more of the same talk of Kafka and the election. I detached, I hoped gracefully, and approached the bar for a refill. As I swaggered over, my phone began seizing. It was a call from a local number I didn't recognize. I answered, instead of letting it ring out to voice mail. I had a suspicion about who was trying to reach me. The numbness in my mouth and on my skin where prior to the party I had sensation was sufficient enough to embolden me to confront my pursuer, face to face, so to speak. I stepped onto the patio before pressing the green button.

"I need to see you," a soft, high-pitched female voice intoned. "What are you doing?"

"Getting wasted," I said.

"Are you at home?"

"Campus thing." It was colder out here than my drunkenness and the surge of adrenaline the shuddering phone had brought out of me led me to suspect initially. I leaned my head in the direction of my shoulder to keep the phone in place and pressed my arms as close as I could to my sides. "Open bar, unlimited bacon-wrapped scallops, conversation, career advancement, no papers to grade. In short, everything academics dream about." I gazed through the casement doors into the buffet room. Grad students still marched the procession along the route of silver domes, which covered the chafing dishes. They lifted the lids to peer down at the picked-over contents, which probably remained still somewhat heated by the last of the hydrocarbon jelly that burned away in Sterno cans between the dishes' legs.

"Come to the Days Inn," Talia said. "I got a room for the night."

"How about if I just go inside?" I slid away the porch door and returned to the warmth. Shortly thereafter, T. Stoddard, mouth purple-red and flecked with black, entered via the hall connecting the bar to the cloth-covered folding-table buffet of pillaged hors d'oeuvres. He was speaking unintelligibly, to no one in particular.

"Are you going to come or not?" she asked. The impatience in her voice made me feel appreciably weakened, despite my surplus of alcoholic bolster. T. Stoddard here, facing me, lifted a partially depleted bottle of warm Cabernet from the particleboard sideboard. He brought the bottle to his lips, tilted his head back, and drank without stopping to breathe until the wine—at least a quarter of the bottle, by my estimation—had decanted into him. He burped. He raised the empty into the air like a sword. With a French accent, T. Stoddard declared, "I will honor my member!"

"What room?" I asked Talia, which I immediately regretted.

"I'll meet you outside."

"I'm not waiting in front of a hotel that's within walking distance of campus," I said.

"Why the fuck not? It's not like I'm still an undergrad," she said. She had a point.

"My entire department is out tonight," I said.

"Paranoid Hapworth," she said.

The booze had made me superhuman in the depth and range of my aggression with my colleagues. It had allowed me to blithely transgress in front of my superiors. But on the phone with Talia, it rendered me sensitive and susceptible to offense. Instead of steeling me, my drunkenness magnified her offhanded casual insult to a level meriting righteous indignation. It also reminded me I shouldn't have been talking to her in the first place. "I'm hanging up," I said.

"No, wait, don't," she said. Her tone once again was gentle and frightened. "Wait for me in the parking lot," she implored. "The farthest, darkest corner you can find."

"Okay," I said. "I'll be there in twenty minutes. And I'm only waiting around for you for ten after that. It's freezing outside."

"It's not that cold," she said.

I ended up in the parking lot, in a far, dark corner, passing out in the old Mustang. On an algid Chicago winter night, that I went without suffering serious hypothermia injury or dying was remarkable, especially so considering how drunk I was. It was after one in the morning when I awoke. The nap and the profound embarrassment that coursed through my ravaged veins had sobered me up. I got out of the car and faced the hotel. My attention was focused on the small, curtainless windows of a room. It was one of few with its lights still illuminated.

"Talia!" I yelled, as loudly as I could. My voice was raw and dissonant. "Talia! Talia!!"

Snow now hurtled down upon me. I stood there shouting until a yawning security guard came waddling out of the hotel and across the parking lot. He entreated me to get into my car and off of the property before he'd have to detain me and call the police. I, grumbling, shivering, obliged.

I drove to a bar I knew in Humboldt Park, my old neighborhood. I was crying now, and continued to blubber until I got there. Talia didn't want me back then. She didn't want me now. She obviously wished nothing more than to destroy my life, now that I finally had one. Was I really going to besmirch my marriage *forever* with this, this fucking crazy girl? It made no sense. What the hell was I doing?

At The California Clipper I ordered a vodka and soda, but drank first the glass of water the bartender brought over after he mixed my cocktail. I'd become acquainted with the old, greasy, orange-lit bar in college. It was a destination worth the schlep from Hyde Park: the management was willing to eschew the carding of minors. It was surprisingly populated for this time of the morning. Second-shifters unwound. Widowers drank away heartache-induced insomnia. Prostitutes took their breaks. Crack whores who'd exhausted their stashes and couldn't score more drugs tonight were now trying to come down with the balm of cheap alcohol. The jukebox spun rhythm and blues dusties, Etta James, Miles Davis, Nat King Cole, Ella Fitzgerald. I listened to the analog-scratchy, plaintive songs and thought about how little time had elapsed from my first meeting Izzy to the present, and yet how much had transpired within that short time. We'd gotten together, engaged after a handful of weeks, and married—*married*—not long thereafter. How had a guy who'd gone a decade without a relationship that had lasted more than eight weeks found himself hitched for life?

What an idiot I'd almost been. What I felt for Izzy existed for no other person. Not now, not in the past, never in the future. And she'd taken certain vows before a judge that affirmed she felt the same for me. But as much as we might have hoped for the opposite, our relationship could only protect us intellectually. Falling in love and getting married were lofty and necessary conditions to getting the past out of our systems, at least in theory, but not enough. They weren't an entirely sufficient defense when actually faced with a face from an epoch preceding. So she'd gone to Pacer Rosengrant's place a couple of times. If Talia had had an apartment in town, I might have done the very same thing. A restaurant wasn't the venue for the sort of conversation that had the power to untangle with any kind of finality. I couldn't believe I'd almost ended up in a hotel room with Talia. This spectacular aberration had resulted in one small, good thing, though. Here with (or, more precisely, without) Talia was our denouement. At that moment, I truly wanted to believe that with Pacer, via a circuitous and only mildly untoward route, Izzy had also found that story's unknotting. I felt then that the worst was behind us. Quite frankly, what could be worse than what we'd already (not) done?

"Trouble with yo' lady?" the bartender asked.

"Several."

"It's last call," he said. He poured another vodka soda and placed it beside my empty glass. I didn't want another drink. I had no idea how I'd even had the stomach to finish the first here, but what the fuck.

My phone vibrated. I expected it to be a text message from Izzy. I was surprised it had taken her this long to wonder after me. She must have been freaked out I hadn't come home yet. I hadn't been out this late without her since we met. But the message wasn't Izzy's. It wasn't even Talia writing to taunt me. The many screens had come from Berkal. *R U still up? We just closd Parthenon. Crashed a wedding there aftr din. Ask yr somm what the hell Retsina is. Must never drink again. What happened 2U? U took off like u were gng 2 see @ girl.*

Talia, I typed.

Oh shit, he returned.

"I'll pay the check now," I said to the bartender.

"Ten bucks," he said. "And your car keys."

"Excuse me?" I asked.

"Man, you were wasted when you got here," he said. "I ain't risking losing my license or getting sued because this was the last place you drank before you go plow into a delivery truck."

"Fine," I said. I reached into my pocket for the Mustang key. "I'll take a goddamn taxi."

"Goddamn right you will," the bartender said. He guffawed meanly. I turned and sipped my weak drink.

10

IN RETROSPECT, I'D SAY THAT SOMETHING BESIDES THE SHAME ABOUT spending part of the night passed out in my car worked to keep me from returning to the Biscuit Factory that morning. Something besides the anguish I felt for almost breaking my half of my not-even-month-old marriage covenant outside, or inside, a cheap hotel.

The taxi that the imperious Clipper bartender had shoved me into took me to Berkal's place in Little Italy. There I passed a fraught few hours hardly asleep and not entirely awake on a standard-grad-student-issue green IKEA couch steeped in old whiskey. Once I made it back to Pilsen, I expected a hassle getting into the apartment. I recalled with a cringe as I walked that the bartender had relieved me of my keys. When I finally reached the building, the main entrance was unlocked. I climbed the stairs with heavy legs. Ironic that at a moment in my life when I had the most: a wife, a job, property, a dog, I couldn't recall a time when I felt more like I had less.

Strangely, our loft door was also unlocked. I was about to go inside when I heard Ishiguro gamboling down the stairs. He breathed quickly and sneezed and bounced on his hind paws. His fore patted my dark hipster jeans. I couldn't wait to get out of them. More than twenty-four hours of leg cinching was long enough to know they were better suited for a scrawny Italian kid than an aging Jew who really should have gone to the gym more than once a year just to visit the smoothie bar.

"What's going on?" I asked the pug.

To catch his runaway breath, he pushed air through his nose. He sprang again and tapped my shin. Wide-eyed franticness beseeched me.

"Were you at the Laheys'?"

He moved around me, as though dodging the question, and we stepped inside. The disarray in the living room was something to which I'd become recently inured. Still, this morning's aftermath caught my attention. There were more empty wine and cheap domestic beer bottles than Izzy could have drained on her own. She didn't even *like* beer that much. An overflowing ashtray also sat on the coffee table. I didn't even know we owned an ashtray. All the butts, as far as I could tell without digging into the cremains, were of the same brand: American Spirit. I surmised Izzy had hosted a raucous late-night gathering for a bistro bunch. It made little sense for them to come here. The front-of-house reprobates could have just as easily and happily drunk and smoked and commiserated the latest Yelp review-reported guest indignation post-shift at a dive bar. The sight of Izzy's stockings and skirts and inside-out blouses strewn over the couch and the coffee table was both annoying and perplexing. What kind of evening would have called for costume changes?

Ishiguro followed me down the long hallway, to the back bedroom. The door was partially closed. The pug pressed ahead, through the crack, which widened the opening enough for me to enter. There was a crude shape buried beneath the blankets. It brought to mind the pile of laundry a child tries to hide from his parents, who pretend they can't see it for the first few moments after finding. Ishiguro stood on two feet and pressed his stomach against the edge of the bed frame. This was how he gestured his desire to be hefted. I picked the dog up and placed him on the mattress. Ishiguro went right for the protuberance in the center. He poked it with a front paw. Izzy didn't stir.

"Do you want me to make you some coffee or something?" I said. I could hear the contralto chagrin in my voice. My own late night notwithstanding, I hated seeing my wife this way, sleeping into the morning. She was supposed to be the respectable one. And here she'd failed to feed the dog, shirked work, me. It was like she was a frivolous and unattached twenty-three-year-old who'd stayed up too late partying.

The "Mmmm" that the sarcophagus sounded was a considerable number of octaves below that which Ishiguro was expecting to hear. I was just as shocked as the pug was. He issued a panicked bark and skittered over to me with a serious get-me-down-right-now expression on his face. His brown eyes, as round and large as a teddy bear's, had me couching my own reaction and quickly opening my arms in triage. I lowered Ishiguro to the floor. He bolted out of the room and down the hall. I was left to investigate on my own. The contents of my stomach rapidly liquified. Acid refluxed in my chest. My palms were sweaty. The shape was now loosening itself from the rigid semicircle of its repose. Straightened out, it was a much longer and wider form than Izzy's.

I knew what my next move had to be. I really didn't want to make it. I gasped when I pulled back the covers. Taking careful backward steps, my subjected eyes never veering away from their object, I kept moving until I felt the bathroom door halt me.

"Who the fuck are you?" he asked.

"Who the fuck are you?" I returned reflexively. But it was pretty obvious. Short, black hair in a spiky, hipster style (though sleep had been unkind to his faux hawk), earrings in both ears, three or four days' worth of black beard growing on his face, parti-colored tattoos on his bicep and chest. His taut and defined stomach made me, even in this moment of supreme incongruity, somewhat jealous. I stood there a little self-conscious, sucking in my mini-gut, stuffed into my imported skinny jeans.

Of course I knew who he was before he introduced himself. I recognized him from Facebook. He had a pretentious name. I'd thought so the very first time I'd heard it. Now that I could ascribe it to an actual person, *this* person I instantly despised, it rang even worse.

Pacer Rosengrant rendered me completely irrelevant by lighting a half-smoked cigarette. I couldn't believe it was my own voice I heard when I asked the intruder, "Do you need an ashtray?"

"Yeah, dude, thanks," he said.

I went for the ashtray in the living room. I delivered it empty, the glass lined with a skin of carcinogenic dust, to the bedroom. The rogue sommelier still lay in my sommelier's bed—*my* bed. I watched Pacer Rosengrant smoke. I phrased and rephrased a question in my head while I waited for him to finish.

He stubbed out his cigarette. I asked him, "Um, do you think you might, I don't know, put on your clothes and get the fuck out of here?"

"Hey, bro, don't take that tone with me."

"'Tone'? You were sleeping in my bed. I think this 'tone' is perfectly justified."

"Look, dude, this isn't what you think."

"A little hard to believe when I see you there naked."

He lifted the sheet. It revealed that his bottom half was still dressed. He wore dark Diesels that resembled the pair I'd slept in. On Pacer Rosengrant they fit much more like I supposed the designers had intended for them to.

"Well, you're still without a shirt. And you're in my bed. And I suspect my wife was probably in it with you fairly recently."

"She wasn't," he said. "She slept on the couch."

"So, what, this was just a little slumber party?"

He pulled a T-shirt over his head. It bore the homemade silk-screened logo of what I supposed was a local Chicago indie rock band. He shod black boots. I followed him out of the room. I was conscious of my feet traversing the hallway, like *I* was the guest. In the kitchen, he unhooked the door of the dishwasher. A torrent of steam escaped. Once my glasses had cleared, I saw that the entire compartment was full of wine stemware. He stared at me, as though this was the perfectly platonic explanation I sought. His boot-elevated height increased the emasculating disparity between us by a good four inches.

"You did the dishes?"

"No," Pacer Rosengrant said. "We had a blind tasting."

"A blind tasting?" I asked. "What?"

Pacer Rosengrant seemed to take my consternation to mean I needed clarification as to what a blind tasting *was*. He explained, in a grammatically challenged "dude"- and "uh"-laden discursive monologue, the gist. Last night, here in the apartment, Izzy led some of the advanced sommeliers in the city through a deconstruction of six wines they knew absolutely nothing about at the outset. This critical analysis and the discussion that followed were practice for their upcoming Court master-level sommelier exams. Under her guidance, Pacer Rosengrant had passed the service portion before he left for Nevada. Tasting and theory were the remaining two parts of the triptychic crucible. They were also the most difficult. He had so far failed to rate on either.

Successful completion of all three components was nearly impossible. Only three percent of the countless thousands of worldwide examinees ever became master sommeliers. Izzy had reared one victor before. She could have handily ascended into the Court pantheon herself, if she'd wanted to. She was regarded as having one of the most discerning palates in the industry. And she'd figured out everything the hundred or so masters knew—on her own. She'd learned about wine from waitressing, from tastings, from books she'd read about clonal selection. She'd studied maps of the wine-growing regions. She'd perfected presenting, opening, decanting, and pouring the window-table regulars at Bistro Dominique their speciously authentic '82 Petrus. Yet the same strategy hadn't worked as well for Pacer. An autodidact he wasn't. He wasn't nearly as smart as she was. He still desperately needed to know what she knew. He still needed Izzy's help.

Here Pacer Rosengrant produced a form entitled "Sensory Analysis." It broke identification into three main categories: "Visual," "Nose," and "Taste." It demanded assessments of criteria like the wine's brightness, clarity, color, rim variation, power, weight, depth, fruit, vinosity, spices, herbs, botrytis, sugar, alcohol, tannin, acidity, texture, length, and balance. The examinee only had a mere four minutes to gather this empirical data from a single one-and-a-half-ounce pour out of a bottle wrapped in identity-concealing brown paper. New or old world? Cool or warm climate? What country? What level of quality? What grape variety? How old? The answers to the questions comprised a preliminary conclusion. Then a final conclusion about region and appellation and vintage was to be declared. A single wrong decision at any point could derail the entire exam.

I had no idea what "rim variation" referred to, outside of, perhaps, the context of a pornographic film. I couldn't define words like "vinosity"—the measure of a wine's wineness? I stumbled in pronouncing "botrytis" a couple of times.

"It's exhausting just reading the blank sheet," I said.

"I know, dude," Pacer Rosengrant said.

Also lying out on the counter were pages and pages of hand-written notes. These mostly illegible paragraphs and grids presumably resulted from the tasting sessions. I found I could more or less read a sheet I recognized Izzy had filled out. *Clear, youthful. Fruit-forward, green apple, Bosc pear, white flower blossom, bay leaf, river stones. Residual sugar, earth, no wood.* Her conclusions: *old world, temperate climate, Riesling or Chenin*, and, finally, *Germany, Riesling, QBA, Mosel, 2007.*

It went on and on like this for two more whites and three reds.

"Can I show you something?" he asked.

"What is it?"

Pacer Rosengrant went to a pile of last weekend's newspapers on the couch. He took from it a thick leather-bound sheaf. It had been shoved between the unread Sunday *Times* sports and business sections. He gave me the document. It was Bistro Dominique's wine list. "La Carte des Vins de Bistro," it read in elegant wedding-invitation script on the front. In the bottom corner, "Chef Patron C. Dominique" was embossed. It was heavier than I'd expected. I needed two hands to flip through it. The sections on the first pages, Vins Blancs, were broken up into regions: Bourgogne, Côtes du Rhône, Loire, Nouvelle-Zelande, and Bordeaux dessert wines (sec, liquoreux). Burgundy contained easily sixty wines, not even including the reds. And the prices were staggering. If a dining guest wanted Montrachet, the Louis Latour from 1997 was $790. The '92 Laboure Roi was a relative bargain at only $330. There were two hundred red Bordeaux wines before I even made it to the Americans and the Italians. A bottle of '86 Chateaux Margaux was $980 (or, approximately, three months' rent on my first off-campus studio apartment in Hyde Park). Though a half bottle of a less estimable vintage, 1995, could be had for only $98. The Chateau Haut-Brion from 1953, the year my father graduated high school, was $1,800.

"I've never seen this before," I said. "Did Izzy really choose all of these?"

His nod looked as awestruck as I felt. It was dizzying to read the scores of names and prices. I couldn't imagine what it took for Izzy to physically inventory the bottles, to say nothing of selling them. It astonished me that she knew the infinite subtle variations so well that she could discern one wine from the next by criteria more complex than vintage and cost.

"What's the tip on dinner with a bottle of the '53 Haut-Brion?" I asked. "A Volkswagen?"

"She's really something. People call her a prodigy," Pacer Rosengrant said then. It was as though he were telling me about someone phenomenal I'd not yet met. Shouldn't I have been the one extolling my wife's virtues to someone who didn't know her as intimately? The role reversal was galling enough to snap me out of my amazement-induced reverie.

"We were just tasting wines," Pacer Rosengrant mumbled, his eyes trained on the floor. He seemed genuinely frustrated by my unwillingness to be convinced. "But whatever. I'll get my stuff." He started back down the hall. Ishiguro, suddenly a defector, ran after him.

"Did she even ask about me?" I shouted into the increasing space between us. My voice was still raw and shaky from last night's parking lot performance. Only the pug was moved enough to stop and look in my direction. "Did she even wonder why I hadn't come home?"

Before he left, Pacer Rosengrant stood at the door. He asked, in a child's voice, if he could "borrow" his tasting notes. I stared at him and briefly considered setting the pages on fire or tearing them up. But a strange wave of empathy came into me. I couldn't even completely hate Pacer Rosengrant for having slept here. Izzy may not have mentioned that she had a husband. He might have been so wasted that he never even noticed she lived with somebody. Little of the furniture and the belongings in the apartment were mine. Few of our mutual possessions bore any traces of my personality. It wasn't beyond the realm that Pacer Rosengrant truly believed she resided at the Biscuit Factory alone when he came here and decided to spend the night. I handed the sheets over. Pacer Rosengrant mumbled good-bye and walked out.

Ishiguro scuttled back to me. He looked particularly apologetic. He seemed truly sorry for not having done a better job intervening last night—or this morning. "It's not your fault," I told him. "If I'd managed to get myself home any earlier, I probably would have gone upstairs to sleep at the Laheys', too." I fed the pug. Five seconds later, he finished eating. He was long overdue a morning nap and I ushered him into his crate. Then I went to the Starbucks a few blocks away for a grande cappuccino. The barista gave me a sympathetic once-over when she took my order. She offered to add a third mercy shot at no additional charge. I gave mute, but heartfelt, appreciation.

Back in the loft, the oaky, putrescent effluvium of oxidizing wine was heavier in the air than I'd first noticed. The stale smoke on the furniture was newly asphyxiating. Could Izzy really have led this tasting and then fucked this ridiculous Pacer Rosengrant in our own home? The beers, the cigarettes. Had they busted a few rails? He was probably one of those lucky twelve-inch bastards who could screw on coke. (I'd tried to do it, and failed, once in college.) I didn't want to believe this, to see this, to smell this. And I dreaded tonight, when Izzy would turn up. I tried to imagine her lying on the rumpled couch, where she'd purportedly slept. I had conveniently avoided saying anything after I discovered his apartment a few blocks from here. But now, now that I'd met Pacer Rosengrant, could I still get away without confronting her?

I found a box of American Spirits on the couch with one cigarette left. I lit it. The last time I'd smoked was with Talia, on the porch of my old sublet. It had followed the last time we'd ever sleep together. After that night, she stopped returning my calls. I heard from other former students that she'd begun sleeping with a fellow twenty-year-old with whom she could listen to indie rock. I'd also later find out she'd gotten into grad school. She hadn't told me about either development when we were involved. Instead, she started building a series of distances between us. And I'd built my own share of distances. I said it wasn't serious. All along, part of me had hoped to find someone else—and I met Izzy shortly thereafter. Was my ambivalence the weakness that had not only drawn Talia to me but also driven her away? Was it having the same effect on Izzy? Still, there was no way I could confront her about last night. This was no buried pile of laundry. This was my fault. I'd led her to believe I was fun and confident. I'd referred to myself as a swashbuckler, in the e-mail that started it all. I wanted her to think I was easygoing when we were first getting to know each other. I wanted to be those things, be the person she seemed to see that night we first looked at each other. And for a while, with her help, I'd become that person. Somehow along the way, though, I'd devolved. What if the confrontation's outcome was that she'd decide to leave me? We'd obviously have to sell this place. She'd probably move back into Chris's, or take up residence with Pacer Rosengrant. With no real savings in the bank, no significant income, where would I go? There were no professors with apartments to sublet or ex-girlfriends to whom I could present myself left. My first and last cigarette had burned down to the filter, and I stubbed it out.

I still hadn't showered or changed out of last night's clothes. But the wrinkled shirt and blazer comprised the uniform in which, playing the role of taciturn domestic, I'd begin to restore order—a superficial order, but a sense of order nonetheless—to our flyblown domestic life. I started by cleaning up the mess in the living room. I threw every bottle and butt and food container into the garbage. I hung up all of Izzy's castoff and crumpled garments. I vacuumed the rug and floor. I emptied the dishwasher and stowed all of the glassware. Then my Timex beeped. I had thirty minutes until the office hours slot I couldn't seem to commit to memory this semester. I was fairly certain I'd have no visitors for the duration of my sentence. It would have been a better use of my time to take a nap. Further incentive to blow it off: the pug had set up rawhide-decimating camp atop my socked right foot as I stood at the sink. Still, I raced away.

When I got back from school and reclaiming the pony car that had been clipped from me the night before, Izzy was home. I followed a newly laid trail of her shoes and stockings and skirt and underwear and blue sommelier coat and blouse and bra down the hall to our bedroom. I hadn't been in here since my unsettling ante meridiem discovery. She was in the bathroom, wearing only a towel, blow-drying her hair. She suspended work once she saw me standing in the door frame. Her eyes cast a disbelieving glare in the mirror. "That must have been some party."

I looked down at my white Oxford and the skinny jeans into which I barely fit. The whole of my outfit was disheveled. I pressed together my empty palms. "Yeah, about that."

"You could have called me," she said.

"I know. I'm sorry. I had too much to drink."

"You've never not come home before. I was really scared something awful was happening."

I thought about Talia, how easily I could have ended up in her hotel room. "So was I," I whispered to my shoes.

"Where did you sleep?"

"Berkal's couch."

"Lovely."

"I'm sorry," I repeated. I looked at our bed and remembered the dismay that smacked me when I found Pacer Rosengrant in it. It was unlikely my absence had genuinely given her much cause for concern last night. My compunction about my own misadventure and embarrassment over passing out before anything could even come to pass with Talia receded. My residual regret was quietly fermenting into low-voltage anger. "You could have called me, too, you know. If you were so concerned. It's not like you don't know how to send a text."

Her forehead became a noteless staff. "I didn't want to make you feel like I don't trust you. I never really pictured myself becoming a nagging wife hounding you while you're out with your friends."

"What kind of wife did you picture yourself becoming?" My hands were restless and too cumbersome for my squeezed Italian pockets. I turned my wedding band around my ring finger.

"What's that supposed to mean?"

"Look, I made a mistake. I don't see why you're making such a big deal of it. I've never given you any reason not to trust me, Izzy."

"What did you mean, 'what kind of wife'? I'd like to know what you're getting at."

Though it would have been a perfect opportunity to do so, I just couldn't bring myself to tell her that this wasn't actually the first time I'd been home today. It was easier to let Izzy think I'd stayed out all night. It was easier for me to let her believe that Pacer Rosengrant had risen on his own sometime after she'd left for work. I was almost starting to believe it myself. He could have been the one to rid the apartment of the incriminating party arti- facts and hang up all the clothes. If he'd gotten up earlier—if he didn't run on restaurant time—he would have disappeared long before I came around.

She returned to the business of her hair. I stood there, watching her. It was a two-handed operation with a brush and hair dryer. She ran the brush through section after section as the hot air blew down on it. The curls, though reluctant initially, eventually com- plied with her wishes and straightened out. After she finished, her hair was long and dark and shone brilliantly. She set aside her tools and asked, "When did you first fall in love with me?"

"When I first saw you," I said.

"That's not possible," she said. "It must have been later, like on our first real date. At Osteria Via Stato. When I had my hair down."

"Then, too," I said. "Also the first time I heard you laugh."

I went to check on Ishiguro. Izzy emerged some time after in a robe. She hugged me. I had to steady myself so as not to lose my footing. She pressed her face to my cheek and inhaled. She took my head to do the same thing in a wavy copse of hair.

"You smell like perfume," she said after she released me.

"What?"

"Yeah, like the nineties." She took in another quantity of the air between us. "It's Exclamation."

My heart began to thump a gangster rap bass line. I flashed on the scene when Talia came to see me on campus. I could tell she had on her old scent when she sat in my office. How could it possibly have clung to me this long, throughout all the places and fragrances I'd passed between the previous afternoon and now? It seemed so impossible. Then again, with Izzy and her preternatural powers of olfaction, the impossible wasn't only probable but inevitable. From her earliest days sneaking tastes in the liquor store, to her first restaurant waitressing job serving Denny's patrons who ordered White Zinfandel when they wanted to drink something "exotic," to her inaugural tours of cellar inventory duty in the basement at the Cattle Company, to the bistro and beyond, she'd been amassing and cataloguing scent memories. She could recall any of them instantly. Trying to refute her would have been tautological. I almost confessed to save myself from escalating heartache.

"The party," I said then, practically blurting it out. I cleared my throat to try to cover over my panic. I feared it was too late to go unperceived.

Izzy, surprisingly, looked at me as though acknowledging this were a plausible scenario. It prompted me, like a caught criminal, to continue bolstering my alibi with details to make what I said sound more convincing, even though it would accomplish anything but. "All the girls were overdressed and over-scented. Grad students. So considered in matters of their diction, yet always so mannered in their aspect. Their idea of style is Edith Wharton's."

"Were you dancing?" she asked, though not in an accusatory way.

"No," I said tentatively. "But these sorts of fetes are attended by a lot of mawkish hugging and hand-talking."

"It smells like it was close to you."

"What was?"

"I don't know. Temptation."

"I thought you said it was Exclamation."

She looked at me searchingly. Her mouth was poised like she wanted to say something. I barraged her with more unnecessary details. "We had a heated debate."

"About what?"

I prefaced with a simper. "Marisha Pessl."

"Well," she said, almost sounding playful, "it must have been pretty serious."

"I don't think it was," I said. "Only in the moment, fueled by alcohol and departmental party anxiety. But not after."

She smiled a white flag. It was evidence that her momentary apprehension had relaxed. "As long as you got it out of your system."

My mind breathed a sigh. "I did. I definitely did."

She smelled me again. "Yeah," she said, "it's definitely fading."

"You want to get some dinner or something?" I asked.

"Nah," she said. "I don't want to stay up too late."

"I'll walk Ishiguro, then," I said, and reached into my back pocket to check for a sandwich bag. There I felt the index card Berkal had given me. "Shit. I shouldn't stay up too late, either. I forgot I have to be on campus early in the morning."

"Why? You're not teaching tomorrow, are you?"

"No," I said. "Stupid meeting with Schultz. I guess I'll find out if I'm getting any summer classes."

"I hope you do," she said.

"Why's that?"

"Because . . . I don't know. It's what you do."

"Yeah," I said, with low-slung bitterness.

I found the statement mildly insulting, despite its veracity. It was what I did. That was true. But had it been a foregone vocational conclusion? What if I hadn't become an academic? I wondered then. What if my training had come from a wine cellar instead of a lecture hall? If I'd spent my salad days brunoising turnips and chiffonading basil instead of sitting in a dusty booth at the C-Shop explicating Hemingway and Fitzgerald in spiral notebooks, where would we be now? Izzy might have stayed out of trouble if I'd grown up to be a guy who swaggered, who took women as if they were wine, without asking and drinking directly from the bottle. I could have ended up a ballsier version of myself, someone more like Pacer Rosengrant, minus the inarticulateness,

I hoped. What if I had been the one who did what he wanted without any guilt or fear? What if I'd been a real restaurant person, instead of just someone who imagined them?

"It would be like me not being able to . . . taste wine," Izzy said.

"Heaven forbid," I muttered.

She looked at me like she didn't hear what I'd said, but avoided asking me to repeat it. Instead Izzy just flashed some bright teeth, as though happiness—feigned or otherwise—was really the panacea everyone pretended it to be.

11

I LET MYSELF INTO SHELLEY SCHULTZ'S OFFICE. "IS THERE A PROBLEM, Peter?" the adjunct coordinator asked. The sternness in her voice was patently theatrical. She scowled at me. She attempted, I supposed, to look authoritative. Sadly, her *Stella Got Her Clothes Back* dark-blue, clingy turtleneck and short skirt life-affirming costume of the recently divorced didn't imbue her improvisation with much verisimilitude. Her curly-bordering-intractably-frizzy shoulder-length hair kept me from feeling too threatened. I imagined she had a similar failure to affect the affable, veneered, pacemaker-equipped widowers and scheming financiers she sat across from on eHarmony dates at Highland Park restaurants. I also suspected these dates ended before nine o'clock as an anticlimactic result.

"I thought you wanted to speak with me," I answered.

She stood up and retrieved a sheet of paper from the top of her gray filing cabinet. She pressed the document to the table. With three fingers, she pushed it a measure closer to me.

"Thanks," I said. It was an agenda for another new hire orientation. Ostensibly the meaningless, hour-long meander I'd just missed.

The border she chose from clip art was suitably incongruous. Her design was more appropriate for a homemade wedding save-the-date reminder flyer than it was for outlining the proceedings of a serious pedagogical discussion.

"Sorry you couldn't make the event. I thought it would be useful for you to meet the new teachers."

"Useful for me? How?"

"To get some perspective on teaching methods."

"I have my own methods, and they're fine, but thanks."

"Well, I'm not so sure about that. I think you might want to have a look at this." She slid over another piece of paper. This one was tattered and wrinkled. It appeared to have been folded and refolded multiple times. Ink bled through from one side to the other. A grease stain adorning a corner called to mind a middle school election nomination petition.

I opened the note. It was the multiple-choice midterm evaluation form I'd handed out a week or two earlier. On the back was an anonymous complaint letter from one of my students. The handwriting looked familiar, yet I'd been so disengaged this semester, I couldn't attribute it to a source.

An absolute waste of time. Hapworth simply goes through the motions of teaching, recycling the same curriculum over and over again, regardless of who his students are. His grading system benefits the young and inexperienced and the class material is too similar to topics previously studied. The only A's he gives out are to those that he deems morally worthy. Any challenge to readings or thinking outside of the box will put you in the "trouble" corner. He seems to only like good, quiet, female students. The years of negative feedback on RateMyProfessors.com have gone nowhere. Bummer of a course.

I folded the note and slid it back across the desk.

"Do you know who wrote this?" she asked.

I shrugged. "Not really. To be honest, I'm not terribly concerned."

"You're not?"

"No," I said. "I'm not."

"And why's that?"

"Shelley, I've been here a long time. I've come to expect that one or two students every midterm evaluation will, for whatever reason, express dismay with my—what did she call them?—'curriculum' and 'grading system.'"

"How do you know the student is a she?"

It was pretty obvious by the penmanship. The thugs' cursive didn't tend to prance through a garden of curlicues and I-dotting circles. Not to mention, who else besides a female would accuse me of favoring the girls? But I refrained from answering. I didn't really give a shit. The complaints had no bearing on me. And if Schultz was this oblivious to the bigger issue of campus ethos at the end of the leader decade of the twenty-first century, whatever it was called, in which education had become commodified and students felt that entitled them to the right to consumer-driven expectations about the "service" the instructors provided, for which they'd paid, and to voice their perceptions on the quality of it in ungrammatical Yelp-restaurant-review-like performance evaluations twice a semester, I couldn't really do much to help her.

"And that's all you have to say about this?"

"I think the student should be sent to the 'trouble corner' for failing to realize that 'good,' 'quiet,' and 'female' are not coordinating adjectives."

Shelley Schultz looked at me blankly. I highly doubted that she knew what a coordinating adjective was. I was fairly certain she would have taken a *Longman Handbook* from her window ledge of unread complimentary desk copies—essential for decorating the set of an educator's office—and searched for the definition, had I not been sitting before her.

I was aware I had two choices here of how to proceed. I could apologize and throw myself at the mercy of the coordinator. This would require fabricating a story about a stressful semester. If I added details about finding my famous spouse's ex-boyfriend in our bed yesterday to portray myself as a pathetic cuckold, she'd have sympathy. It wouldn't even be that difficult of a method-acting exercise. The encounter, in short retrospect, regardless of Pacer Rosengrant's protestations, made me feel like Izzy had cheated on me. I could do that and protect my job. Or I could take a completely different approach.

I thought about Izzy. We'd been to so many places together: the wine festivals, the seminars, the speaking engagements. She made speeches I always listened to intently, no matter how many times I'd heard her deliver them, in Kohler or South Beach or Seattle or Jacksonville. Audiences wanted to pay attention to her. They were compelled by her knowledge and her charm—and her ability to fuse the two made her a true commodity. And I didn't mind being there to support her, with nothing to offer except my presence. It was what she wanted. It was what she needed. She asked for little in return now, but eventually she'd have to want me to be something more than just a travel companion who genuinely laughed at jokes she told rooms over and over and gazed at her lovingly from a seat in the front rows. What if by then it was too late for me to achieve anything of significance? It hit me that toiling away like this, semester after semester, had gotten me nowhere. It was also turning me incredibly dull and unimaginative. It was astonishing that it had taken this long for me to realize I was going to have to take a stand, once and for all. Do something that couldn't be undone. That's what my life with Izzy was, since the moment we first met. What we'd done together had been—and would always be—consequential for that very reason. None of it could be taken back. Not easily, anyway. All this time here, all this shiftlessness, all this buffoonery, I'd been doing nothing more than decathecting from a job that was never truly meant for me. I didn't really want to teach. I never had. What I needed to do was *learn*! My adjunct comp instructor sentence had come to a syntactic full stop.

And Schultz confirmed it with what she told me. I'd asked about the summer classes. Her tiny, hard eyes bulged. Then her face flooded with heat.

"We have nothing for you, Peter, I'm sorry."

"What about the fall?" I asked.

"Those course assignments, as you know, have yet to be made, to be approved of, there are budgetary constraints, grad students who need to have teaching assistantships as part of their tuition waivers . . ."

The equanimity I'd been convincing myself I was experiencing throughout this meeting all at once fell away. "When were you going to tell me?" I asked, half angry, half brokenhearted.

"We were going to distribute memos at the end of the semester." She paused. "Peter, it wasn't—it isn't—personal. The economy has been going through some rough times. This is a temporary situation. Maybe the best thing for everyone is if you took a furlough."

She pressed her thin lips together. Her eyes decamped for the back of the office door. I wondered if she'd arranged to have someone escort me out. But nobody came. It was just the two of us, employer, so to speak, and employee, so to speak.

"You are such a piece of shit, Shelley."

"Don't you dare—I still am—"

"You only care about yourself, about making sure your stupid sections are covered. Admit it. You weren't going to say anything because you knew I'd walk out of here and you didn't want to have to trouble yourself with finding a sub for the rest of the semester."

"You're right about one thing," she said evenly. She now looked at the computer screen, as though reading lines she'd prepared ahead of time for a situation exactly like this. "I'm going to have to find a substitute to cover your sections for the remainder of the term. And you're right about something else: You're walking out of here, and, if I can have anything to do with it, you'll never be back. You're fired, Peter."

I didn't even bother to clear out my desk. Berkal could keep all the tchotchkes masquerading as instruments of education. I'd never again have any use for the dry erase markers, pens, and pencils. The campus organization–sponsored mouse pads, the *UIC Flame* articles that had turned from newsprint to parchment that I'd clipped and had hanging, they were just disparate and hollow relics of my meaningless tenure here. I didn't even want to retrieve my Apple Holler mug, the one I got with Izzy on the way back from Kohler. It had been irreclaimably tainted by its employment here. Just like I was. I took the elevator down nineteen floors without it stopping to pick up anyone else. I revolved through the University Hall door, exiting the Waffle for the last time. As I bounded away from the lecture centers on the quad, I felt like I was reclaiming essential, lost pieces of myself. The more distance I got between the blurry academic persona I'd been freed of and the bon vivant I was now, the more it seemed liked the future was coming into focus—though I had no idea yet where I was headed. To trumpet my "furlough," I dropped my Orwellian laminated identification badge and the unduly cheerful lanyard to which it was clamped into a garbage can at the corner of Harrison and Morgan.

I stopped in a Greek diner. Nobody was at the host stand to greet me. I slid into the first of a long row of empty booths. After receiving a cup of black coffee I hadn't yet ordered, I took out my cell phone to ring Izzy. I had to tell her, right? I dialed. But before the call connected, I hit END three times in rapid succession.

12

AND A COUPLE OF WEEKS LATER, I STILL HADN'T TOLD IZZY WHAT happened. I couldn't tell her. She wouldn't understand. She'd only ever known me as an employed adjunct professor. She'd think I'd been a baby, that my grievances were imaginary. She'd say that people who existed in the real world had to subject themselves to worse things, greater indignities. She'd be right, too. How could I dispute the fact that in the real world it didn't matter who used "affect" or "effect" correctly? So each morning she'd expect me to, I left for school. I'd have coffee and read the *Times* at a corner bodega. Today, instead of taking a bus to campus to sit in the library when I finished, I returned to the apartment. I wanted to look for jobs.

The MacBook awoke from its slumber quickly. Izzy, the last to use the laptop, hadn't shut it down. I sifted through my documents, found a recent copy of my vita, and cleaned it up.

Firefox wouldn't kick in when I entered the *Chronicle*'s URL. I closed the window and opened another, but couldn't connect to the Internet. In despair, I pulled down the Apple menu, selected Force Quit, and terminated the browser process. There were other applications running, too. Safari, Microsoft Excel, Address Book, Adobe Reader, Bluetooth File Exchange, and Preview were all open. Jesus. Really, was it that hard for Izzy to exit a program when she was finished with it?

To a detached *Vintage Attraction* Excel production schedule, I chose not to save changes. I closed Adobe and Preview in a command-Q flash. Then came Bluetooth Exchange. Before terminating, I instinctively scanned the open transaction history file. Izzy must have been synching her BlackBerry e-mails and calendar from the bistro's server. I discovered she had, inadvertently, maybe intentionally, downloaded data to the hard drive. In the factory-installed Outlook client on the desktop that I thought nobody used, I could view all her messages.

There must have been some reason for her pathological indifference of late, skipping the dog's meals and walks, not turning the TV and the lights off at night, the parade of shoes and clothes down the hall. Judging by the number of her e-mails that originated from the same sender, I had a pretty good idea now of the cause of her carelessness. She couldn't be bothered to cover her computer maneuvers probably for the same reason she left the faucet hemorrhaging water for ten minutes when something called her attention away from her cooking or toothbrushing. Probably for the same reason she stopped coming home directly after working a night at the bistro. Probably for the same reason that she could never go out for one drink and really mean it. Someone I'd hoped could vanish back into the past without my having to confront Izzy about him in the present was still preoccupying her. And they'd been corresponding.

Off and on, since Ishiguro alerted me to Pacer Rosengrant's return, since I met Pacer Rosengrant in my bedroom, I'd entertained both the possibility that I was overreacting, as well as the possibility I wasn't reacting enough. Perhaps perspective on the situation was what I lacked most conspicuously. I needed a voice of reason, or at least objective, disembodied words. So I closed the laptop and texted my old student Ari Marks, the journalist. The last time he and I talked, Izzy's and my relationship was going well. We'd just gotten married. Ari was putting his piece about the sommelier and her new restaurateur husband for *Daley Machine* to bed. It was difficult to imagine having to say that things were fucked up, that I'd found Pacer Rosengrant in our bed and, now, on Izzy's BlackBerry so short a time thereafter.

I think Izzy's cheating on me, I typed. *Call to discuss.*

Ari rung me an hour or so later. An editorial meeting awaited him in a conference room, but he wanted to talk anyway. "What happened?" he asked.

I told him what I knew, up to the point of the morning following the department party. "Wow," Ari said, as though scandalized. I heard clanging, then rustling. "Sorry. I'm eating a Clif Bar." He partially muffled his crinkling. "How did Izzy take your finding the guy?"

I already felt like a loser for revealing this much. I wished we weren't having this conversation and were, instead, trading anecdotes about the ineptitude of his columnist colleagues and my students and the analogous poverty of their intellects, like we used to. I'd give anything to have unflattering scenes of gracelessness and missteps that I committed on Internet dates for him once again, instead of this.

"Well," I began, "that's the thing. I didn't actually tell her I found him."

Ari was aghast. "You didn't say *anything*?"

I shook my head, but then remembered he, on the phone, couldn't see me. "No," I had to say to fill the space. "I mean, I haven't found the guy here again or anything, but now I'm suspicious of everything. Her behavior has been very . . . textbook. Absences, evasiveness, distraction, aphoristic speech." On the verge of tears, I told Ari about the downloaded e-mails and BlackBerry messages waiting to reveal everything, there on my MacBook, beckoning, taunting. It was almost as though Izzy were daring me to catch her.

Ari paused for a moment. I could hear him typing something. Then he said, "Well, you have to start reading."

"The texts?"

"The texts, the e-mails, everything."

"I don't know."

"How do you not know?"

"Because I never wanted to turn into that guy. The jealous, possessive, spying type. That's not me."

"Professor, don't be a fucking idiot. You have to see the evidence before you make any pronouncements. Would you have let me get away with a move like this in a short story draft for workshop? The character wants the reader to give a shit about his being cheated on, he needs some proof."

"You're right."

"You're goddamn right I'm right."

Even with Ari's convincing exegetic argument, I still felt like it was wrong to invade. At the same time, I couldn't say at that moment I trusted Izzy, either. No matter what emotional and platonic excuses I wanted to generate on her behalf, no matter how hard I tried to put it out of my mind, ever since my wife had brought another man into our Rabbi Ethan Allen–sanctified marital bed, I only thought the worst. And that was her fault. Her treachery alone had to justify my incursion.

This wasn't the first time in my life I'd suspected someone I was in love with of cheating on me. I thought something was going on when I dated Sydney and she started hanging out with Greg, her summer-job doorman. It was before our senior year of high school. She revealed that fall she'd smoked pot with him and slept with him once when he worked the overnight shift and came upstairs "hungry." In undergrad, there was a point I started to feel like my girlfriend Amy's new engineering major friend Christos Utrecht from the Honors College was someone more than just an acquaintance with whom she was starting a "literary magazine." A Neil Young show at Mandel Hall she secretly attended with him during a long weekend I'd gone back to New York confirmed it. I'd never told her I knew about that concert. I never let on that I was aware of the saved drafts of letters she'd been writing him, which I'd found on her old IBM. Unsummoned, she never confessed. And most recently, Talia. I sensed, before anyone informed me, that she'd taken up with someone else, and he turned out to be her indie-rock idiot. All of this was more experience than I cared to admit I had. It had left me with the unfortunate and sobering knowledge that once enough pall-casting doubt amassed between two people, there was never any redemption. It was much like when TCA bacteria infiltrated a wine cork, which then corrupted the entire bottle. Izzy often got *Vintage Attraction* guests with questions on the subject. Whether or not consumers realized it, one out of every ten bottles plugged with a natural closure was affected. It didn't take a lot of the tri-chloroanisole compound to "cork" wine and make it taste like wet newspaper. Mere parts per million—a drop in a swimming pool— and humans could detect it. Even those without professional noses. Besides, we were way beyond misunderstanding here. Though Izzy had been conveniently absent at the high-thread-count unveiling, I'd still found Pacer Rosengrant *in our bed*. It didn't matter whether he'd just fallen asleep there shirtless and alone after an arduous night of blind-tasting wines at the Biscuit Lofts as he'd claimed, or if between those hemstitched linen sheets he'd committed actual adultery with my beleaguered spouse. Either way, it was pretty fucking bad. Comportment was out the window. We were operating under martial marital law now.

I pressed ahead through the downloaded files. I faintly hoped I'd uncover evidence here that Pacer Rosengrant's interest in my wife was simply a professional one. I wouldn't even have minded learning that her involvement with him amounted to nothing more serious than just one of those stupid phases when someone relegated to the far reaches of romantic nostalgia manages to insinuate himself into the present moment. I'd recently weathered a Talia crisis of conscience. If Izzy's liaison with Pacer had turned chronology momentarily on its head, it wouldn't have necessarily concluded that she'd permanently damaged trajectory—our trajectory.

When I reached the text messages received over the past weeks she'd imported, I discovered what Pacer Rosengrant wanted wasn't merely to learn about wines from an accomplished industry professional. I now had the data to correct certain crucial recent misperceptions. When she'd sat beside me, not paying attention to the important Swedish film I'd Netflixed—too tired to read the subtitles, she claimed—but alert enough to react when the Black-Berry buzzed, and then respond to a line of text with another she clicked out, touch-typing furiously with two thumbs, it wasn't Chef Dominique who'd contacted her. When we were at brunch and she said she was letting her coffee cool down before drinking it—ten minutes after it was served—hands and eyes in her lap, they were the words of Pacer Rosengrant that had invaded.

> *Wut r the subdistricts of rioja*
> *i kno ur at brunch but i need to see u n study*
> *w/service ok it's theory that fucks me up*
> *i miss u taste smell my hands all over u body*
> *yes i am serious said service not a prob lol*
> *im just gonna sit here n stroke throbben cock til u answer*

How was she able to read this shit and eat peanut butter and banana pancakes? How could she talk about the honey that was too thick on the biscuits with Pacer Rosengrant sexting her lap? How could she tell me she had a headache from the night before while she was getting these subliterate linguistic lures and I ordered her another Bloody Mary? How could she sit there and field this fuckalogue and patronizingly agree with my unoriginal and likely flawed analysis of Bergman's contributions to cinema's auteur period? It was staggering.

That evening, I discovered Izzy's BlackBerry pressing uncomfortably against my spine between the couch cushions. Not even caring enough to take the thing with her was yet even more evidence of her baffling late-onset heedlessness. But it gave me an opportunity to conduct a more thorough investigation of her private digital life. I spied pointlessly on group gluten-free-reservation alerts from Chris at the bistro, address book entries belonging to no one I didn't already know. I paged through the camera-phone album. Each frame I advanced compounded the panic over what I might turn up. I feared a picture that would expose just how much more serious an entanglement with Pacer Rosengrant existed for Izzy than I realized. But the shots weren't incriminating. The reel was mostly wine labels and portraits of me from our festival trips. Perhaps fortunately, perhaps unfortunately, I found in the device nothing beyond words to render additionally damning what Pacer Rosengrant's sexts so eloquently limned.

She'd been filming today, which meant a Citron and soda or two at Mamacita's or The Lodge would follow the wrap. Izzy found solace in the lack of artifice and warmth at these neighborhood joints. The Spanish she didn't understand was a welcome contrast to the all-too-comprehensible noise above our apartment, her putative reason for needing to stay away from here for as long as she could. But it was getting late.

Izzy came in an hour later looking like a Kabuki character, still in her studio makeup. She had on black mascara, which simultaneously narrowed and enlarged her eyes. Her skin had a foundation of plaster. Her lips were painted a deep garnet. Offstage, wearing this much on her face was absurd, especially when juxtaposed with her vintage gray-and-silver Chanel embroidered silk dress and black cashmere sweater. Yet the presentation was strangely, alarmingly, alluring. At a moment I didn't even want to be in the same room she inhabited, I couldn't think of anybody I wanted to fuck more.

"So that's where that was."

I was holding the BlackBerry. It was encased in a protective, dark watermelon–colored plastic overlay, which I'd bought her. I hadn't reflexively ditched it when I heard her key in the lock. I hadn't even tried to hide it behind a pillow on the couch where I sat. My thumb twitched over the trackball. She caught me red-handed, literally. I'd predicted it was going to end up exactly like this the moment I picked up the thing.

"Izzy, I know you've been seeing Pacer Rosengrant."

She squinted as though I was a flickering image. But there was no shortage of clarity in the room. Light bounced off of the windows, black with night on the other side. The glow heightened the convenience store sensation. With a formidable intake of breath, she respired her olfactory mucosa, which elevated snot into her brain. I suspected that illicit trafficked agents had spent the better part of the night up there colluding with her latent lower-minded impulses.

"Do you have to have every fucking bulb in the house lit up?" She hated when I didn't keep the place dark. She often commented on feeling like a suspect in an interrogation room. Each month, she scoffed about the electric bill.

"I was trying to read."

"Yeah, I can see that."

"Did you fuck him?"

"Do you really think I'd do something like that?"

The truth was I had no idea. "When I found him here, he said nothing was going on."

She seemed to hear this as though information she already knew. Pacer Rosengrant must have tipped her off about the encounter. "Well, nothing was going on," she said carefully, her tone betraying nothing.

I still imagined a lie-detector needle going crazy, spraying its scroll with hostile ink, after absorbing a blatantly false statement. "What's with the texts, then? He obviously is less interested in theory for his Court exam than he is in practicing with you. What's he even doing back in Chicago?"

She sat down beside me. Apparently she was not at all concerned with maintaining confrontation distance. "Hapworth, have you never been with someone who had . . . that kind of hold on you?"

"He's such a loser, Izzy. You're the one who's important. You're the one who's sought after. He's never going to pass the rest of that exam. He's a hack. I read the Yelp reviews of that Vegas place. An assistant wine director who showed some promise once but is so in love with himself and his fantasy of being a master sommelier that he can't even work the floor or put together a decent list."

"Are you sure you're not describing yourself?"

I was stricken. "Is that how you see me? I'm not in love with myself."

"You stop caring just when you're supposed to start doing. I've never seen you once prepare for a class or actually read a student's paper you graded."

"Part of me has never cared about teaching. What's the point in caring when nothing comes of it?"

"Well, when you really care about something, you're not done after three sentences. You can't just throw it away and move on to the next thing. People lock themselves into your brain. Whether or not your experiences with them were good or bad is irrelevant. Once they're there, they're there. So, yes, rationally, logically, I should be able to walk away from him. I should have walked away long before I met you. And I did, in a way."

"But?"

"But he came back. He showed up. I wasn't planning it."

"You aren't the same person you were when you dated him."

I'd been speaking to the Stil de grain yellow rug that underlay the coffee table, and now lifted my head. Ishiguro had come over and sat before me. He stared in my direction. Though the dog just bore the solemn expression he always did, his eyes and pout seemed imbued with deeper melancholy. I imagined this was how Casshole felt when his parents fought. Scott and Sheryl were uncharacteristically quiet tonight, probably with their sensationalistic pierced ears to water glasses.

I turned to Izzy. She was busy with the BlackBerry she'd reclaimed. I asked, "So what about me?"

She spoke to the device's small screen. "Come on, Hapworth."

"No, seriously, Isabelle. If things were really so good between us, you wouldn't have been so weak to Pacer Rosengrant's surfeit of charm and pleasing aesthetics."

She looked up at me, like I'd said something terrible. "You never call me Isabelle."

I tried to laugh. I put an arm around her, which she didn't reject. "I just wish you'd be honest with me."

"I wish you'd drink with me."

"Fine. Make me something. I'll have what she's having."

She excused herself to the bathroom—"To get out of this armor," she said—and Ishiguro and I watched her advance down the hall until the vantage offered her no longer. I couldn't help imagining her going to fortify her flickering vodka buzz with a couple of lines. The pug climbed onto the couch. Likely he was endeavoring to distract me from my cynicism. He positioned himself in my lap. Then he stood upright, and with a paw on each shoulder to balance himself, set about licking my face. He painted with his tongue rapidly, in sweeping strokes. I kept turning in the direction opposite the dog's focus in order to keep from being suffocated. Barely able to speak, I asked Ishiguro, "Are you happy? Do I give you a good life?" The dog's face was almost completely upstaged by his propeller tongue. He was undeterred by the question, and kept on licking, perhaps by way of response.

Izzy's return signaled the conclusion of Ishiguro's facial. Her opening of bottles and slamming of ice cubes into shakers chased the pug into the kitchen to seek cocktail hour *amuse-bouche*. For some reason, she was still wearing the clothes she'd left to take off.

She presented me shortly with an amply filthy dirty martini. I took an immodest sip. It occurred to me that by drinking it I was forgetting to perform crucial parts of my recently developed and in progress improv sketch.

"I have to go e-mail my attendance list. And grade some papers."

She was angling for the place between the dog and me on the couch. "It's okay. You don't have to keep me company." She looked genuinely disappointed.

I didn't move to exit right away. Instead I continued to sit beside her, drink in hand. She sipped hers and scanned cable channels. She advanced past each offering without even considering it. It was as though her flipping was just an exercise for her thumb. I hated to have to keep pretending to be a teacher. I'd hoped I was leaving academia behind when I walked out of Shelley Schultz's office.

I finished half of the martini. This, I figured, was a fair compromise. I kissed Izzy on the cheek, gathered the MacBook from the breakfast bar, and took it to the guest bedroom. While the computer booted, I withdrew a stack of essays from the desk drawer. These were final papers I'd collected at the close of an earlier semester, without any intention of reading or handing back. I'd forgotten I still had them until recently. Now they served as props to perpetuate the myth that I was employed. I could still taste brininess in my mouth. I longed to finish the glass I'd abandoned. No matter what you wanted to say about Izzy, her power to compose and execute flawless cocktails, almost rivaling her dexterity in wine, could never be shaken. But I needed to remain in control of my inhibitions. I sensed I'd drunk too much on an empty stomach when I contemplated just telling Izzy everything I'd been hiding. I felt like such a hypocrite railing about her deceit. I'd probably trumped her, if not in magnitude, in number of concealments: what had almost transpired with Talia, what had happened on campus to my job. Even what I was doing right now instead of grading papers. I had an unlocked folder of images open on the computer. I'd appropriated the pictures from Facebook. They depicted some of my female student "friends" in salacious poses of alcohol-fomented informality. I hadn't jerked off much over the years. I hadn't done it at all since moving in with Izzy. I couldn't remember the last time I'd even felt the need to before I got fired.

She came in. She found me with my jeans pushed down my legs to the floor. My dick stuck through the hole in my trout boxers. Izzy asked, "This is what you call grading?"

I cracked up. I wasn't actually throttling it when she entered. I was, in fact, appraising one of the Lindsays in the wanton Jamaican spring break bikini semi-nude at the moment my wife broke in. "Sorta."

The fact that this was the first time she'd found me like this over the course of our relationship betrayed no revulsion in her tone. "I'm not good enough? I can put out."

I sighed and exited my dick center stage. "I wasn't—"

"Maybe not yet."

"I don't really feel like doing anything."

"Nothing?" Now she was flirting.

What kind of a person was I if I let her know she could want Pacer Rosengrant and me, too? Shouldn't she have had to choose one of us or the other? I'd often trolled for a threesome when I was Craigslist dating. Now that I was married to someone who got top billing, I couldn't picture myself in a supporting role.

I let her lead me to bed. She pulled with drunk confidence. She'd probably finished both martinis and then made herself another round. I didn't mind. When she took charge of me like this, it reminded me of the early days. There was something vaguely thrilling in being able to return, if even for a moment, to a less convoluted time. Life was simpler when we knew less about each other, when we'd done less together. When had everything we knew and didn't know and had and hadn't done become so goddamn consequential?

I started to help her out of her costume.

"Rip it off me," she said.

I laughed uncomfortably. The Chanel was expensive. I had no interest in shredding it for the sole purpose of advancing some sodden half-blinkered impromptu fantasy. "Can't you—I—just take off your dress first?" She resisted. She countered. She evaded. When

I tried to still her, she squirmed away. Her elusiveness reminded me of the game Ishiguro played every time someone needed to put on his harness. Finally she capitulated. She lay splayed out on the mattress. The sheets were bunched into an archipelago around her. She panted. Sweat glossed her forehead. It broke up some of the hardened studio makeup in its ascent.

"You used to be romantic," she whispered.

"Destruction is not romantic."

"Spontaneity used to be."

"Izzy." Now that I had the dress, and she only her dark undergarments, I wanted to start again. But it was too late. The vacant way she panned her head made it seem like she was thinking about everything else except me, which she probably was.

Then we heard the back gate outside clatter up. A heavy vehicle came in. Izzy shivered when the gate rattled its way down again. Given the number of car doors opening and closing, I knew it was the Laheys. They'd been gone all night, not eavesdropping. The sound of their return suggested the outing had not been a happy one for the nuclear family. Sheryl and Scott yelled back and forth to each other in harsh, underbred Midwestern registers. Cassidy issued his shaky-voiced disapproval for his parents' carrying-on in guttural, shrieking caws. I almost felt a little sympathy for him. He must have been exhausted. I didn't remember being awake at this hour until I was ten years old.

Izzy and I listened to the full theater-in-the-parking-lot production. She waited for the Laheys to pass our deck on the stairs before commenting. "*Après* them, *le déluge*," she said.

We didn't have long before the encroaching footstep and impolite voice clatter would make its way to their oversubscribed apartment and accordingly, by the architectural mandates of shitty cheap construction, down into ours. Once the Laheys were upstairs, our chances of getting further for the evening, if not longer, would be completely tyrannized.

"Nothing like a circus to get you in the mood," I muttered.

Izzy took hold of my sweaty, throbbing hand. I had the feeling she was about to say something tender. But when the toddler detonated upstairs, Izzy turned away from me and drew deep into herself. She went to a place where I once might have been able to find her. Now I had no idea where to even begin looking. The ricocheting vehemence reached Ishiguro in the living room. It caused him to come seeking his mama and papa. Izzy was oblivious to the dog's urgently unrelenting effusion. So I got up to answer the scratch pleas on the other side of the door.

13

THERE WAS THE BISTRO DOMINIQUE OF THE EVENING, WITH ITS DIM lights, delicate sounds of silver tinkling, din of reserved, measured fine dining conversation, and precise choreography of waiters and bussers and captains and managers at "service." This was the Bistro Dominique that had won its awards. This was the Bistro Dominique that the regulars touted. The Bistro Dominique at which they spent a thousand dollars on a single dinner. I didn't know this Bistro Dominique very well. I was more familiar with the Bistro Dominique of the morning and the sloppy, sloshing dissonance that marked it. The days she wasn't filming, the world in which Izzy had to inventory Chef Dominique's wine program and meet with prospective speaking-event clients and show sponsors and audition future *Vintage Attraction* guests was a world anything but placid. It sat in stark contrast to the night's refinement. The bistro when customers weren't there to be horrified abounded in curse words over bollixed produce orders, impatient creditors, reservation line tangles, bags of Doritos, and oily Potbelly sandwich wrappers. Being here when people entered and exited carrying clutch purses instead of clipboards felt like an elaborate deception. An outsider who knew a time at Bistro Dominique had existed when the dress code was Land's End boots and hooded sweatshirts instead of suits and ties didn't belong here. The valet staging Bentleys at the curb where liquor delivery and linen-laundry trucks had idled only ten hours prior seemed an act that worked to convince me I'd somehow imagined all of the diurnal disarray.

I waited outside the restaurant to pick up Izzy. It was a new Dr. Phil–inspired plan for intervention of mine. If she couldn't make it home in a timely fashion on her own, I had no problem guiding. She was supposed to have finished fifteen minutes ago. Finally, out of patience and needing to piss, I had to go inside. Izzy's old room-mate, Chris, in his manager's charcoal suit, looked disapprovingly at my jeans when he saw me. He touched his shiny scalp, seeming to weigh his options. Then he snuck me past the host stand. I knew my way to the wood-paneled water closet from there.

I washed my hands with a fresh bar of French-milled soap and dried off with a thick towel, which I dropped into a minimalist hamper. For once, I wasn't completely disappointed with the image the mirror presented. I took a deep breath, corrected my posture, cracked my knuckles, and let myself out.

Instead of turning back into the dining room, I went in the opposite direction, to the kitchen. I'd been in here before, but never during service. It was suddenly rather abundantly clear why I hadn't. This was no place for me. The air was heavy with intensity and unwavering faith in the operation and commitment to relentless precision. Every face was sweaty and bore a cemented expression of seriousness. Every sleeve was tightly rolled up. Every waist was apron-cinched. And it was anything but quiet. It was actually loud as hell. Maybe it was hell. I found an otherworldly tornado of move-ment and noise behind those swinging doors: sous chefs on the front line, snatching tickets, firing this and that course, slamming down iron pans, clanging whisks, scratching spoons, and pounding mallets. They wielded knives, doled out baby spoonfuls of caviar, reduced sauces in pans, poached speckled eggs in water at a rolling boil. They plunged thermometers' probing ends into meat, sliced portions, sauced, and arrayed the components. They wiped napkins around the perimeter of finished plates one last time before shouting them ready. For the handoff, waiters queued at attention in a chorus line frozen by cognizance. They knew better than to speak or to breathe. An inconsequential interruption, anything that had even the remotest potential to distract, risked breaking anyone's concentration, which in turn could dismantle everyone's. So stolidly they came forward when their orders were up and took the plates. Immediately they turned and endeavored to leave without bumping into the jammed pastry chefs, who'd ended up losing the battle for a fair share of counter space. More tickets came down, more proteins were Frisbeed from one white-coat to another out of the refrigerator and onto the iron to sear. Every burner on the stove raged blue and white, whether or not a pot or pan sat on top. The whole place at all times was at least two hundred degrees because of the internal and external fires ceaselessly erupting. This was the kind of environment from which the weak and strong alike came and went cursing and screaming and crying, as happy and as sad as they'd ever been in their lives. Plate after plate, night after night. If they survived, they'd get to go home at the conclusion thoroughly spent, as though having given birth or fucked like crazy. They'd leave simultaneously exhausted, starving and through with it all, and coursing enough adrenaline to fuel another turn. They'd leave wanting nothing more and nothing less than to reenter the civilian world that revered them but, on the other side of the doors, had no idea what any of it was really like. Marathon runners. War heroes. Then my eyes fell upon the stool at the end of the line. It was the seat from which the director of this made-for-TV epic—Chef Dominique—was supposed to expedite, to lead his cast and crew, to guide them, to encourage them, to be the last to make sure that every course that came out was perfect. The stool was empty.

Seeing all that was going on back here, all of this labor, all of this passion, the sweat, the fear, the self-flagellation, and to know *he* was the sole beneficiary of every reward that could possibly come of it, drove me mad. I hated Chef Dominique for the ridiculousness he subjected Izzy to, under the pretense of advancing her career. I hated him for the grueling *Vintage Attraction* episodes he made her film without paying her. I hated him for booking her appearances at events and taking a hefty cut. I hated him for claiming he did all of this because he was looking out for her interests. I hated him for providing himself at her expense a means to avoid having to concern himself with his restaurant. But at that moment the thing that got to me barely had anything to do with Izzy. At least when she was on the floor, she was the sommelier. She was famous in her profession and on TV. Bistro Dominique's Gordon Gekko–era cuisine owed the vogue it was experiencing to Izzy's celebrity. But what of those whose white chef jackets were unembroidered? What of those nameless kept faceless in the back of the house? The guests were oblivious. Beyond what popular nonfiction and stylized and purchasable food television were capable of revealing, they had no frame of reference. When they had Chef Dominique's scallops and eel terrines and poached prawns and tenderloins of beef and duck breasts and foie gras, they proclaimed their lives forever changed from the experience. But it was these cooks who'd actually executed their superlative courses. Not Chef Dominique, the symbol, the figure, the metonym, the caricature, who was getting all the credit. That was infuriating above anything else. The least he could have done in return was to have *been here* with them, with her. I was even more determined now not to let the proprietor's conduct with Izzy continue to go unchallenged.

"Where is Chef Dominique?" I asked a black-suited waiter. He didn't seem to find my presence in the kitchen troubling.

"He was here?" the waiter said. "But then he go?"

"I wanted to speak to him."

"He will maybe come back?"

"Have you seen Sommelier?"

"She, I do not think?"

"It's okay. Thank you."

I scanned the kitchen one last time before leaving. I couldn't get over how these people worked. It was overwhelming: the way they prepared, every ingredient perfect, the way they served, every piece of china respected, the way they didn't let a single detail go unattended. I didn't think anyone on the line had broken from his or her trance long enough to notice I was even there. The level of concentration, the degree of commitment, the faith it took to pull this off, it was pretty hard not to find it inspiring.

I returned to Chris at the podium. "Are you okay?" he asked.

Before I could answer, Izzy appeared. I expected her to admonish me for entering the restaurant uninvited, for wearing sneakers and jeans. Instead, her face was lit with excitement. She turned over a business card that had a scrawled inscription on its previously blank reverse. "I'm so glad you're here," she said to either Chris or to me. Her eyes darted from one of us to the other. "I have some news."

I steeled myself. I sensed, illogically, that she was going to tell us something unpleasant. My throat went dry. I pointed at her hand. "What's that?"

"Oh, just a note from one of the guests."

"What's it say?"

She read from the card. "'*Brava*, Miss Conway, *brava*. The pairings tonight are outstanding. You're unusually knowledgeable about wine.'" She continued to stare at the words after she finished reciting them. She was silent, moored to the truisms therein, as though the message was a revelation.

"So, what's the news?" Chris said. His measured and unemotional dining room voice escalated with exasperation.

"We got invited to Greece," Izzy proclaimed.

"What?" Chris and I said in unison.

"There's a trade trip at the end of the month. For ten days. It's sponsored by the Greek Wine Council." She said this looking at

Chris, as though he were the one who'd accompany her. "They send a group of sommeliers and buyers and distributors and reporters to tour the vineyards and meet the winemakers and taste through the portfolios. You want to know the best part?"

"Um, real Greek food?"

"Even better. Hapworth and I'd only have to pay for airfare. They cover everything else. The meals, the lodging, everything."

"That's some trip," Chris said stiffly. He turned to me. "Are you sure you're ready for something like this? Do you have a passport?"

His remark annoyed me. "Yes, Mom."

"I wanted to surprise you," Izzy said sweetly, this time to me.

"It sounds . . . I mean, it sounds—"

"Perfect, right?"

"Actually . . . Yeah, it does sound perfect."

Then her face got sad. "There's just one problem," she said.

"What could possibly be wrong?"

"Dominique. He's never going to let me get away for that long."

"Izzy, are you kidding?" I asked. "He owes you some time off."

"Hapworth, it's complicated."

"It doesn't have to be that complicated. We get on a plane. They take care of the rest."

"Let's talk about this at home."

"Fine." I couldn't believe she was really going to let him get in the way of this.

A waiter then came over and whispered something in her ear. "I have to go," she told me. "I'll meet you outside."

She was off before I had a chance to ask her how much longer she thought she'd be.

"Is everything okay?" Chris asked again. He'd apparently been following my trailing Izzy until she disappeared.

"Sure." I patted the pockets of my jeans. "I think I left my keys in the bathroom. I'll be just a moment."

I climbed the stairs beside the kitchen that led to Chef Dominique's office. I'd seen the space before, on my inaugural visit to the restaurant. I learned on the unofficial late-night tour that the glass top of the chef's narrow rectangular desk was a favorite after-hours spot for coke snorting. It made sense, if you thought about it, the need to unwind and become anonymous after a harrowing service, privacy, the darkness, the vast expanse of shiny surface, not a stray invoice or Micros report or pastry chef resume anywhere in sight. But now, midway through the second turn, the door was open and the lights were on. The formidable executive chef sat behind the desk. Izzy had once told me the only thing he did up here was to monitor the dining room's activity on the OpenTable Internet client. It provided in real-time-feed reports on which reservations showed up, which cancelled, how many tables were booked for subsequent nights, how statistically analogous the evening's turnout was compared to the same evening of the week seven days ago, a month ago, two years ago. He now typed on a BlackBerry Pearl that looked even smaller than it was below the single sausage finger that poked it.

He seemed to sense my presence. "May I help you?" a hunched Chef Dominique said automatically, crossly. When I failed to answer, he pressed his shoulders against the ergonomic adjustable back of his Aeron chair. "Oh, Peter Hapworth," he said then. "It's you." He squinted at his miniature screen. "What are you doing here?" he asked the BlackBerry. "Sommelier is busy with a private party."

I took a step inside the chef's office. "I don't think you should have made her work tonight. Or any of these nights."

"What can I tell you? She is popular. She is what they want."

"You have her for fifty, sixty hours a week making your television show and doing speaking engagements. Don't you think this takes a toll?"

"On you, perhaps."

"Yeah, on me."

"You believe you have some sort of claim on her."

"Yes. I do. We're married, Chef. Remember that?"

"You saw a judge. You said 'I do, I do.' And because of this you believe that you know what she wants and needs?"

"I like to think so. I know that it would be too much for anyone to be with you all day and then here all night. Izzy may be a celebrity, and she may not let you know when she's tired, but trust me, she gets tired. She needs to be away from all these people who demand thing after thing."

"What do you want me to do?"

"I want you to stop making her do all of this shit. You have three perfectly qualified sommeliers. Don't make her work the floor."

"Why is it that if she is so . . . overwhelmed she doesn't tell me?"

"Are you kidding? She thinks she *owes* you. She still hasn't gotten over the fact that you hired her in the first place. And the TV stuff. Whatever you say, she's going to do. I've tried to convince her that you're really just exploiting her, but she refuses to believe me."

Chef Dominique stared at me until I had to look away.

"*Ecoutez*, Peter Hapworth," he said, his voice carefully measured, "an unhappy sommelier is the last thing I want."

"Same here."

"So we are on the same team, no?"

"I thought we were, but you never let up. You take and take and take and it's just too much. It's just too much. She hasn't had a vacation in three years."

"And has she wanted one? Did she come to me and say, 'Ah, Chef Dominique, I am tired, I need to go to Martinique, may I have the time off, Chef?' No. She says nothing like this. Am I a psychic? Do I sit with the crystal ball and know what people want before they don't tell me?"

"You're not always supposed to make people ask for what they need. You're supposed to think about things and reasons why your staff may not want to tell you directly, and then make concessions so they don't have to. Appreciate their work once in a while. Have you ever thanked them? Have you been to your own kitchen lately? Do you know what goes on down there? It's a fucking sight, Chef.

Your back-of-house is one of the most meticulous and dedicated in Chicago. Probably *the* most. And you have nothing but heartache to give in return."

Chef Dominique stood up. He pushed his palm out in front of him, as if to signify he'd heard enough. "Peter Hapworth, I no have time for this. I have restaurant to run."

"If that's what you call it," I said. "You don't deserve this anymore. You don't deserve her. You never did. And as far as I'm concerned, you can run your restaurant into the ground without us."

Outside ten minutes later, I was still waiting for Izzy in front of the restaurant. I stood and watched a couple moving west on Webster Avenue. The rangy boy with a small head and his narrow girl ambled without urgency. They'd likely just finished having dinner somewhere nearby, someplace casual and forgettable, like Café Ba-Ba-Reeba! They collided as they talked and came apart at the pauses. They moved as though following the momentum of their mutual desire. They were attracted to each other as it rose. They repelled when it fell. And they were oblivious to everything else around them. The night I met Izzy, I was so drawn to her. We must have resembled these two, save for Chef Dominique trailing behind us. As we moved from the Metropolitan Club to Wollensky's for burgers, I, like this guy, didn't want to stop looking at my date, even at times when not observing the road ahead could have proved perilous and maybe did. I was just that in love with her. It didn't matter if the traffic light were red or green, if keeping my eyes trained on her meant I'd end up standing in a roar of northbound cars and limos and city buses. Ardor was propelling me, steering me, but not, though I wouldn't find this out for months, protecting me.

I kept wondering where Izzy was. Like the dining room, the street was empty. Most of the card shops and boutiques had shuttered long before now. Cars drove by and I tried to time the intervals between them to distract myself. Finally, she emerged. I waved, but Izzy didn't acknowledge me as she descended the stairs.

She came to my side. Her eyes were directed to the sidewalk. I also looked down. I found there a black spot and a green bottle fragment and a pale, sticky smudge.

"He fired me."

My heart bounded. "Because I spoke to him?"

"You shouldn't have gone to him, but it's not because of that."

"What is it, then?" Pacer Rosengrant, lying almost naked in our bed, tangled up in the sheets and comforter that, up until then, had touched nobody else but Izzy and me and the pug, flashed before my eyes. She got caught with him in a private event space. The closed-circuit cameras trained on the cellar picked up footage of him fucking her from behind. A jealous waiter wrote an anonymous complaint.

"I voided a bottle of wine tonight for some old regulars," she said. "The bottle was two-eighty on the list, but only thirty wholesale case price. It doesn't matter, though. He says that's stealing."

I was aghast and turned to face Izzy. "He's that fucking cheap? He fired you over comping one thirty-fucking-dollar bottle of wine?"

"Because I *voided* it. If I'd comped it, he said that would have been one thing, but because I hit 'void,' it's theft. And he has a zero-tolerance policy. He always has."

"With the fucking busboys, sure, Izzy. With the fucking idiot in the coat check who pockets a handful of dollar bills from the tip snifter. But not you. You're his celebrity. He has you on fucking television. Without you, there is no *Vintage Attraction*. Doesn't he realize that?"

She shook her head slowly, as though comprehending none of this. "It's over," she said stolidly. "The restaurant, the show, it's all over. We are no longer partners."

I pushed forward. "Fine, so you don't work at the restaurant anymore. But how can he pull you from the show? You just began the new fucking season. He may be a mercenary, but he can't be stupid."

"Hapworth, don't lecture me. *You* shouldn't have fucking talked to him. After your stunt, he probably couldn't wait to find an excuse to punish me."

"He needed to be spoken to, Izzy. He's been bullying you unchecked for way too long. This is a French restaurant in Lincoln Park, not a Nike sweatshop in Vietnam. He has a lot to learn about what's fair to expect from people."

"Well, you didn't have to be the one to teach him." She kicked the sidewalk with the fascia of her feathered Chanel open-toe pump.

"Why didn't you just comp the wine properly? You've done it thousands of times."

"I don't know," she growled. "I hit the wrong fucking button. Let's say that."

"That doesn't sound completely unreasonable. Can't you tell him it was a mistake?"

"I'm not going to tell him anything ever again."

I couldn't believe she'd been fired. How had we *both* managed to lose our jobs in the same month? We were now as good as destitute, inextricably bound to a mortgage and a myriad of bills. Given our irresponsibly scant savings, these were bills that would soon turn into debts. The debts would suffocate us. We'd be quicksanded to a bankrupt death before the end of the year. The countdown had likely begun the moment Izzy climbed down the bistro's elegant staircase. Yet as I stood on Webster, envisioning the most dire of straits, the thought of Izzy no longer working for Chef Dominique was somehow a relief. I breathed more oxygen than I could recall having inhaled in a long time. I was light-headed.

"You're free," I said softly.

She smiled, almost imperceptibly.

I put my arm around her shoulder. "Do you want to go home?"

She pivoted and raised a contemplative finger to her lips. "Let's get a drink."

"Where?"

A Japanese restaurant glowed in the distance. Its neon window "We Delivery" sign pulsed a quiet yet persistent red and blue current, which beckoned us to come closer. "There."

The warm restaurant smelled of rice wine vinegar and was empty of customers. Dour-faced Japanese children filled a four-top by the entrance to the kitchen. They chopsticked ramen out of shiny green-and-yellow bowls, looking abundantly bored and like they were counting the minutes until their parents finished up the evening's work and could take them home. We took two seats at the sushi bar. Izzy waved off the nigiri selection card and dull-tipped pencil that the annoyed chef offered. She requested the wine list. Without responding, the chef sidestepped away. A white-shirted waiter came between our seats. He proffered a faux-leather folder. In it was bound a single sheet of plastic-coated paper. Izzy sized up our options in one pass.

"Medium—no, wait, large sake. Two cups. Please."

"Hot or cold?"

"Cold."

The waiter bowed and shuffled whence he came.

"They serve shit when you order it hot," Izzy explained.

"Why?"

"Because you won't taste the difference."

"Good to know."

Our waiter wordlessly returned with a tray. He placed the elements he presented in the empty space between us. Izzy reached for the ceramic decanter. She poured sake into the two tiny cups that accompanied it. She tried hers. I pounded mine like a shot. Then she set her cup aside and took my hand.

"I haven't been out of a job since I was, like, sixteen."

"Izzy, you'll get another one."

"How can you be so sure? I'm thirty-two, with a high school diploma."

"You had some college."

"A couple of English classes. It doesn't count."

I grinned. "No, not for anything practical, anyway."

"I'm a fucking has-been. When this gets out, that I got fired from the restaurant, from the show . . ." She sighed. "And who knows what *he's* going to say the reason is. He's going to make up some-thing: I became a diva, I have a drinking problem, he caught me with drugs. Oh my god, do you know how much he could destroy me? Getting fired is nothing compared to how that fat man can wreck my reputation in the media. Who's going to want to hire me?"

"I can't believe you think anything he could say could come between you and . . . all that you've done. Izzy, you're thirty-two years old and you've built this empire. Have you seen how excited people get when you walk into a room? You made Bistro Dominique what it is. You're the reason there's a waiting list and a case of James Beard and *Wine Spectator* awards. Who led *Cellar Temperature*'s 'Top Sommeliers of the Year' three times in a row? None of this is because of . . . of him."

She refilled our cups. "Good thing the Greeks e-mailed me directly instead of going through Chef," she said.

"What?" The trip. "Can we still—I mean, isn't it all contingent on . . . you know."

She rubbed her hands together. She drew her eyebrows close. "I'm still a wine professional. I'm just unaffiliated. A consultant. Yeah. That's it. I'm a consultant. And while everything may go to hell in Chicago tomorrow, I really don't think word is going to spread five thousand miles before we depart."

I thought it wiser not to mention the Internet. "You're right."

The sake disappeared. Izzy's despondency left along with it. I knew it was time to tell her something I'd put off far too long.

"What? You got all sad suddenly."

"Izzy, there's something we should discuss."

Her face tightened slightly. "What is it?"

I sensed a presence behind us. A woman was making her way over. It sped up my heart. The deranged expression on her face and the fact that she was talking to herself made me immediately defensive as she drew closer and closer to the sushi bar. My panic dissipated when I spotted the Bluetooth headset screwed into one of her ears. It returned when it became apparent that the fragments she was now repeating, "*Vintage Attraction*," "Channel 23," "the sommel-*eer*," were directed at us. Izzy kept her eyes fixed on the empty sake decanter.

"Excuse me," the woman said. She was now wedged between us. The ass of her chenille pantsuit hovered millimeters from my face. "You're Isabelle Conway, right?"

I imagined Izzy projecting an honorable mention of a smile.

When the cab driver stopped the car in front of the black wrought-iron gate, we flew forward. We had to brace ourselves against the bulletproof divider. I thanked the driver and Izzy over-tipped him. He drove off before we got inside.

Upstairs, Ishiguro was in a snit. I always could tell when the pug was pissed off that we'd been gone longer than he deemed appropriate. He scampered indignantly up and down the long hallway. His nails against the cherrywood tinkled like house keys strummed on a glass coffee table. After no fewer than two laps, he deigned to acknowledge us. He sniffed Izzy, then me. He howled, sneezed, and yawned. He hadn't forgiven us exactly, but had then found he'd ended up beside a stuffed toy in the shape of a diamond engagement ring that was in need of taunting. His inconsiderate humans were now completely immaterial.

"Ishiguro, do you want to take a walk?" I asked him wearily. To say I was exhausted would have been an understatement. My eyes burned. I had a headache that choked the whole of my brain when it throbbed. I was drunker than I'd initially assessed. It wasn't the fault of the sake, strictly speaking. The amalgamation of the evening's beverages and emotions had finally caught up with me. My debilitating gestalt had also been somewhat aggravated by the frenzied body slam of a taxi ride.

Izzy had already collapsed on the couch with *The Tonight Show*, which she'd programmed to automatically capture on the DVR, and her BlackBerry. "Can you catch him?" I pleaded. She didn't answer, concentrating intently on the tiny screen. She was sifting through the e-mails and texts from purveyors and fans and bank vice presidents and production assistants she'd been unable to answer while working at the bistro. It meant tuning me and everything else around her out.

Ishiguro and I took two turns around the block. He seemed more distracted than usual as we went. He refused to move along for more than a few feet at a time. He stopped to appraise shrubs, black from being pissed on so much, and smashed children's toys. A discarded paper Subway drink cup with balled-up detritus from a consumed cold cut trio foot-long shoved into the Pepsi-sticky cavity required even more fastness of intrigue than usual. He completely ignored me as we went. I tried not to take the dog's disaffection personally.

Izzy was still where we'd left her when we got back. Now she faced the television and flipped pages of the on-screen guide. In the upper-right-hand corner, there was Jay Leno, pompous head bobbing, hands drilling the pockets of his shiny suit trousers, delivering his canting monologue. It was as annoying to behold with the sound muted as it was when you could hear the words.

"Anything good on?"

"Of course not."

"Want to go to bed?"

"What did you have to tell me before?"

"Before?"

"At the sushi place. You said there was something we had to discuss."

I unfastened Ishiguro's lead. I lost my grip on the dog and he took off before I was able to free him from his mesh. I sat on the edge of the couch. Izzy looked up at me. She was braiding a section of her hair.

"It's not a big deal."

"Well, tell me the small deal."

"I don't know how to say this."

"Just say it."

"I got fired, too."

"What? What happened?"

I hadn't thought to prepare an explanation. I should have expected she'd want details. It couldn't possibly be enough to say, "I got fired" and have her not need to know how and why. But sharing the truth was out of the question.

"Nothing happened."

"Something must have happened. Look at me."

I raised my head. By doing so, I telescoped the distance between our eyes.

"Don't lie to me. You only look like that when you're lying."

When had she suspected me of lying? This was the first time she'd articulated an accusation, such as it was. "Listen," I said carefully. I didn't want to let my diction betray frustration. It was too easy a sign of equivocation to detect. "I was downsized. Enrollment's been dwindling for semesters. There are just so many sections of these shitty classes. There wasn't enough left for the adjuncts."

"For a semester. Right? Things could change? Right?" she asked with exponentially compounding franticness.

I shrugged. "I guess. In theory. But there's also the issue that—"

"Peter, I know how you feel about working there. I know how you scorn Shelley Schultz, how you're pissed off the department never took you on full-time."

I resented her reduction. Is that how she saw me? "I don't think that's exactly accurate. I've never applied for a full-time position."

"Never?" Her exaggerated suspicion felt mocking.

"A long time ago. But what does it matter?"

Izzy's BlackBerry buzzed. She turned to conceal her reading. She issued a subsequent reply in a blaze of thumb strokes.

I heard myself ask, in the voice of a sitcom father, "Who is that at this hour?"

"Pacer. He found out about what happened at the bistro and wanted to make sure I was okay."

"How considerate."

She blotted the corners of her eyes. "Hapworth . . ." She began unwinding her solitary braid.

"But you're married to me," I said.

She sniffled. "I just don't know what to do."

14

It had once been my role in our marriage to attend to the day's earliest imperatives. I got up first. I walked and fed the pug. I allocated ibuprofen tablets for Izzy. I brewed coffee and poured nonfat organic milk over bowls of Kashi Go-Lean! Crunch. I periodically checked on my wife to make sure she didn't oversleep. It had been a glorious but fleeting era of familial responsibility. I'd always completed my tasks expeditiously. There was only so much time before I'd have to leave for school. Now that I no longer had anything to do by a certain hour, nor a need to pretend I did, I'd been finding it increasingly difficult to rise. This morning I remained in bed and watched Izzy. She was an unwound vacuum cleaner cord, one long, twisted, gray shape lying opposite me. Even Ishiguro appeared to have lost his sense of weekday urgency. He snored between us. When he finally got up, well after eleven, he was anxious to go outside. I threw on a pair of jeans and a sweatshirt.

We wandered into a block where retail and residential commingled. It was a part of the neighborhood I knew the pug preferred for the variety of scent textures that his fellow canine denizens left for him. The sidewalk ephemera the humans flung as they moved along the street was additionally fascinating and occasionally edible. It was over here among the bodegas and narrow, boarded walk-up apartment houses where the laborers who'd been reared in the neighborhood still outnumbered the benevolent public-radio-listening, text-messaging hipsters with advanced degrees over on our side by the Starbucks. The true locals carted laundry, shambled into and out of bars and taco emporiums, carried on conversations in Spanish, bought churros, apples, and iced *café con leche* from sidewalk stands. Our chorizo came from Whole Foods. When I taught, a time I now called "my previous life," I was always in a rush. In an effort to make it to class or office hours or meetings, I passed this section with little notice to the surroundings. It was only now that we could ramble like pugs that I'd really had the chance to stop and take a look at the twenty-four-hour Laundromat, the donut shop next door, and the alderman's ward office with faded committeeman election posters in its windows. Ishiguro, too, seemed quietly appreciative of the opportunity to take his walk at an unhurried pace that allowed for so much experiencing. I kept an eye at all times on the pavement a few feet ahead. I didn't want the dog experiencing any of the green and white glass shards or unextinguished cigarette butts.

We found Izzy in the kitchen upon returning.

"What are you doing?" I asked.

"Making coffee," she said. It didn't appear as though she'd made much progress beyond boiling water.

"Let me."

She smiled and put down the bean grinder cord. "I was hoping you'd say that."

Izzy, Ishiguro, and I lay together for the rest of the morning, piled up like a triple-decker sandwich on the couch. I got up to get Izzy water when she asked for it. We watched TV. The general state of pleasant inactivity in which Ishiguro's humans found themselves was apparently contagious. The pug took long naps. In between, he occupied himself on the floor with a blue plastic duck and a length of multicolored rope.

That afternoon, Izzy, still in her pajamas, baked peanut butter cookies. She served them to us with two small glasses of tawny port. We watched more TV. The emotionally overwrought complainants sought what they imagined to be justice in the parodic courtroom sets of Judge Mills Lane, Judge Mathis, and Judge Judy. The low-budget commercials for debt consolidation hucksters and attorneys in search of clients for bankruptcy and mesothelioma class action suits between the acts got us laughing.

"I feel better," she said.

"Me, too."

"It's nice spending time with you like this."

"I agree."

And, as she'd done for a significant portion of the week, she even ignored her BlackBerry for most of the day.

But in the evening, after she'd exchanged coffee and water for vodka and wine, she became restless. This domestic reverie no longer appeased her. She checked her messages, all at once capitulating to what—or, more precisely, whom—I knew she'd been working intently on staving off.

"Pacer Rosengrant?" I asked.

"I have to go get a drink with him. He has a job prospect for me."

"Where?"

"He wants me to meet the people who are financing Atom Bomb."

I groaned. "You really want to go from being a sommelier in a fine-dining restaurant to . . . I don't even know what you'd be doing in a nightclub. And plus, how is he even involved?"

"He's doing mixology consulting for them. They'll serve wine, too, you know. They need somebody to buy it."

"They don't need someone of your caliber."

She snorted. "Please. I lost my 'caliber' almost four days ago. I don't have any 'caliber' left. Someone has to make money."

It was a conversation I once would have done anything to get out of having. Now, somehow, I could stand up to it.

"Look," I said, almost pleading. "I don't want you to leave. You have to get a hold of yourself. Okay, you're not screwing around. But you just can't run when he calls."

"You still don't believe me that nothing's going on, do you?"

"Can you honestly say you don't feel anything for him? That he's not feeling something for you when he calls to help you plan out your future in the nightclub wine-buying business with him?"

She turned her head.

"Just stay with me." I took her arm.

And she remained right there, for a moment. A long moment. Long enough to make me think she was willing to go along with me. But then, as though a contrary spirit blew into her, she wrenched her arm away and stood up.

"What if it's my only chance?"

"It's not."

"I'm scared, Hapworth. Goddamn you. You don't understand. I can't even count on you now, now that you're not bringing in any money."

She sighed and took the seat farthest from me on the couch. Ishiguro had become alarmed and now went over to her. He jumped in her lap and revolved himself several turns before condensing. Izzy smoothed out one of his velvet ears. He was too adorable to resist even in the most emotionally freighted of moments. I moved closer to them. She didn't accept the hand I offered her to hold. She jerked her knee when I attempted to touch it. I retreated without hesitation.

"Things would be different if you had a job," she said.

"I'll work again." Doing what, I had no idea.

"I don't know if I can shoulder the burden of supporting this entire family," she continued.

"We can make some changes. Take out the cable. Buy inorganic. There are things we can do to save money."

Without obvious impetus, Ishiguro dismounted the couch. He took off for a distant corner of the living room with the speed of the chased. I gathered he'd been following the conversation and didn't want to end up a budget-tightening casualty.

"This just sucks," she said.

"It may," I said, "but that doesn't mean you need his help."

"I need someone's help."

"You have mine."

She smiled weakly. "For what it's worth."

I chuckled. "For what it's worth."

Even this late in the season, winter still had a stranglehold on Chicago. Hard snow; slick, muddy ice; and abrasive wind hadn't yet surrendered the city to the felicities of spring. Izzy refused my offer to drive her to the Atom Bomb space. She bundled up and left for the bus to meet Pacer Rosengrant. I let her go without much protest, but followed behind, in my Mustang.

Instead of ending up at an under-construction bar in Bucktown, Izzy's destination turned out to be an apartment building in Lakeview. In front of my disbelieving eyes as she went toward it was the penultimate installment of the e-mails Izzy and I had exchanged over the better part of an afternoon just five months ago. I'd always said that series of messages had effectively launched us. One could argue, given what was unfolding here on Kenmore Avenue, that really it had *ineffectively* launched us. The concluding line in my mind as she got closer to the building and farther from me was *This invitation is all based on the assumption that you are not a psycho killer stalker with unmarked graves in your backyard.* And ever since then I'd been careful. I'd measured my steps. No matter how close we got, I'd kept my distance, to an extent. And I'd done it out of fear. I didn't want to come on too strong in the beginning. I never wanted to crowd her. Once things had taken a turn for the bleak after we eloped, I was especially reluctant to. I'd followed her lead because I didn't want to lose her, then or now.

As she treaded the gangway, heading to what I suspected and would later confirm was her old boyfriend's newest residence, I wondered if her disassociating words had really just been an instance of sublimating repression. Her hard-hearted conduct recently could very well have been an expression of Freudian *wunscherfüllung*. She had a wish I wasn't fulfilling. She'd really wanted me to trail her, to protect her, to save her, hadn't she? She was mine now, my responsibility, my love, so why the hell was I just sitting here watching her fall apart from afar?

I got out of the Mustang and shouted, "Izzy," before she touched the intercom. "Stop." She turned around, hands in her coat pockets. She began to come in my direction, but she wouldn't look at me. I couldn't see if it was out of fury or regret. I went on, in a lower voice, "You don't want to do this." Then she got in the car. I drove her back to our apartment, but she said nothing, not one word to me, the entire way. After we got home, I walked Ishiguro. Twenty minutes later, she still wasn't talking to me. It wasn't until I'd gotten the dog out of his gear that Izzy finally spoke.

"How do you expect me to live like this?" she asked.

"I could ask you the same thing," I returned. "Let's not even try to have this discussion right now." But I couldn't help myself. "Do you think this is right? Do you think behaving like this is fair?"

"When you say 'behaving' it makes me feel like a child. Like you're one of my fucking arrogant foster parents. Like I'm sixteen and stayed out past curfew and now you're threatening to send me 'back,' even though there's no 'back' willing to take me."

Ishiguro made for his water bowl.

"I can't do this anymore," she said. "Maybe we should just split up."

She didn't pack the suitcase I expected her to then. And when I went to bed, instead of taking a pillow and blanket to the living room, she climbed in also. She wrapped her arms around me. The pug drilled himself between. We slept like that until the following afternoon.

Even though she had feelings for someone else, I didn't want to split up. We didn't need to. Separating wasn't going to solve anything. Whether what was going on between Izzy and Pacer Rosengrant was personal, whether it was professional, whether she'd slept with him since we'd been married, or whether she'd just hovered around the regressive temptation and had been inching closer and closer to cheating on me without yet doing the deed, I just couldn't accept that what Izzy and I had together needed to end simply because of his presence in our lives, because of him. This wasn't a soap opera. We were married. We had a thirty-year fixed-rate mortgage, for Christ's sake. In making promises to each other, we'd also made certain implicit pledges to a certain furry foot-and-a-half long pug novelist who depended on us to remain united in emotional sickness and in health. Tumult aside, I didn't hate our life. Rather, I was quite fond of it. I ate and drank well. I dressed in suits and ties for occasions that weren't funerals or job interviews. This was the only reality I'd ever know, aside from reading other people's novels. This was the only chance I'd ever have to experience something real and true, something that existed outside of myself, beyond the conceptual. Breaking up couldn't possibly be the answer. Whatever the solution was, I was sure coming to it would be the result of careful consideration. The solution would require interpretation from myriad angles. The end result would be a product of dispassionate (albeit still passionate) deconstruction. This was just like spending a semester analyzing a dense and unyielding passage of text and, at long last, unlocking its wisdom. It was just like tasting wine, when everything seemed to suddenly click.

"Greece," I whispered, mainly to myself.

"What?"

"We should still go. On the trip. Together. I mean, we can take separate rooms or whatever, if you want. Regardless, we could use the time away."

"You think?"

"Well, it's not like we have jobs to keep us from doing it. Besides, you did already book the tickets."

She smiled, in spite of herself. "Go get my bag."

"Why?"

"Just get it."

I brought over her Timbuk2. She withdrew from the front compartment a folded set of stapled pages. "You want to hear what we're doing?"

We sat there together, in bed, discussing the plans. We Googled wineries. We looked up the indigenous grape varieties on Wikipedia. It all sounded so foreign to me. I'd never even considered a trip to this part of the world. Usually when polled about dream European vacations, predictable destinations came to mind. I'd planned to return as an adult to places I'd dimly previewed as a teenager on holidays with my parents and older sister, like Paris and Barcelona and Rome. My dreams never were set in cities called Thessaloniki, Naoussa, and Metsovo. I'd never heard of them. I knew nothing about Greece. I could only vaguely picture it on a map. Was the country part of the EU? Google confirmed it was, and that the national currency was the euro, which was an exchange rate conversion relief to me. The math involved in turning francs to dollars in 1986 was more than my verbal brain could handle.

Izzy had been on wine tours before, in Australia, in France, and regaled me with a preview, stories of sorting machines, bottling lines, fermentation tanks, barrel samples, and tasting rooms. We became delirious with information and imagery. In so doing, the bitterness and animosity between us seemed to fall away. If it didn't disappear entirely, at least it got for the moment relegated to the background. The more facts we amassed, sitting there, taking turns reading from the MacBook screen, the more we lost ourselves in this mythical land of myths and, apparently, ideal viticultural conditions. In Greece grapes could grow as they did in the celebrated regions of the wine world. Yet since the country was largely overlooked in the marketplace consciousness (an ironic state, given vinification's ancient Mediterranean origins), the varietals needed to be hand-sold. Via a trade trip, like the one on which she and I were about to embark, powerful international sommeliers, like Izzy, could potentially be able to turn the wine-tide and lead the charge. At the very least, taken for granted in America, the wines Greece exported were affordable. That fact resonated for both Izzy and me. In our stupor, we forged a truce.

"I really want to go on this trip," she said.

"So do I," I said.

"I want to go on this trip *with you*."

I nodded solemnly, took her hand, brought her close to me and kissed her forehead. "Me, too."

"This is going to be so useful for your restaurant concepts."

I couldn't believe I hadn't even considered that. In all the craziness, I'd failed to make the connection. She was absolutely right. A new culture's customs, habits, private and public idiosyncrasies, not to mention their food and beverage—it had no choice but to inspire me. It had been a long time since something had. I'd almost given up on conceptualizing, without even realizing it.

Veritas
15

Friday, March 21
Thessaloniki

THE THESSALONIKI THOROUGHFARE WAS BUSY IN THE AFTERNOON.
College students traversed on scooters and in compact cars. The
taxi let us off on Monastiriou Street, in front of the Capsis. The hotel
fronted tenement apartments that had laundry dangling from their
windows. I steered our rolling suitcases. Our new friend George
went ahead to the desk to check Izzy and me in with his Greek Wine
Council credit card. The hotel lobby was foggy with cigarette smoke,
and covered in mirrors. It had a long bar off to the side. A white-
shirted bartender brewed espresso. There was also a jazz lounge
behind the narrow elevators. The place seemed something out of
the early twentieth-century French Riviera I'd often read about in
novels. I could imagine Scott and Zelda staying here.

The forms Izzy signed at the desk had been prepared on a typewriter. The key she received to our room was founded of old-fashioned brass. But I was pleased to discover when I powered up my MacBook, the hotel had free WiFi available. While I logged on, Izzy washed her face in the bathroom. I did the same after she'd finished. The soap was harsh and unscented. The towel I dried off on was starchy. Abraded, dazed, we fell onto the low-standing full-sized bed.

When the dinner wake-up call came through, I answered it at the room's corner desk. I remained to check my e-mail and Facebook. No messages. The only update was one made on Talia's profile. She'd changed her affiliation status from "it's complicated" to "in a relationship." I hadn't before realized that the two categories were mutually exclusive in her life. More important, I was relieved she hadn't tried to contact me.

I showered and shaved. The beach-town humidity and late-day warmth made hair styling difficult. I stepped into the room with a towel wrapped around my waist.

Izzy sat on the edge of the bed. "How are you?" she asked.

"Out of sorts. But the shower helped."

"We'll feel better after we eat something."

I flipped through the TV channels while Izzy got ready. I bypassed the English cable news station. The local offerings included movies in Greek, weather reports in Greek, Greek infomercials. I settled on a soap opera. The actors seemed even more maudlin when you couldn't understand their words. Izzy came out with a turban on her head. She cracked up when she saw what I had on the screen. "What?" I said, feigning offense. "I'm trying to immerse."

"You're crazy," she told me.

In the lobby, we sat on a rattan love seat and conversed with George, now our tour guide, who had also taken a shower and shaved. He'd changed into a dark-blue button-down shirt, which was tucked into faded jeans. We were soon joined by a large, rosy-faced man named Dick. Dick was a franchiser, he explained without anyone's needing to prompt him. His background was in fast food and convenience stores, but he had recently made an enological foray. He'd built up a bottle-shop chain that spanned one-hundred-fifty wine stores in twenty-six states and several locations in Mexico and Puerto Rico. Dick's wife, Medea, shortly arrived from their room and took a rattan chair. "Call me Maddie," she told us. In contrast to her imposing husband, Maddie was a petite, delicate woman, with dark hair and dark eyes. She'd been raised in New Jersey by Greek immigrants. Dick and Maddie now lived in Florida. They weren't having any trouble adjusting to the Mediterranean heat.

"So what is it you do, Hapworth?" Dick asked.

"I'm a conceptualist," I said. My voice was so uncertain that I had to clear my throat and repeat myself, in case I'd only imagined having spoken the first time.

Dick brusquely interrogated, "What does that mean?"

"I invent restaurant concepts."

Izzy interjected, "Give him an example."

The first thing that came into my head: "Life's the Wurst. It would be a gourmet hot dog stand and therapeutic facility."

Izzy revised aloud. "In a clinic. Like an upscale mental hospital snack bar."

I looked at her. "Hey, that's good," I said. I scanned the end tables for a pen. Sadly, I couldn't find one.

The others smiled and nodded perfunctory measures of approbation, but Dick refused to yield and play along. "And you make money on that?"

"No," I said. The small voice had returned. "Not yet."

"So, what's the point?"

I held an imaginary object between my hands—an old classroom lecture idiosyncrasy—as I tried to construct a sentence in my head. "I guess that fine dining is too serious, and that it should be about fun?"

"How is eating in a hospital fun? Or fine, for that matter?"

"Maybe that was a bad example."

"I like it," Maddie said.

We moved along Monastiriou into Thessaloniki. Sidewalk kiosks were jammed with cigarettes and tourist trinkets, newspapers and magazines, and, of course, beer and wine options. This was Europe, after all. We peered into the windows of bars and beach clothing shops and strip clubs. George narrated, mainly to Dick and Maddie, the significant historical, architectural, and cultural details. He was a walking *Fodor's* guide of our route. He pointed out the new subway stop. The line had been built for the Athens Olympics four years ago, and construction to extend all the way to Thessaloniki was still taking place. At every intersection, bags and bags of garbage were piled up. The bags surrounded light poles and completely blocked the flow of sidewalk traffic in places.

"There's a strike," George said.

"How long has it been going on?" Dick asked.

"Almost a month now."

"Jeesh."

The restaurant was by the water. We entered through a path in the deck seating, which was empty, save for a few occupied tables. The dining room was completely vacant. The locals ate after nine o'clock, George told us. We'd have the place mostly to ourselves for a couple of hours. The host led us up some stairs to a table in a semi-enclosed space where two men and a woman sat. They greeted George in Greek. He introduced Constantine, the Boutari winery president, and his nephew, Stellios, the sales manager, to the rest of us. Between the two was Constantine's wife, Nikki, a genial woman with a broad smile and a mane of wavy blonde hair.

The Greeks had ordered the meal before menus even reached the table. Shortly, waiters brought bottles of wine Stellios selected. The first served were regional light whites. Moschofilero was very similar in style to Sauvignon Blanc. Malagousia reminded Izzy of white Grenache. As we swirled and tasted, *mezedes*, small canapé portions, began to come. There were baskets of grilled black and sesame breads, onto which we spooned *taramosalata*, a pink-colored spread made of fish roe. I liked it right away. Another spread, *tsatsiki*, was flavored with garlic. Everything was flavored with garlic. A vegetable plate of spinach, beets, broccoli, cauliflower, slices of ginger-glazed carrots, and olive oil followed. I wanted to go slowly, pace myself, but Izzy kept feeding me. She'd take a round piece of bread, paint on a bit of *taramosalata*, have a bite, and pass the rest to me, almost unconsciously.

Then the heavier courses began to tumble out. There was a deep-fried fish, which we had whole, head, tail, and all. There was very tender octopus. Snails came in tomato sauce. I selected two small lamb chops from a platter. I tried to eat them with a fork and knife out of politeness. Doing so was impossible, given their size. I abandoned the silver when I saw the others using their hands. I attempted to skip the sausage and tomato when it came around, but the waiter insisted I try some. I forked up a portion. Then there was more lamb, this time in the form of grilled nuggets in a cream sauce. This was called *souvlaki* and served on very thin pita bread. With these dishes we had a local red, Xinomavro—"Casino-mavro," Dick said to his glass, which he held by the bowl.

By dessert, I was full and ready to go back to the room and pass out. I was aware my trip's host and my surrogate guides from Boutari were watching me, and I didn't want them to think I wasn't having a good time (or tired), so I ate a slice of chocolate mousse cake. I also had several bites of *halvah*, the crumbly cashew pastry. In the States it was often found in dry and terrible versions, so I always avoided it in Greek restaurants back in Chicago. Here, *halvah* was quite desirable indeed.

The Greeks had abstained from smoking the entire meal, out of deference to our allergenic American temperament. Now they could no longer contain themselves. "Does anybody mind?" Constantine asked. Nobody objected.

Izzy caught me longingly eying their Marlboro Lights box. "When in Rome?" I said.

"You're not in Rome. You're in Greece." She took my hand under the table. "Happy birthday, Hapworth," she whispered.

I looked at my watch. "I don't even know if it still is. I like that I got to lose most of it in the time change."

"What do you think of the pairings?"

"Everything tastes so good. It's like the food invented the wine, or the wine invented the food, you know?"

She looked pleased. "There's a reason for that. What grows together goes together."

Izzy released my hand when Dick poked her shoulder. He wanted to show her an old wine bottle he'd pried from a display of plates and other decorative artifacts on the wooden shelves behind us. She laughed generously. I could tell she was uncomfortable with our new franchiser friend's third-grader propriety.

"What do you think of the wine, Dick?" Izzy asked.

He returned the bottle he'd taken to its shelf. He offered Izzy his empty palms. "It's good, I guess, I mean . . . You're the expert. You tell me."

"Well, do you like the ones we've drunk so far? Do you like how they taste?"

"Sure," Dick said. He crossed his arms over his chest. "I don't know if that means they're good or not. I know retailing. I know how to set up a business. I don't know the first thing about wine."

"You know what you like, right?" I asked. Dick exhaled through a partially closed mouth, flapping his lips. "So, you know the first thing."

Dick looked at Izzy.

"He's absolutely right."

Dick and Maddie let the Boutari people take them back to the hotel after dinner. Izzy, George, and I walked in the opposite direction. We went to an outdoor bar that overlooked the beach. Even though the space was small and crowded, the scene was still quaint, charming. The music was loud and the air saturated with smoke, but it wasn't unpleasant. George got us a round of ouzo shots. The small glasses of Greece's most famous anise-flavored liqueur arrived along with a bowl of almonds and tray of olives. "We didn't order this," I said. The waiter didn't speak any English, but he seemed to sense something was awry. George shook his head at the waiter to signal that everything was fine. "That's how they serve drinks in Greece," he told me.

We listened to the soundtrack—"All Out of Love," "Get the Party Started," "Show Me Love"—for a while because it was too noisy to talk. I was exhausted but tried mightily to stay awake. It was after eleven. I'd probably only had three hours of sleep in the previous twenty-four. And I was thirty-eight now, so, by default, elderly.

Saturday, March 22
Thessaloniki

IZZY AND I HAD PASSED OUT PROMPTLY UPON RETURNING TO OUR ROOM. We were a heap of limbs on a flat, unforgiving surface. I got up a few times during the night to piss and to drink handfuls of warm water from the bathroom faucet.

I stood and went to the phone when our wake-up rang. "*Kalimera!*" intoned a discrepantly fervent desk clerk. I thanked her and returned to bed and dozed off. It wasn't until George called, concerned we hadn't made it to breakfast, that we wrenched out from under the sheets. Despite my redoubtable engorgement last night, I was starving. We got dressed in a panic and raced downstairs.

George was waiting for us with the others in the lobby. His black hair looked even darker from post-shower wetness. He handed out bottles of water and led us to the tour bus. It was a sixteen-seat Mercedes Sprinter. Dick and Maddie were already on board. They sat together in the back. Izzy, in her sunglasses, took a row toward the front for us, on the driver's side. The driver, a taciturn Albanian who wore a coat and tie, had a long name only George knew and could pronounce. Izzy and I privately decided we'd call him Mike, after a waiter at Bistro Dominique with whom he shared a resemblance. Mike took off the parking brake, depressed the clutch, and put us in gear. The Sprinter stuttered under the weight of the passengers. As we pulled away from the curb, it began to gather momentum.

We were headed to Drama, in Macedonia. On the way out of Thessaloniki, we passed tenement apartment building after building. Laundry hung drying on their terraces. Boys who didn't seem to have jobs or school smoked sullenly on corners. Then we were on a highway, bordered by green. Twingoes and Honda Civics and motorcycles sped along with us. There were olive groves that looked like apple orchards. A body of water shimmered beneath the hills of Mount Falakro. If winter had been here recently, there was no sign of it having ever shouldered in. Izzy had her head on the window, her eyes shut. Dick also ignored the scenery. He prattled on about retailing without let.

I started to zone out. The highway landscape was meditative. Restaurant concepts began to take shape in the cognitive twilight of my receding consciousness, the vicinity of the most vividly imagined scenes. The sound of Izzy's voice soon returned me to the present. "I was thinking about what you said last night."

I searched my mind for an apparent referent, but came up with nothing. "What did I say?"

She looked annoyed that I didn't recall instantly. "Your restaurant philosophy. It's like my wine philosophy."

I waited for her to continue.

"How, like, you don't want fine dining to be so stuffy, so serious. How your concepts make it easy and accessible. That's what I've always wanted to do with wine. Arm people with information, but not the kind of information that makes them irritating and snobbish. Just well prepared. Prepared so they don't have to feel intimidated. So they have *fun*. I think we're trying to accomplish the same thing, just you're doing it with restaurants, and I'm doing it with wine. Don't you think?"

I didn't know what to say. I reached for her hand. I laced my fingers between hers and left them there like that, atop her thigh.

Ktima Pavlidis, the winery, was the only building on the sprawl of green grass that fronted the acres and acres of vines. It looked like a giant marble mausoleum. Inside the building, we saw the Pavlidis stainless steel fermentation tanks and walked the long bottling line, which was not currently in service. There was a room where hundreds of full bottles yet to be labeled were hanging out in open-faced crates. Then we were taken downstairs.

Here was the tasting room, in the center of two dark, cool cellars in which wine fermented and aged in barrels. The tasting room had an oil painting of a ravishing fire on a large, rectangular canvas on the back wall. They'd set a sleek mahogany table with benches on either side of it for us. There was a white and a red glass for each person. In the middle sat a silver spit bucket. Pavlidis had eight wines for us to taste: Tempranillo; Assyrtiko, the grape we learned about at last night's dinner; three versions of a product called Thema: the white a blend of Assyrtiko and Sauvignon Blanc, a rosé made entirely out of Tempranillo, and a red composed of Syrah and Agiorgitiko; and three non-trade samples that had been taken out of their barrels within the past four weeks and hadn't yet been tried outside of the winery.

I began with the first wine. I hefted my glass by its stem and spiraled the juice inside. Across the table, Dick and Maddie took their glasses by the bowls. This was a faux pas, the mark of amateurs. But swirling was as far as my impersonation of a wine-industry insider would go. Even though Izzy and George tasted and expectorated into the inelegant reservoir without a second thought, I decided, defiantly, that I was not going to make use of the spit bucket. The wine was too good to waste. How much bad could come from swallowing a few sips of each varietal? As I progressed, I caught myself draining the glasses. The sample pours were *pours*, quite the opposite of those you'd find at a walk-around tasting for consumers, where you'd receive thimbles. In short order, I got quite unmistakably tanked.

My head was a tumult of waves. When spanakopita, a flaky layered phyllo pie filled with feta cheese and spinach, came out for lunch, I gobbled several triangles, but it was too late to counteract the gallon of wine I'd drunk. The cheese was acidic and scorched my throat. I hoped Izzy couldn't tell I was wasted. She was reviewing some notes she'd jotted on the Assyrtiko ("Nervous," "Clean and citrusy," "Goes well with ceviche"). I was glad she didn't look up at me when I excused myself. I climbed a cement staircase and found the men's room. There I puked in a toilet. It managed to restore me. After I rinsed my mouth out with water from the faucet, I returned to the group. I was able to stay composed for the remainder of our visit by keeping my eyes averted from the glasses and the remains of the tasting. I feared reacquainting myself with the instruments of my momentary demise would unsettle my stomach's now-precarious equilibrium. While the others engaged the remaining bottles, I drank water I poured myself from a pitcher that somebody had brought out while I was away.

On the bus, I sweated and slept off the rest of my stupor. We arrived two hours later at our next stop, Nico Lazaridi. Here we'd have another tasting, followed by dinner at the winery. How did people survive this pace? I supposed I was ready to go at it again. Maybe this time I'd go at it a little more cautiously.

Lazaridi was more rustic in comparison to Pavlidis Estate. Here the grass was a little wild, overgrown. A goat roamed around, chewing uncertain comestibles. The tour revealed that the facilities, too, were decidedly less pristine. The tanks were dinged up. Their double convex exteriors were pitted and not as shiny as the ones we'd seen earlier. I could tell the grimy floors had been hastily hosed prior to our arrival. We went below ground to see the caves in which the château's sparkling wines were fermented. The walls were craggy with ancient, mineral-rich golden soil. It was as though they offered a rare glimpse at layers deep into the earth. Upstairs, the tasting room wasn't fancy. In fact, it wasn't really even a tasting room at all. The staff set up guests in a winery conference room with seats that had side panels you could swing up for a writing surface, like those classroom chairs many rooms on campus had been outfitted with and I'd sometimes encountered in my previous life.

In this configuration, it was very difficult to balance one glass while trying to taste the wine in the other. My desktop seemed to be the only one that slanted. We tried a blend of white Monemvasia and red Mandilaria grapes that created a Bordeaux-style dry rose. A sweet white the color of amber sunshine made from the Muscat grape was called Moushk. Perpetuus, a local Dramatic blend of Sangiovese and Cabernet Sauvignon, was much juicier than the comparable lighter varietals we'd had so far. The tasting dwelled on a heavy red called Magic Mountain. It was a mélange of Cabernet Sauvignon, Cabernet Franc, and Merlot.

"That's funny," I said, mostly to myself.

"Why's that?" Dick replied. His big hand seemed to grip his desk more tightly.

"There's this Thomas Mann novel, called *The Magic Mountain*. It's about a guy who admits himself to a TB facility in the Swiss Alps."

"TB is funny?"

"Well, no, but to name a wine . . ." When Dick countered with stony inexpressiveness, I added, "Well, if all else fails, I guess it could be a popular by-the-glass placement at sanitariums?" I evoked a broad smile, which went unreciprocated. "Amusement parks?"

Dick exhaled an audible stream. He directed his attention to the ebb and flow of the Moushk tide in his glass. Here his eyes remained, until someone else stepped in with a remark that more closely resembled insight.

After the tasting, we were led to the winery's art gallery. In the center of the room, a round dinner table had been set for us. Servers began to open lids on chafing dishes lined up on a long cloth-covered folding table adjacent.

Izzy fashioned a tasting menu for me from the buffet. She ladled onto my plate large lima beans in tomato sauce, a heap of stewed greens, and a square of a casserole that looked like macaroni and cheese with a spanakopita topping, pastitsio. On the table awaiting us were the open wines that we'd sampled during the tasting. In between us sat the winemaker and the enologist and the marketer with their modest portions. Dick schemed the pyramid of Corked-4Less, Maddie and Barry brought out pictures of their children, and Izzy talked about running a fine dining establishment and her work on television. As I ate greens and drank rosé, I admired the art around us. The giant oils depicted their scenes in broad strokes. Operatic sailors stood on a thrust stage. A fire raged at a horizon, with geometric structures of pink and blue in the foreground, lots of moons, blazing suns.

At a lull in the conversation, Nico Laziridis, imaginably in an attempt to jump-start things, turned to Izzy and said, "Sooo, Osama? Or Heellary?"

Sunday, March 23
Naoussa

A NEW ADDITION TO THE GROUP, BARRY, SHOWED UP A FEW MINUTES before we were supposed to board the bus to Halkidiki the next morning. In an open-collared, apricot-colored polo shirt and with his rolling suitcase beside him, he introduced himself to Izzy and me. Barry was from upstate New York and worked for a company that provided food service to colleges. His flight to Greece had been delayed two days ago. The delay had cascaded a series of contingencies, which resulted in his arrival late last night. Barry was short, squat, with dark, Italian coloring and a heavy East Coast accent. He spoke in the terse, colloquial, innocuous manner of, I decided after we took our rows, a Little League baseball umpire.

The Tsantali Winery was located in Peligros, Halkidiki's capital, a peninsula sixty-nine kilometers southeast of Thessaloniki. Here we saw copper stills and an unconventional vertical press. The vertical press was a hulking machine of steel and wood designed, we learned, to maximize the "must" (the quantity of juice) that could be derived from the "pumice" (solid grape matter) without compromising quality. Winemaking was always a negotiation between technology and the natural processes that resisted it. If winemakers interfered too much, things could backfire. They'd end up losing valuable extractions crucial to vinification, instead of gaining them. Machinery only helped to a point. Ultimately, one had to defer to the idiosyncrasies of the grape.

Athiri, another new varietal to us, was the first wine we tasted. The managing director who'd taken us around, Angelos, was pleased to hear Izzy's remark that this wine's crisp green-pear flavor made it perfect for American drinkers who'd grown tired of the same old Pinot Grigio. Its floralness was also a point of interest to contrast the ubiquitous Italian standard. Izzy next swirled and took a small sip of a blend of Limnio and Cabernet Sauvignon called Metoxi. It had been poured out of the bottle and into a decanter beforehand. "Licorice," she said. It never failed to impress me how she could detect the flavors and generate similes so rapidly. As soon as she made her proclamation, everyone else could taste what it was she said she found. This was quite the opposite of my experiences as a teacher. More times than I cared to recall, students had looked at me aghast, as though I'd dropped my pants and flashed my Melville, whenever I'd allude, offhandedly, but purposefully, to a flourishing passage in *Moby Dick* during class.

A couple of varietals later, as Izzy gave the room her notes, Barry knocked over a glass of wine. When he went to pick it up, down came a glass of Dick's. Barry apologized profusely for the commotion; he hadn't slept well, he repeated, and was still pretty jetlagged. Izzy had been looking at something in her lap during the interruption. Her BlackBerry.

"What are you doing?" I asked.

"Nothing," she said. She straightened her back and put the BlackBerry on the table facedown. "Just looking up vertical presses on Wikipedia."

"Okay," I said.

In the afternoon, we set out for a two-and-a-half-hour drive to Naoussa, a small town of only forty-five square meters. Naoussa sat off the road linking Veria and Skydra. Farmlands lined our path to the east. To the west, there were forests and the Vermion Mountains.

Izzy slept with her head on my shoulder. This trip had already transformed her mood. She wasn't as volatile as she'd seemed for a while back home, not as tense, as defensive. She'd been affectionate again after we left Chicago and continued to be as we moved through Greece. I wanted to believe she'd left behind all the thorny parts of our past. But I couldn't stop thinking about her with her BlackBerry at Tsantali. Her claim she'd been on Wikipedia felt like a lie.

I needed her phone. As I tried to work out a plan to sneak it away from her, we hit a segment of the highway that was littered with potholes. Izzy was still asleep when the rocky stretch of terrain sent a thunderbolt through the bus. Unconsciously, she pulled away from my shoulder and repositioned her head against the glass. Here was my opportunity. Her unguarded bag was between us. I was able to open it and reel out the BlackBerry. I stuck it in my pocket. A few seconds later, I casually brought it out. I feigned surprise, as though thinking, *Who'd try to reach me now, here?* I openly squinted at the screen and made to take in imaginary information, just as Izzy always did when the device buzzed her with a real e-mail.

I looked first at the sent items. She had been texting Pacer Rosengrant from the winery. Goddamn it. His most recent missive went unanswered. He must have sent it while we were walking or eating, when it would have been too conspicuous for her to respond. I set about sending a reply now. I didn't know how much this was costing. I wasn't even sure a text would go through, out here on a country road, where there were likely few, if any, cell towers. I typed, *What time is it there?* Numbers vibrated back a moment later. It was particularly infuriating he replied so quickly. It was as though her tawdry interlocutor were on call. How could she persist in this behavior, even from here? Was she just humoring me by being amiable and, dare I interpret it, loving? That was the only possible explanation. Either that, or she really was torn between both of us. Then the BlackBerry dispensed, *You get to naoussa yet?* I returned: *On the way.* What came next was *Forgot 2 tell u Check out Domaine Karydas if u can. Kickass Xinomavro. Super good fruit n structure spicy roasted plum wood smoke coffee notes. Had on BTG for a min @ Palazzo.* Was he kidding? *Don't have time,* I typed. *And I can't talk right now.* This text-messaging thing had really gotten out of control. It had jumped bail in Chicago and was now committing international offenses. Was she updating him from every step of the journey? Where did Izzy think this ceaseless juggling of her past and her present was going to lead her, exactly? At some point, the laws of nature and half-hour television dictated, things were bound to take a turn for the catastrophic.

I erased the dialogue and put the phone back in her bag. Then I closed my eyes and tried to nap off my warm, throbbing drunk. It was starting to turn into a nauseated rumble in my stomach. My esophagus and trachea hadn't really stopped pulsing and burning all day.

We checked into the Esperides Spa Hotel, situated among the churches and monasteries and ancient tombs. It was a modern resort that had been designed to look rustic. The rooms were clean and brightly colored. Izzy and I showered and changed for dinner. We decided to have a cocktail on the terrace, which overlooked a beautiful verdant countryside beneath the dwindling sunlight.

"You want vodka?" she asked after we sat down. She'd given me the seat that faced the mountains. So I could appreciate the scenery and maybe get inspired, she said.

A server promptly took Izzy's order. We were the only lounge patrons. "I guess Greeks don't start drinking this early," I mused.

Izzy shook her head. "We're Americans. It's always five o'clock wherever we are. It's nice here, though. Without everybody else. Without a tasting to rush to."

"I know what you mean," I said. "These trips are intense."

"Why do you think I've turned down so many invitations? 'Come to Canada,' 'Come to Argentina,' 'Come to Italy and Croatia and Slovenia.' If I went everywhere I got invited, you'd never see me."

"It was nice of them to let you have me along this trip."

"I insisted."

"Why?"

She looked at me like I'd just asked the stupidest question she'd ever heard. "Why do you think?"

The waiter set our drinks and a small dish of pistachios before us.

"I have an idea why you might have wanted me here at one point, but I don't know why you would now. It felt like we were getting along again, but—"

"But what?"

"Ask yourself, 'But what?'"

"I don't follow."

"Do you still want to get a separation? Do you still want to break up?"

"I don't know." She flipped the clean ashtray in her hands. "Do you?"

"Are you done with Pacer Rosengrant?"

She squinted at her cava. "Don't start with me."

"Why are you texting him?"

Her gaze went stormy and piercing. "Why are you constantly patrolling me?"

I was struck with the vague understanding that it was going to take more than reason to extricate Izzy from the mire. I was going to have to do something, but I didn't know yet what.

Izzy stepped away to the water closet off of the lobby to refresh her makeup. I drained my vodka and stared out the windows, down the expanse of green vegetation. It seemed to stretch out beyond the resort into infinity. I knew it must have had some kind of end point, even if I couldn't conceive of it from here. There was always a demarcation where something concluded and something else began. When I tried to commit the panorama to memory, it made me dizzy. I shivered. Suddenly my throat was dry.

When she came back, Izzy noticed right away that her glass was empty. "What happened to my drink?"

"'I drank it,'" I said. "'Because it was yours.'"

She wrinkled her forehead in perplexity.

"That's Hemingway. From *The Garden of Eden*. When you said . . . well, it came back to me."

"It's a beautiful line, Hapworth."

"You should read the novel."

"What were you writing down at Tsantali?" she asked then.

"Everything."

"Do you feel like you've learned more about wine since we've been here?"

"I do. I'm trying to get as much of it into my brain as I can."

"There's probably a restaurant concept in here somewhere."

I grinned. It was touching how she wanted to help me become something more than just an out-of-work English teacher who followed his famous sommelier wife along on wine trips, made inane comments, and took superfluous notes. She still believed in my potential, even at a point when she had no idea of what she'd end up herself. "I know. They're everywhere. You know, Izzy, I'm starting to think more and more about developing a wine idea. A real one."

"Like a wine bar?"

"A *Greek* wine bar, a restaurant, something like that. I love these wines. You love these wines. We could be a hit."

She inhaled the clean evening air that breezed our way. "You'd still need to convince investors."

"Once I'd tell them about all of this, how hard could it be?"

"You'd have to sell more than just Greek wine, you know."

"I know—but, wait a minute, why?"

"Because nobody knows Greek wine in the States yet. Except for Retsina. And those shitty, dusty, ancient bottles on high shelves at those terrible fake tavernas on Halsted, in Chicago. People admire them and then order a Mythos. To Americans, Greek wine is decoration. And what we've had so far here is the total opposite." She looked almost forlorn delivering this disheartening state of enological affairs.

"You forget about your inimitable way of teaching old Americans new drinks. Isabelle Conway doesn't follow trends. She *starts* trends."

"You really want to open a Greek wine bar?"

"There's nothing else like it in Chicago. We could have these wines, foods we've had here for sale, yogurt strained on the premises. We'd be known for our *dolmades* and our delicious by-the-glass Xinomavro."

"I don't know about a Greek specialty foods shop, too, since, you know, you and I know nothing about Greek food, except how much we like eating it."

"You're an amazing cook."

She shrugged this off. "I can tell you this: I like all this 'we' stuff." She smiled.

"Whatever we did, it would be the only way to do it."

"That's sweet, Hapworth."

"We are married, remember?"

"Yeah," she said in a dreamy tone. "I do."

Aboard the bus, we circled the mountain. We climbed up hilly drives at imperiled angles. Then we plunged into town for dinner. We passed gas stations, some boarded up, others operational. We drove by newsstands, a sporting goods store, and an electronics store. There was a sign pointing interested drivers to a sacrifice site. A large power-tool warehouse had a big banner on a windowless side advertising a Mikita circular saw and FAG brand bearings. The latter product name elicited fervent adolescent twittering from the back rows.

We waited outside while George stepped into a small restaurant to announce our arrival. Izzy told Dick, Maddie, and Barry more about *Vintage Attraction*—their intrigue was boundless—and I watched her. She'd changed clothes again before we left. Now she wore a bright-white blouse with its first three buttons open. She also had on dark jeans and ballet flats on her sockless feet.

George emerged to direct everyone into Manos. Across the room from a polished bar, a long table, covered in a plaid cloth, awaited us beneath low-watt bulbs on spindly cords that dangled from the chandeliers. Some menus lay between the place settings. Nobody except Dick reached for one.

"Just order for us," Maddie said to George. "We've had so much food today, I don't know if I can think about anything more."

"Sure," he said. "Just a couple of things? Small plates, family style?"

Dick thinned his lips. He released the menu he'd taken with a flourish. "I was going to get an entrée. But if nobody else is . . ."

Under the dim lights of the chandeliers, the support branches of which looked like wooden antlers, we ate appetizers. Dick and Izzy talked about the wines we'd tasted earlier.

"So, basically, what we saw today, at Tsantali? I could easily buy the entire vintage for my stores," he said from his seat at the head of the table. Behind him was a wall of a stone mosaic that resembled the pattern of a giraffe's skin.

"How many franchises do you have, again?"

"With Corked4Less? By the end of the year, we'll have two hundred locations in America. Next two years, we're going international."

Maddie spread some *taramosalata* on a piece of bread and ate it without an outward expression of enjoyment. She stared through the windows at some kids skateboarding in front of the restaurant. She'd probably heard this story too many times.

"And so since I can get tremendous discounts straight from the wineries, I can cut out the need for distribution channels, and that's why we can offer such savings to the consumers. Isabelle, that organic Cabernet we had today. How much would that usually retail?"

Izzy said, "I don't know, Dick. Depends on the wholesale cost, of course, but assuming good FOB pricing, after you convert the currency from the euro . . . twelve, thirteen dollars a bottle?"

"So, I'd sell it for seven," Dick said. "That's our ideal price point, seven to fifteen dollars. Anything over fifteen, our customers don't want to bother with it."

"Neither does this customer," I said.

Dick smiled. "I'm sure with this one you don't have to buy a lot of your own wine."

"No, not too much," I said. "But I appreciate a good deal when I see one."

"That's the right way to approach it, I think," said Dick.

"What's your next franchise business?" George asked.

"We're launching a line of self-service tanning bed facilities."

Here Maddie put down her water glass and turned back to the table. "It's called Bronze-o-Matic."

Dick pressed together his lips. "I let her name it." Maddie bowed her head, and Izzy and I applauded.

"What's it . . . so, it's going to be—" Barry began to ask.

"Tanning," Maddie said. "People will buy prepaid tanning cards at a variety of outlets, supermarkets, Walgreens, and then let themselves into the franchises with their cards, just like at an ATM."

"And then just get down and close the lid?"

"Pretty much."

"The overhead is low, and the demand for hastening skin cancer high," Dick said drolly. "From where I sit, it's a gold mine."

"A bronze mine," I said.

"Right," Dick said. He smiled. We clinked our glasses together. "I like this one. He's quiet, but he's on the ball."

Plates began to arrive and circulate the table. From hand to hand went breaded eggplant, salad, *horta* greens, sausage, broiled lamb chops—surprisingly devoid of fat, compared to their American counterparts—pita, and sautéed mushrooms. There were bowls filled with lemon wedges. The waiter encouraged us to each take several pieces. The restaurant recommended, in keeping with Grecian dining practices, that we squeeze lemon juice over all of the dishes, in order to heighten the flavors. To conclude the meal, an assortment of brown and golden semolina cakes, *revani*, appeared alongside chocolate, strawberry, and vanilla ice creams. Everybody claimed not to really want dessert. After receiving it anyway, compliments of the house, everyone forked and spooned steadily until it was gone.

On the return drive to the hotel, in the front seat, working beneath a small light, George went over the next day's itinerary. In the back, Barry tried to fill out postcards when the road wasn't too bumpy. Maddie, in her own row, listened to her iPod. This allowed Izzy and Dick to sit together and talk about business. A few rows ahead, I stretched out, shut my eyes. I breathed Mike's billowing closed-window cigarette smoke and pretended to sleep.

"I have the money, I have the stores, but the thing I don't have is someone who knows what the hell he or she is talking about telling me what wines to stock," Dick said. "It's frustrating. I need a sommelier. Do you consult? I know you're busy with TV and stuff, but do you have colleagues who do that sort of thing?"

"Sure," Izzy said. "Sommeliers are a diverse bunch. Many are in restaurants, but a good number work for distributors, for wineries, do consulting, speaking, buy for hotels, train restaurant staffs, serve as brand ambassadors, you name it."

"I think if I had someone just assess the overall Corked4Less central purchasing operation, I'd at least have a good idea if what we're doing makes sense in the long run, if we're picking good sellers."

"Well, how *are* your wines selling?"

"It's all over the map. We have a couple of core products—Pinot Grigio, for example—that sell consistently well, year-round. Other wines are seasonal, heavier reds in the winter, for example, and lighter styles in the summer. But I think we're limited to . . . a roster of very typical, very safe choices."

"Safe and typical are the least interesting wine descriptors."

"I know. I *know*. And that's why I wanna get someone in to help out."

Izzy was silent during a turbulent stretch of highway. The road leveled, and she spoke again. "I think I might have some contacts for you."

"Good," Dick said. "Give me their names and e-mails when we get back. Or, you know, before the end of the week."

"I will," she said. She spoke obliquely, as though she were thinking about other things.

At the hotel, we said good night and went to our rooms. Izzy washed up. I lay on the bed and flipped through the leather-bound hotel information binder. When she came out of the bathroom, she looked at me with such a serious expression that it caused me to sit up. That her face was disconcertingly pale without makeup heightened the trepidation.

"What?" I asked.

"What's that?" Her gaze had snagged on the information binder.

I read to her from the "Electricity" chapter. *"In case of interruption, luminous lamps lit up sufficiently all the communal spaces until the generator of hotel is placed in operation. During this time it is not allowed to use electronic equipments (TV, P/C). The generator does not provide constant tendency and exists danger of their serious damage."*

"Sounds foreboding."

"I think we're safe as long as we don't use the computer or expect any sort of constant tendency."

She smiled, but I could tell a rival emotion assailed her.

"What's wrong?" I asked then.

"I think I should work for Dick."

Monday, March 24
Amyndeon

AFTER HER ANNOUNCEMENT, IZZY HAD STOOD UP AND WENT TO THE bathroom to brush her teeth. I hoped when she completed her ablutions that she'd pick up where she left off and explain her thinking. I wanted to know exactly what had brought her to this. Instead, when she came back to bed, she worked her way onto me. It was awkward because of our unfamiliar surroundings and unfinished conversations, to say nothing of the as-yet unresolved matter. I could still feel Pacer Rosengrant's ghost haunting every overture. My trouble getting into it only magnified the trouble. The night of dreamless sleep that followed had done little to restore my equilibrium or bring me closer to feeling the optimism, the sense of abundant hope that I'd had when Izzy and I were drinking on the hotel's terrace.

I didn't need her to explain it. I could see why she'd choose Dick as a partner over me. Dick had a corporation. Dick had millions of dollars. Dick could snap his fingers and empty out an entire vineyard's annual yield. I may have had imagination, I may have had the vision, but an unfunded vision with no real hope of gaining any financial backing was pretty much worthless. Especially considering the fact that Izzy was out of work. If she went off and developed the Corked4Less wine program, we'd be able to make our mortgage. We could continue to buy groceries, and rawhides for Ishiguro. I couldn't exactly stand in the way of that, even if it left me with bleak future conceptualizing prospects. With Dick, we'd be certain to have a life. Or at least she would. Who could say for sure if she was still planning on keeping me a part of her life? After all, she had pronounced our marriage over before we left Chicago.

At Boutari, a short drive from the hotel, we began with a 2007 Lac des Roches. It was a regional white of the Peleponnese that was well balanced, uncomplicated, and easy to drink. "*Perfect* for Pinot Grigio people," Izzy whispered to Dick. He had sat beside her, likely for this very benefit. He circled the wine on his spec sheets.

Next came the 2003 Cambas cava. It was a nutty, more oxidized vintage of the wine Izzy had on the terrace last night. When the cork popped, the sound triggered a deluge in my brain. I wasn't going to let my wife, or Pacer Rosengrant, or both of them, end this. If Izzy and I could just get past whatever was fucked up right now, we'd emerge at the end of the storm—our vinification—stronger than we could have been if we'd decided to go off separately. Wine-making was like love, if you thought about it: sort of improbable, at least in its earliest evolution, really fucking difficult sometimes, schizophrenically rewarding and punishing, deifying and humbling to the point of humiliating, and yet those truly meant for it had never given up on it. Now look at what was going on here, and all around the world.

And if Izzy wanted to work for Dick, so be it. I just wanted her happy. We'd eventually be able to build a restaurant together. I didn't know how it would happen, but we'd find a way. Maybe I'd have to start ahead.

Amplified brain or not, some of what I thought, some of what I felt, made sense.

Didn't it?

So as Izzy and Dick continued to discuss marketing strategies, I started to really pay attention. These delicious and interesting wines would have made for excellent list additions even without the shockingly low retail price points Dick's circumventing outside distribution afforded Corked4Less customers. The only thing that stood in their way in any US market was their obscure and difficult-to-articulate grape varieties and trade names. I nodded when Izzy and Dick lamented how big a role the fear of the unfamiliar played in the driving of most consumer choices, especially where wine was concerned. After all, it would be an issue of consequence for me if I planned on getting into this business someday.

As we traveled again that afternoon, the sky swallowed the day's sun in imperial swaths. It rendered our already treacherous highway route even more so because of the added factor of darkness. Despite appearing to be only millimeters away from Naoussa on my brightly colored, toddler-complex map of Greece's wine regions, Alpha Estate was, in 1:1 scale, far. Amyndeon, located to the north and east, was almost three hours away. Rain began to fall, and kept falling.

Mike the driver remained stolid, imperturbable. He knew little Greek and no English, and thus didn't speak. It was hard to get a read of his emotional landscape. I had no idea if he was pleased we were moving along on schedule, frustrated because of the weather, bored, annoyed with the ever increasing quantity of spec sheets and brochures and kitschy promotional detritus from the winery visits that accumulated in the bus's overhead storage area, on the empty seats in unused rows, the discarded water bottles rolling down his once tidy aisle. When rain arrived in a blast, he acted as though it was no big deal. That the massive windshield turned translucent for long seconds before the wipers could catch up and restore visibility (even so, the view wasn't that much to speak of) didn't seem to bother him at all. He was, I decided, a paragon of fearlessness. That was comforting during this spell, and would be in others ahead.

We tottered back to the bus after Alpha Estate. I'd had way too much of the verticals they presented us of ripe, fruit-forward Syrah and full-bodied, yet juicy, Xinomavro. The wines were so good I felt I needed to finish several glasses of Izzy's share of the vintages as well. I longed to lie down at the hotel. The landscape that lined the road was a vast expanse of fallow ground. The wild weeds and grasses were dotted with decaying structures. Here were dingy balconied low-rise apartment buildings and ramshackle garages with walls that appeared poised for inward collapse. New constructions were frozen in early building phases. They'd likely remain nothing more than exposed concrete, projects never to be completed, untenable results of financial crises. The desolation eventually gave way to the inhabited and cared for. We passed modest houses of tan and pink with blue Twingoes and red Fiats parked on the steep streets in front of them. This signaled we'd reached the charming little town.

It was six thirty when we arrived at the Aethirio. Izzy got a key to our small country bed-and-breakfast-style room. It had a four-poster bed in the corner. The sink in the bathroom was so compact that I wondered if I could fit both my hands under the faucet at the same time. There was also complimentary WiFi. Izzy hopped online and checked her e-mail.

"People are already writing in to complain I'm off *Vintage Attraction*," she said.

"How does anyone know? Aren't new episodes you already did running?"

"Gossipy PR assholes," she said, eyes on the screen, "and then bloggers who recycle their 'exclusives.'"

"I bet you Dominique will keep replaying all the episodes you hosted. He's not going to make any new ones. His beloved *Vintage Attraction* is over. There's nobody on TV in the city he could replace you with. The investors will take their money out the minute he tries. Viewers would never stand for it. They're fans of yours, not the show's. I think it's going to be you on that program, virtually, forever."

"Yeah, and I won't see a dollar for it."

"Well, at least you'll be out there."

"You say that as though it's a good thing."

"Isn't it?"

"I don't know." She closed the laptop with a sigh.

We showered together, as best we could without a dedicated stall, glass, or curtain to keep the torrent of warm, soapy water that ran off us from spilling out of the bath and into the room. Even though it was only Monday and I still wanted to ration my clothes for the rest of the week, I put on a clean white button-down shirt and a navy-blue blazer. Along with my dark jeans, this formed an outfit identical to that which most of the Alpha Estate staff wore at our earlier tour.

As Greece-usual, I was a dinner table profligate. I refused nothing anyone offered to eat or drink, and took as much more as I could get away with from every dish and bottle within reach. Shortly after Mike brought us back to the hotel, Izzy and I crawled into bed and passed out. I woke up suddenly at three forty-five in the morning. It wasn't because of a sound. I didn't think it was the result of a bad dream. My bedmate, known well to me for her own fractious sleep, had not, as far as I could tell, thrashed out at an acetylcholine villain and conjured me in the process.

My throat burned from the previous day's higher acid wines, and it kept me from falling back to sleep. I went to the bathroom for water to try to neutralize the uprising, since I had no Zantac. Above the vanity, Izzy's BlackBerry hung from its knotted cord. It siphoned power from the razor and hair dryer outlet. I picked it up. Several trivial and theretofore unopened text messages from Pacer Rosengrant lay underneath the previous date's header. The texts ranged from the insipid ("*watchin the bachelor cant believe he gave ashlee the rose*") to the suggestive ("*if u here wouldn't need tv*") to the disturbingly knowing ("*this dick doesn't sound like one ha ha maybe it would be cool to work for him*"). I selected the lot and deleted them all with one click of Izzy's convenience key, which she'd recently programmed to perform this efficient eradication.

I stood there in the dark and wished I hadn't done that. If I wanted to address the matter, to confront her effectively would require the actual evidence. Now it had vanished into the Greek night. Would telling her I knew have even done any good? She'd have found a way to evade. She'd draw attention away from her indiscretion by focusing on *my* misdeed: spying on her. No. The proper course of action seemed inevitable to me now. I returned to the bedroom and sat down at the desk. My ears filled with a hiss of wind outside forcing itself through microscopic fissures in the walls of the hotel as I depressed the spacebar to light the screen of the laptop. The thing to do was to appropriate their chosen medium of surreptitiousness and circumvent, reroute. How hard could it be to fool a guy who watched the fucking *Bachelor* on his Monday off?

I can't do this anymore, I typed. *I love Hapworth. I'm sorry. This just isn't right. Please don't contact me again.*

Not bad, I thought. For a first draft. I went back and exchanged the capital letters for lowercase ones. I removed the apostrophes and periods. I replaced the stilted "contact me" with the more contemporaneously pedestrian "txt." I considered the implications of "please." In the end, I decided to include it. I hoped that Pacer Rosengrant might read undesirable pangs of desperation into the word.

I hit send.

Izzy had claimed that she was only responding to his advances, not initiating their dialogues. If that was true, this puerile intervention was precisely the way to go to decisively rid our lives of this uninvited guest.

Tuesday, March 25
Metsovo

AN ALARM CLOCK BLARED A HERALD OF THE NEW DAY, EXCEPT IT wasn't an alarm clock. It was like the morning was being strangled and calling for help, to no avail.

"What the hell is that?" Izzy said. Her eyes were closed. She still clung to sleep but allowed herself to step far enough across the threshold of consciousness to acknowledge the baleful cries.

I finally comprehended what the hell it was. "A rooster."

She sat up in bed. "Tell it to stop." She combed her hair with her hands, as though attempting to prove to the animal that couldn't even see her that he could consider his mission accomplished, that she was awake. When this failed to elicit any cessation, she said, "Fine. I'm up." Izzy then decamped for the bathroom.

She was already too far into the shower stall to hear me, but I said out loud anyway, "I had the most delightful dream last night."

As had become something of a custom, we got dressed and rolled our packed suitcases to the dining room. We had coffee and a little bread and ham and cereal and strained yogurt with honey at Dick and Maddie's table. George read a Greek newspaper and took several calls on his cell phone, each announced by an idiosyncratically Eastern European disco ringtone. Barry, under sunglasses, met us in the driveway after Mike had begun his stowage ritual with our baggage.

We took our usual rows on the bus, and the tour set off for Metsovo. Izzy slept against the window. I was tired, but couldn't keep my eyes closed for long. As we went, I tried to get the highway asphalt or the unfurled green that surrounded it to hypnotize me. When I got bored of staring, I leafed through spec sheets and brochures Izzy and I had been stuffing into the seat pocket in front of me each time we boarded the Sprinter after a winery visit.

The mountains got bigger and the ravines more cavernous. The peaks were blanketed with white. Winter still clung to Metsovo. I'd visited Colorado once with Jessie, my grad school girlfriend who had penchants for skiing and pot brownies. I thought it looked a little like Breckenridge here, but without the prodigious gleam. These peaks were drier, more weathered. The roads curved and narrowed. The turns Mike provoked the bus to make became increasingly treacherous. Fewer and fewer cars chased behind. Only the heaviest of vehicles dared to pull alongside us.

I'd rolled up my sleeves before we left, and now it was cold enough to warrant having them back. The temperature was dropping by the minute. The bus struggled up the slopes. If we slipped, if we slid down from here, we'd die for sure. The drop distances on either side of the miniscule road were easily kilometers. It was pretty, though, and so quiet. As we climbed higher still, houses began to appear. There were barns, shacks. I made out something that resembled a bus stop, which surely couldn't have been in service now. Mike followed a red tarp–covered pickup on the two-lane road until the truck driver got ballsy enough to pass the vehicle that crawled along in front of him. Fortunately no cars were headed down in the time it took him to swing back over right again. I was glad I wasn't helming our bus. My stomach lurched as my body weight involuntarily leaned with shifting gravity. Izzy was still asleep beside me. My balled-up coat functioned as a pillow in between her head and the frosting glass.

The cabin warmed again, with the bright sun streaming in. More snow piled on the mountains and the exponentially enormous pine trees and rendered the road perilous. Yet the Mercedes bus wheeled along, like a dutiful German, indifferent to the fluctuations. As we pitched and pulled, I had to press my right shoe into the plastic footrest to keep myself from falling out of the seat. We'd definitely driven back through time and into December. There was enough snow now to ski. The copy of *Proust Was a Neuroscientist* Izzy had discovered in a compartment of her suitcase and brought along for the four hours we were scheduled to spend on the route fell from her hands. The slam startled her awake.

"Where are we?" she asked.

"Winter," I said.

"Where the fuck do they grow the grapes?"

Trucks headed downward in the left lane came close—very close—yet Mike impassively persevered. I tried to push the phrase *too fast for conditions* out of my mind.

In the back, Maddie, Dick, and Barry whistled "Sleigh Ride."

"When were you going to wake me up, Hapworth?" Izzy asked. Her digital camera snapped away our vantage of the mountains, which was filtered by frozen and melting ice and snow on the window.

Another rig almost sliced off the left side of the bus. A small car zipped by in a blink. An orange salt truck lumbered ahead. Aside from the exteriors of vehicles that hadn't been already covered, the color was completely drained from this landscape. Everything that wasn't moving was white and gray. The windows began to fog. It was like we drove in an avalanche now. The brightness up here became surreal. We were pushing deeper and deeper into a white, soundless dream. The climbing had us level with the snow on the tops of trees we'd passed at their roots roadway rungs below when we'd begun plunging. Soon I couldn't see anything on either side of the bus.

Mike downshifted. The bus felt unsteady. It rocked a bit beneath us. A spray of ice brushed against the right side. I wasn't certain that the wheels were actually making contact with the slippery ground.

We passed over a river through which water tumbled. "Do you want to stop?" Mike called out in Greek. The first words he'd spoken the entire time.

After an uncertain pause, and without consulting anyone, George yelled back in English, "No, they don't want to." I stared out the window in the same direction George peered. Black signs with faint white arrows lined the curve we were chasing.

When we reached the town of Metsovo, the storm began to recede. It didn't appear we were anywhere close to the winery. After a turn here, and a climb there, before long, we were pulling off the road again. Mike lit a cigarette. The smell in the cold reminded me of taxis I took on the Upper West Side growing up, or piloting the Mustang around the slick Hyde Park streets in college, late in autumn.

In the driveway of what looked like a ski lodge, we got off the bus. We clambered, snow engulfing our shoes, into the Katogi winery, which was also our hotel. We settled at tables around a small bar behind the check-in desk. Helen, a Katogi employee, began preparing coffee, Nescafe, and cappuccino to order.

The desk clerk gave Izzy a castle skeleton key, though the room we unlocked with it was quite the opposite of antiquity: flat-screen Sony television, aromatherapy candles, IKEA lamps, and other Scandinavian-inspired furnishings. Izzy washed her face and reapplied her eye makeup. I changed into a black T-shirt and a blue hoodie, lay down on the bed, and closed my eyes. I felt a hand shoving my shoulder a millisecond later.

"What?"

"We have to go, Hapworth."

"Already?"

"Yeah," she said, and inspected her silver watch. "It starts at three."

"Okay," I groaned.

Helen, the staffer who'd first greeted us, gave a tour of the facility's lower levels. She described the history of wine production here in Metsovo. In the late 1950s, Evangelos Averoff, an admired intellectual and onetime prominent politician, had planted their first Cabernet Sauvignon vines on the slopes of the Pindus Mountains, down the Balkan Peninsula. These inaugural grapes were crushed and fermented and bottled in the cellar—*katogi*—beneath Averoff's house. Given the region's low-temperature climate and consistent humidity, the basement offered effortlessly ideal conditions for aging. It continued to do so for its current armament, consisting of hundreds of French oak barrels. The winery here also served as a local resort hotel.

Following the tasting, we had dinner in town with Sotiris Sotiropoulos, the winemaker, and Katogi's managing director, another Sotiris, who also happened to be Averoff's son-in-law. The wood-paneled restaurant was decorated with iron and copper plates and brown tapestries, and reminded me of a Viking meal hall. From there, we went to see Averoff's house. It had been turned into something of a Metsovo history museum. We strode, single file, past sculptures and paintings, animal pelts and primitive tools, a medieval kitchen on one floor, a room containing a desk staged with pens and papers and a telephone on another.

In the Katogi hotel lobby bar, Helen brought out a large bottle of ouzo. She seemed to have an infinite supply of energy, despite the late hour and the long day we'd shared. The sight of the tray of small glasses she presented next prompted Dick and Maddie to say their goodnights. George, Barry, Izzy, and I sat at a rounded booth and drank and chatted with Helen. She shared enthusiastic anecdotes about Averoff and Katogi. I was touched to see how moved she was by the lore. After she poured the *digestifs*, she asked about my line of work. I told her about some of my sillier restaurant concepts, like the Quiet Café.

She was clearly intrigued. "So people, they do not speak?" she asked.

"Exactly," I said. "That way guests can concentrate on what they're reading." I could see Izzy shaking her head in my peripheral vision. Thanks to the ouzo, I didn't register it as hostile and continued forth.

"How do they make their orders?" she asked.

"In a separate part of the café."

"And nobody hears them?"

"No. It's, like, across the hall."

"We're still working out some of the details," Izzy interjected.

Wednesday, March 26
Oia, Santorini

BREAKFAST AT ONE THOUSAND SIX HUNDRED SIXTY METERS WAS AN alluring and jeopardous bounty. There were spanakopita rectangles and slices of breads and cakes and flaky pastries on one table, ham and sausage and cheese and hard-boiled eggs and an assortment of teabags on a second adjacent. That afternoon we had a flight to Athens, where we'd board another plane that would take us to the island of Santorini. With a few free hours this morning before travel, we could dine here at the hotel, for once without stint, and later, do some things that didn't involve tasting wine.

When we finished, we got on the bus, which lumbered into Metsovo's town. There we lazily toured the Averoff Art Museum. The museum had a collection of ancient-era Greek paintings, as well as a number of rooms displaying the work of modern artists. I was struck by the skillful strokes and poignant symbolism of an oil depicting a male figure bowing his head to a healthy green tree, which leaned toward him. Between man and tree there was a bond, electricity moving in both directions, a communing between intellect and nature. It seemed to aptly convey my connection to this Mediterranean land that I was discovering. The Averoff staff gave us catalogues to take home, thick, bound coffee-table volumes that we appreciated receiving, even if our oversubscribed suitcases wouldn't.

At the foothills of the snow-blanketed mountains, we dawdled while Mike the driver, in a proper gentleman's hat and long coat and small black gloves, affixed chains to the tires of the bus. The hulking vehicle had no chance of making it back up the hill without some reinforcements. To while away the time, we wandered souvenir shops. I browsed a store's magazines. There were a number of English titles, in addition to the primary Greek offerings, on the spinning kiosk: *Truck and Machinery, Business Week, Playboy, Art and Decoration, DVD and CD Mag.*

George disappeared for a while and came back with exciting news.

"The Olympic torch relay is coming through the square." He pointed at a makeshift stage at the top of some stairs leading to a park. "The lighting's in ten minutes."

This explained the throngs of people that had been gathering since we got to the museum. They'd filled in the open cobblestone-paved areas around the parked cars and lined the pedestrian paths police kept clear for the proceedings. Dozens of children waved plastic Chinese and Greek flags. I had an unobstructed view of the cauldron that the traveling canister of flame was to kindle.

Everyone watched silently, triumphantly. Izzy put her arm around me, and we stood together while the ceremony took place. Every step was carried out meticulously: the coterie of runners behind the torchbearer moved in time, paused synchronously. I struggled to hold back tears. I couldn't even comprehend exactly *what* was so profoundly affecting. And there it was. The cauldron lit up and the flame had made its first official stop.

After an hour and a half on the road, we reached the Ioannina airport. We gathered our brochures and tasting notes and other accumulated detritus from the in-cabin stowage compartments of the bus. Mike returned to us the luggage he'd stacked neatly in the rear hold. Then it was time to say good-bye to our driver. We'd been together so long that it was a little sad to know we'd have to go on without him. I, of course, could only communicate how crucial I felt he'd been to the journey thus far by shaking his hand. Once Mike had finalized some details with George, he got back into the bus. He pulled the Sprinter out of the small airport driveway and was gone.

We checked in and passed through security. The plastic tub-seated chairs we took looked like leftovers from the 1970s. I was still thinking about Mike. "I wonder if he's going to miss us," I said to Izzy.

She smiled at me. "I'm sure . . . he's off to his next tour group. You know?"

I looked around. There were Dick and Maddie, a few rows away. They worked at reorganizing their parcels, which had been disrupted during the security screening. There was Barry, who stood by the pay phones, holding a bag of oregano-flavored Ruffles. He appeared incredulous as he counted the coin euro change from his snack bar visit. There was George, on his cell, a vision of equanimity, our leader.

"We meant more to him than just any old tour," I said.

When we landed in Athens, we claimed our baggage from Aegean, checked it once again, and settled into an Olympic Airlines flight to Santorini. Izzy put her head on my shoulder. I leaned my head against hers. We both closed our eyes. We got in around eight and reunited with our things. Outside, George hailed two taxis. A BMW with a more capacious trunk took Barry, Maddie, Dick, and their profusion of baggage. Izzy and I got into a Mercedes. George gave both drivers the name of the hotel, Laokasti, in Oia, and climbed into the front seat of our car.

"Ee-yuh," George corrected, after I mispronounced the name of the village. "The 'o' is silent."

Our driver added that Oia was considered the most beautiful of the Santorini villages. It was situated eleven kilometers away from Fira, the capital, at the top of a cliff. Oia offered visitors an impressive view over the Palia and Nea Kameni volcanoes, which sat in a geological formation known as the Santorini caldera, as well as of the Thirassia island.

Across a cracked tile veranda and through a garden of olive trees and fragrant herbs, we located the seafood restaurant where we'd have dinner, Saltsa, which sat along the water. Our reservation was for a perfectly locally acceptable nine P.M. Izzy and I took places in the middle of a long table that had been set for fourteen. It stretched from one end of the restaurant, beside the bathroom, to, nearly, the other, by the main entrance. I sat facing the kitchen's window, which was festooned with flogged octopi that dangled from brass hooks. The winery we'd visit the next morning, Sigalas, had sent reps to greet us. Some of our Boutari friends, whom we'd met last Friday night in Thessaloniki, were also here. They'd brought with them some local sommeliers and wine spectators.

The party emptied several bottles of Boutari Santorini while the courses came out and circulated. This Santorini wine was made from Assyrtiko grapes, and—perhaps heightened by our new geography—tasted lush and rich, like ripe pear and apple and cream, with spicy and smoky notes. Izzy remarked that the wine was a perfect match for the foods we had, the charcoal-grilled seafood specialties for which this region was famous. I ate octopus risotto; grilled sardines; cod in a cornflower crust, done with caramelized beetroot and fava beans in garlic; and fillet of bream with crawfish sauce. For dessert, there was panna cotta with strawberries; chocolate mousse; and *loukoumi*, an ice cream served with caramelized rose petals.

Back at the hotel, Izzy took off her clothes in the bathroom. She lay on the made bed in a white terrycloth robe of unknown provenance.

"What do you think of Dick?" she asked me. Her voice was a little tremulous, shaky from drink.

"I don't know. He's growing on me, I guess."

"You realize if I went to work for him, we'd move to New York."

I said nothing.

"And you don't want to. I can tell."

"It's not that I don't want to, Izzy, it's just—"

"Do you know how much money I could make with him? Way more than from that stupid restaurant and the TV show. No Chef Dominique to take seventy-five percent of everything because he was under the impression that he was the most important part of the equation."

"I still don't know how you ended up with that shitty of an arrangement."

"Because I was an idiot," she said in monotone. "But I'm a different person now. I'm smarter. I've learned. And Dick is a success. He doesn't need to exploit me. He needs me."

"You could make Corked4Less a real thing. With you, their wine would become significant. They'd be known for more than just the chain shop to go to for cheap Sauvignon Blanc housewives serve with before-meal cheese and crackers."

She giggled. "Dominique would flip out when he would hear people ordering cheese as a first course." In the chef's comic accent, she asked, "'Cheese is for after dinner, no?'"

"Did you tell him they weren't dumb, just American?"

She snickered. "Something like that." She took a deep breath of the sea air that permeated our little parti-colored hotel room. "So what if he wants to hire me? Do we pack up and go?"

It was a good question. I'd never dreamed I'd end up back in New York. I'd resisted the pull of the city, which mainly came in the form of my parents' nudging, for so long, for so many years. I'd gotten the sense from the occasional conversations we'd had in recent months that now they finally conceded I had a legitimate excuse to live a thousand miles away. They'd read the newspaper and magazine articles they Googled about my wife. I had Izzy, and she had a significant life in Chicago. But this was something completely different to consider. If we moved, Izzy and I, together, it wouldn't just be a regression, a capitulation, going back to Mom and Dad. It wouldn't be an admission that they'd been right about the lunacy of my academic choices and the pathologic impracticality of my resulting career as an adjunct, and that I'd been wrong. This would be a change for both of our futures. It would be a chance for Izzy to become an important buyer for a major corporation. Her name and face would be in Corked4Less shops throughout the Northern

Hemisphere. People in dozens of countries would serve the wines she'd have selected—wines like those from Santorini—at myriad dinner tables. It would also be a chance to start anew domestically. We could sell the terrible loft in Pilsen and never have to worry about our noisy and meddlesome neighbors again. We'd be so far away from all the text that was unpleasant in our lives. And Pacer Rosengrant. We'd be chapters beyond him, too.

"There has to be a reason," Izzy said, "that we're on *this* trip at *this* particular junction, that Dick's here and his company's expanding and that he needs someone like me so badly, at *this* particular moment. I know we like to say everything's random and things just happen . . . but an opportunity like this . . ."

It had to mean something. This was not only the right time for us to move ahead. This was probably the only chance we'd ever have to pick up and start all over again. It was fate.

"So, we'll go. We'll go to New York."

"You really would?"

"Yeah. All I've ever wanted is to make you happy," I said. The line echoed in my head like someone else had said it and I'd merely overheard a platitudinous remark.

"It's not just about *me*, Peter."

"You always sound so serious when you call me 'Peter.'"

She laughed a trill. "I *am* being serious. What's good for me may not be right for us."

I asked a question I'd been putting off for some time. It seemed like the right thing to do just then. "So you still want me to be part of your us?"

"Don't be silly. And it's not just 'my us.'"

Gently, I spoke. "I remember talk about separating, Izzy."

"Well, I don't always mean what I say."

"That's not exactly reassuring."

She growled at me, but playfully. "You know what I mean."

And to this end, after we got in bed and I turned out the lights, I found Izzy, a few moments later, climbing on top of me. I'd closed my eyes, but, wordlessly, she began to cajole the decision-maker into keeping the rest of my body awake a little longer. Neither it nor I made protest. It felt good to be this close to her again, no longer adversaries, after what seemed a decades-long disconnection. The moves were our same old choreography, yet it was somehow different enough in this context to surge my limbs with the adrenaline of unfamiliarity. It was as though she were someone with whom I had never before been intimate. Her body seemed no longer indecisive, torn. In this bed, she pleaded for me and me only. And she was the only one I wanted. For the first time in a while, I was *with* Izzy, not wondering when the Laheys were coming home or agonizing over teaching assignments or how we were going to pay the mortgage, not fantasizing about former students, or missing Talia, once again restored to virility, once again a man. The electricity between us cleared my mind of anything beyond sweaty skin and grating foreign sheets and taut ligaments. We were plunging further into the depths than, quite possibly, we'd ever been.

Thursday, March 27
Oia, Santorini

I GOT UP BEFORE IZZY AND EXPLORED OUR ROOM. I OPENED EACH of the cabinets in the kitchenette. I took out plastic plates that had been washed and rewashed so many times their glaze had been reduced to a shine barely perceptible. The small refrigerator, standing against a column that matched its width, was empty, just humming away. In my mind, I transformed it into a proper minibar. I filled the shelves with imaginary single-serving bottles of Assyrtiko and Moschofilero and ouzo. It occurred to me that some of this might be worth documenting. Who knew when I might come up with a restaurant, the décor of which needed to replicate that of a Greek island villa? With Izzy's camera on auto-timer, I snapped a photograph of me standing in the little bathroom brushing my teeth over the sink, the wall-mounted hair dryer holster millimeters away from my ear. After I dried my mouth on a tiny gray towel, I logged more digital exposures of the rattan love seat in the sitting area and its dusty cushions encased in floral print. Out on the veranda, I took pictures of our twin chaise longues.

Izzy caught me lying on a chaise with the camera lens trained on the tip of my nose. "What are you doing?" she asked. She stood in the doorway and rubbed her eyes.

"Nasal gazing," I said. I stood up and dusted off my jeans. I set Izzy in electronic sights and shuttered the tiny shutter.

"It's pretty here, huh," she said, looking out into the murmuring blue.

Against the idyllic backdrop, Izzy was astonishing. Beneath the blue sky painted here and there with cumulus humilis, standing high above the glittery, intensely dark Aegean water, she was absolutely angelic. She smiled at me when she caught me fixing her in my viewfinder and zooming in and out for the perfect balance of sky and white buildings to comprise her background.

"What do you think about all of this?" she asked.

"I really like it here," I said, "on this side of paradise."

She chuckled. "Listen to you. You've become F. Santorini Fitzgerald."

I patted my belly, which seemed poised to overhang my belt. "I'd say more like Santorini Claus."

"I told you not to eat so much last night."

"I didn't want to be rude. And everything was so delicious."

"Nobody held an octopus to your head."

"I kind of wish somebody had."

After breakfast, we moved through the mall of souvenir shops. Collarless brown-and-white shaggy dogs sauntered alongside us. In front of several neighboring agencies that offered hourly, daily, and weekly rental rates on everything ambulatory from donkeys and bicycles to watercraft and SUVs, two taxis awaited. Down and down the volcano we went. We traversed the plain of Oia for two kilometers.

In an area called Baxedes, we reached the Sigalas property. Unassuming winemaker Paris Sigalas met us at the gates and took us around. The Assyrtiko vineyards (like most of the other Greeks, Sigalas pronounced them "veen-e-guards") were in character markedly unlike the others we'd seen. Instead of walking aisles between wire-caged vertical canopies trellised to heights nearly our own, here there lay on the ground rows upon rows of tangled vine nests. The vines had defensively wound around themselves in order to capture the moisture they needed to thrive. There were hundreds and hundreds of these baskets. They extended all the way from the edge of the road to the green side of the volcano in the distance. The vulcanized rocks in the deeply sulfuric soil crunched under shoes as we tried to find a vine coil that had the beginnings of some grapes. A leafy basket revealed a bunch of green fruit smaller than my thumbnail. I imagined its trajectory, starting out here, maturing, going through its vinification. And that resulting Assyrtiko bottle could end up anywhere in the world: on a grocery store shelf in London or an Abu Dhabi hotel room service tray; on a Union Square wine studio by-the-glass list in New York; at a Corked4Less in a Peoria, Arizona strip mall; in the refrigerator of a rural Midwestern shared apartment in which resided a young waitress with big-city sommelier dreams, working to learn as much as she could at her chain restaurant's staff trainings and beyond.

In an understated room of long wooden tables with plenty of light streaming in through the windows, we tasted the Sigalas '07 Assyrtiko-Athiri first. It was a good balance of the two grape varieties. Their association yielded a crisp green-apple flavor, with very light minerality. The '06 vintage that followed was a little sweeter, and somewhat more aromatic. Next they poured us a vertical of Sigalas Santorini, which was one-hundred percent Assyrtiko. This was the same wine we had with the octopus risotto last night. The 2006, Izzy said, would go well with a lobster roll.

The '03, when it came, was too cold. The colder the wine, the less of its components and aromatics could be detected by tasting. Temperature was a common problem with white wine served in the United States, not just with reds. As the 2000, an appreciably darker gold from the additional years of oxidation, warmed, the nose began to resemble a gas station. Dick grimaced and pushed aside his glass, but I found the note intriguing.

"Petrol," Izzy told the balkers on the evaluating panel. "I know it's a little weird, if you're not used to it."

"And people buy that?" Barry asked.

"Oh, yeah," she replied. "Wine geeks love it. The scent actually gets stronger as the wine ages." She swirled and sniffed her pour again. "This varietal reminds me so much of Riesling."

"It must be an acquired taste," Dick said. "But I'll trust the sommelier."

Izzy smiled for the room and pressed her hand against my leg.

At the end of the line came the Sigalas Apiliotis. It was made completely using Mandilaria, a grape variety we hadn't yet encountered. The 2004 vintage tasted like maraschino cherries, acidic but sweet. "Welch's grape juice," Dick said. He seemed, more and more, to find his tasting voice in the final bottle or two we were shown at each winery.

"Cherry Heering," Izzy said. "The Danish liqueur."

"'The lady doth protest too much, me thinks,'" Dick said. "I'm kidding. You got it." She laughed, and they pantomimed high-fiving each other across the room.

"Nice work," I said. I patted her knee. "I bought a bottle of that stuff on a dare in grad school. I think I might still have it. There was a war over whether or not it was pronounced 'hearing' or 'herring,' which went on for two semesters."

"This is a crazy wine," she said.

Izzy's cheeks were rosy with alcohol, her eyes big. She never failed to get a charge out of having a crowd like this, with their rapt gazes and unselfconscious murmurs of approbation. They really, truly, cared about everything she had to say, and wanted to listen, to learn from her. Just as I always had. And I liked seeing her happy.

A Bob Dylan song started playing on a shelf stereo behind the wine bar while we gathered our things. *"You say you're looking for someone / Never weak but always strong / To protect you an' defend you / Whether you are right or wrong."* The marketer said Mr. Sigalas was a big fan.

We reconvened, after lunch and a nap at the hotel, for a short trip to Gaia, a boutique winery also on Santorini. The sparse facility was housed in a converted tomato-canning factory that resembled a parking garage or remote book warehouse. There was a small tasting room in the center of it that was lit by dim fluorescents overhead. Candles were on the easeled old barn door that served as a table. Their small but elegant portfolio didn't take long to get through. At the end, Leon, the enologist and co-winemaker, drove us into town for dinner. The empty restaurant had plates displayed on the wall above the window to the open kitchen and shelves of local gourmet products decorating the dining room of green tables and chairs. Eleven familiar and unfamiliar dishes Leon had ordered ahead arrived in rapid succession. I filled up before many of them made it to our end.

Izzy, too, it appeared, had begun to feel the deleterious effects of our furious consumption. I poured her a glass of Thalassitis, which she didn't drink. She sipped bottled water and ate some of the fava puree on a slice of baguette but little else. I ended up finishing the ladder of octopus and island of *taramosolata* and dismantling the "meet pastie" statue that remained on her plate.

"Are you stuffed?" I asked.

"Yeah," she replied absently. She was looking at something in her lap that was shining a digital light on her expropriated eyes. Damn it, I thought, Pacer Rosengrant got to her again. Had he informed her of, or had she deduced independently, the text "she" sent? It had been days since she'd even picked up her BlackBerry. I'd been hoping she'd left it in her suitcase and stopped caring about it.

"What are you reading?" I asked.

"Just e-mail."

"Anything good?"

"Junk."

"That's one thing I haven't missed too much since we've been away."

She smiled at me tightly. She pressed her free hand against my knee and patted it several times.

Over dessert and espressos, I offered her a spoon of my panna cotta. She shook her head. She twirled her fork aimlessly through an untouched bowl of fettuccine with shrimp and octopus I didn't recall having been passed. She still looked preoccupied, disengaged. I stared at the circumference of the ceramic and its flecks of dark, wilted parsley.

"What's bothering you?" I finally asked, when we were back at the hotel.

She let out a long sigh. "This e-mail I got."

I didn't want to hear the name I was almost certain she was going to enounce. I gritted my teeth, squinted my eyes, and stepped across the living room and into the bathroom to read the sign about towel service.

Izzy's next words were there unintelligible to me. I returned to her and asked her to repeat what she'd said.

She was now logged onto WiFi from my MacBook. On the desk, her BlackBerry lay on its face. "It's from Chef Dominique's lawyer."

"What does he want?"

"For me to call him. I can't believe it. I think I'm getting sued."

"Izzy," I said. I sat down on the dusty rattan-encased couch. "He can't sue you. He fired you. It's not like you quit."

"Maybe he's pressing charges about the voided wine."

"Do you really think somebody as cheap as he is would want to spend thousands of dollars to reclaim that little?"

Her eyes were glassy, her face suddenly pale. She let the computer screen hypnotize her, as though she were alone in the room.

"Izzy," I said. "Izzy," I repeated. "Izzy!"

"What?" she snapped.

"Talk to me. Don't talk to the fucking computer."

She shook her head. "Okay, okay. Look, I'm fucking worried. Is it too late to call?" It was ten thirty. "Twenty-two minus eight is what?"

I was too exhausted to compute. "Why don't you e-mail now and ask him what's going on?"

"You're right. That's a good idea. I'll just say I'm out of the country, and with the time difference—"

"Yeah, yeah. There's nothing he has to tell you that he can't tell you in an e-mail."

"You're right. You're right. You're right," she said, fingers assailing keys in a touch-type fury.

Friday, March 28
Athens

IZZY KEPT HER HEAD CEMENTED TO THE TAXI WINDOW AND HER EYES shut the following morning. She had slept poorly and eaten little of the cereal and yogurt she took from the buffet. It was silent in the car, save for the intermittent soggy drag of the windshield wipers. As the driver descended the mountain, I once again kept myself entertained by snapping digital pictures. My day's study was the exposed rock and deep volcanic layers we passed. It was difficult to make art out of the blurry exposures.

We got to the airport for our flight to Athens, which was to be a relatively brief forty-five-minute hop, checked our luggage, and passed through an amusingly lax security screening. The rumpled attendant seemed more concerned with impressing his pretty female counterpart than he was in preventing the carry-on baggage smuggling of weaponry and contraband. Still sitting in the terminal thirty minutes after our scheduled departure, amid a growing sense of travel futility, we watched rain swallow up the sun and envelop the island in gray, wet darkness. In contrast to the labyrinth of deceptive maneuvers that the American airlines went through to stave off any potential traveler uprising and refund demands by keeping passengers uninformed of the bad news for hours, the flight to Athens, a voice over the loudspeaker announced in Greek then, quite indifferently, was canceled.

For the first time I could remember since being in Greece, we were without a plan. "It never rains in Santorini," George said. He shook his head as though dumbstruck and looked about the terminal. The displaced Greeks surrounding us didn't seem terrifically concerned they might not get to Athens today, just mildly annoyed that they'd gone through the hassle of checking their bags and arranging their boarding passes when they could have been smoking or off having coffee or a glass of wine someplace more convivial.

There was talk of climbing back up the mountain, which we descended only hours ago, and returning to Oia. We could secure rooms once again at the Laokasti, have dinner, and put off trying to leave the island until tomorrow. Then George made a call and conferred in Greek. He got off the phone and shared the idea that had overtaken him: we could still get to Athens today, if we went by sea. He proclaimed, "There's a three forty ferry departure. We're going to the port!"

But first we were directed into a large baggage terminal. Instead of moving along in an orderly fashion on the motorized conveyor belt, all the passengers' checked items had been scattered around the room. "It looks like they just threw the fucking luggage down," Izzy said. I unzipped the front pocket of my suitcase to feel for the miniature ouzo bottle Maddie had given me that I'd stashed. Not broken.

Athens by sea was to take eight hours. Dick, reddened, visibly frazzled already by the day's contingencies in course, lit a cigarette when we got outside. He smoked in full view of everyone, not even bothering to step away for a modicum of privacy or to preface his transgression with his usual jovial euphemistic "I need to walk the dog." We piled into a Toyota van taxi George hailed. It took us from the airport, around the volcano, and down to the port. When we reached the dock, the taxi parked in between commercial vehicles loading cargo to be shipped off to other Greek cities and international destinations. Dick, Maddie, Barry, Izzy, and I stayed in the taxi while George ducked through the rain and into a tiny office to secure our transit. He bought us all tickets in the highest business class available, which would afford access to the VIP eating, drinking, and working sections of the ship. We also were assigned staterooms. I doubted I'd sleep, but appreciated the generous gesture George made on our behalf.

We skittered into the ferry's terminal and through big windows watched the Aegean for the ship to come in. The narrow room was already crowded. I recognized many passengers from the canceled flight. Most looked like refugees, as though they'd been traveling a long time, chalky faces, dirty hair, narrowed eyes. A couple of dogs roamed through and greeted the young mothers with babies and senior citizens with walkers. Local teenagers and backpacking college students wearing American university sweatshirts sat and chatted or stared at the walls or read or slept or sent text messages from the QWERTY panels of their Sidekicks.

George distributed Dramamine ahead of boarding. It took twenty minutes to kick in, he explained. I declined the tablets when the medicine bottle came around to me.

"I don't get seasick," I told Izzy.

"How do you know? When was the last time you were on a boat?"

An image of a summer camp cruise I took as a teenager came to mind. "A while ago. But I remember."

"Okay," she said, "but I reserve the right to make fun of you when you're leaning over the railing, Admiral."

On and on the ship susurrated. The sound reminded me of the constant tremble of an excited heart. It was difficult to hear much amid the vibrations beyond a battery of siren signals and ceaseless chatter in a panoply of dense, throaty languages. It was equally difficult to move around in any direction other than zigzag, because of the waves rocking against the ship and unsettling the floor. I couldn't get used to the fluctuating gravity, unable to master throwing my weight in the opposite direction of the heave. My instincts were off. I pushed when I needed to have been pulling. I had to concentrate intently on each step to avoid colliding into anyone or his cigarette or his beer or his baggage.

We fell into chairs in the lounge. Cinereous rain sheeted down the window beside us and hid the opaque sky.

"This is like *Master and Commander*," Izzy said.

I asked, "Was that a movie?"

"Yes," she said. "It only was nominated for, like, fifty Oscars."

"I seen it," Barry said. I was somewhat surprised to find he'd joined us. The last time we saw him he was negotiating through gestures with a white-capped porter the stowage of his oversize suitcase. Barry's forehead was sweaty and he looked pale. It awakened my sympathy such that I decided to overlook his rurally permissible, but nevertheless improper, verb tense conjugation.

A taciturn server delivered a pile of plastic menus. I was grinning when Izzy handed one to me. "I could get used to this," I said. "It's like a floating hotel." She giggled and searched the wine list for an acceptable varietal. The thundering sound of the waves made it impossible to relax my clench on our context for very long. I peered out the window and saw a ship employee on the deck in an acid-green hooded slicker wrestling with a length of intractable hose. The unrelenting downpour was drenching him. Before long, two large bottles of Perrier and the wine Izzy chose (the very floral 2007 Tsantali Athiri) showed up. The waiter brought it all on one tray. He did it and spilled nothing, not even a wobble or a flyaway cocktail napkin, an amazing feat of nautical virtuosity. The wine had me almost forgetting we were moving, that the course we took was in a lot of ways rudderless.

Barry couldn't eat anything. The sea was hitting him hard. He left for his stateroom to lie down. Dick and Maddie finished their sandwiches. Then they had to go to their room. I had a half turkey baguette and a section of spinach pie. I had potato chips. I slugged Athiri without fear. Izzy cautioned me, "You're going to puke if you keep drinking." "Nonsense," I said. My stomach was fine. I couldn't handle a lot of turbulence in life, but for some reason, being on the water wasn't something that unsettled me. George, too, was fine here, but nothing could unhorse him. Izzy paced herself. She sipped her Athiri slowly. She didn't seem interested in pushing the limits of her Dramamine. At the moment, it was keeping her insides unruffled.

Izzy and I had more wine and chips and watched the Greek version of *Extreme Makeover* (here it was delicately entitled *The Swan*) above English subtitles on the televisions banked into a wall. It started to seem as though this ferry to Athens had been the transportation plan all along. When our waiter returned to the table to refill our Perrier glasses, George put down the Greek paper he'd found to confer with him.

"We may have to stop in Naxos," George said. "Because of the weather. This rain is very unusual."

Izzy poured the rest of the Athiri. "In case of emergency, empty glass," she said. I laughed.

The lounge got smokier as the night moved on. Everybody's patience was running out. Izzy was now in a bad mood. She was annoyed about how long we'd been sequestered. She'd also been unsuccessful in her attempt to check e-mail from one of the ship's Internet kiosks. "They not work when it is so stormy," a nearby tobacco and phone card stand operator had tried to explain. I suggested we go check out the cabin. We lay together on one of the four available Murphy bunks. We had to press tightly against each other and intermingle limbs in order to both fit on the narrow mattress.

"Fucking motion sickness," she said.

"Is your stomach okay?"

"I'm fine. I didn't mean me. I wanted to talk to Dick, and now that opportunity's shot."

"Well, maybe once we get to the hotel."

"I'm starting to get the feeling that he doesn't really want me, not seriously. He just wants a free consultant."

"You'll never know until you ask."

"You make it sound like my not saying anything is the only thing standing between here and there."

"What are you saying?"

"What if we don't really want to move to New York?"

"I don't think we can decide until there's an offer around which we'd have to make a decision. You know?"

"What if we can't go?"

"Can't? Why couldn't we?"

"If Dominique is suing me. Maybe there'll be a long trial. An injunction. A lien on the loft. He has money and lawyers. They could bankrupt me and make it so that I never work in wine again. Not to mention the public backlash."

"That's another thing we're not going to be able to discuss intelligently until we have all the facts. You need to get in touch with that Schwartzstein guy. First thing when we get to Athens, you have to e-mail again."

She heaved a sigh. "My voice of reason."

It was raining in Athens, too. We emptied out into a chaotic, wet port. Fewer taxis were lined up here than weary travelers who wanted them. Fortunately, George had secured two cars ahead of time. Our drivers stood now holding signs for the Airport Sofitel.

We were probably an hour away from the hotel. It sounded like an intolerable length of time to spend in another vehicle, but what else could we do? The driver looked like an amply disheveled Oliver Stone. He plowed through the sloping rain-slicked avenues. It was dark. There were few streetlights. The only real road illumination came from the signs above stores.

"It's hilly here," Izzy remarked. "And the cable car lines. And all these little shops. It reminds me of the Bay Area." It was true. It felt like we were headed up Market Street.

"I love America," the driver replied. Even at this late, sodden hour, he wanted to chat with his exciting American charter. "I've been to United States, three, four time. I've been to Floreedah, San Francisco. Like to travel. See world. When I was eighteen month— year old, I go to Avanah, Coobah."

George said Cuba with an American accent. The driver echoed the "cue." Then he reverted to his initial pronunciation when he repeated it. "I am eighteen-year-old and I get thrown in preeson and they think I am spy because I go to Avanah." He wasn't an agent, just a young navy petty officer with a taste for adventure and a healthy disregard for the staid codes of off-base conduct. He continued, "They ask me each day why I go to Coobah. Every day they ask me. Finally, I tell them, 'You wanna know why I there? I go to make sexy.'"

In the backseat beside me, Izzy was cracking up. She squeezed my hand. I, too, was amused, but more reservedly. The odometer distracted me. One hundred kilometers, one-hundred-twenty an hour it went. We moved so fast that the water pools on the highway splashed high enough to cover the windows when the taxi's tires dove into them.

He went on, "I like America. I like America women. Greek like all the ladies. Dutch, the French, German, the Spanish. Except the Chinese."

George caught the driver's attention and used the opportunity to inquire about our route. It seemed a course that deviated from the one he'd expected us to take. The driver spoke to George in Greek now. He gestured wildly and looked at George more than he did the highway. Good thing the lanes were mostly empty. George translated, "This is a ring road."

The driver, in English: "Fifty, fifty-five-kilometer, circles Athens. You can't go else, just around Athens. Is the most fast." He was quiet for a moment and managed to remain focused just long enough to catch the exit for the airport.

Izzy looked panicked when the driver swerved into the sharp part of a slippery bend. He'd had his eyes in the back of the cab, talking to us during a treacherous turn. He, too, sensed her discomfort. "Miss, do not be concerned," he assuaged. "I have twenty-two year experience driving cab. Eleven as personal driver."

Still, it felt as though we might slide off the earth at any moment. Izzy breathed deeply. She stopped watching the road ahead. Her window had clouded with gray condensation and she rolled it down. The driver looked back, concerned. "Are you haht?" He pronounced the "ha" like the slightly constricted, throat-clearing sound of the Hebrew "ch."

"No," she explained. "I just wanted to clear the fog."

Driver: "Fhag?"

"The mist," George added. It only served to further confound.

"Fag? Fhag? Fuck."

Izzy and I started laughing, which encouraged the driver. "Fuck, yellow fuck," he chortled.

Around curves we went. The driver ignored cautionary lights. Exhaustion heightened my anxiety, but I did my best to will myself into a relaxed state. I let the recognizable shapes of billboards, supermarkets, and gas stations comfort me with their evocations of ubiquity, despite their bearing strange text. We were spinning into the Airport Sofitel before long. The location was immediately familiar to me. This was the airport we flew into, and then out of shortly after, to get to Santorini. Now that trip felt like a lifetime ago.

Saturday, March 29
Athens

THE NEXT MORNING IZZY WAS QUIET. HER SPOON SURFED A CUP OF coffee, and she spent most of our meal staring at a terrible framed hotel print on a long, mauve wall across the dining room. Meanwhile, I had smoked salmon and eggs and tiny chicken sausages in the grandest version of the complimentary hotel continental breakfast we'd encountered yet. When we were through, she obtained from the front desk an access code for the public Internet station off the lobby that would afford her a fifteen-minute free pass. With nervous hands, as though racing against dwindling time, she logged into her e-mail.

"He wrote back," she said.

"So, read it."

Her mouth gaped at the screen. I kept asking, "What happened?" but she didn't respond. Finally she said, "Dominique is dead."

I was aghast. "Dead?"

"Dead." She looked at me. "He had a heart attack. I guess it happened very quickly."

"At the restaurant?" I envisioned a chaotic scene in the dining room. Maybe it occurred upstairs in the office where he and I had our own blood pressure–escalating exchange.

"I don't know."

"So, what's the lawyer want?"

"He left me a cellar in his will."

"A cellar? Where? In his house?"

"In a liquor store. I guess he had a part-ownership in this seedy place on Chicago Avenue."

"The one with the lottery tickets and forties of Mickey's?"

"That one. With all the neon."

"It's kind of a wine shop, right?"

She shook her head. "I guess. Holiday Liquors is the name of the other half."

"And you get the whole store? Or just the inventory?"

She thwacked the mouse button to advance down the page. "I can't really tell."

"What about Dick?"

"What do you mean, 'What about Dick'?"

"Well, now that . . ." Even though I broke off, she looked at me like she knew exactly what I was reluctant to say.

"It's not like I—*we*—could run a store."

"Why not?" I paused. "Wine not?"

She laughed. "I still can't believe he had a wine shop I never knew about. Fucking Dominique and his vintage attraction." She logged out of her e-mail and closed the browser window.

"Vintage Attraction would be a good name for the store."

"There's not going to be a store. I just won't accept it. When we get back home, I'm going to see this Schwartzstein and tell him I don't want to have anything to do with this."

"And then go work for Dick in New York?"

She rubbed her ear contemplatively. "It's a possibility."

"But running this together isn't."

She looked at me tenderly.

"Just don't rule anything out, okay? No relinquishing of inherited property yet, okay?"

Possibly the word *inherited* reminded her of the reason for the discussion. "I can't believe he's dead."

"Izzy, he weighed close to four hundred pounds, if not more. I'm surprised his heart held out as long as it did."

She shook her head slowly, as though the stun of the news was viscous, physically hard to move through.

"He was the first person who really took a chance on me, Peter. He saw something in me. What we did . . . in the restaurant, the television show." Her eyes went glassy. "I just wish . . . I wish things hadn't ended up like they had. You know? Having him spend eternity thinking I'm a thief and a horrible person. That's not what I want."

"Not that I believe in shit like eternity, but what if running his wine shop is how he wanted you to make it up to him?"

"It could have just been an oversight. He probably forgot he even had that in the will. God, this is going to kill his wife, if it hasn't already. She always thought we were screwing."

I winced internally, and tried to elicit a good-natured chuckle. "You should call the lawyer. I'm sure George would let you use his cell. Or do it down here with my credit card."

"Later," she said. "I just want to think about this for a minute."

But Barry was thrumming his knuckles on the glass door of the Internet station, conveying, in an ungainly charade, that it was time for us to go.

"Where are Dick and Maddie?" I asked, when I didn't see them in the lobby.

"Skipping out," Barry said. "I guess Dick's still not a hundred percent."

We sped along to the center of Athens in another yellow Mercedes taxi. Mountains with low-rise complexes and houses jammed into the cliffs thronged the highway. The satellite radio played Red Hot Chili Peppers and Greek pop.

Above the music, Izzy and Barry made brief geographical conversation. George debriefed us about the next day's departures. I pictured my final breakfast buffet and tried to plan the most efficient way to consume the largest quantity of smoked salmon before we'd have to go. The mood was somber until George pointed out the exit for Papagou, a residential area in the northeastern part of Athens, where he and his wife, Sofia, planned to live. He remarked proudly, "We're building a house there." The topic instantly cheered us. The glimpse into a bright future brought with it a contagious feeling of hope, at least for a gray moment.

From Fidippidou Street and Mesogeion Avenue, we took King Constantine Boulevard and swung over to Queen Olga Boulevard. The city was clean because of the rain. We passed through the old royal park, Zappieon, and saw the huge columns at the ancient Temple of Olympian Zeus. George showed us the moldering *stadio*, Kallimarmoro, which was the home of the original modern Olympics. Motorized bike riders pulled in front of the taxi, without even turning their heads. Beyonce sang "Crazy in Love" as we drove the Pagrati neighborhood. It was, as we'd first noticed last night, a lot like San Francisco here. The residential streets were lined with eight- and ten-story buildings. Narrow shops and stores cluttered the main avenues. No space was wasted between commercial and residential. Everything had to nearly overlap in order to fit in as much as possible.

The Acropolis guide we met at Hadrian's Arch was an affable elderly woman, Athena. She'd been giving these tours for centuries. A pair of Londoners on holiday with expensive digital SLRs swinging from their necks asked if they could tag along with us. Athena looked to George for permission. He didn't mind. They paid her twenty-five euros each. A stray golden hound also followed along our climb up the stairs.

We saw the Parthenon, the Propylaea, and the Erechtheum. All the ancient, crumbling structures were imperial and majestic and conjured eons. These were scenes from old canvases and heroic couplets and frames from Richard Burton and Rudolph Maté studio system epics and childhood crayon-and-charcoal coloring-book lore. Athena circled us around the site of the old Acropolis Museum, where a future museum was now under construction. It was being built of period-correct marble and bronze. At each tour interstice, the Brits frantically fired dozens and dozens of haphazard shots, shuttering and flashing away as though Santa Monica paparazzi with mere seconds to immortalize a dazed actress before she'd stumble out of their OVFs and into Starbucks refuge. The dog happily offered to pose in the pictures the tourists took of the monuments.

As we straggled, Athena told stories about the Golden Age and Greece under the rule of Pericles. We learned of developments under Mnesicles in 437 B.C. The Peloponnesian War brought an interruption in progress. Our guide gave us an overview of the Roman Period. We contemplated the Byzantine and Ottoman empires and sympathized with the Greeks when we heard of the Venetians' seizure of their art and valuables during the Morean War in 1687. But it wasn't until Athena concluded the tour that she spoke perhaps the most resonant information. As we looked out over Dionysus's theater, ruined, yet still stately, Athena told Izzy and me Dionysus was the god of wine and words.

"One god for both of us," Izzy said. She smiled at me with eyes I hadn't seen since the day we got married. All at once I felt closer to her, figuratively, and literally, as she stood a little nearer to me. The back of my right hand and her left swung in close proximity at our respective sides. "How do you like that?"

The exit route was lined with tour groups. Italian girls in pastel, hooded zip sweatshirts giggled and elbowed and texted. Spanish families and Russian college students waited on line to claim our places. Older Japanese women queued up in a harrowed huddle. They had surgical masks over their noses and mouths, as though fearful of catching any contagious antiquity.

Izzy, Barry, and I followed George down cobblestone streets. More unaccompanied dogs chased each other. We passed scoundrel taxi drivers looking for unsophisticated tourists to exploit with tantalizing off-meter fares for "a bargain." A gray-haired pastry cart vendor who wore a blazer and tie looked toward our tourist patronage hopefully. In town, the graffiti and its range of expressions impressed me. I saw sparse, perfunctory Greek messages in purple and gray on the walls of residential buildings with motorcycles parked outside. Closer to the restaurants, the messages were brilliant, passionate rebellion in myriad colors. We proceeded up Metropolis Street, a path that contained a cathedral fronted by a marble square. George told us, "Nearly every stone used to make this church came from an older church or other ancient building. The stone from Galilee, where Jesus changed water into wine, is supposed to be here." Agios Eleftherios was the Byzantine church to the south of the cathedral, a Thorne room in comparison.

This road turned into Pondroussou Street, which emptied us onto Monastraki, the area known for its flea market and profusion of shops. For sale were sunglasses and calendars and maps and sea sponges and worry beads in yellow and orange and blue

and black and pink and aqua and playing cards and baskets full
of ouzo miniatures and ceramic busts of gods and kilned, glazed
pottery bearing mythological scenes and marble chess sets and
leather purses and plastic purses and women's sweaters and jackets
and pornographic illustrations of ancient copulating figures
and T-shirts. Carts teemed with bunched bananas, pyramids of
oranges, apples, pears, a billion loose strawberries. Alongside the
carts, men hawked silver and gold rings from boxes that hung
in front of their chests on embroidered neck straps. Izzy bought
a small bust of Apollo at a narrow trinket stall. She thought he
looked a little like me.

Then it was time to go. George met us and led a speed walk to
the Metro. At times he was just a dark leather–jacketed blur with
a backpack. We swept through the immaculate marble-walled and
granite-floored neoclassical facility. A sign boasted it had been built
at the end of the nineteenth century.

The Metro station, like most of Greece, had been overhauled
before the last Olympics descended. It now presented various artifacts encased in glass. George, though hurrying so we wouldn't miss
the train, couldn't resist stopping to point them out to us.

"What is that?" Izzy asked.

"Relics," George said. "Bits of columns and archeological finds.
They discovered all of this when they were digging down to build
the subway."

Here there was, literally, an underground museum. Pieces of
antiquity were juxtaposed with modern works. Izzy and I wandered over to a tactile mosaic fashioned out of petrified earth and
stone. It resembled a relief map. "That's the bed of the Eridanos
River. It's twenty-five hundred years old," George told us. "Hard
to believe we can look at it, just like that. But there you have it.
Anyway."

"I can't believe there's art down here," Izzy said. "In Chicago,
the only things on display in our Red Line stations are crumpled
Cheetos bags and chicken bones."

Down another escalator and through another long corridor we went. We reached the platform two minutes ahead of schedule. George could relax.

A half hour later, a Sofitel desk clerk begrudgingly issued Izzy another fifteen-minute free Internet pass. She checked her e-mail in the lobby. There were more details from Chef Dominique's lawyer. Chef Dominique had bequeathed to Izzy the fifty percent he owned of the liquor store, the wine cellar, and all his wine-related assets, including the name "Vintage Attraction." She could, if she desired, run that side of the business. There was nothing stopping her, or us. It was what Chef Dominique would have wanted.

That night we had a big dinner with a number of winemakers whose properties we didn't get to visit. Our group said good-byes afterward. The parting words were gracious and sincere. There in the Sofitel lobby was talk of domestic reunions, maybe in upstate New York. A Greek viticultural roadshow was making a Chicago stop in May, and there we'd get to see George and some of the winemakers and marketers we'd gotten to know here. I felt immeasurably grateful to George for not disinviting Izzy to Greece when he learned she'd been fired from Bistro Domi- nique. She'd planned to keep it a secret. But Izzy had, I found out tonight, confessed to him when he called her as we shuttled on the Blue Line with our suitcases and a bag of sandwiches to O'Hare almost ten days ago. In spite of the fact that Izzy had lost her wine program, George knew she wasn't going to be out of the business forever. He wasn't going to let her—or me—pass this up. That afternoon, we had airline tickets to Munich and a connection to Thessaloniki awaiting, but beyond leaving the country, we were still largely uncertain about where we were truly headed. And tomorrow we'd return home. So much and yet so little had changed.

We wandered into elevators and upstairs to the rooms. Izzy was already beginning to fade. I followed her to bed. Then the phone rang. It was George, dialing up from the lobby. He needed back the power adapter he'd lent us for the charging of our numerous American-voltage electronics. Back on went my shoes.

George stood downstairs in front of a glass display case containing wine bottles, which incongruously included an old Condrieu. I gave him his adapter. We shook hands and hugged, as though we hadn't done so shortly before.

"I'm glad to know you, Peter Hapworth," George said. "You're a rare breed."

"Thanks, George," I said. "You have a lot of energy. I really admire what you do here. These wines deserve a voice outside of this country, and you give it to them."

He laughed tightly. "I don't know if I *give* it to them, but I guess I help them get heard."

"I'd say you do."

"Well, now you have to tell everyone you know about Assyrtiko and Agiorgitiko, my friend."

"I want to do more than just talk, George," I said. "I think that's the biggest discovery I've made here. I've spent too much of my life just talking about things."

"It's time you started pouring," he said. He grinned like he knew something I didn't. "Anyway, speaking of time, it's changing tonight, you know. Spring forward."

"Yeah, don't remind me."

Sunday, March 30

THE CHILD WAILING ROWS BEHIND US ON THE AEGEAN FLIGHT to Munich provided a reminder the next morning of just how disagreeable being uprooted and entering into the confining situation of air travel was. We'd gone to sleep late and gotten up very early—even earlier than the clock read, technically, because of the time change. The undigested aftermath of my last battle with the continental buffet glut bounced around inside me. The crying and screaming also externalized the perplexing intersection of my conflicting emotional states. I was eager to get back to Chicago, to sift the junk mail that had accumulated at our doorstep, to watch cooking shows and new *Vintage Attractions* I'd DVRed, to reunite with the pug I longed to see, to be with Izzy. Also part of me was dreading our return. In Greece, Izzy and I had become a real couple again. But because of almost-but-not-quite resolved domestic disturbances, I feared things could once more become just as fractured as before we left. We also lacked resolution in matters of our future, and economic means of having one. Takeoff only drowned out the unceasing caterwauling by a negligible degree. I appreciated the escalating sonic competition nonetheless. As the plane gradually ascended, the familiar landscape left focus and effectively came apart. It rendered itself vaguer and vaguer and less and less ours with each kilometer we amassed. The mountains became hillocks and then black smudges of earth. The city turned into small white boxes as we climbed some more. Then it was blue and white and nothing else.

The wailing faded away. Now only the engine rumbled. Izzy was tired and wanted to sleep. I talked her into one last drink in Greece (so to speak, anyway, in case we'd already unknowingly crossed into Italian airspace) when the first beverage service rolled through. We shared a split of Greek sparkling wine. It was Moschofilero done in the Charmat method. We toasted and I sipped my small portion gradually. The wine, Izzy said, bore a similar tart lemoniness to Asian apple pear and quince.

"Chef Dominique would have liked this one," I returned. Our first conversation at the Metropolitan Club before he and Izzy took the stage came to my mind.

She agreed. "But he would have gone insane if you called it Champagne." She did an impression of the chef berating a waiter. Her cheeks were distended and her upper body swayed to simulate his waddle. Maybe because of sleep deprivation, I found it hard to stop laughing.

"Do you miss him?" I asked.

She nodded shyly.

"He wasn't so bad."

She turned, first to the clouds, then to me. "You really think we should do it? You really want to change your entire life and run a wine shop with me?"

"Izzy, of course. I've been changing my entire life since the night we met."

"It hasn't sucked too badly, has it?"

"No. It hasn't." I started to cry. "I'm whole because of it. Because of all of it. Because of you."

"Hapworth."

I took off my glasses to blot my eyes on a sleeve. "So, you're going back into the wine business."

"*We're* going into the wine business."

"We're going into the wine business."

"I guess there's only one more thing we have to discuss."

I sniffled, heart stuttering. "Okay."

"What's Ishiguro going to think?"

Vino

16

WITH IZZY'S OVERSIGHT, I ACCEPTED THE STOCK DELIVERIES. I organized the inventory. I'd found on eBay several used poster-frame marquees to announce purveyors' "new releases" and wines "coming soon." The frames were festooned with lightbulbs to maximize their attention-grabbing powers—and they still worked. A colleague of Ari Marks's, from the *Daley Machine* art department, volunteered to spearhead the store's graphics effort for wine movie–poster ads and other point-of-purchase signs. We'd retained, for the most part, the original wooden wine shelving around the perimeter of the space. We had also acquired several double-sided, mobile, wire-mesh displays of the kind used in video stores. The same fixtures that once accommodated rows of VHS rentals, when that sort of thing still existed, could now, after a bit of adjusting, be used, quite splendidly, to feature varietals. I embarked on a long project arranging the product out on display in the store for optimal customer browsing by style and region.

One morning, I was finally finished arraying. Izzy surveyed the surroundings with a wary (but amused) shake of her head. "Wine shop meets Blockbuster."

"Hey, be kind, re . . . wine," I replied.

She followed me over to a perpendicular bank of shelves we'd designated the Greek corner. It was embattled with gleaming bottles. We admired the spectrum of grape varieties we now carried. Athiri, Malogousia, Roditis, and, below, Agiorgitiko, Mavrodaphne, and Xinomavro. We also had Greek cava and some ready-to-go Assyrtiko and Moschofilero in the cooler.

The decision to sell a lot of the wines we'd discovered on the trip had been difficult for Izzy to make. She'd spent days with the numbers, contemplating financial and logistical realities. Our wholesale cost for the few cases we were able to keep on hand at any one time were higher than the margins would have liked. A Corked4Less-scale big-box store operation this was not. But I held fast. It was important to me that one of the cornerstones of this undertaking was to pay homage to the country and its products that had gotten us here. The usual three-time markup applied to these wines would result in a retail price that would discourage those customers unfamiliar with the grapes. They'd end up purchasing cheaper bottles they already knew they liked. Izzy, after a period of industry knowledge–induced balking, eventually agreed with my logic. It didn't make business sense. It would be easier for us to generate income selling a lot of Pinot Grigio and California Chardonnay. We might even *lose* money by taking risks on the boutique and the daring. But it was, I intuited, a calculated risk. The only way to get people to set aside their provincial consumer fears and explore and discover was to just bring them the wine. And wasn't learning something new the ultimate goal?

I could tell Izzy was impressed with what I'd—what we'd—accomplished in a relatively short period.

"I love it," she said.

"I think Ishiguro's bed should go here. It's a perfect corner, out of the sun, near the wine bar."

"You know he's not going to lie there," she said. "He's going to want to help sell. And this 'wine bar' you mention? You really plan on holding tastings at the counter?"

"Of course," I said. "And not just eyedropper portions of old wine we opened days earlier and want to be done with. I want people to have a *glass* while they shop."

"Isn't that a lot?" she asked.

"They'll buy if they've been drinking."

"True. A sober browser comes in and, buzzed, leaves a customer."

"My theory exactly."

"Well, you and Ishiguro get to do the dishes."

"Deal."

Vintage Attraction opened, in preview mode, with little fanfare, a couple of days before the publicized grand celebration. It wasn't as though I expected an influx of shoppers to come spilling into the store the moment I turned the Closed sign around. But couldn't even a solitary drunk transient working on delirious memory have inadvertently stumbled in for a lottery ticket? I took a deep breath and went about my business as though I had some. I arranged a few glasses on the counter. I opened a bottle of Moschofilero and poured myself a small amount to smell (I had to make sure it wasn't corked, after all). I emptied the Xinomavro I pulled the cork from next into a crystal decanter one of the reps had given us as a gift. The wine was relatively young and the tannins were still aggressive. Decanting, as I recalled observing when we were at Alpha Estate in Amyndeon, would help relax this one and open it up a bit. As I watched the dark purple—almost black—color of the wine sheet down the distended sides of the glass, I couldn't help thinking about how different I was now that I knew about things like age and tannin and the powers of aerating wine. Even though I was still learning, and probably would forever be learning, I took here a measure of pride. I was on a course to having purpose, a direction. These were the makings of a real life.

"Is that Cabernet Sauvignon?" Izzy quipped when she came in. "Because I *only* drink Cabernet Sauvignon. Please, sir, a bottle of your *finest* Napa Valley Cabernet Sauvignon. I simply won't settle for anything less."

"Very funny."

"Good idea decanting the Xinomavro," she said.

"You want some?"

"I think I'll start with your white." She took the Moschofilero from the refrigerator and poured herself a modest glass. "Mmm," she said after a sip. "I think we're going to have a hard time keeping that in stock."

I noticed something flat and square and brown extending from her handbag. "What is that?" I asked.

"Oh," she said. She lifted out a framed portrait of a relatively youthful, jaunty, and only moderately overweight Chef Dominique. "It's the photo from when Chef was featured in *Chicago* magazine in 1995," she said. Here, before a pastel-and-geometric-patterned backdrop, sat immortalized the restaurateur at the zenith of his powers. This was about five years or so before he'd become the embittered, resentful profiteer with whom Izzy had had the fortuitous misfortune of becoming entangled. "Schwartzstein gave it to me."

"Why?"

"I wanted it. I thought the store should honor him in some way."

I pointed to a narrow space between the end of one display case and the "coming soon" movie poster frame. "Let's put it over there."

She looked at me gently, gratefully. "It means a lot to me."

"To me, too."

We hung the picture up. Ishiguro barked at the beaming chef. This was his first design disagreement in the renovation process. The pug and I studied the photograph. In 1995, the chef was estimable. He was likely optimistic about his future. Just as I was right now about my own. I'd never thought we'd had much in common, besides Izzy, but maybe we had shared similar hopes and dreams, just not contemporaneously. Ishiguro declared, in his characteristic shake, exhale, sigh, and sneeze manner, Dominique was free to remain, as long as I made sure not to pattern any of my professional ethics after the chef's, to never take for granted the person because of whom there was a shop for me to stand in now. I silently assented. Then the pug returned to the ledge to resume his nap.

Predictably, the door chime sounded shortly after Izzy went out to get us lunch. I was making a last-minute revision to the order of chilled bottles and had my back to the store. Adrenaline cinched my throat. But there was no way out. This was real now. I turned bravely to face my first guests. It was T. Stoddard and The Pregnant Lady, my erstwhile UIC English Department drinking buddies. I immediately relaxed.

"What are you guys doing here?"

"I think the question is more like, what are *you* doing here?" T. Stoddard's words slurred. True to character, my old friend, with one more class to teach ahead of him today, was hammered well in advance of cocktail hour. He produced a silver flask. Then he turned to The Pregnant Lady and offered it to her. "Something to go along with your Diet Coke?"

She looked at him strangely, though kindly. "But . . . I'm not drinking a Diet Coke."

He nodded, a grave expression on his ruddy, lined face.

The Pregnant Lady unwound her scarf. From an eye-level shelf, using the glass between an Egly-Ouriet's front labels as a makeshift mirror, she handed a slight restoration to her windswept, spiky blonde hair. "So, Peter Hapworth, of all the liquor stores in all the towns in all the world, we walk into yours?"

"We prefer the term 'wine shop.'"

T. Stoddard choked a little on the whiskey he'd slugged. "'Wine shop,'" he repeated in a British accent.

"You look like you've gotten some color," The Pregnant Lady said to me.

"We were in Greece."

"It is the color of someone living his life out in the world," T. Stoddard said.

"How are things going at school? I miss my students."

"They ask after you," The Pregnant Lady said. "Schultz has me covering your 161."

"What did they say?"

"Nothing, really," she said. "You know how stoic undergraduates like to pretend to be."

"Until you tell them they're waitlisted," T. Stoddard added. "Then, let the melodrama floodgates open."

"God," I said, eyes pointed at his sneakers. "I can only imagine how Shelley's been badmouthing me since she let me go. Did she circulate a memo about my 'breakdown'?"

"I'd call it a 'breakout,'" The Pregnant Lady said, "and you needn't worry about any of it. Nobody really pays too much attention to her gossiping and general dithering. People were shocked at first, but, ultimately, only thrilled for you, that you escaped."

"Way to go, Hapworth," T. Stoddard said. "A rare University Hall refugee."

The Pregnant Lady gave me a hug. "You definitely look good here," she said.

T. Stoddard, it seemed, had just about all the mawkishness he could take. He asked me, "Where is this celebrated spouse of yours, anyway? She leaves you here alone?"

"With a pug, in point of fact," The Pregnant Lady added.

"That's Ishiguro," I said. "My new boss."

"Fair enough," T. Stoddard said. He paced the aisles like a trial lawyer. "So, let me ask you something, and please excuse the, er, indelicacy of my syntax: between the former English teacher and the furry novelist, who the fuck is supposed to help customers differentiate between"—he reached up two bottles, additional Greek wines I'd opened and put out on the counter—"this one and this one?" He handed me the Athiri and filled an empty stem with Agiorgitiko. He drained the glass before even stopping to smell it.

"I guess cocktail hour is over and wine service may commence. I hope you're not lecturing today," I said.

"In-class writing. And a lot of it." He blotted his mouth with a tattered corduroy blazer sleeve. "The prompt is:"—he cleared his throat—"'Describe, in no fewer than five hundred words, the meaning of life.'" He paused to pour more wine. He then drawled, "That oughta keep 'em busy until the Ritalin wears off."

"Please excuse *Leaving Las Douglas Hall* over there." The Pregnant Lady spoke in an exasperated register.

I refilled my own glass with Moschofilero. I swirled it. I raised the wine to smell, but suddenly could only detect the store scents: musty wood, dust, Ajax, new paint. "He has a point," I said. "About me running this place. What am I supposed to do when Izzy's not here? How do I tell people the difference between Pinot Grigio and Pinot Gris?"

"What is the difference?" T. Stoddard asked.

"It's like Shiraz and Syrah."

He beckoned with index and middle fingers. "Meaning?"

"Same grape, different provenances, some style variations."

T. Stoddard applauded. "Bravo, Professor Hapworth, bravo. Just use words like *provenance* and *style* and you'll prevail in any battle of enological retail wits."

Of course they left without buying anything. Adjuncts.

"What are you looking for?" Izzy asked that evening when she found me in the guest room. I had the closet open and was riffling through unpacked boxes left over from our move.

"The camcorder," I said.

"Your old one? Why? What do you want to film?"

"What if we made little informative segments on wine topics and played them in the store when you're not there? It would be kind of like having you around, even when you're off doing a speaking engagement."

"*Everything You Always Wanted to Know About Cépage * But Were Afraid to Ask*?"

"Exactly," I said. "I won't have to feel like an idiot when a customer wants to know what kind of wine to serve if some of the dinner guests are having salmon and some are having steak and she doesn't want different varietals." I stood up from the box with the unearthed camcorder bag in my hand. "What would you suggest in that scenario, by the way?"

"Depends on how the salmon's prepared, but if it's grilled, you could get away with Pinot Noir. Heavy enough to go with the steaks, but delicate enough not to overwhelm the seafood. Or, if you really wanted to be adventurous, Tsantali Moschomavro."

"See what I mean? That's perfect."

"I have to tell you, I think it's a really fucking good idea."

I bowed my head and doffed an imaginary hat, in an approximation of a butler. "Why, thank you, madam. Do we have any sparkling wine?"

"Yeah," she said, "there's a magnum of Billecart-Salmon in the hall closet."

"We can use it as a prop."

"A prop! I think an angry mob from Mareuil-sur-Ay would assemble outside this loft if anyone heard you say that about a Champagne."

"I'll film you opening it. That's something every wine drinker should know how to do, right?" I unzipped a pocket of the camera bag and drew out a FireWire cable. "You plug one end of this into the camcorder and the other into the MacBook, and—presto!—video ready for the delicious streaming to our future customers."

"And what are we going to do with an entire open magnum after that?"

There was something I'd been considering recently. I'd refrained from sharing it with Izzy for fear she'd charge me with treason for even suggesting it. I decided, in that instant, to take a chance. Wine not? "Don't hate me for asking this."

She looked at me.

"Should we invite Scott and Sheryl down for a toast?"

"Oh, god," she said. "No. Absolutely not."

I took this in with a smile.

"In this apartment?" She was coming to temperature.

I nodded.

"The very apartment they've assaulted over and over with their shoes, platitudes, flood insurance pamphlets, and Fisher-Price toys?"

"Yes, here. Come on, Izzy. They've been behaving, right?"

"No," she said, "but we've hardly been around." Something gave her pause. "We've been working on the store so much that I kind of forgot all about them."

"So we inadvertently discovered a means of coexisting. What if they've really been trying?"

"Okay, fine," she said. In appreciation of her beneficence, I planted a small kiss on her cheek. "But only for twenty minutes."

"It's Champagne," I said. "It will be gone faster than that."

Izzy was turning the magnum in its ice bath when I got off the phone. "So when are they arriving?" she asked.

"*She*," I corrected. "Apparently Scott is watching Casshole for the evening. At his apartment."

Izzy spun around, her mouth agape. "*His* apartment?"

I nodded solemnly.

"I'm shocked," she said, sounding like she very much was and also wasn't that terribly.

"I guess that means no more fights," I said. "No more treadmill."

"And every other weekend Casshole-free."

"Probably some weekday evenings, too. Every other Christmas."

"Let's hope we're not still living here for too many 'other' Christmases."

"You want to move again?"

"I don't know, I've been thinking about it," she said. "Looking around on the Internet, very informally. I haven't even called Leslie or anything. I'm just . . . I think we should keep our housing options open. You know?"

"What have you seen? Anything good?"

"A little of this, a little of that."

"Just in Pilsen?"

"Actually, *not* in Pilsen."

I was astounded by the possibilities. For so long I'd believed Izzy would only live in this neighborhood, but now that she had broadened her search criteria . . . I pictured us in various scenarios. There we were after a party, ascending in the mirrored elevator of a Gold Coast high-rise, Izzy and I drunkenly colliding into each other along a carpeted hallway, laughing, like the modern-day Fitzgeralds. There I was following Ishiguro up the stone stairs to a Lincoln Park town house. I'd wake early Sunday morning and go outside our single-family home in Roscoe Village for the *Times*, a garage in the back for the Mustang and a front yard in which I could play Dino with the pug. A crumbling mansion in Kenwood could be a project, something we'd restore together, one Sunday undertaking at a time. There was always the possibility of trying out another loft, but in the stroller-free Fulton River District on the West Bank, on the top floor . . . .

"It would be nice to live closer to the store," I said. "Or, you know, wherever."

"I think we'll end up exactly where we're supposed to be."

"This isn't it, is it?"

"No," she said. "But you know what? I don't think anymore that the Biscuit Factory was a mistake. It was something we *needed* to do."

"A test of some sort. Endurance. Fortitude. IQ."

"If our marriage can survive living here, we can make it through anything."

"I feel kind of sorry for Sheryl," I confessed.

"I do, too. But she married the wrong guy. It was bound to come up sooner or later."

"I'm glad you didn't marry the wrong guy," I said.

She put her arm over my shoulder and gave me a kiss.

We got to work while the wine chilled. Between rehearsal takes, Izzy's BlackBerry rang. The affable voice she used in answering had me figuring it was Sheryl. But soon the call began to seem serious. Izzy was largely silent, listening. Her acknowledgments were dull, faint. Then she disconnected and returned the BlackBerry to the breakfast bar. She told me, without my having to inquire, that it had been Ken Fredrickson, a master sommelier. Ken had cashed out of the casinos and now ran a distributorship in Las Vegas. He'd called with intelligence, of sorts. The top-tier master-level Court exams were held this week in Aspen. And Pacer Rosengrant, his and Izzy's mentee, skipped out on the final and most difficult third of the exam to master: theory.

"After all of that, he didn't even show up," she said vaguely. "I really thought he wanted this. Can you believe it?"

I could, in fact, believe it. And it was more than likely my fault. It was pretty remarkable. As I'd impulsively typed in the Amyndeon hotel room, I had no doubt that my pretending to be Izzy was going to backfire. Yet for some reason, by an act of Dionysus, possibly, the clumsy, transatlantic text transgression had managed to make it past rough draft and the acid reflux I'd been coughing and into Pacer Rosengrant's mind. She didn't hear from him again while we were in Greece. And as the weeks went on with no sign of him, it seemed more and more like I'd really convinced Pacer Rosengrant, albeit in the roundabout ventriloquism that marriage sometimes was, to have a conscience. At the very least I'd driven him away from his master sommelier fantasy and excuse to have Izzy mentor him. I'd run him out of Chicago, back to Vegas, or anywhere else. Most important, I'd put distance between him and my wife—and me. He was out of our lives.

"Maybe it was something I said?" I offered. The closest I'd ever come to confessing.

She was putting herself back on her mark behind the kitchen counter and didn't appear to have heard me. It was no matter. I didn't need her to dwell on it more. There were important things awaiting our attention.

"Okay, places, everybody, please, places," I barked from behind the tripod. I stuck my eye to the viewfinder. I huffed and grumbled to myself, in the character of an impatient director eager to get rolling again before we lost our available light.

Izzy, with fingers sweeping up her hair like an actress, laughed.

By the time we closed the shop for the night following the grand opening, we'd grossed seven hundred dollars. After subtracting what we'd put out in free food and drink for the inaugural festivities, the profit was negligible. But the fact that we drove home at the end, from our new store, together, made it all worthwhile.

I got Ishiguro ready to go. "I probably should get dinner started," Izzy said before we left.

"Should I open a bottle of Xinomavro?"

"Just a glass for me," she said. "We have to get up early and go to work."

"I almost forgot," I said, feigning nonchalance. In truth, I was so excited about the prospect of facing a job the next day, I hadn't stopped planning what I'd do at the store tomorrow since we got home. I couldn't ever remember that happening before.

It was a warm evening and so we ate on the terrace. Pilsen was quiet. Few cars drove down the block. I looked into my wineglass at the ripe, graphite-colored juice. I smelled the oregano and parsley and olive oil on the grilled lamb and dill of the spanakopita. I tasted the lemony acidity between the flaky pastry layers. It felt, for a moment, like we were back in Greece. Yet it was better somehow. We were home, together. We had a life, a promising new business, and things to look forward to. I couldn't remember a time when I felt so much in love, so acutely aware of my good fortune, so at peace with everything. I was no longer hapless. I was happy.

I stood to take in the dishes. I asked Izzy if she wanted to join me inside.

"Let's just stay out here for a little while longer," she said.

"Okay, but one more thing?"

"Yeah?"

"I love you, Izzy."

"And I love you, Hapworth."

I deposited our plates and silver in the sink and let myself back onto the terrace. We could hear gentle Haydn on the digital music station through the screen. Ishiguro came around and sniffed for leftovers. His search yielded none. He settled for climbing up and arranging himself into a cinnamon roll on my lap, where he promptly fell asleep. In our twin deck chairs, Izzy and I sat side by side, facing the street. We held hands and interlaced our fingers. We sipped our wine. Periodically I turned to say something to Izzy, my wife, my business partner—my partner. Sometimes I looked over and just smiled. She knew everything I was thinking and not thinking. And it was there on our little porch, just like this, that we watched the night grow old together.

ACKNOWLEDGMENTS

Special thanks to: George Athanas, Thomas Beller, Iris Blasi, Jessica Case, Belinda Chang, Louisa Chu, Lisa Clark, Marissa Conrad, Jessa Crispin, Ted Diamantis, Tony Dreyfuss, Amie Droese, Erika Dufour, Kevin Elliott, Maria Fernandez, Helena Fitzgerald, Gina Frangello, Ken Fredrickson, Michael Fusco, Phil Gaskill, Judith Gurewich, Claiborne Hancock, Ryan Harbage, Brian Hieggelke, Erica Horisk, KC Ipjian, J. Joho, Caroline Eick Kasner, Justin Kaufmann, Danny Klieman, Michael Klong, Vicki Lame, Maia Larson, Victoria Lautman, Theresa May, Cris Mazza, Jay McInerney, Peter Michelson, Brad Morris, Haruki Murakami, Nasdijj, Lydia Netzer, Mike Newirth, Achy Obejas, Maryanne O'Hara, Edwin Olivieri, Eddie Osterland, Julie Pacer, Chilli Pepper, Sofia Perpera, Liese Ricketts, Mike Rosengrant, Amy Krouse Rosenthal, Eric Schaeffer, Davis Schneiderman, Gary Shteyngart, Rebecca Silber, Alpana Singh, Marc Smoler, Philip Spiegel, David Spielfogel, Liz Stigler, Carolyn Stopka, Jill Talbot, David Tamarkin, Madeline Triffon, Ned Vizzini, Vikki Warner, Burt Wolf, Henry Yee, and Kelli Zink.

ABOUT THE AUTHOR

CHARLES BLACKSTONE is the author of the novel *Vintage Attraction*. He is also the author of *The Week You Weren't Here* (Dzanc and Low Fidelity Press) and the co-editor of *The Art of Friction: Where (Non) Fictions Come Together* (University of Texas Press). His short fiction has appeared in *The &Now Awards: Best Innovative Writing* (Lake Forest College Press), *Metazen*, *Esquire*, *Salt River Review*, and *The Journal of Experimental Fiction*. In 2012 and 2013, *Newcity* named him in their "Lit 50: Who Really Books in Chicago" annual feature. He resides in Chicago, with his wife, Master Sommelier Alpana Singh, and Haruki Murakami, a pug.